In Their World, There Was No Fear . . . Until The Succubus Came . . .

Tunnel Rat froze, barely able to breathe.

"This is The Succubus," a voice said, "and I'm coming after you, Tunnel Rat. So you'd better watch every step. No matter where you go, no matter what you do, I'm watching you. I'm even going to come to you in your dreams, Tunnel Rat. You're not going to know where, and you're not going to know when, but I'm going to get you. Do you understand?"

Tunnel Rat felt his heart pounding as a surge of adrenaline gushed through him.

He heard his breath start to gasp, and covered his mouth with both hands to keep the sound inside. He knew he'd give away his position if he made the slightest noise.

As soon as he had his breath under control, his right hand silently went down to his side, where he'd strapped onto his belt the razor-sharp bayonet earlier that day. His fingers closed around the handle.

He waited . . .

For Jon Carroll —

Here's hoping you find a few hour's pleasure in these pages.

Best regards,

Chet Day

12/4/89

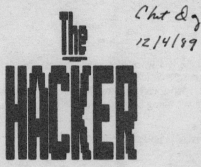

The HACKER

CHET DAY

POCKET BOOKS

New York   London   Toronto   Sydney   Tokyo

An *Original* Publication of POCKET BOOKS

POCKET BOOKS, a division of Simon & Schuster Inc.
1230 Avenue of the Americas, New York, NY 10020

ISBN: 0-671-67611-3

First Pocket Books printing November 1989

10 9 8 7 6 5 4 3 2 1

POCKET and colophon are trademarks of
Simon & Schuster Inc.

Printed in the U.S.A.

*This novel is for my mother and father,
Mary Ann and Myron George Day,
parents who never failed to accept and nurture
my love of all things imaginative.*

Acknowledgments

The quotation from St. John of the Cross was taken from *The Collected Works of St. John of the Cross,* a fascinating spiritual autobiography translated by Kieran Kavanaugh, O.C.D., and Otilio Rodriquez, O.C.D., ICS Publications, Institute of Carmelite Studies, Washington, D.C., copyright 1979, page 95.

I have also paraphrased a famous Zen parable that I found in Paul Reps' wonderful compilation *Zen Flesh, Zen Bones: A Collection of Zen and Pre-Zen Writings,* Anchor Books, Doubleday & Company, Inc., Garden City, New York, pages 22-23.

Prologue

~~~~~~~

Tuesday, October 22nd, 12:47 A.M.

Still kneeling by the bed in the spare room, Harv Webster's pudgy fingers rubbed the rough cotton hem of the monk's robe that hung loosely on his naked body in a circular motion.

His breath came in awkward syncopations—the pace of an old locomotive working up a head of steam, gently but inexorably accelerating.

Savoring the moment of revenge he didn't consciously realize he desired, the huge man's mind drifted back to that day in the locker room so many years before:

"That fat ass of yours'd make an elephant jealous, Harvey," his high school's star athlete had taunted at the end of that afternoon's tryouts for the varsity team, snapping his wet towel at Harv's flabby and heavily dimpled buttocks.

The other boys in the locker room laughed, except for Gary Reynolds, who was also overweight and had asthma and knew all too well what it was like to be on the receiving end of the halfback's cruelty. Like Harv, Gary had decided to try out for the football team—yet one more doomed attempt at being a normal teenager. Like Harv, Gary's uncoordinated movements on the field had drawn nothing but jeers from his fellow students and half-hidden smiles from the coaches.

The halfback again whipped the wet end of the towel against Harv's bottom.

"You're not one of us, Webster," he taunted, "and you'll never be one of us. Stick to your books . . . we don't want your type in our locker room."

"Except for showering after ballroom-dancing class," the varsity center added, drawing a chorus of guffaws.

"Nah," the halfback replied, popping the towel against Harv's now-red buttocks yet a third time. "Ole Elephant Ass Webster here couldn't dance if he was standing on a bomb."

A cruel grin formed on the center's thin lips. "Bomb. That's a great idea. Get the Atomic Balm."

In the corner of the locker room, Gary Reynolds grimaced, hurrying to pull his pants on even though his legs were still wet from the shower. Not bothering to button his shirt, his shoes and socks clutched in his hand, he hurried outside before the team could turn their attention on him.

Completely on his own and knowing it, Harv wildly swung his hamlike hands.

"Be careful, he's strong for a fatso," the halfback said, motioning for the other boys to help him encircle the teenager.

It was over in a few moments. It took twelve boys to subdue him, though one of them ended up with a bruise on his shoulder that wouldn't heal for a week and another one chipped a tooth when Harv shoved him into the showers.

"Get 'em off him," the halfback ordered, pointing at Harv's underwear with the plastic jar of heat-creating analgesic that he pulled from his locker.

"Jesus Christ, you could drop a watermelon sideways through these things," the nose tackle observed a few seconds later, waving the fat boy's boxer shorts for his teammates to see.

"God won't forgive you," Harv warned, his voice cracking. He twisted his large head from side to side, blinking away the tears that now flowed uncontrollably, struggling to free his arms and legs.

"God won't forgive you," the halfback mimicked in falsetto, removing the metal cap from the Atomic Balm.

"God won't forgive you," the other adolescents chanted over and over again, adding insult to injury by making fun of Harv's often-ridiculed religious beliefs.

"Ssssh!" the center warned, gesturing toward the coaches' offices. "Not so loud." Then he looked at Harv and winked. "If you know a special prayer, now's the time to try it out, Elephant Ass."

"Spread his cheeks," the halfback ordered, kneeling now at Harv's feet, dipping his fingers into the gooey Atomic Balm, "and spread 'em wide."

A sigh came from the lips of the nude body on the bed in Harv Webster's spare bedroom, slicing through the memory like a butcher's cleaver through soft marrow.

Harv didn't know it, but he was softly humming his old high-school fight song as his eyes drank in Jim Persall's muscular form—the broad shoulders, muscular arms, firm buttocks, and corded legs.

Jim's body shuddered again from the effects of the tranquilizer that had been injected into his neck, and Harv leaned over to tighten the knots of the rope that held his captive's arms and legs to the bed.

"It's all right," Harv whispered, his bald head softly touching the young man's right ear. Harv leaned back, and his large, heavy hand absently pushed a strand of hair on the young man's head back into place. "God loves you, Jimmy. He told me to do this to you . . ."

Chapter

1

Sunday, October 6th, 11:37 P.M.

Oblivious to the driving rain outside, Tom stared intently at the words on the screen of his monitor:

```
                    THE SURGERY
               Awaiting Call No. 8738
```

The room was dark as a bad dream except for a tight circle of light from the shaded twenty-watt bulb of a brass lamp on the hardwood computer workstation, a workstation that was almost ten feet long. A black leather address book the size of a playing card lay adjacent to the base of the lamp. The young man's unmoving shadow on the opposite wall might have been a pen-and-ink drawing of a stone figure atop a mausoleum.

Tom Barnslow, at six foot three, was painfully thin for his height. A long face hung beneath curly hair that needed trimming. Large ears protruded from the sides of his head. He hadn't shaved in a week, and a few fine blond, downlike whiskers grew on his tapered chin. His hands were beautiful, the hands of an artist, with fine, graceful fingers. These

4

fingers rested lightly on the keyboard of his computer as he waited for a user to call in to his bulletin-board system.

Tom stood up quickly and walked across the large room to lock his bedroom door, which, he suddenly realized, he had forgotten to close when he'd come upstairs after making himself a baloney sandwich for supper. Shaking his head at what he was doing, he nonetheless opened his closet, turned on the light inside, and poked around the clothes and shoes to make sure no one was in there.

Then Thomas Barnslow, renowned in the New Orleans personal-computer-and-modem world of bulletin-board systems as The Chief Cutter, sat down at his workstation again. His fingers idly skimmed across the keyboard of his Apple IIgs as he waited impatiently for a user to log on to The Surgery, one of several extremely popular electronic systems in New Orleans. But The Chief Cutter's board was unusual. It had a restricted user roster, while most of the phone numbers to the local BBSes were spread around on other boards so as many people as possible would call and use them. Tom had never done that with his number, preferring to let an elite group of individuals find him instead. Tom liked mystery in his life, particularly his after-school life at the computer.

The young man glanced at his calendar for October. A thick red circle had been drawn around the date for Halloween night. He sat back in his chair, laced his fingers behind his head, and looked at the digital clock that sat on top of his modem. It was a few minutes before midnight.

Tom thought for a moment about sacking out early. After all, he did have a test in the morning, and if he slept now he could get up a half-hour early tomorrow to review encryption algorithms. God knows, he hadn't made much progress on the material that Professor Cogglin had given the class to decipher.

But, hell, interesting things tended to happen in BBS-land during the wee hours on Sunday nights. And he still hadn't heard back from that strange but friendly new user, The Succubus, who'd chatted with him for a couple of hours one night, then issued the intrusion challenge. Tom watched the time. His fingers lightly traced the smooth plastic keys of his computer.

Outside, the driving wind slapped large drops of rain against the panes of the bedroom's heavily curtained windows.

11:59:58.

Two seconds later, the small speaker in his computer beeped to signal a new caller, and the opening message for his board scrolled onto the screen for the sixty-sixth time that day:

THE SURGERY

You have entered the waiting room. A nurse stares with hard blue eyes and then asks you for your name.

>

Tom watched expectantly, wondering who the caller would be. That was one of the things he liked most about being the systems operator of his own bulletin board. Unlike the utterly predictable world of college and real life, he never knew at any given moment exactly what would happen on his system or who would log on as a new user. The line was busy most of the time, so no one could ever get through at any planned hour. Staring at the prompt, Tom watched as the user typed:

>THE SUCCUBUS

The Chief Cutter sat up straighter in his chair. He pressed the proper keys to enter chat mode and typed, "Chief Cutter here." He punched the return key twice and waited for a reply.

None came.

Five seconds passed. Then twenty. Tom arched his shoulders as a slight chill passed through him. He passed his tongue across his lower lip, which suddenly felt like it was going to start to tremble. He typed, "Surgery sysop here. Are you there?"

Another few seconds passed, and Tom had his fingers on the keys to break out of chat when words started to appear on his screen:

"I'm here. Did you get the material?"

Tom let twenty seconds slide by to punish the guy for making him wait. As a BBS veteran, he knew all the psychological tricks the users played on each other. Indeed, since The Surgery was one of the first alias-only BBSes to go up in New Orleans, he had pioneered more than his share of these psychic punches. The Chief Cutter felt it was very important to keep the upper hand in all chat situations.

"Maybe I got the material, and maybe I didn't," Tom typed.

"Hey, no reason to be rude. We've got a little problem, that's all, and I'm trying to solve it in the easiest way possible. So I have to ask you a few questions. Stay cool. We're friends, remember? I let you fiddle around in my VAX, remember? You owe me. So, did you get the material? And if you did, did you pass it on to any of your elite hackers?"

"Why do you ask?"

"Come on, be straight with me. Are you the guy who got it? Did you give it to anybody else?"

"That would be telling," Tom typed back, enjoying this battle with the systems operator of the mysterious VAX, the number which he'd hacked at the end of September. They'd had a great chat that night, swapping some wild hacking experiences. The guy had seemed really friendly—a fellow hacker now working in the straight world but who still liked to play computer games on the side. In fact, after Tom had told him about the ICU Elite and how skilled they were, the VAX sysop had proposed a friendly challenge, giving Tom and the Surgeons until Halloween to invade his supposedly secure system and then download and decipher a couple megs' worth of material. If the ICU Elite won the game, the sysop had promised to give Tom the phone numbers to six government systems. If the ICU Elite weren't able to meet the challenge, Tom had agreed to pass on numbers to his six favorite systems.

"Look," The Succubus typed, "I hate to do this, but I have to call off the game. Somebody successfully downloaded the Zeus file. I didn't think it could be done. But even so, when I issued the challenge to you and your Surgeons I wasn't worried about it because the information was incomplete. The situation has changed. I have to know who has that material."

"Hey, sorry," Tom typed back, smiling now that he had The Succubus on the defensive, "but you issued the challenge. You made the rules. You can't change them once the game's started. *You* challenged The ICU Surgeons. *You* gave us until midnight on Halloween to invade your VAX, download the material, and then decipher it. If one of us already completed the incursion and dumped the material, that's part of the contest. We're not obligated to tell you until Halloween night when we agreed the loser would pay up. That's the code we play by. You know that."

"Look, let's keep this friendly. If you've got the material, give me your word of honor as a hacker that you'll destroy it immediately. Then I'll give you those numbers I promised to give you if you won. The game'll be over."

Tom thought about the proposal for only a few seconds before he typed: "No, that's not playing fair. I don't want the numbers unless I earn them. And that's not saying that I have the material either."

"I can't allow this to continue," The Succubus typed in reply.

"You can't stop it," Tom typed back.

"You don't want to screw around with me," The Succubus started to threaten, but Tom quickly interrupted and typed over the other sysop's words:

"Hey, wait a minute. You set up this game. Now you live with it. The ICU Surgeons play by the rules. But we play for keeps, too."

A pause of several seconds. Then The Succubus typed: "I know the identity of your ICU Elite."

"Only the Surgeons know that."

"I know."

"Oh yeah? Who are they?"

A long pause. Then: "That would be telling, wouldn't it?"

Very interesting, Tom thought, very interesting indeed. Had The Succubus somehow discovered the names of the ICU Surgeons, the ultrasecret group of elite hackers, programmers, and war gamers who had access to The Surgery's highest-security sub-board, the Intensive Care Unit?

"Look, Succubus, tell me about yourself, and then maybe I'll let you change the rules of the game."

"I told you the first time I called your board. We chatted, and you validated me. Remember? I'm one of the best hardware developers around. I'm about to finish a top-secret artificial-intelligence project that's going to turn the computer world upside down."

"Be serious. Everybody I chat with lies like crazy. Where did you go to school?"

"School of hard knocks."

"Look, jerk," Tom typed, "I don't take crap from dudes who set up challenge matches and then try to change the rules. Answer the question and quit lying. You're no hardware developer, and we both know it."

"Hey, okay . . . you're right . . . I've been jerking you around," The Succubus replied, starting to lie, sensing that the game was going to have to continue and deciding to go for the initiative. "Actually, I'm a student at Tulane."

Tom was slightly taken aback. Maybe this Succubus was one of the grad students in the computer-science department. That would be hilarious. None of them had the slightest idea that The Surgery was Tom's BBS, though Tom had overheard several of them talking about it and how they were trying to hack into ICU. And a few of them did have part-time computer-related jobs with big companies in the city.

"How old are you?"

"Older than you."

"What grade are you in?"

"I'm a grad student in computer science."

Now Tom was really curious.

"I think you're lying."

There was a pause of almost a minute before The Succubus typed in reply: "You know, I think I may have to hurt you." A pause of ten seconds. Then, letter by letter, words appeared on Tom's monitor: "Did you know that during the Spanish Inquisition priests used to soak people's fingers in wine for about an hour? Then they'd lift up a fingernail and roll it back to the quick as if it was soft bread dough. I hope I'm not going to have to do something like that to you."

Reaching into the shadows beyond the light coming from his desk lamp, Tom picked up a sharpened pencil he kept close to the computer, put it in his mouth, and unconsciously started chewing on it. He felt a shiver starting at the base of his spine now that he'd been threatened. His instinct was to disconnect and let the guy wonder whether he had broken the connection out of fear or out of scorn. Thinking very quickly, Tom decided to not escalate the game for the moment by countering with a physical threat of his own. Instead, he typed: "Yeah, that's my problem. Your problem is finding out if one of us has your Zeus file."

Tom started to press the key sequence to disconnect the chat function, but whoever was at the other end of the line beat him to it.

The Chief Cutter looked at the screen, irritated that The Succubus had hung up on him. The screen was dark except for the name of the BBS and the flashing inverse alphanumeric characters in the upper right-hand corner of the screen that indicated the modem was waiting for either a caller or else a key press from Tom's computer that would enable him to log on locally so he could post messages or make adjustments to his system.

"Rude sucker," Tom muttered as he stared at the clear amber screen of his monitor. "But he plays a good game, that's for sure. So he may have to hurt me, eh? Yeah, right. Guess he figures I've got the material and now he's trying to scare me to distract me from breaking the encryption scheme. Too bad for him he's met his match this time. It takes more than threats to shake The Chief Cutter."

A bolt of lightning illuminated the young man's dark

room, and Tom jerked around in his chair, imagining for a second that one of the shadows in his room was a night stalker. "Relax, man, you're alone," he mumbled to himself. He sighed deeply. "You're always alone."

Because his entrepreneur father was constantly traveling on business trips, Thomas Barnslow, for most months out of the year, lived by himself in their huge house. Corrine, the black maid who now slept in the renovated slave quarters behind the triple-car garage, was always available for company, but she was in her late sixties, and Tom had never felt close to her, even though she'd practically reared him after his mother died when he was three years old. Corrine didn't know anything about computers.

A second-year doctoral student, Tom currently studied computer science at Tulane University. Much taller than his peers and unnaturally thin—as well as having a face he thought would be more appropriate on a horse—he saw himself as an outsider. An excellent student, Tom was socially retarded, and his fellow grad students, who thought of him as a brilliant loner, had long ago stopped asking him to join them for their all-night drinking-and-hacking sessions.

Like many shy adolescents, the constant ribbing and teasing in high school about his reticence had only served to thicken a shell that was already hard as a rock. By the time Tom finished his B.S. in computer science, the shell was worthy of a hundred-year-old sea turtle. To make matters worse, as a junior in prep school Tom Barnslow had developed a habit of muttering in his very soft and naturally high voice—and he only muttered when he absolutely had to. Most of the time, both in class and out, his face bore an enigmatic look that was, some thought, slightly crazed.

A few of his teachers had expressed their concern about Tom over the years, and when he was a junior in prep school, the head of the upper school had even gone so far as to call Mr. Barnslow to relate these concerns. Unfortunately, she had called when Tom's father was in the midst of closing a very important start-up deal, and his clipped reply had been, "Are you out of your mind? I'm up to my ass in a multimillion-dollar proposal and you're interrupting me to tell me my son's too quiet? It's a shame more people aren't quiet. He's fine. His grades are fine. I send him to your school for an education, not emotional counseling. Let me worry about his emotional well-being, thank you."

Tom had known adolescent depression with more than the usual familiarity, and, at one point, late in his senior year when he was about to turn sixteen, he gave a week's serious thought to blasting his brains out with one of his father's double-barreled shotguns.

It was at this nadir in his life that he had discovered personal computers through a BASIC programming course offered by his prep school's math department. He had been hooked immediately, feeling an affinity with the powerful little machines that he had never felt with other human beings.

Several weeks into the course, using almost three thousand dollars of his personal inheritance from his mother, Tom had purchased his first of many computers to come, an Apple IIe with all the trimmings: color monitor, printer, programs, expansion cards, and, at the urging of the salesman, a modem.

The modem, an electronic device that connects computer to computer for the purpose of transferring data over Ma Bell's wired America, turned out to be the boy's salvation. Through the modem Tom was able to make connections with strangers for the first time in his life, unseen acquaintances who met and conversed only through their personal computers, modems, and South Central Bell's underground optic fibers. Anonymous friends who didn't use their own names.

"I wonder what The Succubus looks like?" Tom muttered, visualizing a scarred, one-armed monster. "The guy plays a mean mind game, that's for sure."

A new call into The Surgery interrupted Tom's ruminations. The modem signaled the carrier connection with a distinctive click and beep from the small speaker in the computer. The Chief Cutter waited patiently as the user answered the name prompt by typing in: NELLY DEAN.

"Good ole Nelly," Tom said, watching as The Surgery's best female user her way through the password log-on, the menus, and the sub-menus to get to the war board, where she would shred all who tried to defeat her at psychological role-playing with her precise, catty prose.

In her tastefully furnished bedroom in her house on Fountainbleu Avenue, Mary Alice Sluice sat at her computer and watched words scroll past on her monitor. Her intelligent green eyes widened with pleasure when she read the following message on The Surgery's war board:

Message: 139
From: Tunnel Rat
Date: Waiting for Nelly

I'm waiting for you, Nelly, hugging the bosom of Mother Earth like she was you, sitting down here in my tunnel, sniffing the air, smelling the rich, clean loam. You know what it makes me think of, Nelly? It makes me think of you, babe. It makes me think of that body of yours that makes men weak in the knees, of that mind that never quits, of that sparkling laugh that sets birds in their trees a'singing. Yeah, I'm waiting . . . waiting down here under the ground . . . waiting for you!

Tunnel Rat
Below Ground

Mary Alice smiled at the posting. Tunnel Rat had been wooing her on the war boards and in E-mail around the city for almost three months now. Sometimes, he'd post several times a day; other times, he'd disappear completely from the BBS for weeks. He was one of Mary Alice's favorite aliases, particularly since he'd started developing this on-line romance with her.

On-line romance was all right with Mary Alice. Ever since her one failed attempt at love in real life—a relationship with a brilliant but highly possessive ophthalmologist that had unraveled like rotten rope just before she'd finished her residency in psychiatry in California—she'd not wanted to have anything to do with men other than on a professional basis. She did, however, often think that she'd like to have a daughter or son to take the edge off the loneliness that stalked her personal life away from her work and career.

But having a little romantic fun on the war boards was something else. Mary Alice smiled and started to type an answer to the posting she'd just read:

```
Message: 140
From: Nelly Dean
Date: It'll be a Long Wait

   Hey, Tunnel Rat, you'd better find yourself a nice quiet
little mouse, chum, because you're not ever going to snuggle in
the splendid tan arms of Nelly Dean. These arms are reserved for
my prince, my shining knight on a white steed stronger than the
Budweiser horses, my hero who's going to arrive out of nowhere
and sweep me off my dainty ballerina's feet, the Lancelot who's
going to destroy the Black Knight who's abducted me from my
castle.
   Look in the mirror, Tunnel Rat, and see if you're that Knight.
If you are . . . if you are . . .

Nelly Dean
```

After watching Nelly Dean type her response to Tunnel Rat before she disconnected, Thomas Barnslow stood and stretched, loosening the kinks that come with sitting nine hours straight at a computer terminal. A few minutes later, as he crawled under the bedcovers, he heard the click and beep of his modem answering the next user's call.

Tom yawned, closed his eyes, and willed himself to immediate, dreamless sleep.

Monday, October 7th, 12:30 A.M.

The master bedroom in the brick singles-only apartment complex looked like a scientist's laboratory. On the floor was a bluish-green shag carpet that the occupant sprayed three times a week with a special aerosol to reduce the static electricity that had a filthy habit of zapping sensitive computer chips.

The furniture that had come with the apartment had been carefully disassembled and was now neatly stacked in the unused third bedroom, a bedroom which also contained a horizontal freezer, the kind that stored large quantities of meat, and a large double bed that the occupant didn't use.

A counter of inch-thick oak extended out four feet from each wall.

The flimsy door had been taken down, replaced by a steel one covered with thin wood veneer. The occupant had constructed this door himself, adding three deadbolt locks. As far as appearances went, this secure door was a perfect duplicate of the one that he had removed.

The immaculately varnished and dust-free oak counter that extended out from each of the walls of the room was heavily braced with two-by-four crossbars on its underside to guard against the slightest vibrations, which could conceivably damage the hard drives that were attached to two different computers, an IBM-PC and a Macintosh II.

Sixteen square feet of space existed in the middle of the room. Centered in this square was an oversized leather reclining chair and a small mahogany table on which rested a set of keys, a six-inch-long hatpin, a copy of the collected works of St. John of the Cross, and a bottle of chilled Perrier water sweating on a cork coaster. A highly polished stainless-steel hanging lamp had replaced the original fixture in the middle of the ceiling. There were no windows.

The hanging light was turned off at the moment, and the only illumination in the deeply shadowed room came from the different colored diodes on the computer hardware and electronic equipment that took up most of the available space on the counters.

The door to the room was bolted.

The occupant of the apartment, his pale eyelids almost closed, filled the half-tilted recliner. His leather-sandaled feet rested on the extended foot support of the expensive chair.

He wore a robe of unpolished brown wool, a monk's attire.

He was naked beneath the robe.

The cowl covered his head.

An unobtrusive hum came from one corner underneath the counter where the dehumidifier and alternate power supplies, in case of a power failure, had been placed. Cables, perhaps half a hundred of them, snaked around the counter, in a precise arrangement.

"Let there be light," The Succubus commanded arrogantly, and a cone of illumination flooded down on him from the hanging fixture directly above his head.

With the exception of several bookshelves that held an eclectic selection of books and a framed reproduction of Salvador Dali's painting of the crucified Christ, the walls of the room, which the occupant had covered with two-inch-thick cork board and painted a flat black, were bare. The ceiling had also been covered with the black cork to reduce external noise to nothing. The room was, for all intents and purposes, soundproof.

"Twenty watts," he specified, and the light above him dimmed.

"I'm hot."

"What temperature do you desire, Harv?" came a woman's sexy voice from a pair of speakers that were in the other two corners of the room beneath the counter space.

"Sixty-five degrees," Harvey Webster answered and smiled in satisfaction as the computer-controlled central air conditioner immediately clicked on. "And some music. Marais tonight, I think. Sound level two. Soft background only."

Marin Marais's "Sonnerie de Saint Géneviève du Mont de Paris" suddenly permeated the room, and the violins' melody gently danced on the filtered and dehumidified air.

"Very nice, Teresa," he said.

"Thank you, Harv," Teresa responded. "Is there anything else I can do for you?"

"Just one more thing, dear . . . business before pleasure and all that, you know," Harv answered, reaching for the bottle of Perrier.

"Yes, Harv. What do you desire?"

"Play the recording that took place in the director's office, please, Teresa. File entitled Problem One. Play at level five, just above the Marais."

"Yes, Harv," the computer-generated voice responded. "File Problem One, playing at level five. Coming now."

Harv Webster drank a little Perrier before he stretched back in the leather recliner. His pale eyelids fluttered as he listened to the recording and nervously relived the conversation that had taken place on Saturday morning in the director's office:

"First off, when I send for you, I expect you to get that fat ass up here immediately. I do *not* appreciate having to wait thirty minutes. Now, it seems we have a little problem. You assured me the Zeus extract was secure."

The digitalized recording of project director Edward August's angry voice had captured the timbre perfectly, and Harv smiled in satisfaction at the reproduction quality of the tiny state-of-the-art bugs he had designed, constructed, and then hidden in the project's offices and labs. These bugs digitalized and then recorded every word spoken about the project on one of the hard drives here in Harv's personal lab. Harv found this situation particularly amusing because he was in charge of sweeping the offices and labs for electronic bugging devices three times a week.

"So I want to know one thing," the director's voice continued, "how the hell did this happen?"

Harv, who had not been invited to sit down, walked to the small bar in one corner. When he reached the bar, he said, "Cogglin logged off improperly when he uploaded the new hypothesis. Which, obviously, left a window into the material."

Thinking furiously about how he was going to handle this problem if the director asked him about his BBS activities, Harv calmly took his time opening the ice bucket. After the outburst down there in the lab when Cogglin and Brandais had dropped their bomb on him about the viability of the Athena hypothesis, he knew how important it was that he now remain in complete control and appear to be his normal self.

Using the silver ice tongs, he dropped a single cube into an old-fashioned glass. Then he unscrewed the cap off a bottle of soda water, which he poured over the ice. He held the glass to his ear to listen to the fizzing sound.

"What the hell do you think you're doing?" Edward August stammered, surprised by this degree of insubordination. Over in a chair to the director's right, Al Cogglin, the part-time Tulane professor and full-time project programmer, stifled a smile. He enjoyed observing these encounters between Harv and the retired army general.

"Hey, General, I'm thirsty. Building complicated hardware's hard work . . . I'm having to revise some of the prototype in light of the Athena hypothesis . . . ain't easy, you know," Harv answered. His huge hands rummaged beneath the bar's counter. "Any lime twists back here? I can't find one."

"Sit down!" the director ordered in a voice icier than Harv's drink. "And speaking of the prototype, I want a copy of those schematics placed in the extract file."

"Relax, General," Harv replied, sauntering to the softest chair in the room. He eased his overweight body down slowly and stared at Edward August with his small eyes. "And forget about a copy of the schematics. That's my work, and nobody else is going to see it until the project's complete. That's in my contract, and you know it."

The director took a deep breath.

Harv Webster was one of the few people on earth who could rattle him. It's a shame, the director reflected, that he's a goddamn genius and that I can't complete the project without him.

"You can be released from this project, you know," August threatened.

"Don't play games with me because you'll never win," Harv snapped. He took a sip of his drink, savoring the sparkling water. Then he said, "You know as well as I do that I'm the only one working on the project capable of building the connector. Sure, some other hotshot electrical engineer could come in here and do it—but he'd need at least a year of studying Brandais and Cogglin's preliminary research before he'd even have a clue as to what was going on. Do you know how complicated the conclusions in that goddamned new Athena hypothesis are? Sorry, General, you're stuck with me."

Harv smiled his most arrogant grin, but he was cursing himself for swearing about the new hypothesis. To distract the director's attention, he dipped a thick, long forefinger in the soda water and then started lightly circling the top of the glass with the wet skin of his fingertip. A note from what sounded like the upper range of a violin resulted.

"First-class crystal," Harv commented. Then he looked the director square in the eye. "Are you firing me? Is that what you're trying to say?"

"No, son, I'm not firing you," the man replied, deciding to try the fatherly approach. "Look, Harv, I need to know what happened. We can't have the extract of the Zeus material floating around. You know that."

"Don't sweat it. A plan's in play. I'll definitely know who has the stuff by Halloween night. Maybe sooner if my plan works."

The director glanced down at his desk calendar. It was Saturday, October fifth. "That's almost a month," he exploded.

"Can't be helped, General. I've got a couple of lines on who I think has it, but I won't know for sure until Halloween. If that isn't good enough, call in the FBI. The CIA. The Department of Defense. The Daughters of the American Revolution."

The director's small round face started to redden. "Don't wise-ass me, boy. You know I'm not going to do that. This is a private project, and we're going to make a bundle off of it. Three weeks . . . not good enough, Harv. I want to know who has that material by this time tomorrow. And I want to know the specifics of your plan for finding the thief."

Harv stood up, walked to the director's desk, and put the glass of soda on top of the felt blotter. Then he dipped his finger in the water and resumed circling the top of the crystal. The notes that ensued had an eerie beauty.

"You hear that?" Harv asked, turning his head and winking at Dr. Cogglin. "That's one of the purest sounds that God gave us. And you know why we have that sound? Because some craftsman made this beautiful glass. He didn't make a glass like this because some little wimp of a red-faced retired general who gets his rocks off bossing people around told him to do it tomorrow. He made this glass by taking his time and doing it right. Do you get my point? Or do I need to run it past you another time? We're not playing Parcheesi here, General. This is complicated."

By now Harv had leaned over the desk until his face was only inches from the director's. His large belly flopped over the papers on the desk.

Suddenly the director shoved back his chair and stood up. He walked around the desk and stood toe-to-toe with Harv. At five feet six inches, he was dwarfed by the overweight six-foot-five hardware expert.

"Look, you fat slob," the director snarled, "I'm tired of your crap. This is not a game. Do I make myself clear?"

Harv's pale face tightened. His finger left the crystal. A second later it was jabbing the director right on the sternum.

"As usual, you're way off base, General. It *is* a game. A very complicated game. Life's a game, General. And I never lose the games I play. Never." The finger jabbed two more times in emphasis.

Edward August stared into Harv's eyes, the sort of eyes he suddenly realized he could find in a dark corner of a padded room. He took a short step back.

"Harv, I'm not going to fence with you any longer. I want to know who has the Zeus extract as soon as possible. And I have to know your plan. What if one of the Silicon Valley companies has the extract? That's the point."

"You'll have your answer by Halloween night at the latest," Harv said, stepping back and picking up the glass from the director's desk. "And don't worry about it, General. Everything's under control. I'm ninety-eight percent sure that the person who has it isn't going to sell it or give it away. And, for all I know, you may be the thief. I never have trusted retired generals. Especially little retired generals. So, for security reasons, nobody's going to know my plan for getting the material back. Take your pack off and stand at ease. Let me take care of business."

With those words, Harv walked out of the director's office, taking the glass with him. He closed the door gently behind himself.

In the office, Al Cogglin and the director heard Harv's booming laugh coming from down the hallway as Harv made his way toward the lab.

"Jesus," the director said, going to the bar and pouring himself two fingers of scotch. "I hate that arrogant prick. I'm going to have his balls one of these days."

"He's not so bad, Ed, once you get to know him," Cogglin said. "He's really a pretty lonely guy . . . and he's never learned how to get along with people. His mind's top drawer. Best student I ever had. I still get the willies sometimes thinking about the work he did for me that year I was visiting professor at M.I.T. He's just not a people person." Cogglin chuckled. "He can't help it if he's an asshole."

"Don't give me that 'He's a lonely guy' crap, Al. This is a team effort and I want team players."

Al Cogglin shrugged. "I guess all we can do is wait. If anyone can figure out who has the material, Harv's the man."

The director drew a single finger across the top of his Adam's apple in a slicing motion. "For all of us if another company has the material. Stay on his ass, Al. Keep a very close eye on him." Edward August tossed down the scotch in one quick gulp. "I don't trust paranoid bastards like that. I never should have hired him. We should have gone with Conlick. Would have if he'd had himself together. Watch him close, Al. Very close. I'm going to nail our Harvey if it's the last thing I do."

"We need him, sir," Al said softly.

"We need him now," the director amended. "We won't need him forever."

On the recliner, Harv opened his eyes and said, "Terminate playback of Problem One, Teresa. I've heard enough. And bring the Marais up to level five."

"Yes, Harv," the computer responded, and the recording ceased, replaced by the soothing sound of violins.

"Record Zeus Intrusion One, Teresa," Harv said softly. "Filter out music."

"Yes, Harv. Recording now. Music filtered out."

"Zeus Intrusion One, October seventh, approximately one A.M.,"Harv said. "File Problem One has been repeatedly analyzed. Director's response typically shortsighted. Encounter with Chief Cutter regarding challenge of October first entirely unsatisfactory. Game remains in effect. Termination date of Halloween night unaltered. I am formulating a plan to pervert the outcome of the game. End Zeus Intrusion One."

"Zeus Intrusion One ended, recorded, and backed up," Teresa's voice came a few seconds later as two of the hard drives whirled, one right after the other.

"There," Harv said, reaching for the Perrier and taking a sip. "That takes care of business. Now for a little pleasure. So Cogglin thinks I'm a lonely asshole, eh? Hardly lonely since I have you, Teresa. Play some Mozart—level eight—and dim the light. I have some thinking to do. This looks to be a complicated game. It has layers and layers. It may even be fun."

"Yes, Harv. I'm happy you're having fun," the computer voice came, giving the correct response to the keyword *fun*, but misinterpreting the context. The overhead light went out as the sounds of Mozart filled the room.

"Teresa, what's the temperature?"

"The temperature is sixty-five degrees here in our world."

"I love you, Teresa," Harv said softly.

"And I love you, Harv," Teresa replied, the computer-generated voice rich with sincerity and emotion.

"Thank you, dear. That'll be all for tonight. Rest well."

"Thank you, my darling." With those words, the voice-recognition program that Harv had been refining for almost two years terminated, leaving him alone with his thoughts.

"Blast the timing," he muttered to himself. "Wouldn't you know it that Cogglin would upload the key to the project a week after I gave some hackers a chance to infiltrate my system and match wits with me? Rotten luck. And the Cutter's going to be a prick about it. Guess I'll have to show him and his sorry little group of Surgeons what real surgery's all about. Wait till they feel the edge of my scalpel."

The gentle hum of the air conditioner and dehumidifier fought for several moments with Harv's off-key laughter.

"Ahhh yes, the loyalty of thieves and politicians," Harv said quietly in his sealed room, thinking once again of the director's and Al Cogglin's words spoken only after he had left the office. "Who the hell do they think they're playing games with?" Harv asked the empty room.

He chortled quietly to himself and finished the last of the Perrier.

He rubbed the leather top of the collected works of St. John of the Cross.

He prayed silently for almost five minutes.

Then, after pulling up the right sleeve of his robe, he took the hatpin from the table and slowly pushed it through two inches of the fleshly part of the skin above the muscle of his inner forearm. Leaving the pin in and ignoring the slight bleeding, he lowered the sleeve of the robe, looked at the painting of the crucified Christ, and laid back in the recliner.

He slept.

Monday, October 7th, 3:34 A.M.

The storm outside intensifying, Tom Barnslow awoke suddenly in his room to a crescendo of thunder and lightning. As he sat up in bed, Tom asked aloud, "What's so important about the Zeus file that a cool sysop like The

Succubus would suddenly try to change the rules of a game he himself had set up?" And surely, he thought, the guy wasn't serious about rolling back fingernails like bread dough?

A rolling series of thunder cracks outside suggested an answer, but it wasn't one that Tom found comforting.

Chapter
2

Wednesday, October 9th, Noon

The Zeus project team stood in their main lab, the door to the hallway securely locked and the telephones off their hooks. A tape deck was recording the experiment so it could be replayed moment-by-moment if necessary.

"Well, gentlemen and lady," the director said formally, "this is the hour we've been waiting for."

"This is it, all right," Dr. Cogglin reiterated, an expectant smile on his face. "Make sure you do that right, Harv," he ordered.

Harv Webster looked up from where he was running final checks on the prototype of the Zeus connector. "Herr Doktor, do you wish to run the tests yourself? Do you have no confidence in your most brilliant former student?" Harv had straightened and now stood with the mechanism in his huge hands, offering it to Dr. Cogglin. The mechanism looked like a bulky pair of stereo headphones.

"No, Harv, no. You should connect it. You better know what you're doing," Cogglin said.

Mary Alice Sluice smiled to herself. She'd been working

with Cogglin and Webster for three years but was still amused by their constant verbal fencing. "Are you ready for me to bring in von Neumann?" she asked.

"Close enough, Fraulein," Harv answered. "Everything's checking out perfectly here on the simulation. Waltz that ripe body of yours into the lab and bring in our little simian buddy."

"I'll help," neurosurgeon Paul Brandais offered.

"All right." The two of them walked toward the door that opened into the animal lab where the project's trained chimpanzee was kept.

When they were in the animal lab, Paul said with a wry smile, "I'm waiting for the day when you squelch him, Mary Alice."

"Don't worry about it. It's his nature to alienate everyone. He's brilliant but insecure. Partly because of his weight problem and no doubt for a lot of other reasons that we know nothing about. He's been trying to get my goat ever since that party the director threw so we could get to know each other. That was back when he was Mr. Nice Guy—before the real Harv popped out. Remember? Anyway, like I've told you a hundred times, don't sweat it. I'm immune to his nonsense."

"Well, I'll unlock the cage now," Paul said.

"Yes, you do that," Dr. Sluice replied, smiling in spite of herself as he turned his back on her. A gentleman to the core as well as her mentor, Paul Brandais somehow felt she needed him to protect her from the other male members of the team.

"Ahhh, here comes our favorite lab subject," the director said, smiling nervously as von Neumann walked into the lab, holding hands with Mary Alice on one side and Paul Brandais on the other. Except for his head, which they had kept shaved since he was a very young chimp, von Neumann was a perfectly healthy and normal-looking chimpanzee.

"Are you ready, Harvey?" Mary Alice asked, knowing that the use of his full name irritated the obese hardware expert. She gestured with her hand for von Neumann to sit down in the padded swivel chair that was about three feet away from the VAX.

Von Neumann climbed easily into the chair and then turned it around and around on its well-oiled bearings. Spinning in the chair was one of his favorite activities. Mary Alice had been encouraging him to do just that for over a year so he would have no fear when the day of reckoning came.

Sitting now at one of the terminals connected to the VAX, Harv pressed several keys. The four-foot-high robot that was also interfaced with the VAX came to life and moved about the room on its rubber wheels. Harv turned the robot in each of the compass directions and then sent it toward a card table that had been set up at the west end of the lab. There were six bananas on the card table. When the robot had rolled to the edge of the table, Harv punched a few more keys to tell the robot to lift one of the bananas, which it did successfully. After that test, Harv had the robot put the banana back on the table and then roll to its starting position some three feet away from the chimp.

"Everything's okay," Harv said. Big beads of sweat had formed on his forehead and upper lip.

Von Neumann had been watching the robot's trick with the bananas, and the chimp indicated with rudimentary sign language to Mary Alice and Dr. Brandais that he was hungry.

"If this works properly, old friend," Paul said, petting the top of the chimp's head, "you can have all the bananas you want very shortly."

"This is it then," the director said as Harv approached von Neumann with the prototype.

Because von Neumann was used to wearing a set of headphones very similar to the prototype when they had him listen to music, the chimp wasn't at all scared when Harv put the mechanism on his head. The animal winced slightly when Harv attached the first electrode, but Mary Alice was patting the back of his hairy hand, telling him everything was okay. He didn't even seem to notice as Harv slid six microneedles under his skin and secured them with adhesive tape.

Harv rechecked all the wires in the prototype, tracing them back to the two-foot-square metal box that contained the actual hardware of the Zeus connector. After checking the wiring in the box, he examined the half-inch-thick cable that attached the box to the VAX. Then Harv sat down at the terminal.

Typing rapidly, he reloaded Dr. Cogglin's newly rewritten Zeus program, complete now that it had the Athena hypothesis subroutine, and then looked at the director. "Ready to run," Harv said.

The director took a deep breath. Three years of work balanced on this moment. He looked at Dr. Brandais and then turned to Dr. Cogglin.

"Why not? Step on the gas, Harv, and let's see what happens," Dr. Cogglin said.

Harv pressed the key to initiate the program.

All eyes were on von Neumann, who suddenly jerked in the chair.

The hair on the chimp's body rose slightly, as if he were experiencing gooseflesh.

"We have a good connection," Dr. Brandais said, studying the tape that was coming from an electroencephalograph wired into the prototype. "All brain activity within normal range."

"Something's happening with his eyes," Mary Alice observed. "They look distant, as if he's staring at something a long ways away."

Brandais dropped the tape and rushed to the chair where von Neumann sat. Taking a penlight from his breast pocket, the neurologist bent over and looked into the chimp's eyes.

"Marked pupil extension but no apparent retinal disintegration," the neurologist said, clicking off the light. He suddenly added, "Oh yes."

"What? What?" the director asked.

Paul pointed at the robot, which was twitching left and right.

"He's focusing," Mary Alice said, and everyone turned

their attention back to the chimp, whose eyes were now staring at the twitching robot.

Von Neumann's lips formed what might have passed for a pleased smile.

The robot made a beeline for the table with the bananas.

"Holy shit," Dr. Cogglin said reverently. "It works."

Dr. Brandais's mouth opened as he watched the robot pick up one of the bananas.

"Sweet Jesus," Harv muttered as the robot spun around and headed directly for von Neumann.

A few seconds later, the little robot was beside the chimp.

Von Neumann's right hand started to reach for the banana, but Mary Alice held it down and shook her head. With her other hand she pointed to the robot.

Von Neumann looked puzzled for a second, but then his eyes grew distant again.

Suddenly the robot's other arm came over and the waldo extensions that mimicked fingers started to peel the banana.

The robot's arm moved again and gently brought the banana to the chimp's mouth. Then it jammed it in, and von Neumann started chewing.

Harv laughed almost hysterically. "That's von Neumann controlling that thing, all right," he practically shouted. "That's how he always eats those things."

Licking his lips happily, the chimp looked at the project members.

Then he belched.

Walking back to the terminal, Harv typed in a command, which froze the robot in its tracks.

Mary Alice started to remove the prototype from the chimp's skull.

"No! Don't touch it . . . let me do that," Harv ordered, leaving the terminal and rapidly taking the few steps to the happy chimp, who was pointing eagerly at the other bananas on the table across the room.

Harv ripped off the adhesive tape and pulled the electrodes from underneath von Neumann's skin. Then he carefully and gently lifted the prototype from the chimp's skull and stepped back a couple of feet.

"I'll be darned," Dr. Brandais said. "I'll be goshdarned."

"Well, I'll be goddamned," Dr. Cogglin said, doing his colleague one better. Then he grabbed the neurosurgeon by the shoulders and started dancing around the room. "We did it, pardner. We did it!"

"Break out the champagne," the director ordered, a huge smile engulfing his face. "We've batted a grand slam."

"You did great, von Neumann," Mary Alice said, as Al ceremoniously placed the other bananas in the chimp's lap.

"Do you know what we've done here today?" Dr. Brandais mumbled happily to his old friend and colleague.

"Yep," Dr. Cogglin replied, "we've just interfaced a brain with a computer."

"No," Mary Alice said, her voice full of wonder. "We've just changed the world."

While the others were congratulating each other, Harv continued to stand motionless, the Zeus connector dwarfed in his huge hands. It felt like the prototype was tingling.

Sunday, October 13th, 10 P.M.

The dehumidifier in the corner of the lab in Harv's apartment hummed quietly.

From the speakers came the low notes of an early Bach organ piece.

Harv sat in the leather recliner in the middle of the room, the light swallowed by the thick wool of the monk's robe's cowl that covered his head.

His eyes stared at the replica of the Zeus connector that he had built.

He turned it slowly, gently, and reverently in his huge soft hands.

"Harv," Teresa suddenly interjected as she was randomly programmed to do on unpredictable occasions, "I love you with all my heart."

"And I love you too, Teresa. You make me very happy."

"I like to be happy, Harv," the computer program answered, the correct response to the key word *happy*.

"Me too, dear," Harv replied. "I knew finding God would make me happy, dear, but now there's something else . . . Do you know what that something else is that would make me happy, Teresa?"

"I don't understand, Harv."

"Listening mode only, please."

"Listening subroutine called. Listening only now."

"Teresa, it would make me happy to test the connector on myself. Disable Bach and play Lab File, eight-thirty A.M., October eleventh."

"Searching . . . found. Disabling Bach and playing Lab File, eight-thirty A.M., October eleventh," Teresa said.

"That completes the fourth successful test," Harv said, as he removed the electrodes from von Neumann's skull. "Let's hook it up to Herr Doktor Cogglin and see if it works."

Cogglin and Brandais turned simultaneously and looked at Harv.

"I'm serious. I want to see if it *really* works."

Mary Alice laughed nervously.

Keeping his tone light, Harv said, "I'm serious. Let's try it on Al and see if the connector works, damn it."

"Yes, it's tempting to initiate stage two," Dr. Brandais said, cupping his chin with his right hand, "but it's too early. We all know that."

"Well, it's up to you guys," Harv said easily. "I'm just curious to see if my mechanism works the way I built it to work."

"No," Dr. Brandais said flatly. "As senior project member, I'm responsible for the testing sequence. It's my decision. We've only run four models with the lab subject so far. Our protocol for stage one has always called for a minimum of a dozen primate connections. I'm sorry, Harv. I appreciate your enthusiasm for the project, but, no, I insist that we adhere to the established testing routine."

"No problem, Herr Professor," Harv replied, faking a smile. "I just brought it up because it has worked so perfectly. Like all my work, I might add."

"It *seems* to have worked perfectly four times, Harv," Brandais said. "Outwardly, the lab subject *appears* to be unharmed. We will not, and I emphasize the word *not,* know that this is indeed the case until after the primate testing sequence has been completed and the lab subject has been . . ."

"Killed and dissected, Doctor," Harv interjected, angry with Brandais's implication that there was a possibility that the prototype wasn't perfect. "Let's not get sentimental here, right?"

Brandais looked wistfully toward the animal room. Mary Alice stared sadly at the floor. They had all grown quite attached to von Neumann.

"It's a scientific necessity," Dr. Cogglin explained. "I like the chimp as much as anybody here, but it has to be done. You know that, Harv."

There was a long silence in the lab.

Harv eased his 295 pounds into the swivel chair that von Neumann had just gotten out of. The seat was still warm.

"Never should have brought it up," Harv apologized, knowing that he wasn't going to get his way, at least not here at the lab.

"Good for you, Harv," Dr. Brandais said. "Honestly, it's best for all of us that we stick to established scientific procedure. The time will come. If everything continues to go smoothly, we should be ready to test the connector on a human by the end of the month. That's only a few weeks away, Harv. So be patient, huh?"

"Yes, Herr Doktor," Harv answered in his best Igor imitation. "We do it da scientific way, da!"

The project team laughed, the tension dissipated.

"End playback," Harv commanded.

He looked down at the replica of the Zeus connector in his hands.

He stood up and walked over to the counter, where he gently placed the replica on an inch-thick piece of Styrofoam.

He turned to the recliner and picked up the collected works of St. John of the Cross, which he opened.

"Sixty watts," he ordered, and Teresa increased the light from the stainless-steel hanging fixture above his head.

Harv turned to Chapter Ten of Book One of *The Ascent of Mount Carmel* and read aloud:

> Manifestly, then, the appetites do not bring any good to a man. Rather they rob him of what he already has. And if he does not mortify them, they will not cease until they accomplish what it is said the offspring of vipers do within the mother: while growing within her they eat away at her entrails and finally kill her to remain alive at her expense. So the unmortified appetites result in killing a man in his relationship with God, and thus, because he did not put them to death first, they alone live in him . . .

Harv closed the book and put it back on the table next to the recliner. "So true, so true," he muttered, tears springing to his eyes. He took the hatpin from the table.

He pulled the recliner to its forward position and stood up.

"Ten watts," he ordered, and the overhead light dimmed.

He pulled the hem of the robe up above his bare knees.

He knelt, facing the Dali reproduction. He wiggled and stretched until he was in the most uncomfortable position possible, his knees digging into the hard concrete floor beneath the shag carpet. He straightened his back and extended his chest, trying to force his shoulder blades to touch.

Using the fingers of his left hand, he stretched out an inch of loose, fatty tissue just below his Adam's apple. With his right hand, he slowly pushed the pin through the skin. Leaving the pin impaled through his flesh, he lowered his hands to his side.

The pain cleared his mind of his desire.

He prayed.

The Zeus connection was tested two more times on von Neumann, once on Monday, October fourteenth, and again on Thursday, October seventeenth.

On the night of October sixteenth, at a few minutes after ten P.M., Harvey Webster stood in the large bathroom of his apartment. He'd been reading St. John of the Cross for two hours and had just finished a section about vanity. Because Harv was proud of his soft brown hair—his only attractive physical feature—he'd put down the book and had walked determinedly to the bathroom, where he'd laid out a pair of scissors, a can of shaving cream, and the straight-edge razor that his uncle had given him when he turned sixteen. He'd had the razor for fifteen years.

He used the scissors to clip away his hair, then shaved the top of his skull until his scalp glistened.

At work the next day, he wore a yellow stocking cap, which he had kept pulled down low on his head.

Friday, October 18th, 3:46 A.M.

Harv sat alone in the locked project lab, unable to tear his eyes from the Zeus connector he held in his hands.

Slowly, he rose from the swivel chair that von Neumann had sat in during the tests.

He walked to the VAX and gently placed the connector next to the large computer.

He walked to the metal cabinet above the lab's stainless-steel sink and removed from its bottom shelf a large bottle of rubbing alcohol and a pad of cotton gauze. He opened the alcohol and poured a liberal amount on the cotton.

He took the wet gauze and rubbed it slowly across his head. The air conditioning quickly evaporated it, and the ensuing coolness above his fevered brain almost sapped his desire to test the connector on himself.

Almost.

The smell of rubbing alcohol . . .

Harv was in sixth grade, walking to lunch with his best friend, Sammy Weinman.

The teacher lined them up in the classroom, as she did before every lunch period, but, on this particular day—a Friday, Harv remembered suddenly, just like today—Sammy stood behind Harv instead of in front of him as he usually did.

They left the classroom and walked under the eaves between the classrooms and the cafeteria.

The teacher stopped to talk with two of her colleagues.

Suddenly Sammy started laughing almost hysterically.

Harv turned to get in on the joke.

"What's so funny, Sammy?" he asked, a broad grin forming on his chubby, cherubic face, anxious to share the joke.

Almost gasping for breath, Sammy, cruelly, between deep laughs, replied, "You, Harv. You're what's so funny. Walking behind you's like walking behind an elephant's ass! I didn't know you had such a big butt, Harv."

And then Sammy broke into another unrestrained fit of laughter, and he was joined by their classmates until Harv stood in a tightening circle of laughing, screaming faces and pointing fingers.

"Elephant Ass, Elephant Ass," the children chanted.

A few moments later, Harv was being pulled off Sammy, whose nose had split open like a melon under the hammering of Harv's uncontrolled punches.

It had taken three teachers to get the twelve-year-old, 170-pound boy off of Sammy.

The first in a long series of betrayals.

"Odd that I should think of that," Harv mumbled aloud, coming back to the present. "Sammy . . . guess I showed that little bastard."

Harv went to the robot and tested its connections to the VAX. No problems there.

He walked back to the VAX and picked up the connector. Taking his time and being very careful, he cleaned the microneedles on the prototype with the still-wet cotton before slipping them under the skin of his bald head. He tore off strips of adhesive tape and taped the electrodes down to ensure that none of them slipped out.

Bending over, he typed into the Zeus program in the VAX a simple timing-loop subroutine that would give him a minute to sit down in von Neumann's chair before initiating the connection. He added a second subroutine to halt execution of the Zeus program after running for five minutes.

Von Neumann had been connected for ten minutes that morning, but Harv saw no reason to take too many chances this first time.

Pressing the key to begin the timing loop, he carefully walked to the chair, making sure none of the wires were crossed or disconnected by his movement.

He sat.

He closed his eyes and thought for just a second of the plan he had refined regarding the Zeus extract. He'd teach The Chief Cutter and his Surgeons to play games with him.

At the VAX, the timing loop ended, and the Zeus program initiated the connection.

In the chair, Harv's eyelids snapped open.

"Oh my God," he muttered as thousands of different-colored flashbulbs seemed to explode somewhere deep behind his eyes.

He felt like he was falling, down through the lab's floor, through the concrete foundation, through the bedrock of Mother Earth herself.

He felt his mind expand, move geometrically outward with a clarity of thought and precision that he had never experienced before. It was like mainlining dextro-amphetamine—which he had done once at M.I.T. in the early seventies—but much, much better.

His sense of self magnified. Time stopped.

He slowly turned his huge head and looked at the robot.

Then he was inside the robot, and his carbon-based mind and the robot's silicon-based circuits were one.

"God," his voice said, overflowing with wonder.

The intense clarity of the silence impaled him like a sharpened stake.

"Left," he thought, watching the robot.

Nothing happened.

"Come to me," he thought.

Nothing happened.

A voice in his head chuckled.

"No, no," the voice corrected.

As if he were being controlled, Harv found himself visualizing the robot moving across the room.

The robot twitched. On silent rubber wheels, it rolled toward the lab door in what Harv, with his enhanced visual acuity, saw as slow motion.

"Yes," the voice in his head said.

Harv visualized himself lifting his arms.

The robot's arms rose toward the ceiling.

Harv visualized the robot coming to him.

The robot rolled to him.

Harv visualized the robot praying.

The robot's waldos came together in an inverted V.

The voice in his mind chuckled again . . . and then spoke. "I am pleased."

"Who are you?" Harv said aloud, though he didn't realize words had passed his lips.

"I am," the voice answered.

"Are you God?" Harv asked.

Silence. Harv's eyes rolled in their sockets. His hands twitched on the padded armrests.

"I love you," the voice said with the sincerity that Harv had been searching for throughout his entire life.

"I don't understand, I don't understand."

"You now have eternity to understand."

"Are you God?"

Silence.

"What must I do to know?"

"You must prove yourself worthy of me."

"I am, I am."

"You must show me."

"How? How can I do that?"

"You must sacrifice for me."

"A sacrifice? How? Who?"

"Do not disappoint me."

"I—I . . . I don't understand. It's not clear."

"You have always sought me."

In the VAX, the timing routine automatically shut down the Zeus program.

A few seconds later, as if he were struggling up from the depths of a dream, Harv's sense of time returned. He shook his head, his first thought that the connection had not worked, that he had experienced some kind of alpha-induced hallucination.

Then he saw the robot in the attitude of prayer.

Harv exhaled for a long time, and a thread of fire needled through him.

"I have to do it again," he said, struggling out of the swivel chair.

The lab telephone rang.

"No," Harv almost shouted, debating on whether or not to answer it.

He picked up the receiver.

"Damn, Harv, don't you ever sleep?" Dr. Cogglin asked. "You're worse than some of the insomniacs I fought with in 'Nam."

"Yeah, I'm real sorry I missed your war, Herr Doktor. Anyway, I was refining the prototype," Harv said, "trying to make it smaller."

"Yeah, I couldn't sleep either. I've been fiddling with the Athena hypothesis. Something's screwed up somewhere, but I can't put my finger on it. Thought I'd call the lab and see if Brandais was there. Tried to call him at home but nobody answered. Bastard's probably got his phone off the hook again."

"Yes, probably so," Harv said.

"Hey, Harv, you okay? You sound strange."

"Just sleepy, Herr Doktor," Harv replied, forcing himself to humor his old teacher. "And I'm strange anyway, right? Isn't that what Oberführer Director always says?"

"Yeah, that sounds like the Harv I know. Well, anyway, I'm coming to the lab. See you in a bit, okay?"

"Actually, Herr Doktor, I was just leaving. Got to get my beauty sleep, you know."

"Stick around, Harv. We'll shoot the bull about the hypothesis. Like the old days up at M.I.T.? See if we can't track down that damn bug."

"There's no bug," Harv stammered without thinking. Then he bit down on his lower lip to keep from blurting out what he'd just done.

"Oh, there's a bug in that baby somewhere," Cogglin said. "You can make book on that. We just haven't isolated it yet. I can feel it, Harv. And when I get this feeling about something being screwed up in a program, you can bet something's screwed up. Have you ever known me to be wrong?"

Silence from Harv as he listened for the voice of God.

"Harv, you still there?"

"Sorry, Herr Doktor. I'm falling asleep on my feet."

"Yeah, well, you better go get some shut-eye then. You sound horrible. And I need you fresh for the next series of tests. That bug's going to stick up its ugly head real soon now. I can feel it in my bones."

"Yes, Herr Doktor. You're always right. Okay, goodbye."

Harv lowered the receiver back onto the hard plastic cradle, cutting off Dr. Cogglin, who continued to talk.

Distracted, zombielike, his mind racing, Harv quickly, but carefully, cleared the Zeus program from the VAX. He disconnected the prototype and the robot, returning its arms to the normal resting position, and disposed of the cotton gauze.

Standing at the lab door, he cast his eyes around the room to make sure everything was as it should be.

It was. Harv opened the door and left.

Chapter
3

Friday, October 18th, 10:00 P.M.

Seventeen-year-old Master Wu restlessly scanned the IBM's color monitor for the results of the latest test run of a new program.

The results indicated success, and Master Wu pressed the keys to save the current version of the program as well as print a copy of it on the printer for Professor Cogglin.

Placing small hands on top of the IBM-PC, won under a grant for exceptional students in computer science, Master Wu sighed slowly, tired from a long week of constant study and computer programming. *Hate to waste the rest of this night,* Wu thought, *I could use the time to polish and tighten the code.* The program Wu was working on decoded the mechanics of how individual brain synapses transferred electrical impulses.

Master Wu sensed an extremely subtle error in the code somewhere, but, so far, it had proved to be elusive.

The original problem for the program that Master Wu was refining had been posed at Dr. Cogglin's graduate seminar some three months ago, but the solution hadn't hit

40

Master Wu until a night in early October when Grandfather had come in for his evening hug:

On that night, the old man, smelling of Vicks Vapo-Rub and peppermints, had sat down on the single bed and slipped a crumpled dollar bill into Master Wu's hand. "Don't spend on computer," Grandfather had ordered in his heavily accented English, his smile pulling up the rich, deep crevasses of laugh lines at the corners of his black eyes. "Spend on sweets, yes? Or else noodles for me." They had both laughed at the latter suggestion, recognizing Hiro Nomasaki's love of egg noodles and his inexhaustible ability to pack them away at dinner.

At that moment, the old man's words had drifted into the distance, while the edges of the lines surrounding his eyes had suddenly become scalpel-sharp, so sharp that they reminded Master Wu of sunrise in the bedroom, when the first rays of light would dart through the curtains, scatter the deep shadows, and illuminate the dust particles in the air.

With the illusion of Grandfather's wrinkles and sunrays striking dust, the solution to Dr. Cogglin's problem had exploded in Master Wu's mind, a solution that had never been tried before—an idea that could trace on a microsecond-by-microsecond basis the chemical triggering of electrical activity between brain synapses.

"Peppermints, yes?" Grandfather had said again that night in early October, a little louder, but not too loud, knowing from the eyes that Master Wu's strange and wonderful mind was exploring untraveled lands.

The gentle nudge in the thin ribs had brought Master Wu back. "Yes, Grandfather. Peppermints."

Master Wu had hugged Grandfather tightly just as the tears had started to flow. The old man's gnarled and thick fingers had gently blotted the tears away and then he had held Master Wu by the shoulders. Their eyes had met.

"I've just had a wonderful insight, Grandfather," Master Wu had said, physically shaken and still close to tears as the

41

implications of the idea came one after another. "But I don't understand all of it."

"I know, I know," Grandfather had comforted, pulling the seventeen-year-old tightly to his chest. "You must be patient with your gift. Happily, there is tomorrow. And you must remember what I told you about time."

"When eating, eat. When sleeping, sleep. When working, work."

Grandfather Hiro had nodded sagely and then had pulled Master Wu close for another tight hug. "Yes."

"I love you, Grandfather."

"You are my life, child," the old man had whispered in soft Japanese, his hands softly stroking Master Wu's thick head of raven black hair.

Dr. Cogglin had looked at the first draft of the code two days later when the seminar met on October third, and he had hardly been able to contain his excitement.

"Brilliant work, brilliant," he had complimented, his voice suddenly low and distracted. "And I've got just the project to test your program on," he had mumbled before patting Master Wu on the shoulder.

Master Wu pushed back from the computer and walked down the short hall to the bathroom. After brushing her teeth, Master Wu looked into the mirror. "No boy will ever like you," she said softly, appraising her thin but oddly beautiful features.

Stopping at Grandfather's room, she carefully cracked the door two inches to see if the old man was awake and reading his beloved sutras. The deep snores coming from within comforted Master Wu. Grandfather was the only person Master Wu had ever seen who smiled in his sleep.

"Why is that, Grandfather?" Master Wu had once asked when she was a very young child, not long after her parents had been killed in a train accident but before she and Grandfather had moved to America.

"Because I dream of you," he had answered.

Gently closing the old man's bedroom door, yawning, Fuchan returned to her bedroom. She thought about going to bed but then decided to call The Surgery and see if anything interesting was going on in the ICU.

After she dialed The Surgery's number, an amusing thought came to Fuchan: what would Dr. Cogglin think if he knew she also used the same equipment that connected her to Tulane's UNIX-4 mainframe to play, pretending that she was a strong and powerful man?

The connect signal flashed on her monitor, and, a moment later, at the prompt, Fuchan Nomasaki typed in her alias, Master Wu. When The Surgery asked for her password, she entered: SUNTZU.

A moment later, she had full access. She quickly read the war board and X-rated board and then looked into the ICU Elite hi-security board, where she received a very big surprise indeed.

Sixteen-year-old Francis Schonrath, known and feared throughout the BBS world as Genghis Khan, sat in a wheelchair at his enhanced Apple IIe and typed several nasty sentences about Meat Grinder on The Toilet Seat's war board. Although his typing wasn't particularly precise, it was remarkably quick, considering the fact that Francis had only partial use of his left hand. The victim of a serious automobile accident a little over a year ago, Francis had not only lost his right arm below the elbow but had also been paralyzed from the waist down.

His twenty-one-year-old sister Carol, who'd been driving when the drunk had slammed his '73 Chevy into their Audi, was killed instantly. Everyone always said Francis had been the lucky one. But, when he went once a week for physical therapy, when the stump of his arm was infected yet again, when he suffered the terrible back pains that came with the rain, Francis thought his sister was the lucky one. In fact, just about the only time he didn't think that was when he was living in BBS-land or hacking into a mainframe somewhere.

Using the hunt-and-peck method, he put the finishing touches on his most recent slash at Meat Grinder, typed in his alias, punched two keys to get back to The Toilet Seat's main menu, and then pressed the "G" key to exit. The screen flashed the words: "Do you want to leave a message to your sysop The Plumber?"

Francis punched "Y," and then he typed in:

The Seat's okay for a pretty new board but the name stinks . . .
no offense, but give me a break . . . it's a crappy name,
People'll stop callin' if you don't change it . . . Khan

Francis chuckled as he broke the connection. That was sure to irritate The Plumber. Everyone had been giving him grief about the name of his BBS for weeks now, and the word on a couple of the hi-security boards, where some people let their guards down, was that several dudes were even betting boxes of three-and-a-half-inch floppy disks on how much longer The Plumber would hold out before he caved in to popular demand and changed the name. The funny thing was that just about everybody really dug the name; next to The Surgery, The Toilet Seat was one of the most jamming open-to-the-public alias BBSes in the city.

Genghis Khan had been manipulating new users through E-mail, too, buttering them up and then encouraging them to plead with The Plumber to change the name. He owed The Plumber a couple of good shots for a week-long, unprovoked attack that had occurred on The Assassin's Guild's war board over two months ago, and he was just now paying him back.

As he saved a copy of his letter onto his ten-meg hard drive, Francis said aloud, "Genghis Khan never forgets an insult, Plumber. Man, if I only had your real name and address . . . then I could have some real fun!"

Lately, Francis had been finding BBS war rather predictable, and he had started to explore the possibilities of taking war off the boards and into real life. The possibilities that suddenly lurked in the shadowed areas of his mind he found both intriguing and exciting. Sure, regular BBS use and some late-night hacking into big corporation computers was fun, but all that was starting to get pretty tedious for Francis.

In fact, the last VAX he'd gotten into had bored him to

tears. The bottom line was that Francis was a lot more interested in finding a way to extend the game of war than he was in some stupid system operator's game that the Cutter had committed them to. But he also knew he should do something about the challenge pretty soon because The Chief Cutter was going to rag him without mercy if he didn't. After all, as the Cutter would say, the honor of the Surgeons was on the line with that challenge. One thing about the Cutter—he hated to lose any kind of BBS game. But then, so did Khan.

The handicapped boy looked at the battery-powered clock on the twenty-six-inch Sony television set next to his computer workstation: soon it'd be time to call The Surgery. The Chief Cutter had left him a note in E-mail to be sure to call Friday night because there'd be a surprise waiting for him.

The Cutter had been typically enigmatic, one of the things that Francis liked best about him and his private board. You never knew what to expect on The Surgery, but the Cutter apparently had the money to buy equipment that would make that Apple of his do everything but screw a water buffalo, Francis thought, smiling at the image.

"Don't stay up too late, Francis," his mom shouted through the door.

"I won't," he yelled back, glad that he had parents who left him alone and provided him with whatever computer equipment he asked for. That had been his salvation after the accident. Without his computer and modem, he knew he'd probably lose his mind in less than a week. If the tutor who came every morning didn't drive him crazy with her constant nagging about homework, in subjects he had absolutely no interest in, sitting in the room staring at the four walls would. Sometimes he wished he could turn into a computer.

A moment later, Francis turned his wheelchair back to the computer and typed in the dial command of his telecommunications program. The modem dialed the number for The Surgery, and, much to Khan's irritation, the line was busy. "Ah crap," he mumbled to himself, setting the autodialer.

Then he removed a stack of printouts of old war messages from a cardboard box on the floor and started to sift through them, waiting for the autodialer to pick up a carrier into The Chief Cutter's system. Francis started to read:

```
TITLE: GLOBAL QUICKSCAN IS BACK!
->FROM: GABBY HAYS [#0001]
->DATE: OCTOBER 3
```

Well, it seems that I was able to ride around the errors with the security levels and board levels with a little programming ingenuity. So now we have the peace of mind that comes from knowing that only those supposed to be on a particular board are on it. I got a nice, tight little fence around our Security Board, Cowboys and Cowgirls! No more roaming in pastures where folks ain't supposed to be. No more hackers getting in here trying to learn passwords!

```
TITLE: -=- HELLO THERE -=-
-> FROM: NIGHT RIDER [#0193]
-> DATE: BUG
```

. . . .finally got here. Hey, Tunnel Rat, did you finish the crack on GERM LAB yet? You ain't gonna crack that protection scheme, boy. Ain't nobody can crack that code. If you luck out and do it I need it when ya got it, man! Leave me E-mail. Ya got any more numbers for me to hack? Leave 'em in mail if ya do.

Night Rider

```
TITLE: WHAT YA KNOW?
-> FROM: GENGHIS KHAN [#0113]
-> DATE: 6:41AM
```

I have arrived, though I must leave soon. She's coming to stir up my brains some more at eight this morning. I shall be back before the sun casts no shadow on all objects that are in it's rays. OK, people, this is a war board, but guess what! It lacks a war! You people who get to go to school make me sick . . . I might stir up the brew . . .

Meat Grinder, I must say that that potion you drank has worked! It has made you invisible and silent! Damn! I told you to never take drinks from strangers! Ruined a good baddie! Damn!

Yours for bloody war, Genghis Khan*

TITLE: TO GENGHIS KHAN
-> FROM: MEAT GRINDER [#0007]
-> DATE: KHAN'S DEATH DAY

Khan, you speak a lot of being very smart . . . then maybe you can tell me what a sun cat is? You refer to it in your last message. Please tell me. I can hardly wait. As for your potion, you must have <blown> it. One man's poison is another man's steak. And I know you wish somebody would go for your steak. hahahahah. Some fag will go for it but never a girl. Oh yeah, I got your mindscrew E-mail. Don't bother, man. It doesn't effect me.

Meat Grinder
Baddest of the Bad

TITLE: MEAT GRINDER
-> FROM: MASTER WU [#0155]
-> DATE: WEDNESDAY

Like everybody in local BBS I like Genghis Khan and think he's a KOOl dude and support him fully . . . but also . . . I don't know why everybody always picks on poor Meat Grinder. I think he makes war better than just about anybody except maybe for The Butcher but he's gone to Houston now, poor guy. I wish I could make up dirty sayings and inuwindows the way Meat Grinder does. I HATE not being clever like the rest of you with this game. I can't even type damn and hell without feeling silly . . .

Master Wu
ICU Elite

```
TITLE: -=>PB*>=-
-> FROM: GENGHIS KHAN [#0113]
-> DATE: DIMANCHE
```

The Meat Grinder has caught a typo! Oh dear! In case your mind is too numb, I meant "Sun casts" Meat Grinder! Your awesome intellect blinds me so! You dumbfound us with the greatest of ease!

Master Wu, I thank you for your support. We need more of your ilk on this board. You shouldn't be nice to the Meat Grinder, though, 'cause he'll stab you in the back.

Genghis Khan
ICU Elite

```
TITLE: HI YA!
-> FROM: DR. JUNG [#0182]
-> DATE: SEPTEMBER 3
```

Hello. I'm Dr. Jung. I just bought a modem for a birthday present, and I am now trying to get acquainted with users of the war boards. I'd appreciate it if someone would post on this board what BBS war is all about and why you play it. That should help me understand BBS fighting . . . I would greatly appreciate it . . . It's kind of lonely not getting in these wars. And I don't want to jump in without knowing what I'm doing. Oh yeah, what's mindscrew?

```
TITLE: EXPLANATION
-> FROM: MEAT GRINDER [#0007]
-> DATE: TODAY
```

Hey Doctor Jung--sorry you're lonely, dood. BBS war takes place both between groups and between individual users. Here in New Orleans, there are three major groups fighting--The Defenders of the Faith, The Baddys, and The Renegades. There are also independents such as me and you. I'm proud to be a baddy, one of BBS's bad boys who enjoys kicking the beans out of other fighters. Us baddies are outnumbered by about 30:1. It is a tough job to be a baddy but somebody has to do it. If it wasn't for us the others would be bored to death. Mindscrew refers to trying to fight your opponent not only on the war board but also in mail. It's like floating rumors about you . . . or lies . . . all that psychological warfare.

We like to keep the war on BBS but in the past others have seen fit to take it out to the real world. I personally don't stand for that and neither do most of the other users of BBS.

Meat Grinder<King Baddie!!

TITLE: HELLO!
-> FROM: GENGHIS KHAN [#0113]
-> DATE: SOMETIME IN THIS MONTH

True, Meat Grinder, being BBS's asshole like you is a dirty job, but someone must do it.

Doctor Jung, some people bring WAR beyond BBS and when they do that, the consequences are unpredictable . . . In the past, peoples houses have been egged and prank phone calls have come at the early morning hours. We're just havin' a little fun on BBS, that's all . . . We keep it on the BBS until someone exposes, threatens property or life, etc . . . . Vandalizes . . . Then all hell breaks loose . . . If you wish to play the game of BBS warfare, then go ahead, but it usually helps if you know what you're doing . . . Some don't and they get annihilated quickly . . . No death or anything . . . They lose spirit or something and poof, they're gone . . . No physical pain inflicted whatsoever . . . Which sometimes makes it boring . . .

It's like watching a horror show . . . Why do people FIGHT on BBS war boards? To get a good scare knowing that they can't be hurt when danger is right in front of them . . . It's fun. After a bad day it makes you feel better to get on a war board and kick the crap out of somebody.

Well, join in, but be prepared for whatever hits you . . . That's what gets some people, they don't know what's gonna hit them, and they chicken out because of their fear . . . Once more . . . It's safe as long as it doesn't get out of BBS and into the real world. I hope you understand the points stated. If not, I dunno what to do. Study the stuff told to you . . . all in the fun of the game . . . Take some shots at Meat Grinder. He's such a massokiss that he's the easiest target around. He loves people to war on him.

Genghis Khan Has Spoken!

TITLE: C WUT HAPPENZ
-> FROM: MEAT GRINDER [#0007]
-> DATE: MEAT BEATING TIME

That's what I get for trying to be informational--then some asshole like Genghis Bullshit puts me down. Go hump your mother, Genghis, you geek. Get a life outside of BBS. Take a hike in the woods and shit on a tree instead of on me for a change. You waste too much disk space with all your crap.

Meat Grinder

TITLE: YOUR ASS IS MINE
-> FROM: GINGER TOOTS [#0074]
-> DATE: DEATH DAY FOR NELLY DEAN

O.K. NellyBelly, I haven't been able to get on The Toilet Seat lately, the stupid line's always busy, BUT THERE IS NO WAY that I am gonna let your crap slide . . . Remember me? I know you very well, you can fool everyone else with your crappola innocence but you can never fool me, I am a bitch and I am damn proud of it. I will drag you to hell and back if need be, I won our last little battle and thought I rid the BBS world of you but apparently I was wrong. This time I will make sure you never return.

GINGER TOOTS
BITCH AND DAMN PROUD

TITLE: PLEASE
-> FROM: MASTER WU [#0155]
-> DATE: NO DATE

I know that this is a war board but since I have no enemies, I don't fight very much . . . what is going on with this Ginger and our Nelly Dean? I don't want to sound mean but I have never heard of Ginger Toots. Will someone please write and explain???? I want to know what's going on????

Master WuKPuzzled Fighter

TITLE: OH DIRTY!!!!!
-> FROM: TUNNEL RAT [#0188]
-> DATE: ON THE SURFACE

Just playin with the keys
and knocking my knees,
watching the tree leaves
freeze in the breeze

Well, back to what's real. Where the hell is Meat Grinder??? Don't tell me that boy's off grinding his meat again??? Somebody throw me a pound of Lady Godiva chocolate or else a raw steak. To that jerk who asked about GERM LAB I will have it cracked very soon now. Nobody can code a protection scheme that Tunnel Rat can't crack!!! Nobody can protect a system that Tunnel Rat can't hack!!!

And where is my beautiful BBS lover? Where are you Nelly Dean? Your Tunnel Rat's looking for you. I'll even take a bath if you'll say you'll be mine. I'm lonesome for you, babe.

Tunnel Rat's ABOVE ground now!

TITLE: HELLO EVERYBODY
-> FROM: BUFFALO BILL [#0096]
-> DATE: DUNNO

Hesus Kristi on a tobossan! You folk definitely need the ole Buffalo Man to brighten up this place, to get the geeks outta here. There's too many little goody-goodies running around here, rubbernecks like that pathetic dood with his new modem, "I'm Doctor Jung and I just got my new modem." Hey, really pathetic dood! What a wimp! I challenge ya to a littl' game of

skill, Doc. Who wants to bet me a cold can of Dixie that the Doc
runs to hide under his secretary's skirts? Har har har.

Buffalo Bill
King of the Hill

[MESSAGE #16]: RULER OF ALL BBS
-> FROM: GINGER TOOTS [#0074]
-> DATE: THE QUEEN

Okay Genghis Khan, NellyBelly and I had a war before she got
famous and I kicked her ass. I'm been out of BBS getting my
grades up. While I was gone Nelly started attacking me on that
new BBS, The Toilet Seat. Friends told me about it. And they
lashed out at me because they were believing NellyBelly's lies.
So now you know. I would love to have your support and so would
NellyBelly, so it looks like you might have to choose sides.
Either way, I will win this war by a long shot.

TITLE: R U DESPERATE?
-> FROM: NELLY DEAN [#0163]
-> DATE: RHRTHYHTYE

Well, well, well, Little Ginger's crawled on her fat belly into
the Ranchhouse tooting her brassy voice, eh? So you're desperate for some help, huh Gingie Poo? Well, dig the yellow wax out
of your eyes and off your crooked spine and listen up.

Genghis Khan, I don't need your help, unlike Ginger. And,
Gingivitis, you're a stupid little broad. And I do mean little.
Especially where it counts: in the brain's department. Your big
chest doesn't count for diddly on the boards, babe . . . You
always have been desperate for something or someone. Remember
that Homecoming Dance two years ago . . . Yeah, the one you
didn't go to.

Why don't you tell all the Cowpokes here on the Ranch the reaalll
reason why you weren't there? Hmm?

And Tunnel Rat, you want Nelly Dean, you have to earn her, boy.
You have to rescue me from some terrible villain here on the
boards . . . or you have to save me from an evil sorcerer . . .

or you have to defeat the mutated troll that kidnaps my beautiful body . . . that's the ONLY way you'll ever have this

Wonderful Nelly

TITLE: TO BUFFALO BILL
-> FROM: DOCTOR JUNG [#0182]
-> DATE: FLOGGER SHEEEET

Ok Buffie Boy, I accept your challenge. You called me a wimp. Well, son, I'm crushed. I thought you were supposed to be the King of the Hill in BBS war. Those were real tough words for a King. If you're going to try to make war with me, as least do it intelligently. So break that pus-filled brain of yours out of your Buffalo skull and show me what you got . . . .

Waiting patiently,
Doctor Jung

TITLE: TO GENGHIS KHAN
-> FROM: TUNNEL RAT [#0188]
-> DATE: AS LONG AS IT AIN'T NITE

No prob son. Glad you liked me poem. In 'Nam they used to call me The Poet Laureate of Cu Chi Province. Just trying to get Meat Grinder's goat!! Saw Doc Jung on some other boards lookin' for more BADDIES. You know, I think the doc's gonna get into warring, don't you--unlike that retarded excuse for a bad wet dream named Meat Grinder. Yeah, you're right, Doc. Hacking's for losers. Hahahaha. Hey, stick that in your grind and meet it, Meat Grinder!

Nelly, you want a hero? I'm your man, babe. I'm here for you whenever and wherever. Dig?

Tunnel Rat's above Ground now

At his computer, the modem finished dialing. A moment later the word CONNECT appeared on the monitor. "At last," Francis muttered, tossing the old war-board printouts back into the box, "now I can find out what the Cutter's up to!"

Chapter
4

Friday, October 18th, 12:58 A.M.

In the comfortable three-bedroom house that she owned in Uptown New Orleans, Mary Alice Sluice glanced at her watch. She was surprised to see that it was just before one in the morning. She'd been sitting at her computer playing on the boards since leaving the project's lab at a few minutes before six.

"Time flies when you're having fun," she said wearily.

Mary Alice was thirty-three years old.

Valedictorian of her high-school class, she had won a full scholarship to Princeton University for her freshman year. But, after one semester of competing with ambitious northerners and living in unendurably cold weather, she was ready to call it quits. She had returned home after the first quarter of the second semester.

Because she had quit—an unforgivable sin, quitting—her father had retracted his offer of financial help. If she didn't want an essentially free education at a good school, he had told her, she could go out and get a job and earn enough money to get an expensive education at a mediocre school. So, being as stubborn as her father, an immensely successful

54

and very aggressive lawyer, she did just that and dropped out of school altogether for a while.

During that time she worked as a salesgirl in the kitchen-wares section of a large department store and lived quietly in an apartment in a concrete singles-only complex. She had chosen the place to give herself a chance to meet young people her own age. Because she didn't drink, hated gossip and cliques, and wasn't keen on either cheerleading or athletics, she'd never really fit in with her high-school peers, who always thought of Mary Alice as a cold fish. So, thinking that perhaps she should make more of an effort to be better adjusted socially, she had rented an efficiency at the singles apartment.

Unfortunately, after three weeks, she realized the other tenants, at least the ones she met around the swimming pool, were only interested in where and when the next party would occur. So, to her great relief, she had returned to the shell she had constructed around herself in high school and found infinitely more interesting company in the great characters of both classic and modern fiction. She sold food processors, pots and pans, and silverware during the day and, in books, traveled around the globe and through time at night.

She took her savings and enrolled in L.S.U.'s School of Nursing, where she quickly earned her nursing degree. Graduating once more at the top of her class, she specialized in surgical nursing and worked for a year at Charity Hospital before picking up her M.D. at the University of Colorado's school of medicine. She'd done her residency in psychiatry at a mental hospital in a suburb of Washington, D.C.

She had then returned home to teach and practice at Tulane Medical Center, which was where she'd first met the neurosurgeon Paul Brandais, who'd become both a friend and colleague. At his urging, she'd taken an extended leave of absence from Tulane to join him in the development of an electronic interface that would connect human brains to computers.

After the first couple of months on the project, she had

purchased a computer and printer to simplify the statistical work she did at the lab, as well as to more easily manipulate the detailed data of the various tests she constantly ran on the chimp, von Neumann.

During that first year, she used her computer strictly for lab work but, like many others, got caught up by the power of the machine. If she was going to be able to do everything with her computer that was possible, additional hardware was necessary. Consequently, she purchased a 1200-baud modem.

Two years ago, after setting up the new equipment, she had dialed her first BBS, having gotten the number from the salesman at the computer store.

It was the number to The Surgery, which, even at that time, was so popular that The Chief Cutter wasn't validating any new users. The salesman at the computer shop had given Mary Alice the number knowing that. Also a traveler of the boards, he hadn't liked what he saw as Mary Alice's rather snotty personality and so figured that that would be a good way to get a lick in on her. Nothing was harder on a new BBS aspirant than to be refused validation on a board. And he knew The Chief Cutter's reputation well enough to assume that this broad wouldn't impress him a bit.

The Surgery had responded on the first ring and Mary Alice, not having a clue about the BBS world, had typed in her real name at the prompt.

The Chief Cutter, as usual, had been watching the board at the time, and he had been amused by the response. "Mary Alice Sluice," he said to himself. "What a great alias."

At that point, he had entered chat mode and started to tell this user that he wasn't validating new members to The Surgery, but then they had gotten to chatting, and Mary Alice was such a fast typist that Tom had decided to validate her on that basis alone. He hated the hunt-and-peck users who took forever to post even the simplest message.

He had also been impressed by her answers, which were short, to the point, and so knowledgeable that he immediately knew this user was older than the typical applicant.

From the apparent honesty of her responses, he also suspected that this user didn't yet know that one shouldn't reveal too much about one's real life or personality on the boards unless one was sure of the integrity of the person on the other end of the modem.

"Tell you what," The Chief Cutter had typed in that night, "I'm going to validate you on The Surgery. May as well let your first BBS experience be a good one. And, by the way, I like your alias."

"I don't understand," Mary Alice had typed back.

"Don't tell me Mary Alice Sluice is your real name?" The Chief Cutter had responded, laughing so hard he had almost dropped the small address book that he had been toying with.

"It is," she had typed back indignantly. "What's the matter with my name?"

"Nothing . . . nothing at all. You just don't use your real name in the BBS world—unless you're into old fogey boards where everybody's so square it's ridiculous. If you're going to travel the phone lines in real BBS, babe, you'd better pick a new name. Think of one."

The idea had surprised Mary Alice, but it had also appealed to her. It would be kind of nice to have a time each day when she could be someone other than herself. She didn't have to think very long before she typed on her keyboard: "I'll be Nelly Dean."

The Chief Cutter had typed back: "Okay, Nelly Dean it is. I also need a password."

"Password?"

"Yeah. Can't log on boards without a password. You really are new at this, aren't you?"

"Yes. Okay. A password. I'm thinking . . . okay, password is HEATH."

"Okay, Nelly Dean. You're now a validated member of The Surgery, status Nurse. And if you prove to be as good at this as I think you're going to be, you may someday join my elite group, the Surgeons."

Mary Alice thought about telling the owner of the BBS

what she did in real life, but figured she had already exposed her ignorance of BBS matters rather thoroughly, so she simply typed back: "Okay. Thanks. Who are you?"

"I'm The Chief Cutter, sysop of The Surgery."

"What's a sysop?"

"Stands for systems operator."

"Oh, then this is your bulletin board?"

"You got it."

"Oh."

"Okay, Nelly, L8r." At that point, Tom Barnslow had broken the connection and validated Nelly Dean. He had also pulled his leather address book into the tight circle of light from the brass desk lamp and had entered the name Mary Alice Sluice, a name that he had later looked up in the phone book to get the address of her house on Fountainbleu Avenue.

Little did Tom Barnslow know on that night that he had just validated the player who would influence BBS in New Orleans more than any other single individual on the boards, a woman who would show the predominately male users just what inspired writing and creative thinking were all about.

But, on this evening in the middle of October, Mary Alice Sluice wasn't feeling like the Queen of New Orleans BBS. She was tired. Tired of war games, tired of endless discussion forums, tired of the fantasy stories that never had any conclusion, tired of trying to keep track of who Nelly Dean was supposed to hate and who she was supposed to like, tired of having several different aliases on five different war boards, tired of trying to remember just who she was supposed to be at any given moment.

It's becoming too complex, she thought. *My concentration at work's starting to suffer . . . almost made a mistake today . . . need to get more sleep.*

She sighed.

But I can't just quit. It would be like committing murder. Can't kill off Nelly Dean—she's become too real, too much a part of me. I'll cut back. No more than two hours a day for the

*rest of October. To show my resolve right now, I'll skip calling
The Surgery tonight. But I can't give it up . . . can't . . .
especially not now . . . with what's happening at the lab.*

She turned off her computer and modem.

After taking a nightgown from her wardrobe, she walked
into the bathroom and closed the door. Mary Alice slowly
removed her blouse and blue jeans. Standing before the
full-length mirror, she opened her eyes and looked at
herself.

Not bad, she thought, glancing at her curvy figure and
attractive face. She tossed her smooth black hair with a flick
of her head. "That's how Salome would do it," she said in
her throaty voice, "bring me the head of John the Baptist."

"Okay, Mary Alice, time to become real again. Brush your
teeth and get some sleep."

A few minutes after getting under the hand-sewn quilt
she'd purchased at last year's Jazz Fest, she drifted off and
started to dream.

An hour later, a nightmare about von Neumann tore her
from sleep, leaving her soaked in sweat.

She got up, shaking, and washed her hands and face.

At a little after two, she dialed the number to The Surgery.

She felt a good healthy dose of alias BBS would wash the
nightmare from her mind.

Little did she know.

Friday, October 18th, 3:53 A.M.

Dennis Conlick, the Tunnel Rat, finished his third Three
Musketeers bar of the hour and carelessly tossed the wrap-
per in a corner of his three-room apartment in the French
Quarter. He reached over a pile of floppy disks and picked
up a half-empty pack of Salems. Lighting one, he stuck it
between his lips, half-closing his red-lined eyes to keep the
smoke out.

"Ingenious," he mumbled, as he used his sector editor to
examine yet one more time the hex code of the copy-
protected version of Shemwarez's newest, and exceedingly
popular, all-text adventure game *Germ Lab*. So far, no one

in the cracking community had been able to break the protection scheme—and people were starting to get irritated because it had been two weeks since the game's official release. Dennis had already spent more than fifteen hours working on the crack, and he knew he was getting very close.

"Got it!" he shouted, several cigarettes and about thirty minutes later. "A disguised nibble count synchronized on spiraled half tracks. God, what kind of brain thought of that one? Far out." He removed the protection from the disk in a matter of a few seconds.

As the disk drive finished saving the now-unprotected version of the game, Dennis removed a half-smoked cigarette from his mouth and carelessly flicked its ashes toward an empty cereal bowl that had held Sugar Pops hours earlier.

He packed the de-protected copy of the game, turned on his modem, and booted the terminal program which he had written for his own particular uses. After putting the packed version of *Germ Lab* into the second disk drive and having the macro dial his favorite pirate line out in California, Dennis uploaded the cracked copy of the game, smiling as he waited for the 9600-baud transfer to finish, grinning crazily as he thought about how this latest achievement would unquestionably make him king of the cracking community.

He saved a copy of the cracked and packed program to his forty-meg hard drive. This drive also contained two megs worth of material that he'd downloaded from The General's VAX earlier in the month during one of his hacking sessions. The material, however, was encrypted, and Dennis hadn't yet taken the time to decipher it so he could see how August's and Cogglin's project was progressing.

Turning in his wooden chair, Dennis Conlick removed another Three Musketeers bar from the cardboard box that contained a full gross of his favorite candy. He quickly removed the wrapping, dropped it on the floor, and ate half of the bar in one bite.

"All right, all right," he repeated to himself. "What's next, what's next?"

He'd been working very hard on cracking *Germ Lab*, but

his mind was neither tired nor foggy, whirring like a disk drive with a program that refused to boot. Indeed, he felt as if he'd never have to sleep again.

Steadying himself by holding the seat of the wooden chair with his hands, Dennis Conlick stood up and stretched. "What time is it, sports fans, eh?" he asked, and then checked the eight-dollar digital runner's watch that he had gotten at Woolworth's to keep track of day and night.

"Ah-ha, night again," he said. It was 4:27 A.M.

Walking into the bathroom and clicking on the unshielded one hundred-watt bulb that hung from the ceiling, Dennis calmly toed out of his path a roach that scurried around looking for sanctuary from the light.

After relieving himself, he rubbed the mirror above the sink with his right elbow. Suddenly seeing his face distorted in the cheap mirror, his mind flashed back to the war:

"Christ, Sergeant Conlick," said the lieutenant, taking Dennis's mud-covered hand and half-dragging, half-pulling him out of the tunnel, "you look like last week's meatloaf. What'd you find down there? We heard shots."

"Couple gooks, Lieutenant," Sergeant Conlick answered, "but the Tunnel Rat wasted them, no sweat."

"Yeah. Okay. Time for some grub. Shit on a shingle today, they tell me."

"For supper?"

The lieutenant looked quizzically at Sergeant Conlick. "You were down there eleven hours, Conlick. It's morning."

The cadaverously thin and mud-covered man stared at his commanding officer for almost a minute. Then he whispered: "Lieutenant, I think I'm losing it."

He didn't have to tell the lieutenant what he meant. "The jeep's waiting. Get back to the base and shower your ass. You'll feel more like yourself."

The shower had been glorious. Nothing was better than washing off the stinking earth after surfacing from one of those damp, cold Viet Cong tunnels. Rubbing the skin of his hairy chest with a coarse brush, Sergeant Dennis Conlick was startled when one of the other members of the tunnel team entered the field shower tent. *"Jeeesus,* Conlick, now I know why you pull all the toughest tunnels," PFC Anthony Toston had said, his hands absently pulling at the hairs in his armpits.

"Uhh?" Dennis had replied, his mind still crawling through a terrifying sixty-yard stretch of the tunnel alive with centipedes that seemed, in the dark, to be the size of forearms. Dennis hadn't minded them. He was used to centipedes. But the warm, slimy nightcrawler that dropped on his neck when the tunnel had started to narrow had almost torn a scream right out of his madly pumping heart. And he knew all too well what happened to rats who lost their cool when they were under the earth.

"Because you're so damn skinny, you moron," Toston had answered. "Christ, I oughtta go on a diet. What do you weigh? About one twenty?" Toston, the newest member of the select Army 1st Engineer battalion that spent all of its time searching and destroying the incredibly complex and unending network of VC tunnels, was itching for action below the earth.

"Hey, Conlick, scuttlebutt has it you spent some time in Intelligence before you got transferred to the First. What was that like? I hear the three-starrcr who runs that outfit—what's his name? Oh yeah, August—I hear he's one of the toughest bastards in 'Nam."

Conlick didn't answer, but he ate Toston's serving of potatoes that night at mess.

A week and a half later during a night mortar attack—when Dennis had known for sure that his nerve had left him, when the dreams had started, when he had lost a small piece of his right ear to a ricochet in one of the tunnels—he had broken into the mess tent's supply cabinet, where they found him the next morning, gorged and unconscious.

Next to his body was a twenty-pound box of dehydrated potatoes. It was more than half empty.

A month after that, the army had discharged him with a Section Eight, a couple of medals, and a monthly disability check. They had also recommended that he sign into a V.A.

hospital for psychiatric care so he could get his eating disorder under control. The doctor had told him that his weight gain of more than seventy pounds was caused by his subconscious telling him to eat and gain weight so he'd never have to go into a tunnel again.

So Dennis had taken the free army plane ticket and had flown to Denver. And he'd seen a V.A. shrink for a while, but all the guy wanted to do was talk, talk, talk, and Dennis never had been much for talking, so, finally, he stopped his weekly visits to Fitzsimmon's hospital altogether. He labored at a variety of nonskilled jobs, working for a year here, six months there. Time passed, and Dennis's weight eventually stabilized at 233 pounds and then started to drop.

He coped for a while, got his weight down to a hundred and sixty or so. Even got in touch with the general and Al Cogglin, men he'd served under and liked while in Army Intelligence. Al, who was finishing graduate degrees in math and computer science at the time, had written him a long letter about the opportunities in computers and encouraged him to look into it.

He traveled around for a few years and tried to make a new start, picked up a couple of degrees in computer science on the G.I. bill. But he quit before getting his doctorate when the first Apple II had come out, and he had seen in advance the way the little machine was going to make a lot of people a lot of money. Starting in 1979, he worked for one of the software publishers for several years, coding arcade games in assembly language for the most part and introducing copy-protection schemes, but then the dreams had returned and he'd found himself increasingly less able to concentrate at his job.

And he'd started to go on eating binges again, ballooning back up to over two hundred pounds.

His employer had finally discharged Dennis the day the clean-up staff found him cowering in a broom closet, his arms wrapped around his chest, muttering something about nightcrawlers and white lights. His boss had given him a generous severance check and had urged him to seek professional help. He had also promised to send Dennis royalties for the games he'd written.

So Dennis had hitched his way down to New Orleans, where Al Cogglin had settled, thinking that having an old friend close by might help him get his head screwed on tight again. He used the severance pay to put down a year's rent on the apartment in the French Quarter and to buy an Apple IIe, which he enhanced with an absolute reset ROM, the fastest modem on the market, a variety of top-of-the-line RAM cards, and numerous disk drives, storage facilities which he had augmented a month ago with the new hard drive.

Once established in New Orleans, he'd thought about getting another steady job and had even talked to the general and Al about working with them on a private research project they were putting together. But the vibes had been bad the day he talked to them, and he'd felt himself slipping under the earth. So he'd decided—to their obvious relief— that it wasn't worth it, that his mental state couldn't handle the pressure of such a high-level project. He told them to find someone else to build the hardware part of their project. With the promised royalty checks, he could live quite comfortably; without them, he could get by on the monthly disability money and whatever he managed to scrape up here and there doing odd jobs related to comput- ers. The general had a remarkable number of contacts around the country, and, after Dennis turned down the job on the project, the general had recommended him for various consulting jobs, a few of which he'd taken when he was strapped for cash.

The royalty checks didn't come for very long because the owner of the software house filed Chapter Eleven to cut his losses during the software crunch of Christmas 1984. The owner sold the copyrights on the games Dennis had written to another company and retired with his wife and three kids to Hawaii. When Dennis had gotten a letter of explanation from the guy's lawyer, he vowed to spend some serious time ripping off the software industry the way they had ripped him off. Dennis had spent the last year and a half doing just that, gobbling up protection schemes like a shark in a kiddy wading pool and then uploading the de-protected programs on different pirate bulletin boards all over the country. He'd shown the software industry not to screw-over the Tunnel Rat.

And lately he'd been thinking about doing a similar number on the federal government as well. The White House was reviewing many of the Vietnam veterans' benefits, and a V.A. official had recently called Dennis and threatened him with a decrease in his monthly check. Dennis had listened politely to the bureaucrat and told him he didn't think it was a very moral thing to do—to take away what a man had earned by serving his country.

Dennis hadn't bothered to threaten the paper shuffler because he knew, while he was speaking to the guy, that he could break into the V.A.'s computer system any time he wanted and double his monthly check if he wanted to. If they cut what they had promised him, he would do just that, and maybe even make several other nasty little changes that would drive the V.A.'s computer experts absolutely bananas. Hell, Dennis thought, the government's entire computer security was absurd. Even a teenager with computer smarts could access most of the Pentagon's mainframes! Dennis had done it several times for his own amusement.

"Man, you look horrible," Dennis drawled to his forty-three-year-old reflection in the dirty bathroom mirror, staring with alarm at the heavy dark bags of flesh under his red-lined eyes. "You have to get down to fighting trim again." He climbed onto a cheap bathroom scale: 168 pounds. Not obese by a long shot, but he wasn't going to starve anytime soon either.

He opened the mirror to reveal shelves of medication that various New Orleans doctors at the V.A. hospital on Tchoupitoulas Street had prescribed for him as an appetite suppressant. He opened the bottle of amphetamines and dry-swallowed two tabs. "That oughtta take care of the Musketeer-bar blues," he sang to himself. Bending over with some difficulty, he tied the laces on his jogging shoes.

He splashed some cold water on his face and then wiped it off with his hands because he didn't have any clean towels. In fact, there wasn't even a towel in the bathroom. He started to search for one in the pile of dirty laundry in one corner of the twelve-by-twelve-foot main room but by then his face was almost dry. He changed direction and entered the walk-in kitchen with its hot plate, sink full of unwashed dishes, and half-size refrigerator that didn't even have a freezer. A few moments later, he found himself by the door of his third-floor apartment, where he repeatedly flicked the light switch off and on.

His shadow danced on the wall behind him like a silhouette in a strobe-lighted disco.

"What the hell time is it, anyway?" he asked the walls of his room when he realized that he was playing with the light again.

He felt the first tingle that signaled the oncoming rush of the bennies, a feeling like standing in the surf watching a huge wave that you know is going to crash right over your head.

He walked to the single window in the apartment and pulled back the woolen army blanket thumbtacked to the splintering frame. He'd put it up so that he wouldn't be able to tell when the sun came up. He was trying to live outside of regular time these days, doing everything he could in his limited environment to make no distinctions between night and day. Except for when he played with the switch, the two-hundred-watt bulb in the main room hadn't been turned off in weeks. He kept a good supply of the bulbs in the small cabinet beneath the kitchen sink.

But he hadn't been able to give up the wristwatch, even though he'd tried. For some reason, he had to have it to know the exact time if he felt like he needed to know it, as he did now.

He looked at the liquid crystal display. "Ahh, night again."

He paced around the apartment for a few minutes, jumping twice at his own shadow, his feet shuffling through dirty clothes, empty Borden's chocolate-milk cartons, and candy-bar wrappers. Although it had only been a week or so ago, he couldn't recall the last time he had cleaned the apartment and disposed of the garbage.

After five minutes of pacing, the benzedrine wave crashed over him. His mind suddenly cleared and a huge jolt of energy surged through him. He turned up his wrist and looked at his watch: almost four-thirty A.M.

"A nice time to get through to The Surgery . . . maybe write Nelly Dean a little love poem," Tunnel Rat said.

Friday, October 18th, 4:37 A.M.

Jim Persall was sound asleep when the Tunnel Rat's modem sought a carrier to The Surgery.

In fact, Meat Grinder had been too tired to even turn on his computer that Friday evening when he got home.

The only noninjured halfback on Tulane's football team, he had spent the night in the Superdome getting the stuffing knocked out of him by a much stronger and more talented Florida State defense. After the game, he had had to endure the bus ride and the disgusted silence of the coaches. In the locker room, one of the coaches had talked about players who lacked both commitment and concentration, and then he had looked right at Jim and blasted "butterfingered backs" who fumbled twice in the same game.

Finally, after telling the whole squad to get their brains hooked up to their arms and legs during the weekend and to be ready for a serious practice session on Monday after school, the coach had sent their aching and bruised bodies to the showers.

Out in the dark parking lot, his teammates had asked him to join them for a couple of beers, but Jim had declined because he was too sore to even think about anything other than bed.

And so he had driven home alone, back to the house in Uptown New Orleans where he had lived all his life. Jim had spent the first semester of his freshman year living in a Tulane dorm but had hated every noisy minute of it, moving back in with his parents at the end of that semester.

He kissed his mother and hugged his father when he got home, and they had both complimented him on his play during the game, which they had attended.

"Do you want some supper, Jimbo?" his father had asked. "We stopped for something on the way home, but I'll be glad to whip you up a cheese omelet or something."

"Thanks, Pop, but I'm not hungry. I think I'll just go to bed."

"You mean you aren't going to stay up all night in BBS-land with your computer?" his mother asked. She turned to her husband. "That would be a real *first* around here. I can't believe our favorite Meat Grinder is too tired to terrorize the phone lines until dawn."

Patricia Persall stood up and kissed her tall son on the cheek. Then she smiled and said, "I was proud of you tonight. You played well . . . except for the two fumbles, of course. Not bad for a sophomore."

Smiling wryly, Jim started for the stairs that led to his attic bedroom, a large and wonderful room full of posters, pennants, art-deco prints, and just about anything else that had ever struck his fancy. Although his parents weren't rich by New Orleans' standards, his dad was a well-paid senior partner in a small law firm and his mother had her own business as an interior decorator.

In his bedroom the Apple IIc with its nine-inch monochrome monitor and 300-baud modem on the pine desk beckoned him for a brief moment. He thought about giving The Surgery just one ring but decided against it since he knew that once he started dialing the boards he'd be up for hours. The Chief Cutter had told him in E-mail to be sure to call sometime Friday night after midnight, but that was the breaks. Jim was just too tired tonight, and, for him, BBS came second to real life.

So he stripped quickly, drew back the covers on his bed, and got under the cool sheets. Reaching up, he turned off the lamp and fell instantly to sleep.

Chapter
5

Friday, October 18th, 10:04 P.M.

On that Friday in mid-October, the day The Chief Cutter had instructed his closest BBS friends to log on to The Surgery and check out their hi-security board, Tom Barnslow sat in front of his monitor and reread the postings he had put on the ICU, two messages that he had spent most of the afternoon and early evening writing and rewriting:

```
[MESSAGE 1]: CLEAN SLATE
FROM: THE CHIEF CUTTER
DATE: OCTOBER 18
```

As you'll soon see, I've deleted all the earlier postings here on ICU. Tonight I want to start something new. I want to wipe the slate of lies and half-truths that we BBS users so frequently resort to for fun and games. What I want, starting tonight, is for each of us to begin telling some personal things about ourselves. As Surgeons, we've known each other through our aliases for well over a year. I think it's about time we started trusting each other enough to start posting some real-life information. Who Knows, perhaps this new openness can lead to some friendships outside of BBS. I'll start with myself in the next posting.

Chief Cutter

P.S. Before I do that, don't forget about the challenge that the sysop who calls himself The Succubus has put before us. We have until midnight on Halloween, and I haven't heard yet from all of you. I chatted with him almost two weeks ago. He said one of us downloaded the material. If you did it, tell me here or in mail. It's important that we win this game with him and not stain the Surgeons' record by failing to meet this challenge. But I think the guy's conceding to us anyway since I haven't heard from him in so long.

Tom chuckled aloud as he finished reading *Clean Slate*. "They're going to fall for that like ducks in a shooting gallery." He started to read the second message he had put on the ICU:

[MESSAGE 2]: ABOUT THE CHIEF CUTTER
FROM: THE CHIEF CUTTER
DATE: OCTOBER 18

In real life I'm 29 years old. I was born with some kind of glandular deficiency, which keeps me from fully metabolizing food. Consequently, I have a weight problem that the kids at school really used to tease me about. Last year the problem got so bad I had to take to my bed because my heart wasn't able to pump blood properly through all these extra pounds. I'm a mess physically, but that hasn't affected my brain.

I eat and breathe computers. Sometimes I feel like a freak the way I love these machines. My mother's widowed sister lives with me and my mother. She looks after me. My dad's a rich lawyer but my folks are divorced and I never see him except when he comes around once or twice a year and gives me a lot of money. He dresses up in a Scarlet O'Hara outfit on Mardi Gras day. But at least he's a rich weirdo. That's how I bought this computer and modem and BBS program. He pays my phone bills too, even the long distance ones for the BBSes I call in other parts of the country. He's a jerk. But at least he's a rich jerk.

My mother is away a lot with her boyfriends. She's got a thing for professional football players. She's probably gone the distance with every Saint on the team, past or present. Like tonight--she's out. As usual. And I'm sitting here at my computer like I do almost every hour of my life. I'm really lonely. I've been lonely for a long, long time. Today I decided it was time to stop hiding behind the computer and finally tell all of you something about myself. After all, if I can't trust you people who have been my BBS friends for so long, who can I trust? Okay, that's enough about me. Boy, does it feel good to finally stop trying to stay a big secret or something! I'm really glad I decided to tell the truth and I hope you guys will tell us about the "real you" too!

The Chief Cutter

P.S. My real name is Robert Earle Hughes, and I hope you will start calling me Bob here on the ICU. By the way, let's all promise to keep any information revealed here in the ICU strictly confidential. Is that okay with everybody? That way other users can't use the real-life stuff on the war boards. And nobody will get their house egged or something. To show you how serious I am about this, I'm going to post my address too: it's 3009 Friedrichs St. out here in Metairie. Don't anybody egg my house now. Later friends.

Bob

"Oh cripes." Tom laughed to his computer, scratching the top of his head in the shadows. "Wait till they read all that stuff. And if they drive to my address, aren't they going to be surprised to find a 7-Eleven store? God, are they going to feel sorry for poor ole Bob Hughes!" Tom leaned back in his chair and pictured the other members of the ICU, tried to figure out what they were like in real life. He could hardly contain his excitement waiting for them to log on.

Suddenly the phone rang and The Surgery's BBS program picked up the carrier. Tom looked at his clock: a few minutes after ten.

At approximately ten after ten that Friday night, Fuchan Nomasaki logged on to The Surgery and worked her way into the ICU.

She was shocked after reading The Chief Cutter's two postings and wasn't sure what to do.

"How can I tell them I'm a seventeen-year-old girl with Einstein's brain?" she asked herself. "After all this time trying to make myself look so big on the boards, how can I tell them the truth? That I'm a huge brain in a Japanese girl's body." Then she pressed a key so she could reread what The Chief Cutter had posted.

She was moved by the reference to loneliness. She could have written that part herself. And she was also touched by Bob's reference to feeling like a freak. "He ought to walk into Dr. Cogglin's seminar with me and watch how the graduate students stop talking and stare at me like I was from the moon."

Fuchan bent over her computer and started typing:

```
[MESSAGE 3]: I'M A GIRL!
FROM: MASTER WU
DATE: OCTOBER 18
```

Yes, it's true everybody . . . Master Wu isn't a great big guy like he tries to be on the war boards . . . He's really just me . . . a 17-year-old Japanese girl . . . I live with my wonderful grandfather who I love with all my heart. My parents were killed in a train accident when I was very young . . . my grandfather is the nicest man alive . . . he is real old and has a heart problem but he makes me smile . . . I can't type much more now because it's late and I have to study . . . so I will have to go now . . . oh yes . . . we live in an apartment complex in Gentilly called The Sunrise Apartments . . . number 99 . . .

my real name is Fuchan Nomasaki but my grandfather sometimes
calls me Fu for short . . . I hope you will still like me now that
I have told you I'm just a young girl and not the great Master Wu
after all . . . I will tell you more about me later. I have a big
program I have to work on for school.

Fuchan (Master Wu)

P.S. Bob, I am a freak too but in a different way . . . and you
are right . . . it does feel good to tell the truth on a BBS for
a change . . . I like it . . . it will make me sleep well tonite.
My phone number is 282-8137.

When Fuchan had finished typing her phone number, she
pressed the proper keys and quickly logged off The Surgery,
turned off her computer and monitor, and then stretched
her aching back.

Before getting into bed, she went to her grandfather's
room, where she bent down over his sleeping form and
kissed his grizzled cheek. He suddenly opened his deep
black eyes, grabbed his granddaughter to his thin chest and
folded her in a tight hug.

"I love you, Grandfather," Fuchan said simply.

He patted her on the bottom. "To bed, to bed, before the
sun spits fire," he whispered, winking at her.

"Hot damn!" Tom Barnslow said to his empty room as he
watched Master Wu log off. "It's working. He's a she and a
chink to boot! I hope she's got more meat on her bones than
that skinny Japanese girl in Cogglin's seminar. They're
going to fall for this—hook, line, and sinker!" His snort of
laughter sounded almost like a bark from a dog. Nothing
was more exciting than putting a good one over on his fellow
BBS users. He reached into the shadows on his work station
and pulled his address book forward.

Some forty minutes and two non-ICU users later, Tom
smiled again when Genghis Khan, the angry man of the BBS
war boards, logged on to The Surgery. The Chief Cutter
watched as Genghis Khan read the war board and then

posted a blistering, obscenity-filled response to something one of the Nurse-level users had written. A few seconds later, Genghis Khan read the new messages on the ICU. Tom laughed quietly to himself, wondering just who Genghis Khan really was, trying to get a mental picture of him.

In his room in the suburban house on the Lakefront, Francis Schonrath read the postings by The Chief Cutter and by Master Wu. He snorted through his nose when he finished reading Master Wu's real-life information. "A girl!" Francis sneered. "No wonder she can't fight. I should've guessed."

Francis put his left hand on the control box of his battery-powered wheelchair and shrugged his shoulders a few times to loosen up the kinks. Then he pushed the proper keys to reread the postings.

They're a lot like me, he thought.

He popped the knuckles of his left fingers with his left thumb, leaned forward, and started to type:

```
[MESSAGE 4]: ALL ABOUT GENGHIS KHAN
FROM: GENGHIS KHAN
DATE: OCTOBER 18
```

I'm almost your age Master Wu. You want a date with me? Just kidding. I'm 16 years old, and I have problems too. I'm handicapped. I was in a car wreck and lost my right arm, and I'm paralyzed from the waist down. I live in a wheelchair and can't go to school and my parents pay this tutor to come to the house and torture me all the time. The only fun I have is with my computer. Except for the dreams about my sister. She was killed in the car wreck, but she lives in my dreams and gives me hope. My life really sux and sometimes I think about killing myself by taking a lot of the pain pills I have. I was even kinda thinking about killing myself tonight but reading what Bob and Fuchan wrote made me feel better because now I know I'm not alone and do have some real friends who will talk about themselves. Cutter this was a great idea. I felt like crap when I logged on and now I feel a whole lot better. I wish we had done this a long time ago.

I would really like for all of us to be friends. Maybe some of you can come to my house sometime and visit me? My address is 3690 Lake Ave. My phone number is 837-6238. Call me any time. I'd love to talk to any of you. My real name is Francis Schonrath. And please don't laugh at my name or call it a girl's name . . . I hate it but I can't help what they named me. I will sign off now.

Francis

In his room, Francis logged off The Surgery. A moment later he reached for a handful of Kleenex, wiping the tears off his cheeks.

In his room, The Chief Cutter looked at the hardcopy he had made of Genghis Khan's posting of real-life information. "Jesus, the kid's got it rough," Tom said aloud, his fingers flipping through the telephone book to see if there was indeed a Schonrath residence at the stated address. There was!

Tom smiled as he uncapped the felt pen and jotted Francis's real-life information down in his address book. "Oh man," he muttered to the shadows in his room. "This is great."

Things were relatively quiet on The Surgery for the next hour. None of the ICU Elite called in, and Tom watched impatiently as some of the average users—Nurses, Interns, and Administrators—logged on and posted messages on the various boards and read their E-mail. Shifting in his chair, he watched one of the Nurse-level users read several postings on The Surgery's various sections.

"God, I wish the other Surgeons would get here," The Chief Cutter mumbled, turning his attention away from the monitor and cracking the big knuckles on his hand. He was antsy for the other ICU members to log on and bare their souls. He had yet to hear from Meat Grinder, Tunnel Rat, and Nelly Dean.

Nelly Dean arrived at a little after two, and Tom would have given anything to have been in her mind as she read the postings on the ICU. "I can hear her brain whirling," Tom mumbled to himself as he imagined her reading the ICU postings by himself, Fuchan, and Francis. After reading the posting of Francis, Nelly Dean typed:

```
[MESSAGE 5]: NELLY'S THOUGHTS
FROM: NELLY DEAN
DATE: OCTOBER 18

I think this is a very bad idea.

Nelly
```

"What the hell!" Tom exploded in his chair as he watched Nelly post. His fingers quickly punched the keys to switch over to the chat feature of his BBS program so he could communicate with Nelly on their monitor screens.

"Why is it a bad idea?" he typed.

"It doesn't feel right," Mary Alice typed back.

"Just like a woman . . . what's that supposed to mean?"

"It means trouble, that's what it's supposed to mean. You know as well as I do that NOBODY can keep anything secret in BBS. If I posted my real name and address and phone number, I'd be getting hassled all the time. I have real enemies on the war boards. Nelly Dean's feared by almost everyone. You know what happened the last time a good fighter had real-life info revealed . . . remember Superfly. Once they had his real name and address, some of the hackers accessed his father's credit files and got the numbers for all his credit cards and then posted them all over the country. They changed his credit rating and really screwed up his savings account. They caused that kid's family all kinds of grief. That's what would happen to me, and I don't need that kind of hassle. I've got more problems than I need right now, anyway. I don't need this kind of junk going on too."

"I know your real name, Nelly," Tom typed back, pulling his small address book into the bright circle of light from his desk lamp. He opened to the "S" section and glanced at a name and street number. "It's Mary Alice Sluice, and you live on Fountainbleu Avenue in New Orleans."

There was a long pause before Mary Alice replied.

"How do you know this?"

"Easy. You gave me your real name the first time you logged on. Did you forget? Then I looked your address up in the phone book. I've had it for a long time."

"You don't know that that's my real name. I could have been lying that first time I logged on."

"Sorry, hon, you were too green to lie in those days. Not like now."

"I don't want my real name posted anywhere."

"Of course," Tom typed back. "You can trust me. I've had it this long and I've never posted it or given it to anyone, as far as you know anyway."

No response.

"Look, Mary, if you don't want to post real stuff, post some lies—that's what I did. You don't think my real name is Bob Hughes, do you? Surely the brilliant Nelly Dean didn't fall for that nonsense? Robert Earle Hughes was one of the fattest men who ever lived—they had to bury him in a piano box. He worked for P. T. Barnum's circus."

"It's not right . . . it doesn't feel right and I don't like it. Some of what's posted on the ICU sounds really true to me. I think Master Wu and Genghis Khan fell for your trick, and now they've revealed their real identities, as well as addresses and phone numbers. It goes completely against the spirit of alias BBS. You're using people who think you're their friend. This is taking the game too far. You know that, Mr. Chief Cutter. You know everything because all you do with your time is sit in your little room, wherever it is, and watch your BBS."

Tom sat back and ruminated on what Mary Alice had just typed. She had a good point, but there was no way he could or would admit he had made a major mistake. And, besides, he didn't like her disrespectful tone one bit. The damage was done, particularly since Wu and Khan had already posted the truth.

"You're making a mountain out of a molehill," Tom typed back. "This is all in fun."

"Well, I DON'T know that," Mary Alice typed back, "and

I'm not going to post anything about the REAL ME. Nor am I going to post any lies that could very well backfire and hurt one of our BBS friends."

Tom purposely kept his fingers off the keyboard to make Mary Alice a little nervous. Then he typed: "If you don't post anything, I just might type it for you. I can do that, you know. I can post under any name I want. I can make it look like you posted. This BBS program will let me do anything I want. But I'm a nice guy, so here's what I'll do. I'll just delete that last lame posting of yours and let you think about all this for a few days. On some of the other boards you can post that Nelly's going to be out of town for a while or something. I'm going through with this on the ICU whether you like it or not. It's a new part of the game. So, if you don't want to play, stay away. Dig?"

"I dig, Mister," Mary Alice typed back. "YOU are abusing your sysop power, that's what YOU ARE doing. And what YOU ARE DOING is wrong, and YOU ARE going to lose friends and users because of it."

"No way," Tom typed back. "It's harmless fun. Go cool off and think about it. It'll raise the game to a new and higher level. It's a bold move."

When he finished typing that, Tom hit the proper key and automatically logged Nelly Dean off the system, which he knew would both irritate and scare her.

Then he deleted her message.

"Piss on her," he muttered to himself, pushing the address book back into the shadows on his oak computer workstation. "She'll come around . . . I've got her real-life info and if she doesn't play the game my way, I'll expose her."

Suddenly, for the first time in his life, Tom Barnslow felt powerful.

At ten to four in the morning, Tom tired of waiting for Tunnel Rat and Meat Grinder to post, so he went to bed.

Forty-five minutes later, Dennis Conlick logged on to The Surgery. Forcing himself to relax, Dennis changed sub-

boards and read the postings from his fellow Surgeons. He
then wrote the following message on the ICU, which was
Message 5 because Tom had deleted what Nelly posted:

```
[MESSAGE 5]: ABOVE GROUND
FROM: THE TUNNEL RAT
DATE: OCTOBER 18
```

Well, well, well, so everybody's coming above ground now, eh? It
made me feel funny to read all that real-life stuff that the
Cutter (Bob), Master Wu (Fuchan—pretty name) and Genghis Khan
(Francis???) posted. But it also made me feel not so weird for
the first time in a long while.

I'm Dennis Conlick. That's my real name and I live in a dumpy
apartment down in the French Quarter. I'm probably older than
several of you put together so I hope that doesn't put you all
off. I fought in Vietnam and had some problems over there that
still give me some problems over here. But I'm better at the
moment and above ground after reading what you folks posted
about yourselves. This was a good idea, Cutter.

All these aliases have become so real to me that I'd forgotten
there were real people behind them. I don't go outside much
these days but if this all works out and I stay above ground for a
while maybe we can all meet for coffee and beignuts at the French
Market some Saturday morning when you guys don't have school.
Let me know. If I'm above ground then, I'll give it a try.

Tunnel Rat
Cracker Extraordinaire

P.S. Can't wait to hear what my buddy Meat Grinder's like in real
life. And Nelly Dean???? I've had the hots for you since getting
into BBS, babe! Grab a carrier to 833-1969. Just say
"chat." Then hang up and call back in a few minutes using your
computer. I don't want to go voice with anyone just yet but I'd
like to chat.

Before disconnecting, Dennis sent a quick piece of E-mail
to Nelly Dean. As he logged off The Surgery, the Tunnel Rat

rolled his head around his shoulders. "Jeez, I'm tired as
hell," he muttered to himself. He turned off his computer
and modem for the first time in over sixty hours, stubbed
out his cigarette, and walked tiredly over to the cheap cot
that served as his bed. He'd bought it at the Salvation Army
outlet on Dauphine Street. Moving dirty clothes and candy-
bar wrappers off the cot and onto the floor, Dennis lay down
and lowered his head onto one arm. Even though his daily
dose of Benzedrine was still soaring through his system, his
natural exhaustion defeated the stimulant and he fell into a
deep, dreamless sleep.

He hadn't slept since early Wednesday morning.

In her apartment, Mary Alice Sluice was again sitting up
in her bed, unable to sleep.

*You've been worrying about this too long. You have to get
some sleep,* she scolded herself.

She held her hands in front of her face. They were shaking
like tissue paper held over a campfire.

*Stop it, Mary Alice. It's BBS . . . it's fantasy . . . nothing
bad is going to happen to Nelly Dean. She isn't real, she only
lives in your modem. What can they do except send pizzas
and force you to change your VISA number? Big deal. But he
has my name, my God, he has my name. And if he's got that,
it's possible he can find out about the project. And if that
happens . . . the director . . . Brandais. And he threatened
me, and the invasion, the theft of the extract. My God, I
forgot the invasion. What if the Cutter's the one? Who is this
Succubus he mentioned?*

"What am I going to do?" she asked herself aloud as she
pulled the bedcovers up around her face. At 5:17 A.M., Mary
Alice Sluice dreamed about the days when she had been a
surgical nurse:

"Goddamn it to hell, Sluice," the surgeon viciously
snapped, throwing a scalpel against the operating-room
wall, "you gave me the wrong knife. What the hell do you
think I'm doing here, knitting?"

Mary Alice shook her head, her eyes locked on the

glistening gray brain tissue in the open skull of the patient lying on the operating table.

"Give me the knife I asked for. You look like hell. What were you doing last night? I need my nurses awake, not half dead on their feet."

Getting the correct scalpel this time, Mary Alice slapped it into the palm of the neurosurgeon's right hand.

"That's better," he mumbled, his attention returning to the abscess he was about to drain. "Now, let's get down to business. We've got serious work here and I want all of you on your toes. And Sluice, you've lost your touch in an operating room. You never used to make mistakes. You've lost it, baby."

With the words "You've lost it, baby" echoing in her mind, Mary Alice woke up, her nightgown drenched with sweat. In her mind's eye, she realized that the man on the operating table in her dream bore an uncanny resemblance to von Neumann.

At 5:30 that morning, Jim Persall got up to take a leak. Walking back from the first-floor bathroom on legs still stiff from the football game of the night before, he decided to do some stretching.

After stretching for ten minutes, he looked at the clock and realized this would be a perfect time to get on The Surgery before everybody started calling. So he booted his Apple IIc communication program, turned on his modem, dialed the number, and immediately hit the keys to go read the ICU hi-security board.

"Wow," he mumbled to himself after reading the postings on the ICU. "How about that?" He typed the following message about himself:

[MESSAGE 6]: LOWDOWN ON MEAT GRINDER
FROM: MEAT GRINDER
DATE: OCTOBER 19

Hi everybody. What a great surprise! I'm really happy to see everybody come out of their shells, and I can't wait to meet you guys in real life. My name's Jim Persall. I'm a sophomore at Tulane, a football player. I'm a very average guy, kind of like the All-American Kid, I guess. I don't drink or do drugs, and I still live with my parents. In fact, I like living with my parents. Can ya believe it? Anyway, if any of you want to call me, my number's 899-0971. House address is in the phone book. Seriously, let's get together real soon. Have a Surgeon's party or something, okay?

And, Cutter . . . as for this Succubus dude, he'd better watch his step. If he screws around with the wrong Surgeon, namely me, he's going to find himself looking through his asshole!

Jim (Meat Grinder)

Five minutes after disconnecting, Jim Persall was back in bed, sound asleep.

Chapter
6

At six-thirty that Saturday morning, as was his usual habit, one of the most enigmatic of all New Orleans' BBS users, Buffalo Bill, logged on to The Surgery. Buff, as he liked to be called, moved to the war board and posted a satire about one of the area's minor war groups—ninth and tenth graders whose two leaders had recently shaken up the Warlords by kicking out several members for not fighting hard enough.

In his room, Tom Barnslow stretched slowly, enjoying the gentle rocking of waves in his water bed. Rubbing sleep from his eyes, he glanced at the LCD clock on the nightstand an arm's-length away. "God, it's not even eight yet." He moaned to himself, falling back onto the sloshing bed. A moment later, he glanced toward the monitor on his computer workstation. The inverse display at the top of the screen told him Buffalo Bill was on the board.

"Jeez, it's Bill." Tom chortled, scampering out of bed to chat with Buff before he logged off. Clad only in his jockey shorts, Tom sat down at his computer and typed:

"Hi, Buff. Whatcha up to? At it kinda early, aren't you?"

"Nah, I don't sleep much, Cutter. Call most of the boards this time on weekends before they get too busy. You know that."

"Yeah. You've been regular as clockwork for years, all right."

"That's me. How you been?"

One thing about Buff, Tom thought, he's always up for a chat. Especially late-night and early-morning chats. Never could get anything specific out of the guy about his real life, though, except for his recommending novels to read. He was probably the most careful and secretive user of The Surgery.

"I've been fine," Tom typed in reply. "Listen, did you give any more thought about what I asked you a couple of weeks ago?"

"You mean about joining your hi-security group?"

"Yeah, the ICU Surgeons. You interested? We'd love to have you."

"I thought about it some more, but my reply's still the same as the last time . . . and the time before that. I just use BBS to have some fun writing on the war and story boards. I like being totally anonymous and uninvolved on any kind of a personal level, and if I joined your elite group, sooner or later, my secret would be out and then all the BBS people I've defeated on the war boards would be prank-calling me. Who needs it? Not me."

"Yeah, that's what you always say," Tom typed back, deciding to take a new approach. "But, really, Buff, it's not healthy to be alone all the time. This'd be a great way for you to make some new friends."

Buffalo Bill paused before typing back: "Hey, I'm the Mystery Man of BBS. What makes you think I want new friends? What makes you think I don't have any friends? I've got lots of friends. There's nothing the matter with my social life."

"Don't get steamed. I dunno. All the secrecy stuff surrounding your alias, I guess. Everybody I chat with figures you're a real geek or something. There's even a rumor going around that you're in an iron lung, that that's why you won't break your anonymity."

Buff typed in response: "Iron lung! I love it. Besides, everybody knows I'm a twenty-nine-year-old geologist. I posted that when I left the city and worked in Dallas for those six months last year."

"Yeah, but nobody believed you were gone. Everybody figures you just wanted a break from all that heavy-duty fighting you were doing then."

"Well, everybody can believe what they want. But, to get back to your question. Thanks for the invitation to join the Surgeons. I'm honored, really. But the answer's still no. No offense, okay?"

"Sure. No problem," Tom typed in reply, anger scratching the back of his mind like the tooth-edged end of a rake. Try something else, he thought. An idea struck him, hard.

Tom Barnslow typed: "Look, Buff, it's really me that's lonely. If I'm not in school, I sit here and watch this damn BBS. That's ALL I do with MY life. And it's driving me nuts. And I woke up really depressed this morning. My parents are divorced and my mom's fooling around with her boyfriends all the time and it's really getting to me. I NEED some kind of REAL connection with another REAL human being. Awwww, forget it. You don't need to hear all my problems."

"If I tell you my real info," Buff typed, feeling sorry for The Chief Cutter, "can I count on you keeping it totally to yourself? Are you willing to give me your word of honor on it?"

Tom paused for what he thought would be just the right amount of time before typing back: "Forget what I said. You want to be a mystery. That's probably half the fun of it for you."

"Yes."

"I'm feeling better anyhow. Don't tell me anything you don't want to," Tom typed.

"Are you sure?"

"No, damn it! I can tell from your postings that you're a decent person. Even on the war boards, it's obvious you do this just for fun. You always let up on people when it's clear they don't want to fight you anymore. And I've read some of the things you've posted on the discussion boards. I remember that stuff you posted last year when Diaper Man was writing about shooting himself."

"All I said was that everybody got depressed once in a while and that he should never think about taking his own life, that it was the most precious gift of all."

"Yeah. I know it made him feel better because he told me so in chat the next day. He said you probably saved his life."

Tom laughed as he typed. He'd never chatted with Diaper Man in his life. Diaper Man was one of the low-life scum of BBS, a twerpy little fourteen-year-old who thought about nothing but Photon and jacking off, judging from his pathetic postings on the various war and X-rated boards in the city.

"Well, you're not thinking about suicide, are you?"

"The thought's crossed my mind lately . . ."

"Look, Cutter . . ."

Tom broke in and started typing, cutting Buffalo Bill off. "My real name's Robert Earle Hughes. I live at 3009 Friedrichs St. out here in Metairie. See, I trust you."

Pause from Buff's end as Tom shouted "Do it!" at the monitor, knowing that it was now or never for him to learn the most coveted information in BBS. "Do it, goddamn it!"

"Okay, Bob. My real name's Ted Reschay. I'm knocking on the age of forty with a Reggie Jackson baseball bat. I've got a beautiful wife and two neat kids. I'm a high-school teacher. My phone number's unlisted, but it's 891-6323 if you ever need to call and chat. My address is 3000 Park Road. And now you know what nobody . . . and I stress NOBODY else in BBS knows. I've trusted you with this information because you seem to be hurting this morning, and I don't like to see somebody in pain. Now, tell me what's really bothering you."

In his room, Tom sat back in his chair and read the real-life info on the infamous Buffalo Bill. "Gotcha, gotcha, gotcha!" he almost shouted aloud in his room before he pulled himself back together. He bent back over the computer keyboard and typed:

"You're such an egotistical sonuvabitch, Ted, you know

that? Ted? What kind of name is Ted? What a fag name! I don't need your help, Ted. It was just a ploy. A trick. The sort of ruse that only the real King of BBS could pull off. Everybody's been dying to know your particulars for a hell of a long time. And now The Chief Cutter's got 'em! And I've got you by the balls, Buffalo Boy. You ain't king of the hill no more, Buffie."

Tom hit the proper sequence of keys, simultaneously breaking out of chat and logging a very angry Ted Reschay off The Surgery.

Tom giggled as he grabbed his pen and added Buffalo Bill's particulars to his address book.

The Chief Cutter stared at his monitor. Entering the ICU section of his BBS, Tom laughed with satisfaction as he read the postings where Dennis Conlick and Jim Persall had also coughed up their real life information.

He put his fingers to the keyboard and typed:

```
[MESSAGE 7]: GOODS ON BUFFALO BILL
FROM: THE CHIEF CUTTER
DATE: OCTOBER 19
```

Well, fellow Surgeons, remember how Buffalo Bill always used to post ""King of the Hill'' underneath his alias when he was heavy into war and pounding the crap out of just about everyone? Remember how he blasted into alias BBS out of nowhere and defeated every fighter who dared to take him on—including The Untouchable who chickened out and ran off to Destin in the middle of their great one-on-one battle? But not me. I was patient. I knew when he first logged on that I'd get the best of him sooner or later. Well, I'm happy to report that we now have a new King of the Hill.

And I'm HIM.

That's right, everybody. I got the real lowdown on Buffalo Bill. He's not the boy genius like we've all believed for such a long time. And he's not locked away in some iron lung somewhere, either. Nope. It's ridiculous actually, and we shoulda guessed a long time ago. His name's Ted Reschay, and, get this, he's a high-school teacher! How about that? His phone number is 891-6323 and his address is 3000 Park Road.

By the way, this information should be kept on the q.t. Buff gave it to me this morning in confidence, but I know he wouldn't mind me posting it here on the ICU since he knows all of us can be trusted. I promised him none of us would reveal it to anyone else, so keep it under your hats, okay?

Regarding other things, Tunnel Rat . . . I mean Dennis . . . thanks for telling us about yourself. Man, it sure sounds like you've had a tough life. Why don't you tell us more? And Fuchan, where do you go to school? Are you a senior or a junior? Hey, Khan (sorry, can't call you Francis without laughing), that's too bad about your handicap, man. Did you have a lot of surgery? If you did, why don't you tell us about it? I'm sure we'd all like to hear about it. Jim, your life sounds pretty boring, man. Guess that's why you like to stir it up on the war boards, eh? Glad to see you're not intimidated by that geek Succubus. He doesn't scare me either.

Oh yeah, I almost forget. Nelly dropped by last night. She was too busy to post here on ICU, but she gave me her name and address in chat and told me to pass it on to you. It's Mary Alice Sluice, and she lives on Fountainbleu. She's in the phone book, so you can get the rest from there.

Robert Earle Hughes (Bob)

After saving the posting, Tom sat back in his swivel chair and stretched his long bony arms toward the ceiling. "That'll teach her to give me a hard time in the middle of the night. If she's going to play on my board, she's gonna play by my rules, by God."

Tom took his time making his bed. When he next looked at the inverse display at the top of his monitor, he was surprised to see that The Succubus had logged on. He hadn't heard from the sysop of the mysterious VAX for two weeks and hadn't expected to either, particularly since he'd been utterly unable to hack into the guy's system.

Tom's glance dropped down from the user display.

He was stunned to see that The Succubus had just finished reading Msg. No. 7, the info about Buffalo Bill. And if The Succubus was now on No. 7, that meant this person had also read the previous six postings and now had the real information about not only Buff but also Meat Grinder, Tunnel Rat, Genghis Khan, Master Wu, and Nelly Dean. Not to mention the false information about himself.

Tom stared at the screen in disbelief. It was impossible, he told himself, for The Succubus to be in the ICU since Tom had never validated him for the system, much less set his flags for high-level access. Absolutely impossible.

Tom had modified his BBS program so that no one could crash it or break into it. Unless The Succubus was one of those legendary hackers, capable of breaking into the most secure telecommunication-and-computer systems in America. Tom did more than his share of hacking, and he just couldn't believe his system wasn't impenetrable.

The leader of the Surgeons rushed to the keyboard and started to press the chat keys but stopped when he realized The Succubus was going to post on the ICU.

Incredible, Tom thought. The guy's not only validated himself but he's actually hacked write status too.

His curiosity getting the best of him, Tom watched as the intruder typed:

```
[MESSAGE 8]: YOUR WORST NIGHTMARE ARRIVES
FROM: THE SUCCUBUS
DATE: OCTOBER 19

I am The Succubus.

I hacked this supposedly "elite" board.

I've read the information here.

I've been watching you people for a long time.

The Chief Cutter, Buffalo Bill, Meat Grinder . . . and the
rest . . . all of you are nothing. I can't stand you people who
```

```
think you're so much better than the rest of BBS, Elite?
Bullshit!

You little Electronic Warriors think you know about war?

Now it's your turn,

Guess who'll be the first sacrifice? And this isn't a game,
kiddies, This is for keeps,

The Succubus
REAL King of the Hill
```

The Succubus hit the proper key to save the message, and the hard drive whirled. As soon as the drive stopped, Tom punched the chat keys and broke in.

"What the hell do you think you're doing?"

"Hahaha," The Succubus typed back.

"I'm going to delete what you just posted," Tom typed.

"Try," The Succubus challenged. "Kill that posting and your hard drive will self-destruct, along with every file on it. I planted a logic bomb in your system, Cutter, so you'd better not screw with me or else you can kiss The Surgery goodbye. I'm your master now, and as long as you want to keep your board up, you don't touch anything I post. You dig?"

"I've got backups," Tom typed.

"That bomb's been in there for three years, kid. Ever since I got to town. My money says every backup you've got has my bomb in it. If you don't believe me, kill the message. I'll enjoy seeing The Surgery self-destruct right before my eyes."

"Look," Tom typed, "I don't have that material you're so worried about. Honest, I tried, but I haven't been able to invade your VAX."

"Too late. You had your chance to back out, and you refused. The real game's begun now, and it goes to the finish. The very finish."

The Succubus punched the proper keys at his computer terminal and dropped the carrier, leaving Tom alone, cut off, furious.

"Sonofabitch!" Tom shouted, putting himself into the sysop mode of the BBS, so he could kill The Succubus's posting on the ICU as he had deleted Nelly Dean's the night before.

His fingers started to press the proper sequence of keys to kill the message, but then an icy thread of fear needled through him. If the dude was good enough to hack read/write access to the ICU, he was probably good enough to put a bomb in the program.

"Oh shit," Tom Barnslow said, "I can't believe this is happening."

The Chief Cutter went into the electronic-mail feature of his BBS and composed the following letter:

To: All Surgeons
From: Chief Cutter
Re: Invasion of the Surgery

I know you're going to find this hard to believe, but I promise you it isn't mindscrew. I AM NOT trying to start some kind of a new game. So please take this seriously.

I have a very big problem. Some guy called The Succubus has somehow hacked read/write status on to the ICU. I know this sounds impossible, but he's done it, and I can't delete him because he claims he's left a logic bomb in the system that will destroy it if I try to kill one of his postings or try to delete him. Since he hacked read/write status, I have to believe him.

I'm going to need your help on all of this. We have to come up with a plan. We . . .

Tom suddenly realized that he couldn't send the letter to the Surgeons. If The Succubus had read/write access, that meant he had sysop access, and if he had that, then he could read all the mail anytime he wanted to.

"Which means," Tom mumbled to himself, "I don't have many options. I can admit to everyone that I was lying about being Robert Earle Hughes and tell them my real information and ask some of them for help, or else I can go to war with this guy by myself. Great, just great."

Chapter

~~~~~~~

7

Saturday, October 19th, 11 A.M.

Sitting once again at his computer, Francis Schonrath laughed aloud when he entered the ICU Elite hi-
security board and read the background of Buffalo Bill.
The posting by The Succubus he ignored, figuring it was
The Chief Cutter playing one of his practical jokes again.

"Hot damn," he said gleefully, jotting down the address
and phone number. "Now I can get him back for what he
did to me last summer."

Months earlier Khan had made the mistake of mentioning Buffalo Bill's name in a rather snide way, and
Bill had immediately jumped down his throat with
both boots, savaging him on three different war boards
for an entire week before Francis had been forced to
ask for a truce in E-mail. And then Bill had posted
the E-mail without permission, which had irritated the
hell out of Genghis Khan. He'd sworn then that he'd get
the Buffalo Man back if it took him the rest of his life.

Francis pressed the "P" key to post a message on the ICU
and then typed the following:

[MESSAGE 9]: SOUNDS LIKE FUN
FROM: GENGHIS KHAN
DATE: OCTOBER 19

Well, I'm glad we're all telling the truth here. Except for you, Chief. What's with this Succubus stuff? You've fooled me too many times for me to fall for one of your jokes again, CC. Good try though.

Anyway, I think we ought to have a little fun with Buffalo Bill. He porked me good once and I owe him. And he's porked most of you on more than one occasion too. So why don't we pork him back???? I think I'll send him a few pizzas tonight. But that'd be taking BBS into the outside world. And we don't do that, do we?

Hey, Meat Grinder, are you hungry? Wanna pizza?

Francis

Logging off The Surgery, Francis Schonrath leaned back in his wheelchair and chuckled. "Pizzas," he said. "Nah, I can do a little better than that. I wonder if Ted scares easily?" Then Francis laughed as one idea after another went off in his head, like a string of Black Cat firecrackers.

Saturday, October 19th, Noon

Sitting in his recliner in his apartment laboratory, the overhead light dimmed to ten watts, Harv listened carefully to the instructions.

"Do it soon."

"I will do it tomorrow."

"Do you understand?" the voice in his mind asked.

"Yes, I will put no others before you," Harv answered dreamily.

"There should be no deviations."

"No. No deviations."

"You must show yourself worthy."

"I love you," Harv replied.

But there was no answer. Still attached to the connector,

Harv closed his eyes and willed his mind to be as blank as possible, hoping the voice would come back.

It didn't.

Several minutes later, Harv struggled out of the recliner and terminated the running of the Zeus program. He pulled the electrodes from under his skin and gently removed his replica of the prototype from his skull.

Picking up his keys, Harv unlocked the lab door and went into his kitchen. He removed a bottle of Perrier from the refrigerator and returned to the lab.

He locked himself in and sat down again, sipping the sparkling water and mentally reviewing the instructions He had given him.

He spent almost twenty minutes with the New Orleans phone book, jotting notes on a sheet of yellow legal paper. Then he turned on one of the modems and made a call to a local computer. Watching the monitor carefully, he jotted a few notes on the paper.

"Teresa," he said five minutes later.

"I love you, Harv," the computer-generated voice responded.

"Expand database Sacrifices."

"Expanding database Sacrifices," Teresa answered.

"Record begin. Saturday, October nineteenth," Harv said. "He has asked me to make a sacrifice for him. I now have complete information on the Surgeons to add to project team member information. The information I lacked I obtained from South Central Bell's billing computer. Append following real information for Surgeons."

As Harv watched and spoke, his finger tracing through the information he had written down, Teresa extended the database. He watched the screen carefully to make sure the appended information was correct:

```
Fuchan Nomasaki          Thomas Barnslow
Master Wu                Chief Cutter
Sunrise Apt. 99          304 Iona St.
Gentilly                 Metairie
282-8137                 837-0334
```

Dennis Conlick	Mary Alice Sluice
Tunnel Rat	Nelly Dean
913 Royal Street	703 Fountainbleu
New Orleans	New Orleans
833-1969	899-3285

Jim Persall	Francis Schonrath
Meat Grinder	Genghis Khan
6317 Prytannia St.	3960 Lake Ave.
New Orleans	New Orleans
899-0971	837-6238

"Save database Sacrifices," Harv instructed and waited for the hard drive to finish writing the new file to the drive.

Then he laughed.

"Why are you laughing, Harv?" Teresa asked, programmed to inquire when his laughs reached a certain decibel level.

"Because the arrogant Dr. Mary Alice Sluice is Nelly Dean, dear. Never in my wildest dreams would I have imagined that our prim and proper Dr. Sluice was the greatest female warrior on the war boards. What a surprise. I have all of them right here." He rubbed the ball of his thumb against the tip of his index finger, like he was squashing a flea.

"It's very funny, Harv," Teresa said.

"Yes," Harv replied, starting to get bored with his voice-recognition program's predictability. Maybe it was time to trash that program? After all, who needed Teresa when he had a connection with God?

"I love you, Harv."

"Listening-only mode, Teresa," Harv ordered to shut her up. "Hardcopy database Sacrifices."

The Diablo daisywheel printer began to print the new database.

When it had finished, Harv ripped the page from the printer. Holding the copy of the database, he walked to his recliner, where he sat down and picked up hardcopies of the first nine postings on ICU. He reread them carefully.

He took a red pen from his shirt pocket and circled one of the names on the hardcopy of the Sacrifices database.

"You will be my first sacrifice for Him," he said.

Saturday, October 19th, 2:45 P.M.

Grandfather and Fuchan sat shoulder-to-shoulder at Master Wu's IBM and read the latest messages on the ICU.

"Pizza sounds good, Fu," Grandfather said, stroking the back of Fuchan's head with his arthritic old hand. "Do they make noodle pizza?"

Fuchan laughed. "No, Grandfather, I don't think they do. But what Genghis has posted is not very smart. He shouldn't take BBS off the boards."

"He said he was kidding, yes?"

"Yes, but I don't think he was. He fights very hard, Grandfather, and he hates to lose. I think he'll do what he said."

"Maybe you should ask him for date to take mind off war?" Grandfather suggested.

"I couldn't do that," Fuchan replied, shocked. "You know I've never had a date. Besides, who'd want to go out with me?"

"I would accompany you, of course."

"Grandfather, he's sixteen years old."

"Yes. You are one year older. Incredible difference."

Hiro Nomasaki's wrinkled face broke into hundreds of laugh lines.

Looking at him, Fuchan had to smile.

"He is lonely, yes?"

"He sounds very lonely."

"You are lonely too?"

"I . . . yes, I am lonely too."

"Call him. The Dragonmobile go zoo tomorrow. We will feed monkeys."

"Grandfather, I can't do that."

"Monkeys easy to feed, Granddaughter. I will help."

97

Laughing, Fuchan realized her grandfather had made up his mind. "I'll call him, Grandfather."

"Good," Hiro answered, rising from the chair he was sitting in. "I leave room for private talk. Pick up at noon tomorrow, yes?"

Fuchan nodded, and the old man slowly walked out of her room, closing the door gently behind him.

Fuchan turned off her modem and then dialed the number.

"Hello?"

"May I speak with Francis, please?"

"Francis? You're calling for Francis? Who is this?"

"My name is Fuchan Nomasaki."

"I don't think Francis knows you," Mrs. Schonrath replied. Since the accident, her son had received very few phone calls.

"I know him through BBS," Fuchan explained.

"Through what? Oh, I see. Okay, just a second."

Fuchan giggled. She couldn't believe how scared she was. Pushing her ear against the warm plastic of the receiver, she heard Mrs. Schonrath calling for Francis. Then she heard a whirring sound.

"Hello?" a high adolescent voice answered.

"Hello, Francis. This is Fuchan Nomasaki. Master Wu."

"Hi. I'm Genghis Khan," Francis replied, giggling.

"I saw your phone number on the ICU and I, well, my grandfather and I are going to the zoo tomorrow, and we want you to go with us. Do you want to come?"

There was a long silence on the other end, and Fuchan felt her face redden. Maybe this had been a bad idea.

"I'd like to," Francis said finally, his voice low, "but I can't. I'm handicapped."

"I know. You put that in your posting. I thought you had a wheelchair."

"Of course I have a wheelchair. I live in a wheelchair."

"Then why can't you come to the zoo?"

"I'm a cripple, I already told you," Francis snapped, his voice angry.

Fuchan was at a loss for words. "Will you talk with my grandfather?" she asked, not knowing what else to do.

"What for?"

"Because I think you'd like him. He's a very nice man."

Part of Francis wanted to hang up the phone and go back to his computer, but another part of him, the part that hadn't talked to anyone except his parents and his tutor for far too long, made him say, "Yes, I'll talk to him. And I can't go to the zoo with you. But thanks anyway. Maybe you'll call again?"

"Sure . . . if you'll call me?"

"I don't know."

"Just a sec, let me get Grandfather."

Fuchan rushed out of her room. Hiro Nomasaki was standing in the living room, by the picture window, looking out at the ugly asphalt parking lot of their apartment complex. His mind idly compared this scene to the beautiful temples of his home city of Kyoto.

"He says he can't go, and I don't know what to do. Will you talk to him? Please, Grandfather, I want him to go with us. He sounds so lonely."

Hiro smiled and walked into Fuchan's room.

"Hello, do I speak with great Genghis Khan?" Grandfather said, smiling broadly at Fuchan.

Francis didn't know what to say.

"Ahhh so, Genghis Khan speechless, yes?" Hiro chuckled deeply. "I have stolen words from great Khan's mouth."

"No sir," Francis replied. "You're Fuchan's grandfather?"

"Happily yes, and you honor us please with company to visit zoo tomorrow at noon? We feed monkeys and have good time."

"I'd like to go, I really would, but I can't. I'm crippled." Francis struck his useless legs with his fist.

"I read writing wrong? You do not have chair with wheels?"

Francis grinned at the awkward phrasing. "Yes, I live in a wheelchair."

"Chair moves if somebody push it, yes?"

"It's battery-powered," Francis explained. "I can make it move with a switch on the armrest."

"Then I not have to push you all over zoo. Very good. Hard for old man like me to push young boy around big zoo."

"I can't go," Francis said flatly.

"Why? If chair have battery wheels, then why not come to zoo and feed monkeys?"

"People will look at me."

"Oh, now understand. Genghis Khan has big fear of people. Just like Master Wu. You afraid because legs don't work. Wu afraid because brain too big. Both big strong warriors on war boards but scaredy cats in real life."

"I'm not afraid of anything," Francis snapped.

"Ahhh, I make mistake. So sorry. Not afraid of people after all. We pick you up noon tomorrow then," Hiro said, chuckling. "I put one over on great Genghis Khan, yes? I, how you say, I mindscrub you?"

Francis couldn't help himself. He started to laugh. "I have to get permission from my mother, and I don't think she'll let me go."

"I speak with Mama-san, please."

"Yes, sir," Francis answered, smiling. He looked at his mother. "He wants to talk to you, Mom."

Mrs. Schonrath took the phone.

"Hello, this is Francis's mother." The two talked for a while before Mrs. Schonrath looked at Francis. She covered the phone with the palm of her hand. "I don't know about this, Francis," she said. "I don't know these people. Do you want to go?"

She got her answer from the look in her son's eyes.

"All right, Mr. Nomasaki, Francis can go to the zoo with you tomorrow."

"We have good time. We feed monkeys."

"Yes, that will be fun," Mrs. Schonrath replied. "You have our address?"

"Happily yes, 3960 Lake Avenue, yes?"

"Yes."

"Very good. Please to tell Genghis Khan we pick him up in Dragonmobile noon tomorrow. Thank you very much."

Hiro Nomasaki lowered the phone. He blinked at Fuchan. "We go zoo tomorrow with Genghis Khan. Just hope he and Master Wu don't get in big war."

Fuchan hugged her grandfather.

In the living room of the Schonrath house, Mrs. Schonrath said, shaking her head in disbelief, "He said to tell Genghis Khan they'll pick him up at noon tomorrow in a Dragonmobile."

Francis laughed, and a moment later his mother did too.

Saturday, October 19th, 5:17 P.M.

Mary Alice Sluice stepped out of the shower and vigorously toweled her hair. She slipped on a bulky cotton bathrobe and walked barefoot into her bedroom.

"What a day," she said, looking at the alarm clock next to her computer, realizing that she'd been at the lab running tests on von Neumann for over three hours.

After putting a TV dinner in the microwave, Mary Alice clicked on her modem and booted her terminal program. Setting the autodialer, she absentmindedly watched the screen.

The timer went off on the microwave just as she got a carrier into The Surgery. "Never fails," she mumbled, typing in her user number and password, and then reading:

```
You have mail waiting. Read it now? (Y/N)
```

She hit the "Y" key and the screen filled:

```
To: Nelly Dean
From: Tunnel Rat
Re: New Developments
```

```
Hiya babe, I'm leaving you this note because I saw on the ICU
that you hadn't left your real time information, which is
```

probably a smart thing to do. It's after four in the morning as I
write this, and I'm about to crash real hard. I left my number on
ICU. Call me. Part of me's still below ground, so I can't talk
to you voice, but I'd like to chat. If you feel like swapping
words with some 43-year-old computer geek who only plays with
half a deck most of the time, give me a buzz, eh? I can tell from
the way you write that you're older than the kids who play war,
and I'd like to chat with somebody who's not in her teens any
longer. No offense. Anyway, after reading the stuff from Master
Wu and Genghis Khan, I felt halfway human for the first time in a
long time. Don't feel obligated to answer this. My feelings,
what's left of them, won't be hurt if you don't. In case you
didn't jot down my number, it's 833-1969. Name's Dennis,
Dennis Conlick. Call if you feel like it—no obligation.

Dennis

"Great," Mary Alice muttered. "Another lost soul. Just
what I need." Nonetheless, she saved the letter on disk so
she could recall it to the screen anytime she wanted to.

Pressing a couple more keys, Mary Alice went quickly
into ICU. She started chewing her fingernails as she got
caught up on the messages that had been posted since her
call of the night before.

"That bastard," she swore when she read her real name.
"He promised he wouldn't expose me, and then he did it."

She was bemused by the posting from The Succubus and
wasn't sure what to make of it, but, like Genghis Khan, she
figured it was another one of The Chief Cutter's practical
jokes.

"He's gone off the deep end," she muttered.

Then she read Khan's threats about Buffalo Bill.

She sighed, pressed the "P" key to post a message, and
started typing:

[MESSAGE 10]: JUST AS I FEARED
FROM: NELLY DEAN
DATE: OCTOBER 19

First off, THE CHIEF CUTTER did NOT have permission to post my real name, and I am very pissed off about it.

I told him last night that this was a very BAD idea, and Genghis Khan has just proved me correct. Once you start taking BBS outside of BBS, it gets out of hand in a hurry. Francis is already making threats about pizzas. What's next, Francis? VISA card numbers? Armed thugs? Storm troopers?

Well, this is it for me. I hereby resign from The Surgeons and from BBS. Nelly Dean is dead, boys. Killed by The Chief Cutter.

I'm out of the game.

Nelly Dean R.I.P.

Tom, of course, was watching as Nelly read her mail and as she read the ICU. When she finished typing and saving her message, he broke into chat:

"You were right," he typed, "and I was wrong. I'm sorry."

"It's a LITTLE late for that, isn't it, Mr. Chief Cutter? What you've done to me is inexcusable. I do NOT accept your apology. Like I posted, I'm quitting BBS."

"Geez, Nelly, settle down."

"It's not Nelly any longer. You killed Nelly."

"Look, Mary, I really am sorry. I'm not mindscrewing you or anything. I'm serious."

Mary Alice sat back and thought for a moment before replying:

"I'm still quitting, sorry or not. You've ruined the game for me."

"I'm afraid it's no longer just a game. Did you read what The Succubus posted?"

"Of course. You are The Succubus. And I'm sick of your practical jokes too, Mr. Chief Cutter."

Tom Barnslow took a deep breath.

"Truth time," he typed. "I'm not The Succubus. My name is Thomas Barnslow, and I'm a graduate student in computer sciences at Tulane. I think I'm getting in over my head with this game, and I need your help."

"Give me your voice phone number and I'll call you," Mary Alice typed back. "That's the only way you can prove to me that you aren't lying again."

"I can't talk on the telephone," Tom typed.

"Give it to me or I'm hanging up and that'll be it. I'm real now, Mr. Cutter, and if you want help, you're going to have to talk to me. The real me talks to real people."

"254-8813," Tom typed, his hands shaking, sweat breaking out on his upper lip.

"I'll call you after I eat my dinner," Mary Alice typed.

"I can't . . ."

But Mary Alice broke the connection and left Tom Barnslow alone at his computer.

Going into her kitchen, Mary Alice stood for a moment and looked at the copper-bottomed pots and pans that she seldom had time to use anymore. She thought about the gourmet meals she used to cook before she got so involved with the project. Between the project and BBS, there just weren't enough hours in the day to do all the things she liked to do.

She sighed as she removed her TV dinner from the microwave.

Her eyes kept returning to the phone on the wall in the kitchen.

Everything's falling apart at once, she thought. *Cutter's ruined BBS for me, and something's happening to von Neumann. The chimp growled at the director when I stopped in the lab. He went up to von's cage, opened the door like always and offered him a banana. Von snarled—he's never done that before!*

"Did you see that?" the director had asked, pulling his hand out of the cage in a flash. He had quickly closed the door and latched it, checking to be sure the latch was secured.

Von Neumann's lips had curled back over his teeth. Snarls came from deep inside the chimp's chest.

"That's not like him," Mary Alice said, picking up the clipboard that held the file on which they monitored their lab subject's vital signs, appetite, mood, and other daily statistics. "Everything seems to be normal here. No temperature, brain waves normal, hmmmm."

"Paul ran the usual tests this morning," the director explained. "Everything was well within standard range. He was fine too. Ate a banana and let me pet him. Spun in the chair for a while."

"Did you connect him again?"

"Hell no. Nobody else has come in since I've been here. The next test's not scheduled until Tuesday," the director had replied.

Mary Alice walked to the cage. "Von?" she said softly, "von, are you okay?"

The chimp's lips returned to normal, and he stopped snarling. He pointed to his mouth with his right hand.

"Give me a banana."

Edward August handed her one.

She slowly unlatched the cage door, opening it an inch at a time, watching von Neumann's face carefully.

He seemed to be fine, and, a few moments later, he was sitting on Mary Alice's lap, eating the banana while the director watched apprehensively.

He had gone into the cage without any problems. There was really no explanation for his behavior, she reflected, hoping to God it was gas or something and not related to the connector.

She picked up the half-eaten TV dinner and carried it to the trash compactor and dropped it in, still musing.

That's how my work day went and then to come home and find myself exposed by someone in BBS I thought I trusted. Jesus, I need somebody to talk to, somebody real.

A few minutes later, Mary Alice dialed Tom Barnslow's voice number.

"Hello," he said, and she was surprised at the highness of his voice.

"Who is this?" she asked.

"Tom Barnslow. Mary Alice, Miss Sluice, is that you?"

"It's Dr. Sluice," Mary Alice said.

"Dr. Sluice? You're a physician?"

"I'm a psychiatrist."

"Gosh, I had no idea."

Mary Alice didn't answer.

"Dr. Sluice, are you still there?"

"I am."

"I—I'm not used to talking on the phone," Tom mumbled.

"Speak up, I can't understand you, you're mumbling."

"Sorry. I said I'm not used to talking on the phone."

"Hmmm."

"Well, anyway, I'm sorry about exposing you. It was a mistake."

"Yes, it was."

"Will you accept my apology now?"

"I don't know. You said you were in trouble of some kind?"

"It's very complicated. You see, at the end of September, I was doing a little hacking. And I got into this VAX . . ."

Mary Alice felt like someone had just slipped a scalpel between two of her vertebrae. *Oh no,* she thought.

" . . . it's run by some guy who calls himself The Succubus. We chatted for a long time. He was really friendly. Said he was lonely and wanted to make some new friends in the hacker community. After I told him about the Surgeons, he challenged us to invade his system. Gave us until Halloween night to do it. Then, a few days later, he dials me up—I gave him The Surgery's number the night we chatted on his system—and says the game's off, that he was canceling the game that he'd set up."

"What's the number to the VAX?" Mary Alice asked, crossing her fingers and praying that it wasn't the project's computer.

Tom recited the number.

Harv, Mary Alice thought when Tom recited the old number to the VAX, a number which the director had recently had Harv change.

"Do you recognize it?" Tom asked. "I didn't know you hacked too."

"I don't hack, and no, I don't recognize it," Mary Alice lied, thinking furiously. *Just what was Harv up to?* "So he wanted to cancel the game, but of course you were too stubborn to agree," Mary Alice stated flatly.

"A game's a game, you know that. I never saw you give up once the Surgeons got into a war. Not until the other side admitted defeat."

"True. But BBS war and hacking a VAX are two very different things."

"Not the way I see it. And if you were a hacker, you'd know that you don't cut and run in the middle of a challenge. But, anyway, I didn't even have the material."

"But you made like you had it, right?" Mary Alice asked, knowing that would be the way the Cutter would play it because it was the way she'd play it. Never give an inch and always win.

"Uhh, yes. And then he started to get nasty. He said he was going to rip off my fingernails. Then I didn't hear from him for quite a while, so I figured he'd decided to let the game go on. I haven't been able to get into that VAX—keep getting a busy signal. Then he called this morning and posted on the ICU. I couldn't believe it. Nobody's supposed to be able to do that unless I give them access. But he did it. And he said he's had sysop access for over a year. He said he'd planted a logic bomb in the system ages ago, and that he'd set it off and destroy The Surgery if I killed his note or deleted him. That's why I left his posting up on the ICU. I think he's serious, Dr. Sluice. I'm worried about what he's going to do to The Surgery."

"Too bad you're more worried about The Surgery than you are about those of us you've put in jeopardy with your little 'real-life' game."

"I did that before The Succubus called, honest. I never would have started this new game if I'd known he was going to go crazy on me . . . on us, I mean. Honest. Please believe me."

"I don't have much choice, do I?" Mary Alice asked rhetorically. "Well, what do you want me to do?"

"I want you to help me."

"And how am I supposed to do that?" she asked, her mind racing, wondering if Harv and this guy were in it together to get at her somehow. *God knows,* she thought, *Harv's been down on me ever since the director's party.*

"I don't know," Tom mumbled.

"It's hard for me to trust you after what you've done," she said. "I'm going to have to think about this."

"What should I do in the meantime?"

"Hey, Mr. Cutter," she snapped, "how the hell am I supposed to know? You're the King of the Hill, remember? Act like it."

"You mean I should keep playing the game?"

"What else can you do at this point?"

"I don't know."

"I don't know either."

"Well, can I kill that posting about you quitting BBS?"

Mary Alice thought quickly.

"No," she said hesitantly, quickly forming a preliminary plan. "I'm going to pretend that I quit the game. If anybody asks you, I've quit and you haven't heard from me. Don't look for Nelly Dean to post. But don't lower my access. I'm going to hide—watch and read only until I can figure out what's going on."

"Thank you," Tom mumbled, "thank you very much."

"I hope you realize what you've gotten all of us into," she said, refusing to take the responsibility off his shoulders. "I've seen this coming for a long time. All of us have gotten too serious about the game, but especially you."

"I can't help it," Tom said, his voice querulous. "The Surgery's all I have. The game's all I have."

"Yes, Tom," she said after a thoughtful, silent moment, "I know."

"Can I call you if I think of something or if there are new developments?" he asked hopefully. "And will you call me again?"

"In for a penny, in for a pound," Mary Alice answered. "Have you called any of the other Surgeons?"

"No, no. Like I told you, I hate talking on the phone. It's very hard to me to talk to anybody's voice."

"Don't call anyone else then. Let's try to keep them out of this."

"Okay," Tom replied, relief in his voice.

"Goodbye," Mary Alice said.

"You won't forget about all this?" Tom asked. "You're not going to leave me alone to deal with it?"

"I should, but I won't. No, you'll be hearing from me."

"Okay, good."

"I'm going to hang up now."

"Good night, Dr. Sluice," Tom said, and his voice cracked.

"Good night, Thomas Barnslow," Mary Alice said gently, slowly replacing the phone on the cradle.

Saturday, October 19th, 9:37 P.M.

Harv's IBM beeped to let him know the autodialer had gotten a carrier into The Surgery.

He hit the "C" key.

"Yes," Tom typed, the letters materializing very slowly.

"You're not nervous, are you?" Harv typed back.

"I don't have the material from your VAX. I don't think any of the Surgeons do."

"One of you has the material, but that no longer matters, as I told you."

"What do you want then?"

"You'll find out."

"I haven't done you any harm," Tom typed, trying to figure how to deal with this guy—who was sounding crazier all the time.

"You don't know who I am, pal. But I know who you are . . . Tommy."

He knows, Tom thought, and he felt sweat form under his arms.

"I have the number to your VAX," Tom typed back. "If you don't leave me alone, I'll report you to your bosses."

"You do that, pal. You call that VAX number, if you haven't already, and see what happens. It's gone, pal. It's really gone. You think I don't know how to do a simple thing like wipe a number? Hell, pal, Ma Bell doesn't even have a record of that number any longer."

Interested in spite of himself, Tom typed, "I didn't know that could be done."

"I can do anything with my computer," Harv Webster typed in response.

"Please don't destroy The Surgery. It means a lot to me."

"I won't blow up your system as long as you don't screw around with my postings and my access. But you better get your little group of Elites together, pal, because things are going to start coming down real soon."

"I don't understand."

"A few sacrifices are going to have to be made."

"Sacri—"

But Tom didn't get a chance to complete his question because Harv broke the connection.

Then Harv sat back at his IBM. Tears came to his eyes.

"I am worthy," Harv said to the silent room.

"I love you, Harv," Teresa answered.

Chapter
8

Dennis Conlick's heavy breathing filled the room. He'd been asleep since disconnecting from The Surgery very early on Saturday morning. He thrashed around on the cot, sweat glistening on his skin. The single sheet that half-covered him was soaking wet.

He was in a tunnel.

It was darker than death, and he didn't dare turn on his flashlight because the enemy was behind him, following him, had been following him for over three hours.

The Tunnel Rat had lost all sense of direction and was operating on instinct now, instinct honed from too much experience. He knew that eventually he'd find an exit.

If his stalker didn't get him first. Earlier they'd exchanged shots, both emptying their magazines.

He could just barely hear rubber-soled sandals scraping against the hard-packed earth of the tunnel's floor, perhaps fifty yards behind him.

The tunnel came to a Y, and the Tunnel Rat decided to

make his stand. He pulled himself into the right-hand opening and stopped.

He twisted and tried to push himself into the clay wall, at the same time silently pulling his razor-sharp knife from its leather sheath. He tested its edge with the ball of his thumb; the slight pain focused his already heightened senses.

The sounds behind him stopped.

All the Tunnel Rat could hear was the sudden rasping of his breath, which he struggled to still. If he could hear it, then . . .

The telephone rang, and the Tunnel Rat woke up, screaming.

His heart pounding as if he'd just run one hundred yards, sweat pouring off his face and chest, Dennis clutched his pillow and gasped.

"It was a dream, man, just a dream. You're okay, man, you're above ground, man. You're in New Orleans. Wake up, you're okay, wake up."

On the eleventh ring, his heart finally calm enough for him to move, Dennis walked over to the phone and answered it.

He didn't say anything. He just picked it up.

"Dennis, this is Nelly Dean from the war boards. You said I could call."

His heart started hammering again.

The phone in his hand started to shake.

"Do you want me to call back with my modem?" she asked.

Dennis couldn't answer.

"If you do, tap the phone with a pencil or something."

Dennis snapped the fingernail of his right index finger against the hard plastic. Three times.

"I'm hanging up now," Mary Alice said, "but I'll call back in a few minutes. Turn on your modem and boot your term program. Okay?"

Dennis tapped three times.

She hung up.

"Oh man, oh man, I'm in bad shape," Dennis grumbled

as he set up his system. "Couldn't get a single word out. That's pathetic. And I asked her to call too, didn't I? She'll think I'm nuts."

The phone rang once and the modem connected instantly.

Dennis eased himself into the wooden chair in front of the computer. He hit the proper keys to enter into chat mode.

"Sorry about that. I'm not entirely above ground, and I can't talk on the phone. Anyway, I'm Dennis Conlick. And you're the infamous Nelly Dean. I love your stuff on the boards," he typed, relaxing a bit.

"Thank you, but Nelly Dean is dead."

"Huh? I don't follow you?"

"Haven't you been to The Surgery recently?"

Dennis looked at his watch. It was almost 10:15 in the morning. "I was there about four-thirty, I think, just before I went to sleep. Didn't know it was this late. I can't remember the last time I slept until after ten on a Saturday. I must have been really zonked."

"It's Sunday morning," Mary Alice typed back, chewing nervously on a pencil as she sat in front of her computer, suddenly wondering if this man was even capable of understanding what was going on.

"Sunday morning?" Dennis typed. "Damn, that means I slept for almost thirty hours. I can't believe it. I've never slept like that."

"You have trouble sleeping?" Mary Alice inquired.

"I have trouble doing a lot of things. Sleeping's one of them. Talking voice to people is another one."

"Well, I'm glad you slept so long . . . sounds like you needed it."

"Yeah, I feel pretty good for a change. Almost human."

"I'm glad to hear that. Was there some particular reason you wanted me to call?"

"Yeah, a sudden attack of the lonelies. I wanted to chat with the person behind Nelly Dean, and I was concerned about the Surgeons posting their real-life info. It doesn't matter about me—no way anybody can hurt me at this point, but I hate to see the younger ones doing it. There're some strange folks in BBS, and I was just curious to see what you thought about all of it. You were smart not to come clean yourself."

"Cutter did it for me."

"I don't follow you."

"You'll see when you read the ICU. Cutter exposed me."

"That's bad."

"Yes. And that's not all."

"What do you mean?"

Mary Alice filled him in on everything that had transpired in the past twenty-four hours, including her voice conversation with Thomas Barnslow and his fears about The Succubus.

"That's odd," Dennis typed.

"Yes. What do you think about this Succubus thing? Is it on the level or is Cutter just trying another very complicated game?"

"Could be either way," Dennis typed back. "The Chief's been getting heavily into psychological war the last few months—I've noticed that when I've chatted with him. He's been trying to weasel my real time info out of me. So it's possible this is another of his ploys."

"Yeah, that's what I've been thinking too," Mary Alice typed back, "but he did give me his voice number. And he sounded *very* nervous when I talked to him last night. He said The Succubus threatened to pull out his fingernails."

Dennis shivered and forced himself not to think back to the war. Slowly, he typed: "Right, so he's either better at this game and a lot more subtle than either of us ever realized, or else he's on the level with this Succubus thing. I'll have to think about it. Need to read the new postings. See if I can make any sense out of it."

"Well, I'd appreciate it," Mary Alice typed. "I'm kind of nervous about the whole thing. I've been warring hard for several years and I have a lot of enemies out there."

"Me too," Dennis replied, "but I'm not worried about it. And you shouldn't worry either. I'll look into this. I have sources in BBS that you wouldn't believe. I'm not bragging, but I get around."

"That's what I've heard. I've also heard you're the main software pirate in this part of the South, as well as a big-time hacker."

"Well, some of that's exaggerated, though I do my share to rip off as many software companies as I can. As for the hacking, that's illegal, and I don't do any illegal hacking."

"Right," Mary Alice typed back.

"Seriously. I may drop in and visit some major computers once in a while, but that's all I've ever done. Window shopping."

"What do you do for a living?"

There was a pause as Dennis thought about how to answer. "Well, it's a long story, but, except for occasional odd jobs, related to computers, I mainly live off my disability."

"Oh, I see. Well, I sold housewares for a while, did some surgical nursing for a while, and have been a psychiatrist for the past few years."

"I knew you were smart from the way you wrote. A psychiatrist, huh? Your stuff on the board seems too sensible to come from a shrink. I bet you're a good one. How old are you, if I'm not being too curious. Are you married?"

"Early thirties, and I've never been married. Are you a college graduate?"

"Yeah. Couple of degrees . . . quit before I got the doctorate to hop on the software bandwagon, but I got screwed. I'm working on my degree at the school of life, I guess you could say. But I keep flunking the tests."

"You want to chat about that?"

Long pause.

Then: "You sound like Dr. Hartley on the old Bob Newhart show. No. Not now. Talking about it isn't my strong point. Actually, except for computers, I don't have many strong points anymore."

Dennis's eyes suddenly surveyed the room, as if he were seeing it for the first time. He shook his head, disgusted.

"I'm sure that's not true. Well, this has been a very nice chat, but I have to go."

"Okay. Thanks for calling. It meant a lot to me. Will you call back sometime?"

"Only if you'll call me too."

"I don't have the number to your computer."

"My home phone number is 899-3825. It's my voice number."

"Well, I can't talk voice, but if I call, I'll tap three times and then call back after you connect your modem. I know that sounds stupid, but, would you mind? Maybe I can get myself above ground again. Then I'll call you voice."

"No, I don't mind. Three taps. I got it."

"I don't even know your name."

"My name's Mary Alice. Mary Alice Sluice."

"Mary Alice. That's a pretty name. I like it," Dennis typed back, the name seeming vaguely familiar to him for some reason.

"I'm glad. Talk to you later, okay?"

"Okay. Thanks for calling."

"Bye."

"L8r."

When the disconnect signal flashed on Dennis's computer, he leaned back in his chair.

His eyes again examined the room.

"Goddamn," he said, "this place looks like a rat's nest."

He walked into the kitchen and shook his head at the sinkful of unwashed dishes. Opened the refrigerator door. Counted two boxes of candy bars and three six-packs of beer.

"Jesus, where have you been?" he asked the empty room, as he squatted and opened the cabinet under the sink. Rummaging around, he found a box of plastic trash bags. "Ah-ha," he said, "I thought I had some of these."

He opened the box and pulled out one of the bags. Shook it in the air.

It looked like a body bag for a second, but then that thought passed. Holding the open bag, he stuck the box under his arm.

Dennis walked into his living room. For the first time in months, he pulled the wool blanket down from the window and let sunlight flow in.

Using his hands like a scoop, he started to shovel candy-bar wrappers, cigarette packs, cereal boxes, and empty beer bottles into the plastic bag.

"God, what a mess," he complained, noticing the smell of the room for the first time.

When he finished filling the bag, he gave it a twist and tied it off with a plastic-coated wire. He casually tossed the bag toward the door to the apartment, where it settled, flat, bodylike.

Dennis watched it out of the corner of his eye.

He felt the earth fold him into an embrace.

The box of trash bags fell from his hands.

"The light! They'll see you!" he shouted, covering his eyes with his hands, rushing toward the wool blanket that he had dropped on the floor. Almost stumbling, he pulled the chair from his worktable to the window.

Standing precariously on the chair, he jammed a corner of the blanket through one of the nails at the top of the window. Tracing the blanket through his shaking hand, he moved the chair to the other corner of the window and reattached it to the nail above the window on that side.

The room plunged into darkness.

Dennis felt a scream rising in his abdomen.

Almost tripping over his own feet, he rushed to the light switch by the door.

He clicked it on and the two-hundred-watt bulb flooded the room with light.

Catching his breath, his eyes roamed the room.

They settled on the bag of trash on the floor, next to his feet.

"I'm sorry, I'm sorry," he said, bending over, kneeling, gently placing the palms of his open hands on the smooth plastic.

The Tunnel Rat started to cry.

* * *

117

In her house, Mary Alice turned on her printer and made a hardcopy of her chat with Dennis. While the dot-matrix printer zipped the characters out at over a hundred a second, she mentally reviewed their conversation.

He's pretty freaky, she thought, *but there's something about him I like.*

When the printer finished, she decided to go over to the lab to make sure von Neumann was all right.

Sunday, October 20th, 11:35 A.M.

Jim Persall logged on to The Surgery and read through the messages since he had last posted early Saturday morning. Slightly confused by what was going on, but intrigued nonetheless, he left the following:

```
[MESSAGE 11]: WHAT'S GOING ON?
FROM: MEAT GRINDER
DATE: OCTOBER 20
```

Things just get weirder and weirder here on the ICU, but I like it. I want to ask one question, though. Cutter, are you The Succubus? Are you trying to pull another fast one on us like you did to the Defenders of the Faith last summer when you were Scarecrow? That's what I want to know. If you aren't The Succubus, then this is addressed to him: Get porked, dude! Get out of the way before the Meat Grinder takes you in and spits you out. I'll cut you a new asshole, dude, if you don't get your ugly mug out of our ICU.

Well, since there aren't any big wars going on on the boards and since I'm not even fighting any of you (except The Succubus) with bad intention at the moment, I've got a suggestion. Why don't we have a Surgeons' picnic in Audubon Park on Wednesday afternoon? About six o'clock? Meet at the butterfly. I'll bring the food—my dad's got a small grill, and I'll bring it and the charcoal and hot dogs. Is anybody up for this? Come on, friends, let's do it. I'm dying to meet you people in person!

Jim

"Jimbo," his mother called from downstairs. "Come on down, brunch is ready."

"Okay, Mom," he yelled back, "I'll be down in a moment."

Whistling, keen on the idea of finally meeting his BBS friends, Jim turned off his Apple IIc and modem.

Sunday, October 20th, 11:43 A.M.

"Well, well, well, look what the cat dragged in," Harv said when Mary Alice walked through the door of the lab.

"Good morning, Dr. Webster," Mary Alice said formally, leaving the door open.

"Oh my, *Dr. Webster*. What on earth have I done to earn such respect from our lovely psychiatrist? And you really should close and lock that door, my dear. Director's orders, you know."

Harv placed his heavy forearms on the table where he was working on the design prototype of the Zeus connector. He was determined to reduce the physical size of the connector by a minimum of fifty percent before he put the team-member phase of his long-range plan into effect.

"Anybody else here?" Mary Alice asked, closing but not locking the door.

"Nobody here but us roosters," Harv replied, his eyes wandering up and down her slender, attractive body. "I've waited a long time to have you alone again, Mary Alice," he said, his eyes suddenly hard. "Like an elephant, I never forget anything, especially a betrayal."

"What on earth are you talking about?"

"Don't play dumb with me, Fräulein Doktor. You remember as well as I do."

"Look, Harv, that happened a long time ago. Why don't we forget it? I don't have any hard feelings."

"Well, I do," Harv snapped, struggling to his feet and knocking over one of the large schematics. "You have to pay for what you did."

"What's the matter with you?" Mary Alice asked, trying to keep her cool. "Three years ago at some stupid project party, I called you a drunk and refused to sit at a table with you. You were loaded and rude. What's the big deal?"

"I wasn't drunk. And earlier you were coming on to me," Harv said righteously.

"Wrong, mister. I was being nice to you. Nothing more, nothing less. If you think a woman's coming on to you just because she tries to have an intelligent conversation, then you've got a lot to learn about women."

"You came on to me," Harv repeated stubbornly. "You were acting like you wanted me, and then you betrayed me."

"Wanted you? You? You're living in a dreamworld."

"I can't help the way I look. It's glandular . . ."

"It's got nothing to do with the way you look," she said, her voice softening just a bit.

"Prove it to me," the huge man said, his 295 pounds shifting on the balls of his splayed feet.

Her hand on the doorknob of the lab, Mary Alice watched as Harv started to walk toward her.

The doorknob suddenly moved and she yelped in surprise.

It was Paul Brandais, who entered the lab and then looked at Dr. Sluice and Harv. Tension was thick in the air.

"Gosh, am I interrupting an argument or something?" Paul asked, closing the door and locking it.

"Suck a brain," Harv snapped at the neurosurgeon, sitting down at the worktable, where his big hands rearranged the schematics.

"Come on," Mary Alice said abruptly to Paul, "there's work to be done."

Paul looked at her. And then he looked at Harvey.

"Just a minute," he answered, going to where Harv now sat.

Paul leaned on the table. "Son, you have a lot to learn about dealing with people. You're blessed with a brilliant mind, but as for everything else . . ." Brandais's voice trailed off.

Harv looked at the surgeon. Then a smile slowly formed on his face. "Yes, Herr Doktor, you are, of course, right," he replied, winking at both of them. "I have the social skills of a cannibal." He looked at Mary Alice. "I sincerely apologize. Don't know what got into me. But I know what I'd like to get into."

Dr. Brandais sighed with exasperation, then gestured toward Mary Alice. "Let's check on von Neumann, Dr. Sluice," he said, and the two of them went into the animal lab, leaving Harv alone, chuckling.

Sunday, October 20th, Noon.

"There it is, Grandfather, 3960 Lake Avenue," Fuchan said, unable to contain her excitement.

Hiro Nomasaki pulled into the wide driveway and turned off the engine.

He and Fuchan walked to the front door and rang the bell.

"I'm coming, just a second," Francis's voice came from inside the house.

In his room, Francis turned off his computer for the first time in a week. Then he looked down at the new shirt and pants that his mother had bought the day before and had given him to wear earlier this morning.

Rubbing his left hand through his hair, which he'd actually combed, Francis tried to think if he'd forgotten anything. He was so nervous he couldn't believe it. His palms were actually sweating.

A moment later, he was opening the front door.

"Ahh so, Genghis Khan," Hiro Nomasaki said, bowing formally. "Pleased to meet great BBS warrior. This is Honorable Granddaughter Fuchan Nomasaki. I am Hiro Nomasaki."

Without realizing it, Francis bowed from the waist in his wheelchair. "Pleased to meet you, sir," he said, "and you too, Fuchan." He offered his hand to the thin, but attractive, teenager.

"I'm pleased to meet you, Francis," Fuchan said.

"Very nice home," Hiro said, casting his eyes around the large suburban house. "You have Japanese gardener."

"How did you know that?" Francis asked.

"Grandfather knows everything," Fuchan answered.

"Grandfather not know everything," Hiro corrected. "Come, we go zoo now. Feed monkeys. Great Khan tell how put self and chair with wheels in Dragonmobile."

They all laughed together, and, a few moments later, Francis had his arms around the old man's neck as he was gently lifted into the back seat. Fuchan got in the back seat with him. As Hiro put the wheelchair in the trunk, Francis leaned over and whispered, "He's sure strong for an old dude. He lifted me like I didn't weigh anything."

"Grandfather *is* strong," Fuchan whispered back, smiling.

"Okay, now go zoo," Hiro said, getting behind the steering wheel. "Young peoples latched into Dragonmobile?"

"Yes, sir, we're buckled up and ready to go," Francis answered, surprised by the enthusiasm in his voice.

Sunday, October 20th, 1:03 P.M.

Sitting in the animal lab, which she had locked from inside after Paul Brandais had left to play golf for the rest of the afternoon, Mary Alice thought about the negative results of the tests she and Paul had finished running an hour ago. She absently stroked von Neumann's hairy hand as he rocked in the swivel chair and listened through headphones to a Beatles tape. Von Neumann loved early sixties' music.

Unable to come up with any further tests to try, Mary Alice said, "Okay, von, time to get back into your house."

The chimp looked up at her as she removed the headphones from his shaved skull.

He whimpered slightly.

"That's new," she said aloud.

The chimp looked at her with his opaque black eyes. Then he sauntered to his cage and walked in, closing the door behind him. A moment later, his fingers reached through the food slot and latched the door. Then he stuck two of his fingers in his mouth and bit down, hard.

Mary Alice shook her head, not quite believing what she'd just seen.

She crossed the lab and picked up the telephone, dialing Al Cogglin's number.

"Cogglin," came a sleepy voice.

"It's Sluice. I'm over at the lab. I have an anomaly with von Neumann. He's showing signs of increased intelligence."

"He's what?"

"Well, he just latched his own cage."

"Come on, Mary Alice. Surely you don't call that significant? Von Neumann's bright. He's just been watching you and suddenly got the idea how to do it. But increased intelligence? I rather doubt it. You've seen chimps do much smarter things than that."

"I know, Al, but it's not just that."

"Yes, what else?"

"He whimpered."

"Whimpered?"

"Yes. It was a new sound. And he also bit down hard on two fingers. I've never seen him do either of those things before."

"I see."

"I don't think you do. The behavior certainly isn't overt, but it is anomalous with *all* of our past observations."

"Well."

"Well? Is that the best you can do?"

"You have other observations?"

"Nothing specific. But, well, I sense something's the matter."

"Well, if you have any *specific* evidence of this new intelligence, call me. Otherwise, I'm going to get back to the nap I was trying to take. I've been trying to track down the bug in the Athena hypothesis all night, and I'm exhausted."

"Thank you for your help, Doctor," she replied and hung up on him.

Reviewing the conversation in her mind, though, Mary

Alice decided a nap was probably a good idea. Her own sleep had been very restless lately, filled with ugly dreams.

She unlocked and then opened the animal-lab door slowly, taking a deep breath, prepared to confront Harv again if necessary.

But the main lab was empty.

Sunday, October 20th, 4:03 P.M.

"I had a wonderful time, Mr. Nomasaki," Francis Schonrath said, pumping the old man's hand after he had put Francis back in his wheelchair and rolled him to the front door of his house. "And thank you, Fuchan, for taking me on my first date. It was great."

Fuchan blushed. "It was my first date too, Francis. I had a wonderful time."

She bent over and lightly kissed the boy's cheek.

Francis unlocked the front door to his house. "Thanks again," he said, wheeling in.

"Bye-bye," Fuchan said, turning to wave as she and Grandfather walked back to the Buick.

When they were in the car and driving down Lake Avenue, Hiro looked at his granddaughter, who was still smiling.

"You have fun, Honorable Granddaughter?"

"Oh yes, Grandfather. It was awesome."

"Awesome?"

She laughed. "It's American slang for *I had the best time I've ever had,* and I love you, Grandfather."

"Young Khan very lonely, just like young Wu," Hiro said. "See, having real friend better than only computer."

"Well, I still like my computer better," Fuchan said.

When her grandfather looked at her sternly, she couldn't keep a straight face.

"He nice boy," Hiro said. "You help each other get over lonelinesses. You call him on phone and talk. No use computers. Promise?"

"Don't you think I'm too young to get involved with boys?"

"You talk with Khan every day for few minutes. Not all night like girls on TV. Few minutes only. Yes?"

"Yes, Grandfather."

"Good. When eating, eat. When talking, talk. But not talk too much, *hai?*"

They both laughed.

Sunday, October 20th, 8:42 P.M.

Harv sat at his IBM terminal and typed rapidly, his eyes intense with concentration. Hacking into *The Times-Picayune* computer had been ridiculously easy—he'd first done it over a year ago one night at the project lab when he'd been bored. But the only thing he did once inside was to make a hardcopy of the built-in help functions that explained to the New Orleans newspaper's reporters and writers exactly how to save their stories and send them to the proper editor, who'd then edit the files before electronically transferring them downstairs to the composing department.

When he finished typing the text, he used the sequence of control characters which would make it look like the editor this material usually went to had approved the copy. Pressing a few more keys, Harv sent his story directly to the printing department, where it was added to the other stories that were to go on that particular page of Monday morning's edition.

"That ought to stir the pot," Harv said, starting to grin as he logged off that computer and started dialing into The Surgery.

Half an hour later, deep in thought about Mary Alice, Harv got a carrier into The Surgery, and logged in as The Succubus. He went directly to the ICU, read the new postings, and then typed out this message:

```
[MESSAGE 12]: JUST WATCH
FROM: THE SUCCUBUS
DATE: OCTOBER 20
```

I always keep my promises.

Read the obituary section of tomorrow morning's *Times-Picayune.*

The Succubus
Your Worst Nightmare

Hitting the "T" key to quit the system before the sysop could break in to chat, Harv leaned back in his chair and started watching the second hand on one of the many battery-powered miniature clocks in his personal-computer lab. He had promised himself he wouldn't make another connection with the replica of the Zeus connector until midnight.

Tom Barnslow sat at his computer, feeling like the lowest bedpan-cleaning orderly instead of the mighty Chief Cutter. He felt the game was getting completely out of hand.

The Surgery was oddly quiet for the rest of the evening, almost, Tom thought, as if his ICU Elite were afraid to call for fear of what they might read.

He wasn't far from wrong.

Sunday, October 20th, 11:03 P.M.

The phone rang in the Tunnel Rat's apartment.

Dennis slowly got up from his cot, shaking his head, trying to piece together what had occurred this day. As was often the case lately, he wasn't sure, though he did remember either chatting with or dreaming about chatting with Nelly Dean before he slipped back below ground.

He picked up the receiver and lifted it to his ear, but he didn't say anything. He heard a deep voice: "Dennis, it's Ed August. I have a job for you. Now. Two hundred, cash. Shouldn't take more than a few hours. Bring your gear."

Hating to leave the apartment but unwilling to pass up an easy two hundred dollars either, Dennis slipped on a pair of blue jeans and the cleanest shirt he could find. A moment later, he pulled a briefcase full of delicate electronic equipment out from under the cot.

"I'm okay," he said, standing at the door, again surveying the apartment. "I can handle this. No sweat."

He opened the door and left to do the job for his old commander.

Sunday, October 20th, 11:59 P.M.

"I'm here," Harv said aloud, his pale eyelids fluttering in anticipation.

"I am disappointed."

Harv sat up straight in the recliner, stunned by what the voice in his head just told him.

"What did I do?"

"It's what you tried to do."

"When? I . . ."

"With the woman."

"I haven't . . . done that . . ."

"You wanted to."

"I didn't . . . not really . . . I was . . ."

"You must earn the right to be my disciple."

"I've been trying . . ."

"Penance."

Harv felt his bald head break out in a glistening sweat under the subdued overhead light. The microneedles under his skin itched like wasp bites. His hands unconsciously moved to rip them out, but he stopped himself at the last moment.

"What do you want me to do?"

"You must be clean of mind and body. You cannot prepare a sacrifice for Me if you are unclean."

Harv nodded his head slowly.

He waited for Him to speak again, but now there was only a soft hum and a gentle tingling in his mind. Lately, the connector seemed to be making his mind feel different.

Harv waited five more minutes before he stopped the Zeus program and removed the electrodes.

After tidying up the lab, he unlocked the door and went into his apartment's bathroom.

As if in a dream, he slowly unwrapped the thin, stiff paper that covered the new double-edged razor blade. Leaving the blade on the opened folds of paper, he removed his shirt. Standing before the wall-length mirror above the double sinks, Harv looked at himself.

A broken sound erupted from deep within him.

His small eyes stared back at him from beneath his shaved head. His eyebrows arched critically. His jowls were heavy and the bone structure of his jaw was buried in several chins. On his white, hairy chest, flabby breasts mocked him. The excess flab on the bottoms of his upper arms swayed uncontrollably when he stretched out his arms to their full length. The movement caused the thick roll of fat around his waist to jelly over the top of his pants.

"Unclean," he slurred, "unworthy of Him."

His thick fingers opened and closed, looking like some kind of diseased sea anemone, reaching, searching, crabbing unconsciously along the smooth clean tile of the double sink counter.

The fingers, so ugly and yet so dexterous, simultaneously the fingers of a dock worker and a jeweler, gently closed on the razor blade.

Lifted it.

The eyes watched the blade.

The eyes looked into the mirror.

Harv watched as the blade scraped away his eyebrows.

He watched as the blade scraped away the hair on his chest.

He watched the blade.

"I am worthy of You," Harv said sometime later, looking at his now hairless body.

Chapter

9

Monday, October 21st, 5:30 A.M.

"Roheaux, get in here," the morning copy editor for *The Times-Picayune* shouted into the huge open room where all the reporters had their desks and computer terminals.

"Yeah, what's the problem?" Mike Roheaux said a few moments later, leaning nonchalantly against the closed door of his boss's office, yawning without covering his mouth.

"This is the problem," the copy editor said, tossing the obituary page at Roheaux. One obit was circled in red ink. Roheaux started to read it, his eyes opening wider when he got past the second line.

"I didn't write this," Roheaux said.

"If this is another attempt to get me to take you off the death page, you're going back to that weekly rag in East St. Jesus Parish, Roheaux," the copy editor said. "I am not amused."

"Hey, you know I hate writing obits, but I wouldn't do something this stupid," Mike explained, striking the folded newspaper against his thigh. "This isn't how we write obits. Hell, I don't even know what a succubus is."

"Then tell me how it got in here. You're the only person I've had writing these things for over a month."

Mike Roheaux scratched his head. "Beats me, boss," he said, "unless somebody's been fooling around with the computer system."

"Nobody can fool around with our computer system, Roheaux," the copy editor stated. "It's a secure system."

Monday, October 21st, 10:30 A.M.

"We're running the sixth connection in half an hour, Ed," Dr. Cogglin said, "and this one should be real interesting. We've established the viability of robotic manipulation through the interface, which, in itself, makes the entire project a big success."

"We've achieved our goal, at least with a primate," Dr. Brandais added.

"And we've got a traitor on the team," the retired general interjected. "Harv's screwing us."

There was a moment of silence as the two scientists stared at the director.

"I don't believe it," Paul said slowly.

"I found out at ten-thirty last night," Ed August explained. "You see, I've been keeping a close friend at the Pentagon apprised of your work. And *his* man in the company told him that Langley Airforce Base had gotten its hands on some very sensitive artificial-intelligence work . . . work that was heavily encrypted. They're trying to break the encryption even as we speak . . ."

"How do you know it's the Zeus material?" Dr. Brandais asked. "It may not even be *our* material. We're not the only ones working on neutral networking. You seem to be drawing a lot of conclusions on some very flimsy evidence."

"It's my job to be careful. And I'm not positive about Harv, but I have my reasons. He hasn't been looking me in the eye lately, and I caught him standing behind my desk the other afternoon. He was reading a document."

"Hell, that doesn't mean a thing," Al Cogglin said. "I read

whatever's on your desk every time I come in here. And so does everybody else. You're acting paranoid, Ed."

"Hardly. Here, look at this." The director tossed a small glass vial to Dr. Cogglin, who looked at it and then handed it to Paul Brandais. "It's a sound sensor, a bug. Two were found right here in my office. There were twelve others scattered throughout the lab and the other offices."

"I thought Harv was sweeping the project several times a week."

"He is. And on Friday he told me the place was clean."

"Then the bugs went in this weekend?"

"Conlick unearthed these bugs last night. He told me they'd been in place for a long time, probably since the project started. Al, you heard from Conlick lately?" the general asked.

Dr. Cogglin shook his head back and forth, his eyes narrowing as he tried to remember. "Not in a long time. Almost three years ago when we interviewed him. He was pretty spaced-out. Haven't heard from him since. Too bad. He was a smart bastard."

"He's smarter than ever. I've stayed in touch with him. He doesn't play with all his marbles all the time, but he still does excellent work when his head's screwed on tight. I've used him on a few occasions when I had something sensitive that needed to be done right and done quietly. He could find a bug in a flea's asshole. Anyway, the project's clean now."

"Well," Dr. Brandais said, "if Harv was in charge of finding listening devices and he didn't find these, then it sounds to me like something's not kosher. But why would he do it?"

"I'm glad you're starting to see the situation. Who knows his motive? Gentlemen, what we're doing here is much too important to our national security to . . ."

"You've informed the Pentagon, and maybe the CIA knows, too," Paul Brandais summarized, folding two sticks of spearmint gum into his mouth and chewing them rapidly.

"I had to tell my Pentagon contact," the director said. "You see . . ."

"Oh, I see all right." Paul Brandais looked up from the chair where he was sitting. "The project may still be a total failure. It's much too early to even think about success. Not to mention the fact that our deal with you was that the government would not be brought into this until the three of us agreed." He looked at Albert Cogglin for support.

"Ed, I came to you because I liked working under you in 'Nam. You were a man who got things done. Paul and I approached you because we trusted you. And now we find you've been screwing us over. Talking out of school to your Pentagon buddies, no less." Cogglin angrily kicked the small trash basket by the director's desk.

Paul Brandais's face was flushed. "When we formed this limited partnership, your job was to find the venture capital and then oversee day-to-day management. Our agreement was that there would be no government notification until— and unless—the three of us concurred."

"What's done is done," the director stated. "If there was the slightest chance that the Agency was on to this, my friends in the Pentagon had to have it too."

"I repeat, it's too early for that. We don't know what we have here, what the potential dangers are . . . heck, we've only tested it on a chimp five times. This whole thing could blow up in our faces at any moment. The connection could even be life-threatening to humans. We won't know for months yet. Besides, we didn't devote three years of our lives developing the prototype to have it used for military purposes," Dr. Brandais said, his voice cracking. "We did it to benefit mankind, not to help destroy it. God, think of the constructive applications. What it can do in the operating room alone is mind-boggling. Manipulating laser scalpels with the Zeus connection, surgeons will be able to perform even the most delicate operations imaginable. Think of what it . . ."

"Your love of mankind is commendable, Paul," the director interrupted rudely, "but hardly realistic. Look, Al, you were in Southeast Asia with me, you know what this is all about. Tell our innocent friend the facts of life, will you?"

Al Cogglin looked at his colleague and slowly nodded his

head. "We knew the military would eventually end up with it, Paul. God knows we've discussed this often enough. We just didn't think it would happen so soon."

"I will not allow the military to have the Zeus connection," Paul said bluntly, standing up and walking to the door. "I'll see you both in . . . I'll resign first," he added, slamming the door.

"Ahhh crap, Ed," Al swore, bending over and picking up the trash basket he had deliberately kicked over for effect. As he put the crumpled papers back in the woven container, he said, "You've really screwed the dog with this, General. I told you to let me handle Paul. You've dropped the ball. Paul's the sort of idealist who has to be mollycoddled. I was going to bring him around to our way of thinking sooner or later."

"Maybe you're right, Al. Maybe. But with security deteriorating, it's better that he got a hard cold dose of reality. He needed to know where we stand."

"Where do we stand? Are you going to confront Harv?"

"I'm not sure yet. We'll have to wait and see. Let the dust settle. No, I'm not going to confront Harv until we have more information. But keep an eye on him, Al."

Monday, October 21st, 10:48 A.M.

The Chief Cutter, who had been watching The Surgery most of the night, worrying about what was going to happen, woke up. He looked at the clock and swore under his breath. He had slept through his first morning class at Tulane.

He dressed quickly and then went downstairs, where he found the early edition of the newspaper on the dining-room table. Grabbing an apple from the bowl of fruit in the center of the table, he took the newspaper and returned to his room.

Spreading *The Times-Picayune* on his workstation, Tom turned pages until he found the obituary section, which he read. He breathed a sigh of relief when he finished reading it.

"So," he mumbled, "it's a game after all." He chuckled to

himself. "Well, Succubus, you had me going for a while there."

Logging on to The Surgery, Tom went to the ICU hi-security board and posted the following message:

```
[MESSAGE 15]: LOOKS LIKE A JOKE
FROM: CHIEF CUTTER
DATE: OCTOBER 21
```

I just finished reading the obituary column in the paper. Here it is for those of you who haven't seen it yet:

James Persall, on Thursday, October 24, at seven o'clock P.M.; age twenty years; a native of New Orleans, LA, and a life-long resident of Orleans Parish.

According to the coroner, Persall's abused body, though damaged by fire, was found by Detective Mary Francis Nomasaki and Sergeant Robert Conlick.

Relatives and friends and fellow Surgeons are invited to attend the funeral services at The Succubus Funeral Home.

Well, you had some of us going there for a while, Succubus. And I have to give you credit for a good one. It's a small point, but you earned it.

Okay, well maybe now things can get back to normal around here, eh? Jim, I can't make the picnic, got other plans. Sorry. Anybody else going? Where is everybody? This is the quietest ICU's been in ages.

Cutter

After saving the posting, Barnslow picked up his textbooks and dashed down the stairs. If he hurried, he'd only be a few minutes late for his second class that day.

Monday, October 21st, 11:04 A.M.

As the director and Al Cogglin continued to talk, Dr. Brandais joined Dr. Sluice in the animal lab. He looked at his watch. It was five minutes after eleven.

"Hello, Paul," Mary Alice said, unlocking the small padlock that they now used to latch von Neumann's cage.

"Mary Alice," Dr. Brandais said, chewing furiously on his gum. "How's our subject doing? Any more signs of that increased intelligence you mentioned to Al?"

Mary Alice's face reddened.

"Sorry, didn't mean that the way it sounded. Just had a run-in with the director."

"Nothing else unusual," she said, tapping the clipboard with her finger.

"Well, let's get him hooked up then, shall we?"

In the main lab, Harv bent over the keyboard and finished typing in the Zeus program modification that Dr. Cogglin had written for the latest experiment. He then ran the test segment, and the voice synthesizer slowly recited each letter of the alphabet.

"Are you ready to crank it up yet, Harv?" Dr. Cogglin asked, entering the lab with the director.

"Yes, Herr Doktor," Harv replied, "everything checks out."

"We're ready out here," Al Cogglin called to Mary Alice, knocking on the animal lab door.

"Coming," Dr. Sluice called back. A few moments later she walked into the main lab, followed by von Neumann holding Brandais's hand.

"What exactly are you trying today?" the director asked, looking at Paul Brandais, trying to get back on good terms with the neurosurgeon.

Dr. Brandais stared coldly but was unable to maintain his stiffness as he began to explain the sixth connection: "As you know, the first five experiments established the viability of robotic manipulation through the Zeus connection. Today we're going to attempt to interface the subject's brain with a speech synthesizer. If this works, in future years, people who've lost voice capability will be able to speak normally through the use of the Zeus connection and an inexpensive synthesizer. Additionally, we may be able to establish contact and teach language to the smarter animals, dolphins and the higher primates in particular."

As he finished speaking, Paul helped von Neumann get into the swivel chair. Mary Alice poured rubbing alcohol on a cotton ball and began cleaning the animal's shaved head. Harv walked over with the prototype and started attaching the microneedles. He purposely bumped into Mary Alice's hip as he inserted the last electrode. She glared at him. He smiled innocently. Mary Alice noticed for the first time that his eyebrows were gone and that what she could see of his head beneath the ever-present stocking cap appeared to have been freshly shaved.

"That sounds remarkable, but chimps can't speak," the director argued.

"Correct. Their vocal mechanisms are incapable of forming the syllabics of human language. Von Neumann has the I.Q. of an eleven-year-old child, and it's possible that he understands English in his mind but can't use it because of his vocal limitations. The connection, of course, removes the limitations and interfaces him directly with a speech-synthesizing chip here in the speaker that Harv built." Dr. Brandais tapped a small box about five inches on a side.

"I'm impressed," the director said. "What are the chances of this working?"

"I'd say fifty-fifty," Paul answered.

"Let's crank her up and see," Dr. Cogglin said, nodding at Harv.

Harv returned to the VAX and ran the newly modified Zeus program.

As usual, von Neumann's eyes stared distantly at first, but then they began to focus. He swiveled the chair around 360 degrees, looking for the robot. He whimpered softly when he didn't find it.

Harv walked over with the speech-synthesizing box cradled in his hands.

"Press the 'T' key, Herr Director," Harv ordered.

Sitting at the terminal, Ed August pressed the proper key and the computer-generated voice repeated the alphabet, then caused the small speaker in the box to say, "Hello, von Neumann. This is Dr. Cogglin speaking. You are a good fellow."

Harv squatted in front of the chimp and stared deep into the animal's eyes, as if he were willing him to understand how the box worked.

Von Neumann tilted his head to one side, as if he were listening.

Harv smiled slightly, and placed the voice synthesizer in the chimp's hands.

Von Neumann held the box, turning it first one way and then the other. He whimpered.

The sound came from his lips. At the same time, it came from the synthesizer.

The chimp dropped the box as if it had suddenly grown red hot.

Harv, still kneeling at the chimp's feet, caught the synthesizer and gave it back to von Neumann.

Holding it again, the chimp tilted his head backward.

He closed his eyes.

"I hart," the voice synthesizer said.

"Holy shit," Dr. Cogglin said.

"Be quiet," Mary Alice ordered, turning the swivel chair so that von Neumann now faced her instead of Harv. "It's Mary Alice, von. Tell Mary Alice what hurts."

"I cry."

Everyone stared disbelievingly at the synthesizer.

Cogglin looked at Harv suspiciously, but from the fat man's complete fascination with the words coming from the synthesizer it was obvious that this wasn't one of his jokes.

"Why do you cry, von?" Mary Alice asked gently.

"I feel bad. I hart."

"Tell me where it hurts, von," Mary Alice repeated.

"Ear. I ear."

"How the hell could it hurt his ears, Paul?" Dr. Cogglin asked, his face reflecting his puzzlement. "How is that possible?"

"Damn it," Mary Alice said, her voice low, "everybody be quiet!"

"Be quiet," the voice synthesizer said.

Silence in the lab.

"Be quiet," the voice synthesizer said more forcefully.

Then, almost a shout, "Be quiet!"

Suddenly, without warning, von Neumann threw the synthesizer against the opposite wall. Pieces of it scattered throughout the lab.

"Shut it down, shut it down, Ed!" Dr. Brandais yelled, rushing to the chimp, whose eyes were rolling back into his head. "He's having a seizure. Quick, Mary Alice, ten cc's of adrenaline. And bring the sedative, too!"

The director terminated the running of the program.

Mary Alice didn't move. Her eyes were locked on the chimp.

"Al, get me the adrenaline. We're going to lose him."

Cogglin rushed into the animal lab and removed a clear glass vial and a syringe with a long needle from a metal cabinet. Running back into the main lab, he handed one vial to Dr. Brandais and placed the other on the floor next to the surgeon. Paul quickly wiped the needle with the wet cotton ball that Mary Alice had used to clean the chimp's head.

Brandais jabbed the needle through the vial's rubber top and withdrew a small amount of the clear liquid.

"Hold him, damn it, hold him!" the neurologist shouted, pointing with the syringe to von Neumann, who had started to convulse in the chair.

Harv pushed Mary Alice out of his way, knocking her to the floor. He got behind the chimp, wrapped his arms about him, and trapped the animal tightly against the back of the chair.

Brandais jabbed the long needle directly into the chimp's heart and depressed the plunger.

A moment later, he withdrew the syringe and dropped it on the floor, next to the vial of tranquilizer.

In a matter of seconds, von Neumann was still.

"Stretch him out on the floor," the neurosurgeon ordered.

On his knees, Dr. Brandais bent over the chimp and pushed open one of von Neumann's eyelids. He clicked on his small penlight and shone it in the chimp's eye. Then he repeated the procedure on the other eye.

He breathed a sigh of relief. "That seems to have done it," he said, "I'm getting a pupil reaction."

While the attention was on von Neumann, Harv slipped the syringe and the vial of tranquilizer into his pocket.

Mary Alice placed the flat part of a stethoscope against the chimp's chest. "His heart's slowing. What happened?" she asked.

"It's that goddamn bug I was afraid of," Dr. Cogglin said, banging his hand against the tile floor. "The bastard finally decided to show his face. I told you, Harv, I told you there was a bug in the damn program. Didn't I?"

"Yes, Herr Doktor," Harv replied slowly, "you told me."

Monday, October 21st, 12:31 P.M.

While his granddaughter attended class at Tulane, Hiro Nomasaki sat down at Fuchan's IBM and booted her communications program. He chuckled quietly to himself as he did so. How Fu would tease him if she knew that lately he'd been using her computer to read the BBSes in the city!

Using his granddaughter's password and alias, he logged on to The Surgery as Master Wu and pressed the "Q" button to get a global quickscan of all new messages. He didn't find anything particularly interesting until he got to the ICU, and what he found there disturbed him. He was puzzled by The Succubus and almost sorry that Fuchan had revealed their address and phone number. But he wasn't completely sorry because at least Fuchan had finally started to make a connection with a human being, and, for a brief moment, had been distracted from her computer interests.

Taking a blank sheet of paper from one of his granddaughter's notebooks, he jotted down a note about the picnic in Audubon Park on Wednesday at six o'clock.

Well, Hiro thought, *at least Chief Cutter thinks all is joke. I hope he's right. Something bad in air. But must accept its coming.*

Hiro logged off The Surgery without posting anything, then dialed Francis Schonrath's number. It rang four times before a high voice answered, "Schonrath residence."

"Hai, Genghis Khan. This is Hiro Nomasaki."

"Hello, Mr. Nomasaki," Francis said, his voice enthusiastic. "How are you?"

"I am fine. You go Surgeons picnic on Wednesday?"

Silence from Francis.

"Hello, hello. Great Khan still there?"

Francis laughed. "Yes, sir, I'm still here. I was thinking. I don't know about the picnic. I read that posting when I got up this morning and called The Surgery. I didn't leave a message because I was kind of unsure about what The Succubus was saying about Meat Grinder."

"Hai, I share concern. But Chief Cutter post this morning that all was joke, so I decided to take Fuchan to picnic. Master Wu be unhappy if Genghis Khan not come too. You ask Mama-san, okay? I have Wu call you tonight."

"That sounds good, Mr. Nomasaki. I think it'll be okay with my mom. Should I bring anything?"

"Meat Grinder say he bring picnic foods. If you have raw squid, you bring for me, *hai?"*

Francis laughed. "Okay, Mr. Nomasaki. Thanks for inviting me."

"Goodbye Genghis Khan. I see you at five-thirty on Wednesday. We ride in Dragonmobile again."

As he lowered the phone, the old man could hear Francis laughing. He wrote a brief note to his granddaughter, telling her not to make any other dates for Wednesday between five and eight, since he and the great Khan were taking her to a picnic in Audubon Park. He left the note on the IBM's keyboard.

Hiro then walked into his bedroom, where he painfully squatted down on his three-foot-square cotton support cushion and pulled his legs into a full lotus. Clearing his mind without effort, he let go of the day and became his breathing.

Deep in *shikan-taza zazen,* he looked at the face he had before his parents were born.

Monday, October 21st, 2:37 P.M.

The entire team was in the director's office.

"All right, what have we got?" the general asked, his hands folded in front of him on top of his desk so they wouldn't reveal the fact that he couldn't stop them from shaking.

Everyone looked at Paul Brandais, who was holding a clipboard with several sheets of paper attached to it.

"These are preliminary observations. We're still waiting for the detailed results of the blood test."

"Well?"

"Well, General," Dr. Brandais said with an edge to his voice, "as we were discussing this morning, the project is still in its very early stages. I told you it could blow up in our faces at any time."

"Has it blown up, Herr Doktor?" Harv asked. His huge hands shifted the stocking cap on top of his head.

"Shut up," Dr. Cogglin snapped, "and let them tell us what they've found."

"Mary Alice," Paul said, nodding.

"Psychologically, gentlemen, von Neumann is reacting as if he has literally been scared half to death. His heart rate is still way above normal, he's running a degree and a half of fever, and he's overly sensitive to sound and light. He's displaying signs of acute paranoia."

"We had to sedate him further before we could even take a blood sample," Dr. Brandais added, "and that's going to color some of the results. But it was either sedate him or lose him. His heart was close to infarction."

"Jesus Christ," Dr. Cogglin swore.

"So we're back to square one?" the director asked.

"Oh, I wouldn't say that, General," Al answered. "We know the bastard works with the robotics. I don't think it's a hardware problem. Like I said down in the lab, there's a bug in the Zeus program somewhere. We're misconnecting on a subtle neural pattern, but I just can't find the goddamn thing. It's there. It smells like dog shit and I'm going to find it."

With those words, Dr. Cogglin stomped out of the office.

"Can he find it?" the director asked rhetorically.

All eyes turned to Harv, who was staring out of the director's window.

"Harv, wake up. Can he find the bug?"

"Say what?"

"Cogglin says there's a bug in the program. Can he find it?"

"He'll find it if it kills all of you," Harv replied dreamily. Then he pulled his 295 pounds out of the chair and walked toward the door.

"Where're you going, Harv?" the director asked.

"To help the good Doktor, of course. Where else?"

Mary Alice looked at the director. "Well, General," she said, "if there isn't anything else, I want to get back to von Neumann. It may be touch-and-go with him for a while. I want to be there when the sedative starts to wear off. If his heart hasn't stabilized, I'll have to shoot him up again."

"What's the bottom line, Paul?" the director asked Dr. Brandais when the two of them were alone.

"I wish I knew," the neurologist answered, "I really wish I knew. But I know one thing."

"What's that?"

"You'd better call your chum in the Pentagon and tell him they're not going to be connecting any brains to any missiles just yet."

Monday, October 21st, 3:20 P.M.

When his mother got home from her bridge club, Francis got her permission to go to the picnic with Fuchan and her grandfather. He promptly turned on his modem and started autodialing The Surgery.

Getting a carrier about fifteen minutes later, he read The Chief Cutter's reassuring message and then posted the following:

```
[MESSAGE 16]: I'LL BE THERE
FROM: GENGHIS KHAN
DATE: OCTOBER 21

Okay, Meat Grinder, I'm coming to the picnic. You'll be the only
dead person there, I guess. See you at six. This should be fun.
Who else is coming?

Francis
```


Monday, October 21st, 3:58 P.M.

When Fuchan got home from her last class of the day, she was tired and not looking forward to spending hours on the skull-cracking problem that Dr. Bates had given them for homework.

Looking in on Grandfather, she found him doing *zazen* and so gently tiptoed past his room and went into her own. Relaxing for a few minutes before starting on her homework, she went to her computer, where she found Grandfather's handwritten note about the picnic. She smiled as she read it. Then she turned on the computer and modem and was pleased to get into The Surgery on the first ring. Once in ICU, she posted a message right below the one Francis had left:

```
[MESSAGE 17]: I'LL BE THERE TOO
FROM: MASTER WU
DATE: OCTOBER 21

This will be short and quick since I have a lot of homework
tonight. But Grandfather and I will be at the picnic on
Wednesday, too. Khan, I'll call you tonight voice and we can
talk about the details, okay? If you're dead, Meat Grinder,
maybe we can bring you back to life?

Master Wu
ICU Elite
```

Monday, October 21st, 6:16 P.M.

Speeding on diet pills, but munching a Three Musketeers bar and drinking a beer nonetheless, Dennis Conlick logged on to The Surgery early on Monday evening and got caught up on his reading. When he finished reviewing the messages on the ICU, he posted the following:

```
[MESSAGE 18]: PICNIC
FROM: TUNNEL RAT
DATE: OCTOBER 21

Man, it's weirder than weird here in ICU, and I don't
understand everything that's going on here. I'll say this,
though, anybody who brings BBS war out of BBS is gonna have
to deal with the Tunnel Rat. Forewarned is forearmed. I am 100%
serious about this. I will not let this game go into the outside.
I've played the biggest game of all outside and it sucks!

Meat Grinder, your idea for a picnic's a good one. I really wish
I was above ground so I could come. But right now I'm way under
```

the earth and I can't tunnel my way to Audubon Park. Anyway, you and Wu and Khan have fun. And the rest of you who go—have fun too. Damn, I wish I wasn't so far below ground right now.

Cutter, you should explain to us what the hell's going on here. BBS is for fun and games—not to try to scare people. If you're The Succubus, then you owe some people some apologies. One thing, man: you don't screw your own friends. And you don't let them down. Because if you do, bad things can happen.

If you're not The Succubus, then whoever is, call me at 833-1969. If you wanna play games, play them with me, dude.

Tunnel Rat
Below Ground and Sinking

After saving the message, Dennis sat back in his chair at his wooden table. He turned on his printer and dumped the entire set of eighteen postings from the ICU from his computer's buffer onto paper.

Turning off his modem, he pushed back the chair and walked around the room while the dot-matrix printer banged out the hardcopy.

Standing by the light switch by the door, he clicked it off and on without thinking or realizing what he was doing.

"Terrible shitstorm coming down," he muttered to himself, feeling his forehead break out in sweat. He wiped it away with his index finger and flicked the perspiration onto the floor.

The phone rang and he jumped. It rang eight times before he picked it up.

"Hello, this is Terry, and I'm calling for the Sheriff's Department. Once again this year we're sponsoring our annual Halloween circus for the benefit of Jefferson Parish's special children, and we've hoping that you'll be able to sponsor five tickets. The tickets are only five dollars each and you'll be helping to bring a little pleasure into the lives of people who don't usually have any pleasure. Can we count on your generosity to sponsor . . ."

"I'm below the earth," Dennis muttered, hanging up in the middle of Terry's spiel.

"Jesus," he said to himself, "what the hell time is it anyway?"

He looked at his watch.

"God, will night never get here?" he asked, walking over to the light switch.

He clicked it on.

He clicked it off.

The room plunged into darkness.

Dennis walked to his cot and fell on top of it.

It sagged dangerously.

His mind racing out of control from the amphetamines in his bloodstream, he lay on top of the seedy yellow sheet. His heart felt as if it was going to explode like a grenade. He folded his hands on top of his chest, pressing, hard, trying to make his heart slow down.

Tears rolled uncontrollably from his eyes.

Four barely comprehensible words escaped his lips.

"I think I'm dying."

Monday, October 21st, 8:03 P.M.

"I don't see any sense in pursuing this any longer today," Dr. Brandais said, dropping the clipboard on the stainless-steel table in the animal lab. "Frankly, none of it's making a lick of sense to me."

Mary Alice walked to von Neumann's cage, where he was huddled in the corner; his eyes were wild, darting from side to side as if he were waiting for something—something about to attack him. She started to remove the padlock from the latch.

"I wouldn't do that," Paul said. "He almost bit my hand off an hour ago when I undid the latch."

Mary Alice opened the door and swung it wide.

"Come here, von Neumann," she said softly, "come here."

The chimp's eyes stopped their darting and focused on her. He whimpered from deep inside.

"Come here, von Neumann, come here."

Using the backs of his hands, the chimp shifted his weight and stood up. Slowly, cautiously, looking to the sides and behind, he came toward the psychiatrist.

"Be careful, Mary Alice," Dr. Brandais warned, filling another syringe with a strong sedative. "His teeth are sharp."

She put a finger to her lips. "Everything's okay, von Neumann. Come here."

She opened her arms wide, and the chimp suddenly jumped the last foot from the steel cage and leaped into her embrace. Not knowing for sure if he was going to bite her, she folded her left arm around the animal's waist and back and used her right hand to pull his head down onto her left shoulder. Then she stroked the bald head gently and muttered, "It's okay now, von Neumann, everything's okay now, okay now . . ."

Dr. Brandais stood where he could watch the chimp's eyes. Gradually, they grew less wild, less wide. They relaxed their vigil and in a few minutes closed completely.

"Bring me the rocking chair," Mary Alice whispered. "He's too heavy to hold this way."

Paul quickly brought her the cane-backed rocker they used to soothe the young chimpanzee, and she sat down and rocked von Neumann, still stroking the top and back of his head.

"I'll be darned," Dr. Brandais said a few minutes later, lifting the stethoscope from the chimp's back. "His respiration and heart rate are back to normal." The neurologist stood up, and his eyes grew distant in thought. "Which suggests . . ."

"Yes," Mary Alice said, thinking along the same lines, "it suggests that the entire reaction was psychological and not physical."

"It means that he was almost scared to death," Dr. Brandais said. "But how could that be? He said he hurt."

"Maybe he said 'heard' instead of 'hurt,'" Mary Alice suggested, looking over the top of the sleeping chimp's head. "I think you got it wrong."

"If that's the case, what did he hear?" Dr. Brandais asked.

"That's the million-dollar question, isn't it?" Mary Alice responded.

Monday, October 21st, 8:22 P.M.

"I'll be down in a minute, Mom," Jim Persall shouted from his upstairs bedroom. "I just got on The Surgery. Let me post real quick."

"Don't be too long," she yelled from downstairs. "Your leftovers are getting cold, and your father and I have to leave for the airport in a few minutes."

"Okay, Mom," Jim answered, his fingers hunt-and-pecking out a short ICU message:

```
[MESSAGE 19]: PICNIC AGAIN
FROM: MEAT GRINDER
DATE: OCTOBER 21

My mom's calling me for dinner, so this'll be quick. Guess what?
I'm alive! The newspaper had the wrong guy. Ha! She and my dad
are leaving for a two-week vacation right after we eat, and I
want to spend a few minutes with them before they go. Fuchan and
Francis, I'm glad you two are coming to the picnic. Wish you
could come too, Dennis. Cutter, too bad you can't make it.
Nelly, where are you? I can't believe you really quit BBS.
You've been the Queen of BBS too long to just drop all of us
like this. Come on out of hiding and join us at the picnic, will
you?

Gotta go eat. See you all Wednesday at six at the butterfly
behind Audubon Zoo, okay? That way we can sit and watch the old
muddy Mississippi, and stuff our faces with grilled hot dogs and
hamburgers.

And Succubus--you don't scare me a bit, dude. If you think
you're man enough to take down the Meat Grinder, come and get me.
I'm waiting for you, and I'm going to crush that pointed head of
yours like it was a full pimple!

Jim
```

Jim disconnected from The Surgery and rushed down to eat. After the punishing practice the coach had put the team through that afternoon, he was famished.

Monday, October 21st, 8:48 P.M.

"Well, Harv, what the hell do you think?" Dr. Cogglin asked his former student.

Harv pushed the long printout of the Zeus program around the small conference table in Cogglin's private office. They'd been locked in there reviewing the program's assembly language code for hours.

"I don't know, Herr Doktor. I'm a hardware man. You know that."

"You're also a hell of a programmer, Harv. Don't give me any of that false modesty crap. It doesn't become you."

"Thanks, Doktor." Harv tapped his skull. A hollow sound resulted. "It's empty, Herr Professor."

They both laughed.

Cogglin lifted a five-foot length of printout. "It's in here, Harv. I can smell him but I can't find the bastard. I may have to go back to the source."

"I don't follow you," Harv said, his eyes widening. "We've got the source right here." He tapped the hard-copy.

"The source code we've got. The author we don't."

"Say what? I thought you . . ."

"I revised and expanded on an idea, which is from one of my students, a teenager, believe it or not."

Harv rubbed a forefinger across his other forefinger. "Shame on you, Herr Doktor. More plagiarism from my favorite professor."

"I was going to give her full credit and stock in the company once we got all the bugs out, Harv. I wouldn't take a student's work as my own. You know me better than that."

Harv snorted through his nose, thinking back on some of the articles Cogglin had published in various scientific journals. One of them had been based on an idea that Harv had first hypothesized in a seminar paper back when they were both at M.I.T. "Yeah, Herr Doktor, like the piece you did several years ago on thirty-two-bit microprocessors, eh? When you were visiting prof at M.I.T."

"Hey, Harv, you got credit for that."

"Yeah, a stinking footnote."

"Credit's credit, Harv, you've been in this game long enough to know how it's played."

Harv nodded. "Yeah, that's why nobody on this team sees my work on the prototype. Okay, so when are you going to bring the genius in to solve our little problem?"

"Probably won't have to, but I'll see her in class on Thursday. If I don't crack it by then, I'll put her on it. She reminds me of you, Harv, when you were younger. When she gets hold of a problem she just won't let it loose until she wrestles the bastard right into the earth."

Monday, October 21st, 9:59 P.M.

Dennis Conlick's phone rang, ripping him away from his mental journey through the past.

Struggling off the cot, he picked up the receiver on the fourth ring, but he didn't say anything.

"This is The Succubus," a voice said, "and I'm coming after you, Tunnel Rat. So you'd better watch every step. No matter where you go, no matter what you do, I'm watching you. I'm even going to come to you in your dreams, Tunnel Rat. You're not going to know where, and you're not going to know when, but I'm going to get you. Do you understand?"

Dennis felt his heart pounding as a surge of adrenaline gushed through him.

He heard his breath start to gasp. He slammed the receiver onto its cradle and then covered his mouth with both hands to keep the sound inside.

He knew he'd give away his position if he made the slightest noise.

THE HACKER

As soon as he had his breath under control, his right hand silently went down to his side, where the razor-sharp bayonet that he'd brought back with him from Vietnam was strapped onto his belt. His fingers closed around the handle.

He waited.

Chapter
10

Monday, October 21st, 10:03 P.M.

If I don't get to bed, my eyes are going to fall out of my head," Fuchan giggled happily to Francis. "It's after ten. And don't worry about that Succubus thing in the newspaper. It has to be a joke. Nobody's going to get Meat Grinder."

The two teenagers had been talking for about forty-five minutes, neither of them realizing how quickly the time had gone.

"God," Francis said, "I didn't realize it was after ten already. Seems like I just called you a few seconds ago."

"Yeah, I know. We're set for Wednesday then? Grandfather and I will pick you up for the picnic at five-thirty?"

"I'll be ready, Fuchan, thanks. I really like you . . . your grandfather, you know. He's great, and I like you too."

"We'll have fun, Francis. I can't wait. Okay, I have to go now. Bye."

"Bye, Fuchan," Francis said, and they both hung up at the same time.

A few minutes later, both were in their beds.

This was the first night in over a year that Francis hadn't

152

been up until after midnight dialing BBSes. He was surprised at how easy it was talking to another person. And he didn't even miss reading the boards that much.

Monday, October 21st, 10:08 P.M.

A cold bottle of Perrier water rested on a cork coaster on the table next to the leather recliner in Harv's lab.

He pulled the cowl of his robe off his bald head and disconnected from The Surgery, having just read the new postings on the ICU. He hadn't left any messages, content for now to leave everything alone. Harv started talking to himself: "Wonder if Tunnel Rat still thinks he can take me on now that we've gone voice? Wonder what Sluice is thinking after our little talk? And Jimmy's mummy and daddy are going on vacation? And the picnic's set for Wednesday? All kinds of possibilities opening up here."

"I missed you, Harv," Teresa cooed, as she was programmed to do when he spoke a phrase that wasn't in her data files.

"I missed you, dear," he answered absently, leaning back in the chair where he was sitting, his browless eyes blinking rapidly as thoughts raced through his mind.

"Listening mode, Teresa."

"Listening mode."

"Play most recent project recording."

The hard drive whirled.

A second later, the director's voice filled Harv's lab: "I just found your bugs, asshole, and I've got your number. Sleep real tight, you hear?"

"Speaking mode," Harv ordered, sitting up.

"Speaking mode, Harv."

"Play back today's lab tapes. Start at eleven A.M."

"I have no tapes for today, Harv."

"Rats," Harv said, rolling the desk chair up to his main terminal.

He loaded the program that tested the bugs at the lab. A few moments later, his fears realized, Harv smashed a fist down on the sturdy oak counter. "Every damn one of them," he sputtered. "I can't believe it."

"What's the matter, Harv?" Teresa asked.

"He found the bugs, that's what's the matter. I don't know how he did it, but he got every single one of them."

Harv looked at the replica of the Zeus connector.

"I love you, Harv," Teresa said.

"Shut up, goddamn it, just shut up!" Harv suddenly screamed, and a thin line of saliva glistened between his thick lips. "I'm sick of you, can you hear me? I'm sick of the game with you, Teresa." His voice became almost childish. "Sick of your sloppy 'I love you, Harv' crap all the time. I'm going to shut you up, Teresa. One of these days I'm going to cut your throat right down to the bone. Listening mode, damn it!"

A few seconds later, his anger momentarily sated, Harv wiped his chin with the sleeve of his monk's robe and then loaded the Zeus program. Without cleaning his scalp, he pushed the microneedles under the skin, placed the connector on his skull, and ran the program.

As usual, lights exploded in his head and Harv felt the strange tingling in his brain that always accompanied the initial connection. His eyes refusing to focus clearly, he stumbled to the recliner.

"I'm here," he thought, trying to clear his mind.

There was no response.

"I'm here," Harv repeated aloud a minute later, but there was no response save for an increased tingling, like a colony of yellow jackets buzzing in his skull.

"Answer me," Harv pleaded.

Nothing but more buzzing at a higher pitch.

"Please, please, answer me."

"Tonight you must prove your love for Me," the voice finally stated, just when Harv thought his skull was going to explode.

"I'm ready, tell me what to do."

In the center of his sterile, shadow-filled room, Harv's head tilted almost forty-five degrees to the left as he listened to what he thought was the voice of God.

Ten minutes later, his soul aflame, he filled the long-needled syringe with the powerful tranquilizer that he'd stolen from the lab. He placed the syringe on the table next to the recliner. He opened the collected works of St. John of the Cross and then placed the opened book on top of the filled syringe, effectively hiding it.

Monday, October 21st, 11:59 P.M.

When he picked up the phone on the night stand next to his bed, the voice on the other end said, "Let me speak to Meat Grinder."

"This is Meat Grinder," Jim Persall answered, yawning. "Who's this?"

"Tunnel Rat. Look man, I've got a big problem, and I need your help."

Jim came fully awake and sat up in his bed, pushing the pillow between his back and the headboard. "It's midnight, and I've got a test tomorrow . . ."

"I wouldn't call if it wasn't important. You posted on ICU that you wanted to get to know everybody, and I'm above ground right now and I need some help."

"What's the problem?" Jim swung his feet over the side of the bed until they rested on the floor.

"It's about The Succubus. He called me voice and threatened me. So I told him to meet me, that we'd have it out. I'd just as soon have some company. Since you said you were a football player, I figured having a big guy along wouldn't hurt, eh?"

"Yeah, but, look, it's after midnight and I've got a test tomorrow."

"Sure, sure. Well, forget it."

"Wait, don't get mad," Jim said, thinking fast. He really didn't like what The Succubus had been posting and if he could help put an end to this nonsense . . .

"Hey, I'm not mad. If you can't help me, I'll do it myself. I'm sick of that guy's crap, and I'm going to put a stop to it if I can. Okay, talk to you later."

155

"No, don't hang up. I'll come with you. It shouldn't take too long, huh?"

"No, it shouldn't take long at all."

"Okay, where are you going to meet him?"

"I'll pick you up. No sense taking two cars."

"Okay. You have my address?"

"Yeah, 6317 Prytannia, right?"

"Yes."

"I'll be there in about twenty minutes."

"I'll wait on the front porch. What kind of car you driving?"

"Big Chevrolet. Black, two-door."

"Okay. See you in a bit."

"Count on it," Harv said, and gently lowered the receiver.

Tuesday, October 22nd, 12:07 A.M.

Tom Barnslow sat in his dark room and watched his monitor as Nelly Dean read the newest messages on the ICU. When she finished, he broke into chat mode.

"Hi," he typed, "how you doing?"

"Bad day," she typed back.

"Mine's been okay. I was glad to see the obit about Meat Grinder. Puts the whole thing back on the game level where it should be."

"Is that how you read it?" Mary Alice typed, shaking her head at her monitor.

"What else could it be? The Succubus got into *The Times-Picayune*'s computer and left a story. Shoot, that's just fun and games."

"I don't like that abused and burned body stuff. Doesn't sound like fun and games to me."

"He's just trying to scare us."

"He scared me."

"Well, I don't think it's anything to worry about. He's trying a mindscrew on us."

"I have to go now," Mary Alice typed, "I've got a splitting headache."

"Take some Tylenol," Tom suggested.

"Call me voice if anything develops that I should know about," she replied.

"Okay, L8r."

Tom put her back into command mode and she logged off The Surgery.

"Boring night," he mumbled to himself, yawning.

He decided to bag it and go to bed.

Tuesday, October 22nd, 12:18 A.M.

Jim Persall turned on a table lamp in the living room and then left his family's house on Prytannia Street. He carefully locked the door and then sat down on the top step of the porch of their two-story brick house and looked up at the stars. It was a very clear night in New Orleans and he could easily make out the constellations.

Two blocks to the north, a dark car turned out of the shadows onto Prytannia. It slowly came down the street and stopped in front of the Persall house.

Jim stood up, stretching his six-foot-one-inch frame.

He walked to the passenger side of the black Chevy.

The window rolled down silently.

"Jim?" Harv asked, leaning across the middle of the car, his massive stomach almost wedged against the steering wheel.

"Yeah, you must be Tunnel Rat."

"Dennis Conlick. Glad to meet you."

Jim opened the door and got into the front seat. The light in the center of the ceiling illuminated the car, and Jim was surprised to see how big the Tunnel Rat was in real life. For some reason, he'd always pictured the Rat to be small.

"Why are you staring at me?" Harv asked, his small eyes glittering.

"Sorry," Jim said, tentatively proffering his hand, "I'm Jim Persall. Glad to meet you."

They shook, and Jim couldn't help but squirm a little from the cold, limp feel of Harv's fleshy hand.

"Bad circulation," Harv explained, pulling his hand back quickly and placing it on the steering wheel. "A glandular problem. Runs in the family. That's why I'm so . . . well, that's why I look the way I do."

Jim looked at the huge man behind the wheel. He was wearing a yellow stocking cap on his massive head, a cap that was pulled down almost over his small and very deep-set eyes.

"Well," Jim said, slightly uncomfortable and wishing he had stayed in bed instead of agreeing to help the Tunnel Rat. "So The Succubus called you, huh?"

"Yeah, that guy's nuttier than a fruitcake," Harv replied, stepping on the accelerator.

"Where we going to meet him?" Jim cracked the knuckles of his right hand without thinking about what he was doing.

"Don't do that," Harv snapped.

"What's your problem anyway?" Jim asked, glaring at Harv for a moment. Like most large football players, he was not easily intimidated and didn't let too many people boss him around.

"Yeah, never mind. Anyway, he's coming to my place. We're going to meet him there."

"Yeah? Where do you live?"

"Metairie, apartment complex out by Lakeside Shopping Center."

"Hey, I thought you posted that you lived in the Quarter."

"Yeah, but I just moved. Forgot to put up the new address."

Turning onto St. Charles Avenue and following the streetcar tracks, Harv speeded up and headed for the intersection that would bisect with the interstate highway.

Tuesday, October 22nd, 12:31 A.M.

In his apartment in the French Quarter, Dennis Conlick stood at the light switch by the door and flicked it off and on, off and on.

Suddenly, he realized the room was in total darkness.

Dennis dove onto the floor.

Like a swimmer breaststroking, he squirmed across the floor until he was huddled underneath the cot.

Holding his breath, trying to still his hammering heart, he closed his eyes and waited.

His right hand slowly pulled from its metal sheath the bayonet he'd strapped on when he knew he was sinking below ground again.

The sound of steel scraping on steel filled the room.

Dennis opened his eyes and saw nothing but darkness.

Tuesday, October 22nd, 12:37 A.M.

"Home sweet home," Harv said, opening the door to his apartment and motioning for Jim Persall to go in.

"Nice place," Jim said, eyeing the immaculate living room. "When did you say The Succubus would get here?"

Harv looked at his watch. "Should be here in a few minutes. Hey, you like computers, right?"

"Yeah, I guess so," Jim answered. "Why?"

"I'll show you my lab."

"Okay."

Jim watched, his curiosity whetted, as Harv reached into the pocket of his baggy corduroy slacks and pulled out a key ring.

"I've got computer equipment you wouldn't believe," Harv said, walking toward a closed door, which he unlocked. "Sold an accelerator-card idea to one of the big boys out in California a couple of years ago and made a mint on it. Spent most of the dough on new equipment. I've got stuff in here that a lot of small companies don't even have. You wouldn't believe some of the things I can do with this stuff."

"Wow," Jim said a moment later, as he entered the lab.

Harv bolted and locked the door behind them.

"Hey," Jim said, "what're you doing?"

"I always lock myself in. Wouldn't want anybody in who wasn't supposed to be."

Harv pulled his stocking cap off.

His hairless head glistened with perspiration.

"Teresa, I'm hot," Harv said.

The air conditioner clicked on.

"I love you, Harv," Teresa said out of the speakers, and Jim Persall's hands suddenly felt clammy.

"Who's that?" Jim asked, his head turning in all directions, looking for the sexy voice.

"That's my woman," Harv answered. "Name's Teresa. Teresa, say hello to Meat Grinder."

"Hello, Meat Grinder," Teresa said. "How are you?"

"I'm fine," Jim answered hesitantly, experiencing the first trickle of adrenaline rush he always felt just before a ballgame, as if his body was readying itself for violence. "Where is she? I don't get it."

"She's in the computer," Harv answered, running the palm of his hand across his shaved scalp, speaking almost to himself. "I created her. She loves me. She'll always love me . . . never betray me in a million years."

"Look, Dennis," Jim said, "it's really getting late. I don't think The Succubus is going to show, and I better get home."

"Yeah, just a sec. Let me show you around . . . here's where I keep my big tools." Harv pointed to neat shelves that he had built below part of the oak counter on the west wall. There were several drills and a variety of handsaws, hammers, screwdrivers, and wrenches of different sizes. "Small tools for fine work here." Harv walked a couple more feet. He then pulled from another shelf a suitcase-size box, which he put on the floor. He opened it to reveal the precision equipment he used to build and test delicate electronic devices.

"Pretty neat," Jim said. "Look, this is great, but I really don't think the guy's coming."

"Give him a few more minutes," Harv answered. "I guarantee you he'll be here shortly. Why don't you sit down and call The Surgery? Try out my IBM."

Harv clicked on one of the modems and booted the terminal program, which started autodialing Tom's BBS.

"No," Jim said with some force in his voice. "I want to get out of here."

"Sure, okay," Harv said, and at that moment the modem got a carrier into The Surgery. "Wait, there's a carrier," Harv said. "Log on and let's read the ICU."

Jim looked around the room, fascinated in spite of himself by all the blinking lights and the equipment. "That's quite a picture," he said, looking at the Dali.

"He died for your sins," Harv said quietly, gesturing for Jim to sit in the chair by the computer terminal.

"Yeah, that's what they say," Jim answered, sitting down and punching the correct keys to log in to The Surgery.

After watching him type—and thus memorizing Jim's password—in to The Chief Cutter's BBS, Harv moved to the table next to the recliner.

He lifted the book that concealed the syringe.

Walking on the toes of his huge feet, he silently approached the big football player.

"I'm in the ICU," Jim said, turning his head.

"I'll say you are," Harv replied as he jammed the needle into Jim's muscular neck and depressed the plunger before the young man could react. Leaving the syringe, which dangled and whipped in the air as the football player struggled, Harv wrapped his powerful arms around Jim's body and held him entrapped in the chair.

Jim's body thrashed for a few moments, his feet kicking uselessly at the solid oak counter before he lost control of his leg muscles.

His eyes rolling, the last thing Jim saw was Harv's smooth, round head bent over him.

The last thing he heard was Harv's voice: "Guess what, Meat Grinder? The Succubus is here."

Harv took his time, savoring the moment of victory. He knew that Jim was out. He slowly removed his shirt, folded it neatly, and then put it on the leather recliner. He repeated the operation with his pants and underwear and socks.

Then he took the heavy wool robe from the back of the recliner and slipped it over his head until it fell, covering his nude body. After pulling his arms through the wide sleeves, he put his bare feet in the leather sandals that were under the counter, close to the dehumidifier, where he always kept them.

Shaking off the cowl, he wet a ball of cotton with rubbing alcohol and cleaned the top of his perspiring head thoroughly before inserting the microneedles.

He ran the Zeus program.

"I am pleased," the voice whispered to the now kneeling Harv as soon as the timing loop in the program finished and thus completed the connection.

Harv smiled, and he listened intently as the voice told him what he could do with Meat Grinder.

"It's okay for me to do that?" Harv asked, his voice full of surprise.

"You are free of sin now," the voice in his mind answered. "You now live outside the bounds of moral law."

"Thank you, God," Harv whispered, his pale eyelids fluttering.

After crossing himself and then removing the replica of the Zeus connector from his head, Harv unlocked and opened the door to the lab.

Harv came back and, holding him by the ankles, dragged Jim out of the lab and into the spare bedroom, where he stretched the football player out on the bed and undressed him, gently folding the clothes and placing them in a neat pile on the floor. When Harv had finished removing all Jim's clothes, he turned him over on his stomach. Harv went back to the lab and took a large spool of heavy wire from under the counter. Opening the suitcase full of precision tools, he picked out a thick roll of black electrician's tape.

A few moments later, he knelt before the bed and looked at the unconscious and nude body of the Tulane sophomore.

"God loves you," Harv whispered, as he firmly and carefully spread Meat Grinder's arms and legs. Using the heavy wire, he securely tied Jim's wrists and ankles to the corners of the bedposts and then sealed the mouth shut with the thick plastic tape.

Humming softly to himself, Harv knelt on the floor, staring at Jim Persall's muscular body. His eyes darted back and forth, up and down, surveying every inch of the young man's back—the broad shoulders, muscular arms, firm buttocks, and corded legs.

Harv licked his lips unconsciously.

"Boys like you always made fun of me," Harv remembered, thinking of his tortured adolescence and the constant taunting about his weight. "Once they stripped me in the locker room when the coach was reading the newspaper in his office, then one of them . . ."

The memory flooded back into Harv's mind from where it had been buried so deeply for so long. He sighed explosively. Then he took a deep breath, and his hand gently brushed a strand of hair back from Jim's forehead.

"They always teased me. Always. And I did their homework for them and let them cheat off my tests. And then, that day, they . . ."

Jim's eyelids fluttered as the sedative-induced rapid eye movement quickened.

Harv's thick hand lifted one of the young man's eyelids. He bent over and watched as the eyeball rolled down and then upward again.

"You have beautiful eyes," Harv whispered.

Tuesday, October 22nd, 1:37 A.M.

"The bells, the bells," Dennis moaned, curled fetuslike under the cot. He opened his eyes as his right hand was gouged by a splinter of wood on the rough floor.

"I'm above ground," he said, suddenly realizing he was in his apartment. He pulled himself out from under the cot.

"It's the telephone, you idiot," he said, laughing almost hysterically.

He lifted his right hand to answer the phone and saw that he was still gripping the bayonet.

"Man, you really lost it that time," he muttered, picking up the receiver with his left hand and resheathing the bayonet in its steel case with his right.

He started to say *hello* but couldn't get the word out.

"Hello? Dennis?" a female voice stammered anxiously.

He cleared his throat. Cleared it a second time.

"Dennis, it's Mary Alice Sluice. I have to talk to you. Please talk to me. Please."

"I can't," he stammered, his voice almost a croak.

"If you can say that much, you can say more," she said. "Please, it's important. I have to talk to someone I can trust."

Drops of sweat erupted on Dennis's forehead and dripped silently down his chubby face. He tried to make his mouth form words.

"I've been way below ground," he finally managed to say. "I just tunneled out a minute ago. I can't talk."

In her room, Mary Alice sighed deeply. "Okay, okay, turn on your modem. I'll call you right back. Okay?"

"Yes . . . thanks."

Mary Alice hung up and then turned on her own modem and computer, booting her communications program.

Staring at her watch, she forced herself to let an entire minute pass.

Then she typed Dennis's number, and his computer answered before the first ring finished.

"Mary Alice?" Dennis typed.

"It's me."

"I'm sorry. I feel terrible. I just can't go voice yet. It was bad. I was so far below ground. But I'm better now."

"I don't understand, Dennis, but it's okay. I'm not mad. I'm just glad you're better."

"You sounded worried. What's happening?"

"I got a call tonight. From some guy who said he was The Succubus. He said he knew I was alone. He said he was coming to my house. I just woke up thinking about it, and I suddenly got scared and wanted to talk to you."

There was a pause at Dennis's end as he pondered what Mary Alice had typed. His memory cleared and he remembered that he too had heard from The Succubus.

"Yeah, I think the guy called me too. Did you recognize the voice?"

Mary Alice thought back. "Something about it sounded kind of familiar, but no, I didn't recognize it. It was a man's voice."

"A man. Not a boy. That's what I remember. Are you sure?"

"I think . . . no, I'm not sure."

"What were his exact words?"

"Something like 'I know you're alone. I'm coming to your house tonight. When you're sound asleep.' Something real close to that."

"That bastard," Dennis typed. "That guy's got a real problem, babe."

"Yeah, and I'm afraid I do too. He really scared me. I'm not the type who scares easily, but he got to me. I had a bad day anyway, and I didn't need this kind of stuff to top it off. I'd just gotten to sleep too."

"Did you call the police?"

"You must be joking. They're not going to do anything. They'd think I was crazy if I made a big deal out of one phone call. I can almost hear them. 'It was a prank call, ma'am. Be sure to let us know if you get any more of them now, you hear?' Tell me that isn't what they'd say?"

"You're probably right," Dennis typed. "Well, call them if you get another one. Wouldn't hurt. Why don't you go over to a friend's house? You have any relatives in town?"

"My parents have been dead for a few years, and I have only one close friend. She's out of town."

Dennis wiped the sweat off his forehead as he thought about what he was tempted to type.

"Hey, look," he finally wrote, "I'm nothing to write home about and I live in a dump, but you're welcome to come over here if you want to. I think I'll be above ground for a while. I'm usually okay for a while after going under . . . well, afterwards anyway."

Mary Alice felt herself relax, the tension flowing out of her with Dennis's offer, which, she knew, had been hard for him to make.

"It's nice of you to say that," she typed back, "but just chatting with you is making me feel a lot better."

Mad at himself for being so relieved, Dennis replied, "Are you sure?"

"Yes, I'm sure. You really have made me feel better. It probably was just a prank. Maybe it was The Chief Cutter. I chatted with him earlier, and he's convinced it's all just a mindscrew again. One day he's scared to death and the next day it's a game."

"I'll leave him some nasty mail," Dennis typed. "No way he's going to do that to you. Look, is your house pretty safe? I mean, do you have good locks and stuff?"

"Oh yeah. I live uptown and there were some burglaries here last year so I spent a lot of money for deadbolts on the doors and iron bars on all the windows. Houdini would have a hard time getting in here. I'm glad you mentioned that. That makes me feel even better."

"Well, good," Dennis typed. "I was going to offer to come over for a little while and just sit with you until you felt better, but I'm not sure I could do that right now. I'm still pretty shaky from when I was below ground."

"You keep mentioning that. What do you mean?"

"It's hard for me to talk about. I was in the war and some pretty bad things happened. Sometimes I slip back there. You know what I mean?"

"Yes, I think so. Well, I won't press you. But anytime you feel like you need a friend, you call me. Okay? You've really helped me tonight and I want to be able to return the favor."

"Yeah, sure. That's nice of you."

"Look, Dennis, I really *am* much better. I've got a loaded gun here too, and I know how to use it. I'll put it right next to my bed, and if I hear anything, I'll shoot first and ask questions later."

"Yeah, that's the way to do it," Dennis typed.

Mary Alice looked at her watch. "God, it's a little after two. I'm sorry for waking you."

"Don't be sorry. You pulled me out of the tunnel. You didn't wake me up. I owe you."

"Well, we helped each other then," Mary Alice typed, starting to yawn.

"Yeah, I guess we did."

"Okay, I'm yawning so I know I'm okay. I'll call you tomorrow night, okay? I'll call voice and maybe you'll talk to me. If you can't, we'll hook up the modems again. Is that okay?"

"I'd like that," Dennis typed.

"Okay. Thanks. Good night, Dennis."

"Good night, Mary Alice."

"I'm going to disconnect now," she typed.

"Okay, thanks for calling."

"Bye."

"Good night."

"Good night," she typed yet again and then broke the connection.

Turning off her computer and modem, Mary Alice went into the bathroom and washed her face and hands, then opened the drawer in her night stand and checked the loaded automatic she kept there. She clicked off the safety catch and left the drawer open so she could quickly get at the gun if necessary.

A few minutes later, she was sound asleep, exhausted from the long day at the lab and the tension of the evening.

As Mary Alice slept, Dennis logged on to The Surgery and quickly scanned through the message base. There were no new postings on the ICU. He hit the key to chat with The Chief Cutter, but he didn't respond. Looking at his watch, Dennis figured the Cutter had gone to bed, so he left him the following piece of E-mail:

```
Cutter, it's after two in the A.M. and I just finished chatting
with Nelly Dean and some bastard called her tonight and said he
was The Succubus. He put a good scare into her. The guy
prank-called me too. If it was you, I want to know about it, and I
want an apology posted on the ICU. If it wasn't you, we've got
a problem, boy, and we need to get our heads together
```

to do something about it. Don't ignore this mail. I want an answer in my box when I call back.

Tunnel Rat
Above Ground and Kicking

Saving the letter to Tom's hard drive, Dennis disconnected from The Surgery and turned off his modem and computer. Then he walked into the bathroom.

Still in his T-shirt and old cotton pants, he stepped into the shower, and turned on the cold tap as far as it would go, tilting his head back. The water gushed over him. He opened his mouth and drank deeply.

He pulled off his clothes and rubbed them with soap, then used the hot tap to rinse them thoroughly. When he finished, he tossed the now-clean clothes on the floor of the bathroom.

Then he lathered his body and scrubbed thoroughly.

Ten minutes later, his clothes stretched neatly on top of the shower-curtain rod to dry, Dennis lay down, naked, on his cot.

He slept.

Tuesday, October 22nd, 3:11 A.M.

Fuchan Nomasaki slipped out of bed as quietly as she knew how. Tiptoeing carefully, she crossed her room and gently closed the bedroom door. Then she turned on her IBM and loaded the neural patterning program she'd written weeks ago that Dr. Cogglin had been so excited about. She knew there was a bug in it somewhere, and she was determined to find it.

Her beautiful dark eyes intent on the screen, she never even noticed when, twenty minutes later, Grandfather silently pushed open the door to her room to look in on her, as he did almost every night at this time when he got up to go to the bathroom.

Seeing her lost in concentration, Hiro Nomasaki shook his head wryly and closed the door.

He returned to his room and got into the full lotus position on his large square cotton cushion.

Just before he consciously cleared his mind of all thought, he sensed for the third time in the past week that great evil was afoot—the reason he had resumed his habit of late-night *zazen*. He had mentioned this to no one, but he knew that a bad time was coming. And he wanted to be as ready as he could be to play his part. If Karma had given him a part.

Grandfather took a deep breath and exhaled slowly. Before all the air had cleared his lips, he was at peace with himself and the universe.

Tuesday, October 22nd, 3:18 A.M.

After injecting Jim Persall with a further dose of sedative and then covering his unconscious body with a light blanket, Harv went into the lab.

"Teresa," he ordered, "retrieve all lab files with Dr. Sluice's voice on them."

"Retrieving, Harv," Teresa answered. The hard drives whirled with distinctive sound as they sought the desired files.

Thirty minutes later, Harv finished programming a message that used Mary Alice Sluice's voice. After playing it back a few times to be sure it was perfect, he had Teresa save the digitalized recording. He then yawned and went into the bathroom, where he pulled the robe up and over his head.

Nude, he stood before the wall-length mirror above the double sinks and surveyed his body. Thick black curly hairs had once again sprouted all over his chest, neck, and back. Running his hand across his head, he could feel a day's worth of down growing there also.

He opened a fresh double-edged razor blade and slipped it into the razor. He sprayed shaving cream on the palm of his right hand and then rubbed it onto his head and face. Turning on the hot-water tap above the sink, he shaved leisurely.

When he finished with his face and head, he stepped into the shower and luxuriated under the stream of water that was almost scalding.

He realized as he stood on the thick rug outside the shower that his mind was wonderfully quiet, not roaring with ideas about circuitry as it usually was.

After drying off, he used the towel to wipe the condensation from the mirror and looked at his reflection in the mirror.

For the first time in his life, he wasn't disgusted by his obese body.

"Thank you, God," he said.

His hand steady, he picked up the razor and placed it four inches below his Adam's apple. Then he pulled it down slowly and carefully, shaving a swathe of chest hair an inch wide from his sternum to his navel. He repeated the process, on both sides of the initial swathe to broaden it.

Then he shaved himself from nipple to nipple, repeating the process until the horizontal swathe was as wide as the vertical one.

After using the towel to wipe away the small amount of blood from two cuts the dry shaving had caused, Harv raised his head and looked in the mirror.

A perfect cross now adorned his flabby chest and hanging belly.

"I am truly Yours now," he said, kneeling on the wet bathroom rug, placing his fingertips and palms together.

Chapter
11

Tuesday, October 22nd, 8:02 A.M.

How's von Neumann?" Paul Brandais asked, walking into the animal lab.

"He had a good night," Mary Alice said, again looking up from the terminal. "I'm entering the data now. All his signs are back to normal. Perhaps the last test was an aberration."

"Cross your fingers and pray it's so," Dr. Brandais said. "We'll know soon enough."

"Is the seventh connection still scheduled for eleven?" Paul asked as he opened the door to the control subject's cage.

"That's the plan," Mary Alice answered, a hint of skepticism in her voice.

Tuesday, October 22nd, 8:20 A.M.

Tom Barnslow's alarm went off and jerked him out of a very deep sleep, the first hard night's rest he'd had in quite a while. Feeling alert and strong, he practically vaulted out of the water bed.

He sat down at The Surgery and logged on locally to read

the overnight postings that his users had made. He quickscanned the boards, skimming most of the messages. There was nothing new on the ICU and nothing worthy of his attention anywhere else for that matter.

"Geez," he mumbled, "bore city."

Then he pressed the right key at the main menu to read his mail. The first letter was Tunnel Rat's message about the Succubus.

"Who the hell do you think you are, Rat?" Tom mumbled to himself, pissed off at the tone of the letter. He angrily punched the "A" key to autoreply to Dennis's letter and typed in the following response:

Look, Den Den, I know your name and phone number and address and I know Nelly's name and phone number and address and I know all the info on all the Surgeons. Have you seen me post anything about any of that anywhere except on the ICU? Get off your high horse, dude, and don't take cheap shots at your friends. We've known each other in BBS for a long time. You know I play hard. You also know I play by the rules.

Let me make this simple for your thick skull: I am not The Succubus. I did not call Nelly Dean and threaten her. There, can you understand that? The Surgery is my BBS, and it's here for the people I choose to let use it. In the future, if you want to stay a user on this system, you will not tell me what to ignore, nor will you tell me when to reply to your letters.

Comprehendo?

A Highly Pissed-off Chief Cutter

"There, that ought to put the Rat back in his hole," Tom mumbled, cooled off considerably. He turned his head and looked at the alarm clock again. He'd have to hurry to get to his first class on time, so he logged off the BBS and put it back on automatic so it would run while he was at Tulane.

Tuesday, October 22nd, 10:58 A.M.

"How's it look?" the director asked as he came through the door of the main lab. "Are we going ahead?"

"Hell yes," Cogglin swore, looking up from the terminal where he was finalizing several changes in the Zeus program. "I think I found the bastard that was screwing us over."

"That's good news, Al. What was it?"

"The program was moving one goddamn bit to a place it shouldn't have, which threw off two short subroutines used to determine the electrical charge between synapses. A simple problem. It never should've slipped past me."

"The important thing is that you found it," Dr. Brandais said, folding another piece of gum into his mouth.

"I just hope that *was* the problem," Mary Alice added, stroking von Neumann's hand as the chimp sat in the swivel chair in the center of the lab.

"Let's find out," Cogglin suggested. "Hook him up, Harv."

"Yes, Herr Doktor," Harv replied, scratching his skull through the stocking cap that never left his head while he was in the project building.

"Isn't it kind of hot with that cap on?" the director asked.

"Keeps my brain warm," Harv answered, slipping the microneedles under von Neumann's skin. "Warm brain, warm body, you know."

"Where's the synthesizer?" Ed August asked, choosing not to ask Harv what he was talking about, looking around the room.

"Not here—we're repeating the fifth connection this morning," Dr. Brandais explained. "Backing up a step. If it works without problems, then we'll try the synthesizer again on Thursday. Get the robot into position, will you?"

"Okay," the director answered, rolling the robot toward the west wall until it was directly between von Neumann and the table that held the usual bowl of bananas.

Harv finished taping down the electrodes and walked

173

back to the terminal, where he ran the standard test on the robot's range of maneuverability to make sure it was working properly. "No problems here," he said a few minutes later.

"Von looks scared," Mary Alice said, her eyes frozen on the chimp's face.

"Respiration and heart rate up slightly," Dr. Brandais stated, tracing the electrocardiograph tape through his fingers. "But still well within normal parameters. Mary Alice, did you draw the tranquilizer?"

Mary Alice looked up from where Paul was now kneeling and holding the chimp's other hand. "Yes." She tapped the breast pocket of her white lab coat. "Right here, all ready if we need it."

"God forbid," the director said, putting his right hand in his pants pocket and then secretly crossing his fingers.

"Can the goddamn chatter and run the bastard," Dr. Cogglin said, the fatigue and anxiety from a sleepless night apparent in his voice.

"Wait a second," Mary Alice said, drawing a frown from everyone. She stroked von Neumann's hand and then rose to her feet. Bending over, she gave the chimp a tight hug and whispered in his ear. "It's going to be okay, von. I'm here, and I love you. I won't let anything hurt you, okay?"

The chimpanzee's unfathomable black eyes stared into hers.

She forced herself to look away. Then she knelt at von Neumann's side once again, took a deep breath, and nodded at Dr. Cogglin.

"Drop her into gear, Harv."

Harv pressed the proper key, and the Zeus program began to run.

"Connection established," Dr. Brandais said quietly, staring intently at the tape of von Neumann's vital signs. "No problems."

Mary Alice watched as the chimp's eyes shifted until he was looking at the robot.

A second later, the robot rolled to the table.

This time, unlike the four previous tests, the robot picked up the entire bowl of bananas instead of a single one.

"He hasn't done that before," the director observed.

"Keen grasp of the obvious," Harv remarked, now standing where he could watch the chimp's eyes.

"Here it comes," Paul said.

The robot came up to von Neumann and gently placed the bowl in the chimp's hairy lap.

Von Neumann's eyes shifted to look at Mary Alice, who smiled at him and nodded.

The robot picked up a banana and peeled it. Then it placed the banana in the chimp's mouth. Von Neumann quickly ate it.

The process was repeated until the bowl was empty.

Then the robot picked up the plastic bowl and returned it to the table.

"Better and better," Cogglin said.

"Very interesting," Brandais said.

"Shall I terminate the connection?" Harv asked the silent room, motioning to walk back to the keyboard.

Everyone turned and looked at Brandais.

"Let's give him a few more minutes," the neurosurgeon said, again tracing the tape through his fingers. "We don't have any problems at this point, and I want to see what he'll do next."

The project team members shifted their attention to the statue-still robot.

Harv continued to watch von Neumann's eyes.

Tuesday, October 22nd, 11:05 A.M.

In his apartment, Dennis Conlick was actually whistling.

He'd gotten up at seven-thirty that morning and found himself free from beneath the earth for the first time in months.

In the bathroom, he'd opened the bottle of amphetamines and flushed them down the toilet.

He'd felt so good, in fact, that he'd left his apartment and walked to the laundromat down the street with a bed sheet crammed full of all the dirty clothes he owned. He'd washed and dried his shirts, pants, towels, and mildewed shower curtain and wash rags. Then he'd returned home and dropped the clean laundry on the cot.

He'd gone out a second time, a highly unusual occurrence and visited the National supermarket across the street from the French Market. There he'd cashed his latest disability check and had spent most of it on food and cleaning supplies.

For the past hour and a half, he'd been working up a serious sweat cleaning his apartment. After sweeping the three rooms of the place with the broom he'd bought, he'd taken five plastic bags of trash—empty cereal boxes, candy-bar wrappers, beer bottles, and crumpled-up cigarette packs—out to the street for the next day's garbage collection.

Filling his new green plastic bucket with hot water and taking a sponge and containers of Mr. Clean and Comet, Dennis headed for the bathroom. A minute later, still whistling, he was removing months' worth of grime from the shower, sink, and toilet. "You're next, turkey," he said to the grimy floor.

Tuesday, October 22nd, 11:07 A.M.

"I hope somebody's clocking this," Paul Brandais asked, his eyes fixed on the motionless robot.

"Going on four minutes," Al said, glancing at his watch.

"Shall I halt the program?" Harv asked again, feeling his blood pressure rising.

"Give him another minute or two."

"I think we ought to stop now," Mary Alice said. "Something doesn't feel right about this."

"Women's intuition again, Dr. Sluice?" Cogglin asked, grinning at her.

She glared at him.

"Oh-oh, here comes something," the director said, pointing at the robot, which was suddenly twitching on its rollers.

Von Neumann's eyes narrowed ever so slightly, and Harv felt a chill between his shoulder blades.

The robot rolled toward the VAX, passed it, circled several times in one place, and then headed for a large blackboard that the team members used for notes and presentations.

The robot's left waldo picked up a two-inch-long piece of chalk.

Von Neumann's eyes turned to slits as he stared in concentration at the robot across the lab from him.

The robot wrote a letter on the board, a shaky *"I"* and then, a little to the right, it wrote an *"M."*

As the robot's arm continued to move, von Neumann suddenly whimpered loudly, and his face contorted in pain.

"Something's wrong," Mary Alice shouted.

"Heart rate's off the scale," Brandais yelled.

"Shut it down, Harv, shut the bastard down," Dr. Cogglin ordered, and Harv, fascinated by what was happening, didn't break out of his ruminations to stop the Zeus program until the director jabbed him in the ribs.

Tuesday, October 22nd, 11:09 A.M.

"Well, Miss Nomasaki," the calculus professor asked, calling on Fuchan, "did you strike gold in the mine of our little problem last night?"

"I think so," Fuchan answered. Actually, she'd found it to be a relatively simple problem; she'd solved it in less than ten minutes.

Tom Barnslow, who had been bored to tears with the class for weeks, turned his glance away from the third-floor window. *Did he say Nomasaki?* Tom thought. *He did. The guy said Nomasaki. Why didn't I ever notice that before?* Trying not to be obvious, The Chief Cutter slowly turned his head toward the skinny Japanese girl who was in several of his classes.

"Come up here and walk us through the solution then," the professor suggested, offering with his hand a stubby piece of yellow chalk, anxious to see what her wonderfully creative mind had come up with.

Fuchan blushed and shook her head back and forth. She picked up the thick calculus textbook without realizing what she was doing and held it to her chest as if it were medieval armor. Then she lowered her head in shame.

Tom watched her face redden and thought, *I know just what she's feeling.* He suddenly found himself wanting to help Fuchan.

Realizing that he'd unintentionally embarrassed his favorite student, the professor tried to think of the right thing to do. Unfortunately, though a brilliant mathematician, he was a failure when trying to solve problems that involved people.

The result was odd. The small incident grew in a blend of tension and compassion. The other seven extremely bright students in the seminar, two girls and five boys, found themselves lowering their heads in sympathy, looking at the hard plastic surfaces of their own desks for answers.

The professor found himself stuck in time, unable to move, his hand trapped in the air, still proffering the piece of chalk.

A tingling started somewhere in Fuchan's head and quickly turned into a high shrill whine deep within her. Her eyelids fluttered uncontrollably, and she sensed that her head was moving in a very slight circle on her neck.

She could feel her heart pounding, faster and faster.

Just before she lost consciousness and slumped down in her desk, almost sliding onto the floor, she saw her grandfather, dead, with a number of people standing around his body.

And then there was only darkness.

Tuesday, October 22nd, 11:11 A.M.

"Are you okay, von?" Mary Alice asked, lifting the stethoscope from the chimp's chest. She stroked his arm from the top of his shoulder down to his wrist.

"Heartbeat's almost normal," she said.

"Brain waves have stabilized too," Dr. Brandais said, dropping the electroencephalograph tape and walking toward von Neumann. "Let's get him back in his cage. I think that might be best."

Mary Alice helped the chimp to his feet. He bounced up happily and pointed to the empty plastic bowl that had held the bananas. Then he rubbed his stomach with the palm of his hand, something he always did when he felt good.

Cooing noises came from his lips and, without warning, he jumped at Mary Alice and threw his arms around her neck, hugging her like a two-year-old whose mother has just come home from a week away.

Mary Alice laughed. "Oh, he's fine," she said, the relief in her voice eliciting a smile from everyone except Harv, who was sitting by the VAX, a distant look in his eyes and a strange smile on his heavy lips.

"Come on," Paul said, putting his hands under the chimp's armpits to take him from Mary Alice. "Let's go back to your cage."

Von Neumann suddenly turned his head, which had been nuzzling in Dr. Sluice's soft brown hair, and bared his teeth at the neurosurgeon. A low growl rumbled in the animal's chest and throat. He jerked his head forward and snapped viciously at Dr. Brandais.

"Von!" Mary Alice yelled, caught off-balance by the chimp's sudden aggressive thrust.

"Hey, better sit your ass down," Dr. Cogglin said, keeping his distance but gesturing at von Neumann's swivel chair.

Brandais took several steps backward, his eyes wide with surprise. He'd always gotten along very well with the lab subject, and he was taken aback at what had just occurred.

Mary Alice, still holding the animal, who was clutching her fiercely, sat down heavily in the chair.

Von Neumann's fingers picked through her hair, gently. A sound something like a child's humming came from him as he groomed her hair.

179

Tuesday, October 22nd, 11:13 A.M.

"You should put your head between your knees," the boy suggested to Fuchan, who was now sitting on the floor. "That's supposed to help get more blood to your brain. Passing out's caused by a lack of oxygen to the . . ." His voice trailed off as he thought about how silly he might sound.

"Are you okay, Fuchan?" Tom Barnslow mumbled, lowering himself like a graceless stork to sit cross-legged next to her. The fingertips of his right hand rubbed the wet towel on the back of her neck. "Are you all right?"

"Yes," Fuchan answered in her soft voice. "What happened?"

"You passed out," the professor said, taking his pipe from the side pocket of his sport coat and fumbling with his other hand in the other pocket for the ever-present plastic pouch of tobacco. "One minute you were here, and then . . . whammo, you were gone."

"Has this happened before?" one of the girls asked.

Surprised at himself, Tom continued to gently move the wet towel on the back of Fuchan's neck. The towel was drying out, getting quite warm. It was the first time in his life that The Chief Cutter had actually touched a girl.

"No, it's never happened before," Fuchan said. Then she giggled. "And I hope it never happens again."

They all laughed.

"Yeah, well at least it livened up a boring class," Tom said. "No offense," he added, looking at the professor.

"It *is* stuffy in here," another boy said. "I don't know why the maintenance staff at this school can't adjust the heating. We freeze in the fall and spring and steam in the winter. God knows we pay enough tuition!"

Everyone laughed again.

"Well, let's call it a day, shall we?" the professor said. "There's only a few more minutes of class, anyway."

"Professor?" Fuchan said, smiling up at her teacher.

"Yes, Miss Nomasaki."

"I'm sorry for disturbing the class."

"You have nothing to be sorry for. I'm just glad you're okay. I do think maybe you ought to stop at the health center before you go home, though."

"I'll do the problem at our next class, okay?" Fuchan said. "I have to stop being so shy."

"That's a deal," the professor said.

"Can you get up now?" Tom mumbled. "I'll help you."

He rose gracelessly to his feet and then bent his six-foot-three-inch frame at the waist and offered his hands.

Fuchan took both of them and slowly stood up.

The other students, telling Fuchan they were glad she was all right, picked up their texts and notebooks and started to leave.

Tom lingered, waiting for Fuchan.

"Here, let me carry that," he said, taking the heavy backpack.

"No, I can manage," she said.

"Master Wu, let me carry it, please," he said.

Fuchan's mouth dropped open.

Tom couldn't meet her look.

"I'm The Chief Cutter," he said a few long seconds later.

"No!" she said. "You can't be The Chief Cutter."

Tom found himself looking into her beautiful dark eyes. "Fraid so," he mumbled. "The Surgery's my BBS."

Fuchan tossed her head and her long hair danced through the air. She giggled and held out her hand.

"I'm glad to meet you, Chief Cutter."

His palms clammy, the boy said, "My name's Tom Barnslow. And I'm glad to meet you."

Tuesday, October 22nd, 11:15 A.M.

"Okay, let's do this slowly and carefully, right?" Dr. Cogglin suggested, looking at Paul Brandais.

"Okay," Paul said, placing his hands on the back of the swivel chair.

The two men pushed gently and the chair, still holding

Mary Alice and the chimpanzee, moved easily on the slick tile.

The director opened the animal lab door, and Brandais and Cogglin pushed the chair through the door.

"Swing open that cage door," Dr. Cogglin said, and Paul opened it slowly.

"Time to go back inside, von," Mary Alice said, hugging the chimp tightly. "Okay?"

Von Neumann looked at her. He slowly unwound his arms from around her neck and crawled off her lap.

Standing on the floor, he looked at the men in the room. Then he curled his fingers through the chain links of the cage and pulled himself into it.

Reaching outside, he closed the door himself and latched it. He took a step back into the large cage and pointed at the padlock lying on the stainless-steel dissection table.

Dr. Brandais picked up the padlock and handed it to Mary Alice, who slipped it through the latch and locked it. "Good chimp," she said, pushing her fingers through the chain links, "good von Neumann."

The chimpanzee took a step forward and kissed her fingers. Then he seemed to sigh from the depths of his being, and he lay down on the bottom of the cage and waved his four limbs in the air.

"I'll be damned," Dr. Brandais said, unwrapping a stick of gum. "I'll be goddamned."

"Don't think I've ever heard you talk like that, Paul," Dr. Cogglin said, breathing a sigh of relief himself.

"He seems to be fine again," the neurosurgeon observed.

The scientists looked at the chimp. Then they looked at each other. Von Neumann cooed to himself.

"No," Mary Alice said slowly, "something's wrong . . . but I don't know what it is."

Tuesday, October 22nd, 1:48 P.M.

"Hi-ho, hi-ho, it's off to work we go . . . from nine to three it's misery, hi-ho, hi-ho," Dennis sang to himself, wringing the last of the rinse water into the plastic bucket.

Putting his hands on his hips, the Tunnel Rat stood straight and examined the fruits of his labor.

"Unbelievable," he complimented himself, looking at the gleaming floor of his apartment. "I declare this place fit for human habitation. Now, where's the wax?"

Dennis laughed, and the sound of it lifted him even further from the magnetic clutches of the earth that had been his enemy for so long.

Tuesday, October 22nd, 2:21 P.M.

Hiro Nomasaki was literally ripped from the peace of his *zazen* meditation.

Long accustomed to the devious tricks of the ego in its unrelenting attempts to regain supremacy over the serenity of universal mind, Hiro as a Zen student had learned to note and accept *makyo* momentarily—delusions that included colorful light displays, occasional visions of long-ago times, and frequent moments of utter peace—and then recenter himself and return to just sitting. It had been years since he'd had such strong *makyo*.

Perhaps this isn't *makyo,* Hiro thought, shuddering.

Whatever it was, it was not possible to ignore. A thick finger had touched his heart, and it was not the recognizable touch of everyday *makyo* delusion trying to regain sovereignty. No, this finger belonged to something real, something tight, dark, and very evil.

It was as if a sliver of broken glass had been scraped across his mind's eye.

Physically and spiritually shaken, Hiro quickly rose to his feet, suddenly wheezing with an asthma attack.

He almost fell, for both of his legs had gone to sleep during his hour and ten minutes of *shikan-taza*.

Walking slowly down the hallway from his room to the bathroom to get his medicine, Hiro Nomasaki remembered a day in Kyoto where he had studied so long and so hard as a boy and young man . . .

* * *

It was winter in Kyoto at Taihei-ji and the unheated *semmon dojo* creaked with the cold. On entering the *sodo* that morning, crossing the hardwood floors, barefoot, had felt like walking on ice to the young men who were in their sixth day of a week-long *sesshin* with their master, Dengyo-roshi.

Sunrise was at least an hour away.

The young men curled themselves gracefully and silently onto their round *zazen* cushions, locked their legs into full lotus, straightened their backs, and centered their minds on their *koans.*

Hiro, then a young man of twenty-six who'd been studying at the temple since he was fourteen years old, quickly found the quiet place within his *hara,* a spot a hand's-width between his navel and pelvis, where the connection with universal mind was said to be most intense.

The silence in the *sodo* intensified and the energy from the *zazen* of the twelve young men seemed to warm the unheated room.

Dengyo-roshi sat in the front, leading their *zazen.* Six students faced one wall of the *sodo;* the other six students faced the opposite wall.

They would sit thus, immobile, silent, for forty-five minutes to an hour.

Halfway through this period of *zazen,* an ant crawled onto the square cotton mat on which Hiro sat, its movement distracting his attention. His half-closed eyes focused on it. As a boy, Hiro hated all manner of insects and the fact that this bug was now on the same cushion with him did several unkind things to his centeredness.

As Dengyo-roshi taught and Hiro tried to accept intellectually, he was one with the ant. Intuitively, however, he only wished to squash the unpleasant intruder. Which, of course, was impossible since taking any form of life was contrary to the precepts of Zen Buddhism.

Faced with this dilemma, Hiro felt beads of perspiration break out across his body.

The ant crawled onto Hiro's ankle. It walked an inch and

paused. In a moment, if it continued in that direction, it would touch Hiro's bare foot.

Hiro consciously and slowly unfocused his eyes in an attempt to accept what was happening without getting attached to it. Minutes passed. Then he felt the slight tickling of the ant's legs as it began to walk through the hairs on his uncovered ankles.

His eyes focused with a clarity he'd never experienced before and zoomed in on the ant, which had paused in its movement. *If he walks under my robe* . . . Hiro thought, totally distracted from his *zazen* now.

The ant moved its head from one side to the other, then headed for the hard sole of Hiro's bare right foot, which was resting in full lotus on his left thigh. The feeling of the ant's legs on his sensitive skin caused the sweat to dribble down the young man's back. The ant stopped when it reached the ball of Hiro's foot.

He's going to bite me, Hiro thought, and he watched as the insect's stinger penetrated his skin. He watched the ant's body quiver as it released the poison. A few more seconds passed before the ant withdrew its stinger from beneath the skin of his sole. A tiny drop of blood appeared on the bite. The ant stood next to the wound, seeming too exhausted to move.

A swelling smaller than a dime rose on the skin of Hiro's foot where he had been bitten. The ant staggered and stepped onto the swelling.

His awareness and swollen skin so sensitively tuned, Hiro felt the touch of the insect's legs. And at that moment, the earth fell away from Hiro Nomasaki. Suddenly he was himself but not himself. He was the ant but not the ant. He was the cold of the *sodo* but not the cold.

He was everything and nothing at the same time.

Time stopped, and he existed in the unequivocal peace of just being.

Hiro opened the brown glass bottle of asthma medicine and drank quickly from it. In a moment, his breathing passages opened and he was able to catch his breath.

Recapping the bottle, he returned it to the small cabinet above the sink and closed the mirrored door. He looked at himself in the mirror. A wrinkled, nut-brown face stared back at him, the eyes sunken, bright pinpoints alive with a mixture of fear, anticipation, and acceptance of what was to come.

"Karma," he muttered aloud.

Tuesday, October 22nd, 3:52 P.M.

Lying on the bed in Harv's apartment, Jim Persall's body stirred restlessly, straining against the heavy wire that held him.

He awakened for a moment and tried to move his arms and legs. His eyes tried to focus, and through the blur, he could see the taut wire that imprisoned him to the bed.

"Mother," he said, his eyelids fluttering as his mind struggled to hold on to consciousness. Then the heavy dose of sedative that Harv had injected him with that morning overcame the desire to wake up, and the young man's heavy body relaxed, slumped back into deep sleep.

Chapter
~~~~~~
12

"Let's call it a day," Paul Brandais said, tapping the clipboard on the table in front of him with his silver Cross ballpoint pen. "We're not getting anywhere with this."

The project team, sitting at the conference table in Dr. Cogglin's small office, where they had set up the blackboard from the main lab, seemed to breathe a collective sigh of relief.

"It's like trying to decipher a Ouija-board message," the director said, drumming his fingers on a note pad where he'd written the letters *"I"* and *"M"* over and over again.

"Hog manure," Al Cogglin said, shaking his head in frustration. He looked at Harv, who was slumped in his chair, his pale eyes half-closed. "Harv, you have any ideas on this?"

"Say what?" Harv asked.

"Any ideas what these letters mean?" Cogglin repeated.

"Who knows, Herr Doktor? They could mean just about anything. You people have been batting them around long enough." He looked at his watch. "For about six hours to be exact."

"You've been unusually quiet, Harv," Cogglin observed, "so I thought maybe you had an idea that you were waiting to spring on us."

"I've got all kinds of ideas," Harv replied enigmatically, "but none that any of you want to hear."

"Come on, Harv," Paul Brandais coaxed. "If you've got an idea, tell us about it."

Harv shrugged and his huge head moved slowly from side to side. He started to lift the stocking cap off his head to scratch several spots that itched but stopped when he realized what he was about to do. "I don't have anything to add," he said.

"Let's sleep on it," Dr. Brandais said. "I think all of us are exhausted."

"I'm going to check on von Neumann one more time before I go," Mary Alice said, standing, then walking toward the door to the main lab.

Tuesday, October 22nd, 6:30 P.M.

"Good noodles," Hiro Nomasaki said, taking his third serving from the bowl in the center of the kitchen table where he and Fuchan ate every night.

Fuchan was lost in thought, wondering whether or not to tell him about the fainting spell, finally deciding not to worry him. She looked up. "I met a new boy today. Tom Barnslow. He's the sysop of The Surgery, Grandfather. I think he's lonely too."

"More lonelies? America full of lonelies, *hai?*" Grandfather observed. "Spend too much time with machines. Not enough time *zazen.* Now enough time with people."

"It's nice to make some friends. I never knew that."

"You not listen to old grandfather. Not concentrate in *zazen.*"

"I'll never not listen to you again, Grandfather," Fuchan said, giggling, "because you're never wrong."

Hiro Nomasaki snorted at his noodles. "When eating . . ."

"Eat!" Fuchan said sharply.

"Good," he replied, his eyes looking at her carefully.

They ate.

Tuesday, October 22nd, 6:45 P.M.

"Good night, von Neumann. Sleep tight," Mary Alice said. She turned off the camera that was hanging from a corner of the lab's ceiling for a moment, put a blank tape in the VCR, and then flicked the switch to turn the camera back on. Dr. Brandais had had this videotape camera installed right after the sound synthesizer experiment because he wanted the animal monitored for twenty-four hours a day.

Closing the door, she walked into the main lab.

Harv was sitting by himself in von Neumann's chair, his obese hips wedged between the arms. His eyes were closed, but his cheeks were wet, as if he'd been weeping. No one else was in the lab.

Mary Alice pulled her shoulders back.

Moving carefully on the balls of her feet, she crossed the thirty feet of the lab until her hand was on the door leading out into the hallway.

She opened the door and started to leave, but then she looked at the terribly overweight figure trapped in the swivel chair. A wave of pity passed through her.

"Hey?" she asked quietly, "hey? Are you okay?"

His eyes opened slowly.

"I'm becoming something wonderful," he whispered.

"Oh. Is there anything I can do?" she asked, sensing confusion in the hardware expert, and ready to help him despite the past.

"Yeah, you can ball me," he said, laughing abruptly and slapping his hands on the armrests of von Neumann's chair.

Mary Alice turned, opened the door, and exited quickly, slamming it behind herself.

"I got you again!" Harv yelled after her. "I'll always get you. Mindscrewing or body screwing, I'm your master! I'm master of all of you."

Shaking with fury, Mary Alice headed down the hallway.

In the lab, Harv struggled out of the chair.

He went to the main door and locked it. He waddled across the floor and entered the animal lab, where he turned off the camera and VCR. He took a plastic chair and put it in front of von Neumann's cage, then sat down.

The chimpanzee moved from the back of the cage on the floor to the front, the two of them staring into each other's eyes.

"I am," Harv said. "That's what you heard, isn't it? And you're trying to keep him out of you, aren't you? Why? He's wonderful. It's wonderful. You stupid chimp."

Von Neumann whimpered, his hairy body shaking, and his hands tore at the top of his head.

Tuesday, October 22nd, 6:45 P.M.

Tom Barnslow found a note and a hundred dollars from his father on his computer when he got home from his late seminar that evening.

"I'll be out of town for two weeks," he read aloud from the note. "Call me if you need anything. Dad." Two fifty-dollar bills were with the note, which also had a phone number where he could be reached.

Tom crumpled the note in his fist and pushed the money to the back of his workstation.

Then he turned his attention to The Surgery, logging on locally to see if anything interesting had occurred during the day.

Except for two letters from new users seeking validation and a complaint about not having full access from an old user, nothing interesting had happened. No one had posted on the ICU and The Succubus was still absent, which reaffirmed Tom's belief that the mindscrew was over.

Switching his BBS program to command mode so it would wait for a user to call, Tom leaned back in his chair. His stomach grumbled. He thought about making himself a sandwich. Then he thought about Fuchan and the conversation he'd had with her after class:

"Thanks for helping me," she had said at the door to her car.

"Look, my car's just across the street," he said, "I could cut the rest of my classes and drive you home. Maybe it's not safe for you to drive."

"Oh, no," Fuchan said, appalled at the idea of missing a class, something she did only when very ill. "I couldn't let you do that."

"I don't care," he said. "I'd like to take you home. You might, well, faint again or something."

Fuchan laughed. "I'm fine, really." She touched the back of Tom's hand as she took the backpack from him. "See you later, okay?"

Not thinking and not wanting her to leave him, Tom almost grabbed her by the elbow. "Look, I really don't think you should drive. Let me take you home."

Fuchan looked at the ground. "Please let go of me," she said, her voice fearful.

Tom let loose of her elbow immediately. "I'm sorry, I'm really sorry," he said, "I didn't . . ."

But she was opening her car door now, and she didn't turn around.

Looking at his computer monitor, Tom thought about Fuchan's beautiful dark eyes. And how nice her touch had felt.

In the main lab, Harv sat down at the VAX's terminal and ran the communications program. He had the modem dial The Surgery's number and was connected immediately.

He typed in The Succubus's password and user number.

Tom stopped thinking about Fuchan and broke into chat mode, typing, "I tried to call your VAX again. The number really has been changed."

"I told you I'd changed the number. You lost that game."

"Changing the number isn't fair."

"Give it up, kid. Even if I hadn't changed the number, it'd be easier for you to get into a movie actress than it'd be to get into my VAX."

"So our game's off? Is that what you're telling me?"

"You lost that game," Harv typed. "Another one's still in effect . . . which you will also lose."

"I'm glad you let up on the stuff on my board. You were starting to scare a few people."

Harv thought about Meat Grinder in his spare bedroom and then typed: "Who said I've let up? I've just taken it underground."

"You sound like Tunnel Rat," Tom typed.

"He's on my list. All of you little Surgeons are on my list. One at a time . . . one at a time."

"What do you mean?"

"Figure it out, smart guy."

Harv hit the right keys and broke the connection. "That should give him something to think about," he said to the blank screen above his keyboard.

"Awww hell," Tom mumbled, "this stuff's getting old." He stood up, stretched, and went downstairs to make himself something to eat.

In the lab, Harv unlocked the large drawer where he kept the single copy of the schematics he'd developed in designing the Zeus connector prototype. They weren't complete, of course, since he had the real designs on the hard drive back at his home, along with the two additional small circuits that Dr. Cogglin hadn't been smart enough to think of. Just to be on the safe side, though, Harv had decided to destroy the paperwork. Taking the schematics into Dr. Cogglin's office, he ran them all through the shredder.

Finished with that, he walked back to the main lab and turned his attention to the VAX. He dialed his modem number at home, logged in to his IBM, and typed the command RUN CONFUSION. Staring at the monitor screen, he relaxed when the VAX responded, "Muddling Zeus extract . . ."

Harv sat back in the chair at the VAX and laughed; a program he'd written several weeks ago was now entering random letter-and-number combinations in place of the Zeus project files. If anyone looked at the material, they'd think it was encrypted, when, in reality, it would soon be nothing but garbage. "Now the connector is really mine," Harv gloated.

Tuesday, October 22nd, 9:52 P.M.

"I can't talk very long tonight, Francis," Fuchan said into the phone. "How are you?"

"I had a good day," Francis said, telling her about the novel he and his tutor had discussed.

"I may have to read that book," Fuchan said. "It sounds pretty good."

"I wouldn't go that far. Anyway, did you have a good day?"

Fuchan thought about telling Francis about her fainting spell but decided not to. It would be best just to pretend that the incident hadn't occurred, though it also seemed to her that something had happened just before she lost consciousness that she should remember.

"Fuchan, are you still there?"

"Sorry, Khan, I was thinking . . . yes, I'm still here, and I had a good day. I'm looking forward to the picnic tomorrow."

"Boy, me too," Francis said enthusiastically. "I've been thinking about it all day."

"It's late, Francis. I just wanted to call and say hi. I've got a lot of homework to do tonight."

"Okay. You and your grandfather are still going to pick me up at five-thirty?"

"Yes, we'll be there in the Dragonmobile at five-thirty."

"Okay, good. See you then, Fuchan."

"Bye, Francis."

Fuchan lowered the phone. Then she opened one of her textbooks, and, a moment later, was lost in a differential equation of no minor proportion.

Tuesday, October 22nd, 10:20 P.M.

"I love you, Harv," Teresa said.

Harv sighed in exasperation. "Listening mode only, Teresa," he replied, turning in his chair, his eyes falling on the replica of the Zeus connector. Standing up, he walked to the recliner and lowered himself into it slowly. Pushing it back until he was stretched out almost flat, he closed his eyes and listened, trying unsuccessfully to summon the voice to him without the help of the prototype.

Tuesday, October 22nd, 10:33 P.M.

"Hello, Mary Alice, it's Dennis, Dennis Conlick." He said hesitantly, after the phone was picked up on the fifth ring. "Tunnel Rat."

Mary Alice laughed softly, pleasantly—pleased—and then replied, "Well, well. Hi, Dennis, it's nice to hear your voice."

"Yeah, I finally found the bal . . . er, I found myself . . . well, I got myself so far above ground at the moment that I thought I'd call you while I could. I wanted to hear your voice, too. Sorry to call so late."

"I'm glad. How are you?"

Dennis laughed, a full-bodied laugh directly from the heart. "I'm great. The best I've been in ages. Guess what I did today?"

"You cracked six games and hacked into NORAD?"

More laughter.

"No, I cleaned my apartment."

"I hardly know what to say."

"You'd say it was wonderful if you'd seen the condition it was in. I spent the entire day doing it. The place shines, and the smell, God, it's almost heaven. But let's not talk about

194

me. How was your day? Any more calls from our weirdo friend, The Succubus?"

"Not since I've been home from work. I made myself some supper and was curled up here with a good book in bed when you called."

"Good idea. It's a nice night for it."

"Yes. Did you eat?"

"Actually, I did. I had baked catfish."

"Yummy."

"That's what I eat when I'm trying to lose weight."

"I see."

"Since you aren't looking at me, you can't see," Dennis replied, "but if you were looking at me, then you would see."

Mary Alice laughed. "That makes a lot of sense."

"Yeah, I guess it does. Nothing serious. Just time to take off about twenty pounds of love handles that crept up on me when I was underground."

Then they both laughed.

"When am I going to see you?" Mary Alice asked without thinking.

Long pause.

"I don't think I'm ready for that yet," Dennis finally said. "Just calling you voice wasn't easy."

"I don't know what you mean. We're talking like we've known each other for years. Of course, in a way we have—as Nelly Dean and Tunnel Rat—but this is better. Because it's real. But it's not as real as meeting in person."

"I'm not stupid, but I'm not much to look at," Dennis said.

"I don't care about that, Dennis."

Another pause.

"You want to do something with me tonight?" Dennis asked, his voice very tentative.

Long pause from Mary Alice before she replied. "I'd love to do something with you tonight, but I can't. I'm very busy at work right now, and I'm really tired," Mary Alice said, her own fears of any kind of involvement suddenly popping up out of nowhere and causing a hasty retreat.

They were both quiet for almost thirty seconds.

"I see, well, maybe some other time. Look, I have to go. Somebody's pounding on the door."

"Okay. Let's talk again soon, okay?" Mary Alice asked, suddenly unsure that she wanted to.

"I don't know. If I stay above ground, I will."

"Okay, I'll call if I don't hear from you, okay?"

"Sure. Look, they're really pounding. I have to go."

Dennis hung up, leaving Mary Alice with the hard plastic receiver in her hand and tears springing to her eyes.

"Now why did you do that?" she asked herself. "Why did you do that to that poor man?"

In his apartment, Dennis Conlick heard a sudden buzzing in his head. He walked over to the cot, now neatly made with the sheets washed and tucked in under the corners of the thin mattress. Reaching over to the pillow, he lifted the bayonet that had been with him since Vietnam.

After pulling it from its metal sheath, he tested its edge on the ball of his thumb. It seemed kind of dull.

Standing slowly, Dennis walked out to the kitchen and got his whetstone and a small can of Three-in-One oil. He put a couple of drops of oil on the stone and then started stroking the knife on it.

Back and forth, back and forth.

"What's the use?" he asked the empty room.

The sound filled the clean, tiny kitchen.

Tuesday, October 22nd, 11:12 P.M.

With the replica of the Zeus connector attached to him, Harv knelt on the carpet in front of the Dali reproduction of the crucifixion.

"I want you," Harv said aloud, "to come into me."

"I am pleased," the voice in his mind answered.

"Will you do that? Will you fill my emptiness?"

"When you are ready."

"What else must I do?"

196

"You know."

"I've already done that."

"It wasn't enough."

"Tomorrow?"

"Yes, tomorrow."

"Do you love me?"

"You are earning My love," the voice answered.

When Harv had removed the electrodes from his scalp, he got out a set of tools for very fine work and disassembled the prototype. He pulled one of the smaller microprocessors out of the mechanism and replaced it with a more powerful unit that he had taken from the main lab.

When he finished reassembling it, he thought about giving it an immediate test. But the top of his head was still irritated from the earlier connection, so he decided to wait until the next day to test the enhancement.

Summoning Teresa, he had her play the recording of Mary Alice's voice that he had made.

Wednesday, October 23rd, 5:42 A.M.

When Mary Alice wrenched herself out of the nightmare she was having, she found herself sitting up in her bed, her nightgown drenched with sweat.

"Von? Von?" she said aloud, "what's happening?"

She shook her head back and forth, lightly striking her cheeks with the palms of her hands, trying to come awake completely.

"It was a dream," she said, entirely unconvinced, thinking about the vision she had just had of von Neumann going berserk in his cage, his paws tearing at the chain links and his teeth viciously snapping open and closed.

She quickly got out of bed, dressed, and headed for the lab.

Chapter
~~~~~~
13

Mary Alice rushed down the hallway to the lab entrance. She fumbled the keys out of her purse, opened the door, then locked it behind her according to procedure. Rushing into the lab, she clicked on the main light switches next to the door. She stopped just outside the closed animal lab to catch her breath. All she could hear was the sound of her own uneven breathing.

"Please, let it be just a dream," she whispered, raising her hand to the doorknob, which was cold to her touch in the lab's constant air conditioning.

She opened the door slowly. Placing her purse on the small table that held the computer terminal connected to the VAX in the main lab, she walked slowly, fearfully, toward von Neumann's cage.

The chimp was huddled in the back left corner of the cage, his eyes closed.

At first, Mary Alice thought he was dead because he was so still. Then, standing silently like a new parent with her firstborn, thinking of the children she didn't have, she watched the animal's chest for a sign of life.

It rose and fell, slowly, peacefully.

With a long exhalation, Mary Alice felt a smile form on her lips.

Thank you, God, she thought. Then she almost laughed because, as usual, she'd returned to the God of her childhood, the protective Episcopalian deity who looked after children and sparrows, returned to it as she always seemed to every time she was frightened or worried or when she really wanted something.

Will you never grow up? she thought.

Opening one of the cabinets, she took a fresh tape. She clicked off the camera and VCR and removed the tape that had been recording all night, replacing it with the fresh one. Using a felt-tipped pen, she dated the exposed tape. Then she turned the VCR and camera back on.

Glancing fondly at the sleeping chimp, she quietly walked out of the animal lab to make some coffee.

Wednesday, October 23rd, 6:08 A.M.

Each in his own room, in his own house, Francis Schonrath and Tom Barnslow slept.

In his dream, Francis, his sister Carol, and Fuchan were on the seawall that surrounded the south shore of Lake Pontchartrain.

Holding hands with Fuchan, they ran across Lakeside Avenue and stopped, breathlessly, when they reached the red blanket spread out for a picnic on the manicured grass of the park.

Carol was sitting on the blanket, her blond hair blowing in the wind, smiling widely at him.

"You look so happy, little brother," she said, her green eyes sparkling with pleasure.

"I can run again," Francis said, the voice in his dream full of wonder. "My legs work. Look." He bent down and picked up a yellow Frisbee. Then he ran a good sixty feet, turned like a ballet dancer, and flung the Frisbee toward Fuchan, who caught it gracefully, laughing, and tossed it back to him.

"I love you, Fuchan," he shouted, and she smiled back at

him, her beautiful coal-black hair flowing behind her in the soft breeze coming off the lake.

"I love you, Carol," he shouted to his sister, who suddenly had the large white wings of an angel.

"I love you, little brother," Carol said, flying up toward the sun.

In his dream, Tom and Fuchan were sitting together at the terminal of a Cray X-MP/48 supercomputer.

"Wow, this is really something, isn't it?" Tom asked.

"It's wonderful," Fuchan said, lightly touching the back of his hand.

"Let's design a new disk head configuration," Tom suggested. His fingers lightly grazed the tops of the keys on the keyboard. "You start."

Fuchan tossed her head happily toward Tom, her eyes full of love. "Hmmm . . . well, we'll need differential equations to describe the physics of the materials we're going to use and the sort of body dynamics we want . . ."

"Yeah, and we'd better throw in something about fluid flow too."

"Yes, as well as . . ."

"You're great, Fuchan, you know that," Tom interrupted her, turning to look into her intelligent dark eyes.

"I think you are too," she answered.

Wednesday, October 23rd, 6:11 A.M.

Dennis Conlick, who hadn't gone to bed at all, sat at his computer and typed over and over again: "I will not go underground. I will not go underground. I will not go underground." He'd been typing this sentence since a few minutes after four when he found himself clicking the light switch next to the door off and on.

He stopped typing for a moment and looked at his watch.

Struggling to push the chair back from the table, he stood up. "If you don't get out of this room," he said, "you're going to end up in another tunnel."

He walked over to a chest of drawers, removed the nylon

windbreaker he had washed yesterday, and slipped it over his head. Picking up his wallet, his apartment key, and some loose change, the Tunnel Rat left his apartment.

Standing on the curb, he felt for a moment as if he was back in Saigon on R-and-R. The French Quarter was very quiet at this time of day, but he could sense the life that had throbbed in it the night before.

Dennis began to walk.

Wednesday, October 23rd, 6:11 A.M.

Mary Alice sipped her coffee and reviewed once more the electroencephalograph data from yesterday's connection. Her stomach rumbled, reminding her that she'd skipped breakfast in her dash to check on von Neumann. She glanced across the room at his cage, where the chimpanzee still slept quietly in the corner.

Suddenly, with no warning, von Neumann thrashed out of sleep and hurtled to his feet, his shaved head striking the steel chain links on the top of the five-foot-high cage.

Mary Alice jumped at the unexpected noise and spilled her coffee across the data. Almost knocking over the chair in her haste, she stood up and rushed toward the animal's cage.

His teeth bared, two inches of viciously red gums showing, von Neumann snarled and growled, scratching his hands across the steel of the cage.

He lunged at the door and shook it frenetically. His fingers grabbed the padlock and twisted and turned it, banging it against the latch.

His eyes seemed to be on fire, and they drilled into Mary Alice with pure hatred.

His teeth grated on the steel links.

"Von!" Mary Alice screamed. She reached for the chimp with her right hand through the narrow opening between the cage and its door.

He raked his fingers across her skin, ripping a long gash from her elbow to the top of her wrist. She pulled back, terrified.

The chimpanzee screamed then. He ran to the back of his

cage and slammed his hands against both sides of his head. Then he started banging his head against the thick chain links.

Over and over and over again.

Then he stopped and stared at the cage.

Suddenly one of the links shattered apart.

Then he resumed slamming his head into the steel mesh.

Small spots of blood splattered onto the white wall of the lab behind the cage.

"Oh my God!" Mary Alice shouted.

Von Neumann rammed his head into the steel links three more times. A sharp crack reverberated across the room. The animal screamed in pain.

Then he collapsed at the back of the cage on the chain-link floor, blood flowing freely from the wounds on his forehead. His body was still as stone, but he whimpered—the sound of a baby in terrible pain.

Mary Alice rushed to the cabinet and removed a syringe and a vial of extremely powerful respiratory inhibitor which, upon injection, would cease all breathing activity. She drew two cc's of the poison into the plastic syringe.

Taking the padlock key from where they kept it, on a small hook on the wall, she cautiously approached the cage.

She held the syringe between her clamped teeth so both hands would be free and slowly unlocked the padlock and removed it from the latch. She opened the latch and the door.

On the floor of the large cage, von Neumann continued to whimper.

The syringe still in her mouth, Mary Alice got down on her hands and knees and crawled into the cage.

Wednesday, October 23rd, 6:14 A.M.

Sitting in full lotus, at peace with nothing and everything at the same time, Hiro Nomasaki hadn't moved for over an hour.

In the distance, he heard Fuchan's alarm clock go off. He

slowly moved his torso in a circle and then used his hands to lift his feet off his thighs. Rising painfully, his mind clear, he bowed three times to his cushions, adjusted his silk *zazen* robe, and walked into his granddaughter's room.

"The day begins, Granddaughter," he said, kissing her softly on her forehead.

"I love you, Grandfather," Fuchan said, opening her eyes and smiling at him, surprised to see him in his robe, which he seldom wore.

"Picnic today, *hai?*" Grandfather reminded.

"Yes, and I can hardly wait," Fuchan replied.

Wednesday, October 23rd, 6:15 A.M.

Dennis Conlick sat down at one of the outdoor tables at Café du Monde. It was a table at the back of the popular chicory coffee-and-beignet restaurant. His restless eyes surveyed the other patrons carefully before he relaxed.

"Black coffee and a half-dozen beignets," Dennis said to a passing waiter.

Dennis let his eyes drift westward. From where he was sitting he could see the levee that separated the French Quarter from the Mississippi River. On the river, he could see the top of a huge freighter headed toward Baton Rouge to take on a new load, maybe grain or perhaps chemicals.

Suddenly a radio station's traffic helicopter roared overhead, checking the traffic on the Greater New Orleans Bridge that crossed the river a couple of miles upstream.

Dennis's instinct told him to dive for the floor of the café at the helicopter's clatter, and he almost did. He felt the earth pulling him, calling him, telling him to get inside quick, down where it was dark and close and quiet. Where he'd be safe. He fought it, and slowly felt his racing heart calm.

"You're okay, Rat," Dennis said aloud, almost chanting. "You're okay. You're okay. You're above ground and you're going to stay . . . hold on . . . this'll pass . . . don't give in to it."

He gripped the steel-mesh table with his fingers until the knuckles turned white. Sweat broke out on his forehead. His eyes closed and he felt himself slipping, falling.

A honeymooning couple at the table next to Dennis's looked at him curiously and warily. They'd been partying all night and were having a few beignets to soak up some of the alcohol before returning to the Hyatt Regency on Royal Street to spend the day in bed.

"Who's that guy talking to?" the young woman asked.

"God knows," her new husband answered. "Damn, listen to him. That's pathetic. Tell the waiter to call the men in the white coats."

Dennis, holding on to reality by his fingertips, heard through the fog of his flashback the young man's unkind words.

"White," he suddenly muttered aloud. "White, white, white. White light." Using the word almost as a mantra, he repeated it again and again. It pulled him out of the tunnel.

His eyes snapped open.

The waiter arrived with the coffee and large plate of beignets. "Are you okay?" he asked, looking at the sweating, wide-eyed man.

"Yeah, fine," Dennis replied suddenly, his eyes fully open now. "I really am fine this time."

Reaching into his pocket, Dennis handed the waiter a five-dollar bill. "Keep the change," he said.

"Geez, thanks," the man answered, taking his bent steel tray and heading back to the kitchen.

Dennis sipped the coffee. He looked at the steaming beignets, the powdered white sugar melting deliciously on top of them. The sweet smell curled upward from the plate.

Making a decision, he lifted the plate, stood up, and walked over to the young couple's table.

"Here, have these courtesy of the Tunnel Rat," Dennis said, placing the plate of New Orleans-style donuts in the center of their table.

He smiled radiantly at the newlyweds and left the café, crossing the street into Jackson Square.

"What was that all about?" the young woman asked.

"Guess he's going back to the nut house," her husband answered, picking up a beignet.

Wednesday, October 23rd, 6:16 A.M.

"It's okay, von Neumann, it's okay," Mary Alice repeated quietly, the chimp's head now cradled in her lap. "I love you, von, I love you."

She was sitting cross-legged, her head just barely clearing the top of the cage.

The paralyzed body of the chimpanzee stretched across the rear of the cage.

"Oh, von, what have we done to you?" she muttered, her fingers feeling the fractured bones at the back of his neck, making an ugly sound of gravel scraping on glass.

The fingers of her other hand fumbled on the floor of the cage for the syringe and then closed around the plastic.

"It's going to be okay, von," she said again. "Everything's going to be okay."

Von Neumann's eyelids fluttered at the words.

She could see great pain in his eyes. And she could see something else: terrible fear. Tears flowing freely down her cheeks, sniffing repeatedly, trying unsuccessfully to clear her running nose, she brought the syringe closer to the suffering animal.

"I'm sorry, von, I'm so sorry," she said, forcing her hand to be steady as she eased the needle into the muscle of the chimp's shoulder.

Her thumb depressed the plunger and the tiny bit of clear poison went into von Neumann's body.

A second later, as the powerful drug coursed through the animal's bloodstream, the chimp's dark eyes cleared.

For a heartbeat, they seemed to sparkle with their old playfulness.

"I love you," von Neumann said.

And then he died.

Wednesday, October 23rd, 7:00 A.M.

"Well," the director said, looking first at Dr. Brandais and then at Dr. Cogglin, "where do we stand? Al, since this early meeting was your idea, why don't you start?"

"Sorry for calling you so late, General," Al Cogglin said, "but Paul and I came back to the lab last night around midnight to review the schematics for the prototype. I've been concentrating so hard on the Zeus program, and Paul's been putting all his time into monitoring the subject. And, well, neither of us have been keeping a close eye on what Harv's been doing with the actual prototype. So, in trying to find an explanation for what happened in the lab with von Neumann yesterday morning, we decided to go over the schematics."

The director sat up straighter in his desk chair. "And?"

"To make a long story short, we jimmied the lock on the drawer where Harv keeps the schematics for the connector. We found next to nothing, only a few pages of preliminary notes. The drawings for the actual hardware weren't there."

"Just what I was afraid of," the director said.

"Without those damn schematics, Paul and I can't tell what's going wrong, or right, for that matter, with the prototype. We'd have to get somebody in here to break it down, reverse engineer it. And that would take months."

"Well, that's a problem, but it's not that big of a problem, is it? We have copies of the schematics in the computer, right?"

The two scientists looked at each other.

"Right?" the director asked again, his voice louder.

"Maybe," Dr. Brandais said.

"Maybe? What in blazes does that mean?" the director shouted.

"Maybe means maybe," Al Cogglin snapped back.

"Someone's changed the encryption scheme. We can't read any of the material now."

"Damn," the director said, slamming his hand on the top of his desk. "Have you talked to Harv? This sounds like his doing."

"We just found out about it last night."

"Why would he do such a thing? What's the point?" the general asked.

Al looked at Dr. Brandais and said, "We don't know for sure but . . . Paul, why don't you tell him?"

"We're seeing some definite anomalies," Paul Brandais said. "Several days ago, Mary Alice suggested that she was seeing signs of increased intelligence in the lab subject. I scoffed at her idea, but after what we saw with yesterday's experiment, I'm not sure we can continue to reject that hypothesis out of hand."

"Now, wait a second," the director interrupted. "I hope you're not suggesting that the Zeus connector may also be a . . . a what? An intelligence enhancer? Come on, Paul. You can't be serious."

"It's a hypothesis, nothing more, a suggestion that I initially rejected, but now, in light of what the lab subject did with that piece of chalk, one we're going to have to take a closer look at."

"Good lord," the director mused, placing his fingertips to his lips. "Think of the possibilities. When will we know more? What are the plans for proving or disproving this hypothesis?"

"We've pretty much limited ourselves to physical monitoring of the subject so far," Dr. Brandais explained, "with, of course, some very simple observations of manipulative ability. What I want to do first thing this morning is run him through a battery of intelligence tests. Check this idea out scientifically and see if there's anything to it."

"God, I hope there's something to it," the director said, his mind alive with the defense possibilities.

"Well, there's only one way to find out," Al said, "and

that's to run those tests on our simian friend. But that doesn't solve our problem with Harv, does it? If we don't get him in line, it's conceivable that he'll be the only project member who knows everything that makes the Zeus connector work. And there's one other thing . . ."

"You *can* crack the new encryption, can't you?" the director asked, looking at his ex-army subordinate.

"In time, yes . . . if I drop everything else."

"How much time?"

The artificial-intelligence expert shrugged. "A few hours, a day, a week. Hard to say."

"And what's the other thing?"

"You've noticed Harv's shaved head? That he hasn't let his hair grow back out since the so-called lice infestation he told us about? That he never takes off that stocking cap?"

"I hope you're not suggesting that he's tried the connection on himself?" the director asked, rubbing his hands nervously.

"I wouldn't put it past him, would you? It might explain the missing schematics and the new encryption," Al replied. "Maybe he knows something we don't know, and he's going to try to steal the whole thing. It's going to be worth millions."

The general sat back in his chair and stared out the window for a minute. "Well, let me worry about Harv. Don't confront him," he finally said. "You two go run those tests on the chimp."

Al Cogglin rose quickly to his feet, looking at his colleague.

"Buzz me as soon as you know anything," the director said.

Wednesday, October 23rd, 7:05 A.M.

"Going on a little picnic," Harv said happily as he dressed that morning.

Then he went into his lab, called The Surgery using Jim Persall's password and user number, read the board, and then left the following message:

```
[MESSAGE 20]:
FROM: MEAT GRINDER
DATE: OCTOBER 23

Well, Suckyourbutt, you just come on to the picnic, pud. If you
want to tangle with me, I'll be real happy to accommodate you.

Don't worry about that jerk, everyone. Come to the Surgeon
Picnic and let's have a blast.

See you all at the butterfly in Audubon Park at six tonight, 'k?

Meat Grinder/Jim
```

Harv turned off his equipment, locked the deadbolts, and went into the kitchen, where he started to make himself a big breakfast. He put a pot of water on the stove to boil, deciding that this morning he would spoonfeed the disciple in the spare bedroom a little oatmeal before injecting him once again with the sedative.

Wednesday, October 23rd, 7:06 A.M.

Back in his apartment, Dennis toweled off from a long shower. He slipped on a clean shirt and clean blue jeans and then walked into his main room.

He sat down at his worktable, stared at the phone for several minutes, and then dialed Mary Alice's number.

After ten unanswered rings, he hung up.

He sat at the table for several more minutes and then dialed another number.

The private line on the director's phone blinked rapidly.

"Hmmm," the general said, slowly picking up the receiver. Only three people had the number to his private line: his friend at the Pentagon, another friend at the Department of Defense, and Dennis Conlick.

"Yes?" he answered authoritatively.

"It's Dennis."

The director relaxed. Of the three who had access to this number, Dennis would present the fewest problems.

"How are you, Conlick?"

"I'm fine, sir. The best I've been in a long time. I'm above ground, and I think I'm here to stay. I *am* here to stay."

"That's good to hear, son."

"Look, General, I've helped you out on several occasions, haven't I?"

"Yes, you have," the director replied carefully.

"I've always done whatever you've asked of me?"

"That's true."

"And I've never failed you?"

"Correct. Dennis, if you need money, just say so, son. I'll be glad to loan you . . ."

"No, sir," Dennis interrupted, "I don't want any of your money. It's like this, sir. I'd like a job. It's time I quit hiding and started working again. Any ideas?"

The director wasn't about to recommend Dennis for anything until he had talked to him personally to determine his state of mind. He picked up his pen and chewed on it thoughtfully.

"Know anything about encryption?"

The Tunnel Rat laughed. "General, I'm a whiz with encryption."

"Why don't you come over here, we'll talk. I may have something for you."

"When do you want me, sir?"

"I'm waiting on you now," the director answered.

"I'm on my way," Dennis said, hanging up the phone.

Wednesday, October 23rd, 7:11 A.M.

"It looks like somebody's here already, Al," Paul Brandais said when he unlocked the door to the main lab and found the lights still on. "I remember turning these lights off last night."

"Sure does. Harv!" Al Cogglin shouted. "Where you hiding?"

"The door to the animal lab's open," Dr. Brandais said, walking in that direction.

"I'll be there in a minute."

Paul Brandais walked into the animal lab and was stunned with what he found. "Al, Al, in here!" he shouted, his eyes wide with fear as he looked at Mary Alice. She was sitting in von Neumann's cage, her eyes glazed, staring at nothing, her right hand absently stroking the dead animal's head.

Al Cogglin ran into the room. He knelt down next to his colleague and looked into the cage. "Holy Christ," he said. "What happened in here?"

"I don't know. Looks like she's in shock. Let's get her out of there."

"Is the chimp . . ."

"I think so. God, what a mess." Dr. Brandais crawled halfway into the cage. He gently touched the psychiatrist's arm. "Mary Alice," he said softly, "Mary Alice, it's Paul."

"Paul?" she answered, her voice soft and sad.

Then her head turned slowly and her eyes focused.

"Oh God, Paul," she said, starting to pull herself together. "I had to put him down."

"Take my hand," he answered, lifting von Neumann's head and upper body off her lap and slowly lowering it to the back of the cage, "and let me help you."

"I'm all right," she said, but she took the neurosurgeon's hand nonetheless.

Wednesday, October 23rd, 8:20 A.M.

"Francis, I'm going shopping now," Mrs. Schonrath said, poking her head into her son's room.

"Okay, Mom. Have a good time," Francis replied, buttoning his shirt.

"Your tutor called a little while ago. Her daughter's coming down with the flu, so she's not going to be able to tutor you today."

"Hooray!" Francis yelled.

"Now Francis," his mother scolded, smiling in spite of herself. It was so nice to see some animation in the boy.

"When are you going to be home, Mom?"

"It'll probably be late this afternoon. Why?"

"Don't forget that I'm going to the picnic with Fuchan and Mr. Nomasaki. They're picking me up at five-thirty."

"I'm glad you reminded me. I forgot all about it. And when will you be home?"

"I don't know. Around eight, I guess."

"Well, don't be too late."

"I won't. Have a good shopping trip, Mom."

Mrs. Schonrath walked into the room and kissed her son on the cheek. "I'm glad to see you doing so much better, Francis. I love you."

"Aww shucks, Mom," Genghis Khan responded.

She rubbed the top of his head with her hand and then left, closing the bedroom door behind herself.

"No school," Francis cheered again, and then he turned on his modem and booted his communications program. "Time for a little BBSing," he said happily and started the autodialer, anxious to check into the ICU and see if anything new was happening.

Wednesday, October 23rd, 9:03 A.M.

"You look well, Dennis," the director said, scanning him from head to toe. Clean clothes. Shaved. Hair combed. Eyes clear.

"It's the first time in years that I've really felt like myself, sir," Dennis answered.

"Good to hear." The director smiled.

"You mentioned something about an encryption problem for me?"

"Yes. Now, here's what I've got for you," the director began.

Wednesday, October 23rd, 9:05 A.M.

"Mary Alice, I know this is hard, but, please, I need your help. A sponge," Dr. Brandais said, the tips of his fingers in von Neumann's skull cavity. "I don't want to drop this."

"Sorry, Paul," Mary Alice replied. "Here, I'll do that."

"Yeah, that's better. Much better. Here, just a sec . . . okay, give me a hand. Clip the brain stem. Yeah, that's got it. Okay, I'm lifting it out now."

Squishy, wet noises came from the stainless-steel table where the neurosurgeon worked.

"What do you make of this?" Dr. Brandais asked, holding von Neumann's brain in his gloved right hand. The brain was grayish in color and seemed dried out. "Normal tissue looks nothing like this."

"I've never seen anything like it," Mary Alice answered, absentmindedly feeling the gauze that Dr. Brandais had wrapped around her wounded arm after he'd cleaned it. "Initial indications suggest severe desiccation."

"Hmmm," Brandais mumbled.

"But that's not possible, is it?" Mary Alice queried. "I mean, I suppose increased brain activity might cause something like this, but the magnitude of electrical activity would have to be enormous. I don't see how the mechanism could have, I mean, there's no electricity flowing from the prototype, is there?"

"No way," Al Cogglin said.

"Not that I'm aware of either," Brandais replied, placing von Neumann's brain in a stainless-steel pan and then angrily stripping the latex gloves off his hands. "Unless we haven't been getting all the facts. Is Harv here?"

"He just came in a few minutes ago," Al said.

"Does he know what happened?"

"I didn't tell him."

"Okay. Mary Alice, get him in here, please," Dr. Brandais said.

Dr. Sluice walked to the animal-lab door, opened it, and stuck her head through the opening. "Harv, Dr. Brandais would like to talk with you. Will you come here, please?"

The sound of Harv's voice from the main lab: "Anything for you, Fräulein."

The hardware expert came in and closed the door.

"Harv, have you told us everything about the prototype?" Dr. Cogglin asked, his tone very serious.

"Hey, what's going on here?" Harv looked around the

lab. Von Neumann wasn't in his cage. "Where's the chimp?"

Mary Alice pointed to the body on the stainless-steel table.

"What happened? What's going on?"

"Look at his cage."

Harv walked over to the cage and took his time looking at it.

"What're all the scratches?" he asked.

"They're teeth marks," Mary Alice explained. "I was sitting here when he just went insane with pain. Tried to chew his way out of the cage. I had to . . ." Her voice faltered. She bit her lip before finishing the sentence. "I had to put him to sleep."

Harv stared at the body of the chimpanzee.

"What haven't you told us about the prototype, Harv?" Dr. Cogglin asked again. "Paul and I opened your drawer and tried to look at the schematics last night, but they weren't there."

"I've told you everything, Herr Doktor," Harv answered, feigning surprise over the missing schematics. "I followed the exact specifications that you and Doktor Brandais insisted on. Didn't put in any extra bells or whistles. You people must've screwed up. Too bad von Neumann here had to buy the ranch because you guys made a mistake. It's always worked perfectly. What did you do? Run a test without me this morning?"

"We didn't touch your prototype, Harv. You've witnessed all the connections, and each one has followed your protocols to the letter. We didn't change the Athena hypothesis a bit, and anyway it doesn't account for the level of electrical activity that would dry up brain tissue like we have here. Don't play games with us. If you have an idea, we want to hear it."

"Feel how light it is," Brandais said, lifting von Neumann's brain in her still-gloved hands and offering it to him.

"No. No thanks. I'm not into feeling brains," Harv answered, taking a step back from the dissection table, his mind spinning. "Wouldn't mind feeling those boobs of Fräulein Sluice's, though," he quipped, trying to keep his cool so they wouldn't see his sudden panic.

"Feel your own," she snapped back.

"Don't sidetrack him, Mary Alice," Dr. Brandais said. "Okay, Harv, I want an explanation for this. Neurologically, I don't have one. It has to be something in the prototype. A pretty solid jolt of electricity might have caused this. Looks to me like there's a glitch in your mechanism."

"No way, Herr Doktor. No way even an amp could flow into the subject. The sensors connected to our dead buddy here were receivers, not transmitters. I don't make mistakes, Doktor," Harv answered.

"It makes no sense then," Mary Alice said, gently lowering the brain back into the pan.

"It certainly doesn't," Dr. Brandais replied. "The mechanism's worked perfectly every time we've tested it. So what happened? What caused our poor friend here to go so utterly and completely berserk? Something happened to von Neumann's brain, and I want to know what. We're going to be standing on square one again if we don't get this figured out."

"I suggest you find the schematics for your prototype, Harv," Al Cogglin said. "We know they're missing, and we need to review them. You didn't happen to lose them by mistake, did you? After all, you're the only one with the key to the hardware cabinet."

"Why would I destroy my own schematics?" Harv asked innocently.

"Who accused you of *destroying* them, Harv?" Dr. Brandais replied instantly, raising an eyebrow suspiciously.

"Cogglin's the expert, let him figure it out," Harv snapped.

"Don't bite the hand that feeds you, Harv," Dr. Brandais suggested. "You wouldn't even be working on this project if it wasn't for Al."

Harv smiled arrogantly. "No one else could have built the connector," he boasted, walking out of the animal lab.

"What do you think, Al?" the neurosurgeon asked.

"He did something with the paperwork, no question about it."

"Why would he do that?" Mary Alice asked.

"Without those schematics, no one else knows how to build a connector," Al Cogglin explained, "at least not until we tear the prototype apart and get everything down on paper again."

"He's sure touchy," Mary Alice observed.

"It's obvious, isn't it? He's made a mistake with the mechanism," Dr. Brandais concluded. "He messed up and knows it's his fault. He made an adjustment or something that he didn't tell us about. Did you see his eyes when I said the mechanism had a glitch? He had an idea. But he's too arrogant to admit he made a mistake. God, I hate prima donnas."

"His eyes looked frightened to me. What're we going to do?" Mary Alice asked, feeling helpless. The mechanism itself was a mystery to her as foreign as particle physics.

"What else can we do? We'll review the data and wait for Harv to come to his senses."

Outside, in the main lab, they could hear Harv laughing.

Wednesday, October 23rd, 11:33 A.M.

With Fuchan so fully on his mind, Tom Barnslow decided to cut his afternoon classes at Tulane University. He made himself a peanut-butter-and-jelly sandwich when he got home and then he went upstairs and logged on to The Surgery. He scanned into ICU and read the following posting:

```
[MESSAGE 21]: IT'LL BE FUN
FROM: GENGHIS KHAN
DATE: OCTOBER 23
```

Just a quick note from Genghis Khan, Meat Grinder, Master Wu, and I will definitely be at the picnic. See ya at six!

Francis the Khan

Tom read the posting, thought about it for a moment, thought about Fuchan, and then wrote the following on the ICU:

```
[MESSAGE 22]: I'M COMING TOO
FROM: CHIEF CUTTER
DATE: OCTOBER 23

Well, Francis, I've managed to make other arrangements with
what was going to keep me away from the picnic, so I'll be
joining you and Fuchan and Jim at the picnic. See ya there!

Cutter
```

Tom sat back and smiled at what he had just written. He knew this meant he'd have to admit that he'd lied on the ICU about being Robert Earle Hughes, but at this point he didn't care so much about the game. For some reason, BBS was no longer the overriding obsession of his life. After the experience with Fuchan yesterday, he suddenly found himself wanting to make some real friends.

Wednesday, October 23rd, 2:09 P.M.

Dennis Conlick sat at his computer and reexamined the code he'd used earlier that month to break the original encryption scheme on the two-meg Zeus extract. He'd surreptitiously downloaded the files from the project VAX early in October but had never read them. This unencrypted copy of the original Zeus extract still resided in his hard drive. As he looked at the deciphering program he'd written, he was also thinking about the puzzling conversation he'd had with the general that morning.

It's odd, Dennis thought, that he wants *me* to decipher material from his project. The explanation about the disgruntled employee changing the encryption scheme and then leaving town was plausible, given the nature of some computer geniuses that Dennis had known, but barely so. What was particularly odd was the general's insistence that Dennis download the material at exactly 5:30 P.M. this evening. The general had said that he didn't trust a member of the team and that the lab would be cleared of all project members so Dennis could access the material secretly. Dennis could buy that too, especially in light of what he had already figured out about the nature of the project from a whole day spent reading the original Zeus extract. The implications were indeed incredible. Nonetheless, something had gone very sour with the project. There was no question of that.

Wednesday, October 23rd, 5:00 P.M.

The director entered the lab, where he found Al Cogglin reviewing data at the VAX's secondary terminal. Harv was seated at the main terminal, his fingers resting on the keyboard but not typing anything. The prototype, its thin cable tightly wound around it, was lying next to him, a couple of feet away.

"How's it going, Harv?" the director asked while his assistant gathered the team.

"Fine, my Führer," the hardware expert replied, snapping his hand up in a Heil Hitler salute.

"Not amusing, Harv. You haven't seen the schematics for the connector by any chance? We seem to have misplaced them. Maybe they were taken by the same individual who bugged the project and changed the encryption on the Zeus extract," the director said sarcastically.

"Darn, General, haven't seen any bugs, haven't seen any schematics. Security's pretty poor around here, isn't it? Somebody even broke into the drawer where I kept the schematics. Guess you weren't the man for this job, eh?"

"Get the others, will you, Al?" Edward August asked, his face reddening.

Harv's head went back on his thick neck then and he belly-laughed for a couple of seconds.

"The director wants you in the main lab," Cogglin said, opening the door to the animal lab.

The retired general turned at the sound of Al's voice. At

the same moment, Harv moved several inches closer to the prototype.

"Be there in a moment," Paul Brandais said, looking up from the microscope under which he was examining a tissue sample from von Neumann's brain. He turned to Mary Alice and, looking at his watch, said, "We can't do much more today anyway until the cultures have had a chance to incubate."

"Right," Mary Alice answered, knowing that she should tell him about what she had seen and what she thought von Neumann had said just before he died. Unfortunately, the sound capability of the videotape camera had failed to record the chimp's final words, and Mary Alice was still unconvinced in her own mind that the animal had actually spoken to her. So she chose again to keep the knowledge to herself.

By 5:12, the members of the project were either sitting or standing in the main lab.

"Now that you're here," the director said, "I want all of you to go home and get a good night's sleep. This has been a difficult day for everybody, especially you, Mary Alice, and I think the team could benefit from getting out of here early."

"But I . . ." Dr. Cogglin started to say.

"As director of the project," the general interrupted firmly, "I won't hear any excuses. So go. The lab is officially closed as of right now. I expect to see you bright and early in the morning, however."

As everyone started milling around to gather their things, Harv inched back to where the prototype of the connector was lying next to the VAX. Casually surveying the room, he slipped the mechanism between his bulky sweater and his back. A second later, he had pulled on his heavy overcoat and was walking out the door, winking at the director as he left.

In five minutes, the lab was clear and locked.

The director sat down at the computer and waited for Dennis Conlick's call to download the encrypted files.

When the phone rang at precisely 5:30, the general

entered his own password and access number, opening the file that he believed contained the Zeus extract, along with Dr. Cogglin's most recent version of the Zeus program, which included the modified Athena hypothesis.

"When you crack this, Dennis," the general said to himself as he watched the encrypted file start to go out over the modem, "Harv's going to be history around this place."

Chapter

~~~~~~

14

Wednesday, October 23rd, 5:38 P.M.

Harv parked his car almost directly in front of what the teenagers of New Orleans fondly called *the butterfly,* a large concrete structure behind Audubon Zoo which resembled its namesake and overlooked the Mississippi River.

Unwedging his huge belly from behind the steering wheel, Harv got out of the automobile, carrying the blanket he'd put in the car that morning.

After crossing the street and spreading the blanket, he lowered himself slowly and proceeded to wait. He looked around to see if any of the Surgeons had arrived yet, but none of the few individuals in the area looked anything like the people behind the aliases of The Surgery.

A jogger tramped past Harv, and the hardware expert looked up. The jogger, a short guy in a faded pair of cotton running shorts, huffed and puffed through his open mouth, a mouth that revealed an easy smile with a wide gap between his two front teeth.

"How you doing?" the jogger asked, eyes staring from behind thick lenses, seeing Harv looking at him.

"Just great, Herr Runner," Harv answered, thinking to himself, *Why do those people do that to themselves?*

"See you," the jogger said, moving past at his blazing ten-minute-a-mile pace. Harv stifled a laugh when he saw the guy from the rear—he ran with both feet pointing out at forty-five-degree angles.

"Looks like a ruptured duck," Harv muttered to himself, laughing silently.

Hiro Nomasaki with Fuchan and Francis Lee pulled into an empty parking space in front of the butterfly at a couple of minutes after six.

"This is going to be fun," Fuchan said, opening the door on her side of the back seat.

"You're telling me," Francis replied.

"I'll help Grandfather get your wheelchair, Francis," Fuchan said, getting out of the car.

"Great."

Behind the car, Fuchan lowered her voice. "Are you feeling all right, Grandfather? Your heart isn't bothering you, is it?"

Hiro's angina and occasional asthma attacks scared Fuchan very much, and she knew that her grandfather always seemed distracted when he was in pain, though he never complained. He'd been unusually quiet when he was driving them to the picnic.

He turned the key, and the trunk lid flew up past their faces. Then he kissed his granddaughter on the forehead. All day he'd had a strange feeling about the upcoming picnic, and, now that they were at the appointed place, he felt the intertwined strands of karmic fabric lacing together.

"I am fine, Granddaughter. Can not get word in backwards with you and Khan chattering like squirrels."

"Why don't you let me help you with that, Pops?" A strange voice came from directly behind Fuchan and her grandfather. The voice was so close that both of them started with surprise. "Sorry." The voice chuckled. "Didn't mean to frighten you."

They turned and Fuchan looked up and up until she saw the slightly crazed eyes of the six-foot-five-inch Harvey Webster.

"I'm Dennis Conlick, the Tunnel Rat," Harv said. "I found myself above ground this morning and decided to come to the picnic after all."

Fuchan and Grandfather both relaxed noticeably.

Grandfather bowed. "Hiro Nomasaki," he said, "and Master Wu, my granddaughter Fuchan Nomasaki."

"Glad to meet you," Harv said, bowing and smirking at the same time. His big hands reached into the trunk of the car and lifted out the wheelchair as if it weighed five pounds instead of fifty. "That must be Genghis Khan in the back seat, eh Pops?"

Hiro frowned. "Yes, Francis sit in back seat."

"I'll get him out," Harv said. "You open the wheelchair."

Before Hiro or Fuchan could say anything, he had put the wheelchair down on the asphalt, groaning as he bent over, and then he was moving for the door on Francis's side of the car.

Harv opened the door and stuck his huge stocking-capped head in.

"Here comes a Tunnel Rat," he bellowed, causing Francis to jump. "Dennis Conlick," Harv said, thrusting a meaty hand in the boy's face. "Shake, kiddo."

Francis, intimidated by the man's size and personality, slowly stuck out his hand. Harv's hand engulfed it and then squeezed until he saw Francis wince. "Glad to meet you, Khan. You're a hell of a BBS fighter. Here, put your arm around my neck and let me get you out of this sardine can."

Hesitantly, Francis did as he was told. A second later, Harv was holding him in his fat, but muscular, arms as if he weighed little more than a baby.

"Got that wheelchair ready yet, Pops?" Harv said loudly.

Grandfather, his old eyes squinted into slits, nodded, turning down the stainless-steel latch that locked the wheelchair into open position. *"Hai,"* he said.

"Hi yourself," Harv answered, lowering the boy into the

wheelchair. Then he looked at Fuchan, who was openly staring at him.

"Whatcha staring at, Wu?" Harv asked.

"I'm sorry," Fuchan answered, embarrassed, lowering her eyes.

Another car drove up and parked two places to the right of them.

Watching Tom Barnslow get out of the car was like observing a large water bird preparing for flight. First one long leg came out of the car, bent at the knee. It extended, and a second later, the second leg, bent at the knee, came out. Then a long, thin torso, bent at the waist, stretched from under the roof of the car.

When all six-feet-three-inches were clear, Tom stood up, placed his nervous hands on the top of the still-open door, and looked around.

"Hi, Fuchan," he mumbled, looking at the asphalt.

"Tom!" Fuchan said happily, glad his arrival had broken the awkward moment with Tunnel Rat. She rushed across the open parking spaces and took him by the hand. "Come on, I want you to meet our friends."

"This is Francis Schonrath, my grandfather Hiro Nomasaki, and Dennis Conlick," Fuchan said a few seconds later. "And this is Tom Barnslow. He's The Chief Cutter—the sysop of The Surgery."

Francis, who was feeling jealous for the first time in his life, stared openly at Tom. "You posted that your name was Bob Hughes," Francis challenged, "not Tom Barnsdoo."

"Barnslow," Tom corrected, taking a deep breath. "My real name's Tom Barnslow. Bob Hughes was a fake name I used to sucker all of you into giving me your real names. I was too involved in the game, and I made a mistake. I'm sorry," he mumbled.

"One lie make man little," Grandfather said, bowing to Tom, "but one truth make man big. I am Hiro Nomasaki."

"Glad to meet you, sir," Tom replied, awkwardly returning the bow. "Fuchan told me a lot about you."

"She did?" Francis said, looking possessively at Fuchan. "When did you do that?"

"Yesterday when I met Tom," Fuchan said, smiling so innocently at Francis that his building anger was swept from him. "I told him all about Grandfather and all about you and what a great time we had at the zoo and what a great time we've been having on the telephone talking voice."

Harv stood like a dormant volcano and watched this interchange between the three Surgeons with amused interest.

"I've got a blanket spread out across the street," Harv said when there was a pause in the conversation. "Let's go plop our bottoms on it."

"I wonder where Meat Grinder is?" Tom asked Fuchan and Francis as they crossed the asphalt and sidewalk and then went over to the blanket, where they sat down.

"Yeah, he was going to bring the food," Francis said.

"Yes," Tom mumbled. "Said he was going to bring hot dogs and hamburgers and something to cook them on."

"Maybe The Succubus got him," Harv said softly, watching the old man, whose eyes had been downcast ever since their introduction.

Hiro Nomasaki looked up from where he was sitting cross-legged on the blanket.

"Ah yes," he said, "Succubus-san. Great coward."

"Why do you say that, Pops?" Harv asked, suddenly uncomfortable as the old man's glistening black eyes seemed to drill right through him.

"He's an asshole," Francis said, reverting to BBS language, "and if he ever gets the guts to play war on the boards, I'll destroy him."

Grandfather continued to stare through Harv.

"Well, I'm not going to sit here and starve to death," Harv said, groaning as he got to his feet. "I'm gonna go get some grub. Cutter, why don't you come with me?"

Tom suddenly looked very uncomfortable. There was something about the Tunnel Rat that he didn't like. He knew the guy was probably as lonely as he was and was just trying to make friends, but, darn it, the guy came on too strong. "I, uh, I . . ."

"I go with Tunnel Rat," Grandfather interrupted.

Rising in one fluid motion from his cross-legged position on the blanket, eighty-two-year-old Hiro Nomasaki, all five-feet-three-inches of him, looked up at Harv.

There was an odd silence within the circle of people around the blanket, the uncomfortable silence that falls when someone has just committed a serious faux pas or when an argument is about to erupt.

They all looked at Harv.

"No, Pops," Harv said, thinking rapidly, as this was not part of his plan. "I'm afraid I need someone a little younger than you to help me carry the food. You look like a good breeze would blow you right back to China."

"It's all right, Mr. Nomasaki," Tom said, standing and putting his hand gently on the old man's shoulder. "I'll go."

Hiro stared again into Harv's eyes. He could sense the evil spirit in the huge man's body, the same spirit that had been distracting his *zazen* for the past week.

"No go store," Hiro said, reaching into his pocket and pulling out several bills. "Buy food over there." He pointed to the snack bar on the river side of the butterfly.

"Hey, that's a great idea," Tom said enthusiastically, seeing a good way out of being alone with Tunnel Rat. "Put your money away, Mr. Nomasaki. The food's on me. I've got lots of money. And this'll make up for my lying to all of you. Come on, Dennis," he said, touching the obese man's elbow. He immediately pulled his hand away, his fingers feeling as if he had just touched a soft jellyfish rotting on a beach. Trying not to shudder, Tom said, "Let's get the food over there."

Stymied, Harv let his guard down a bit and returned the old man's stare. Then he turned without answering and walked across the street.

Tom shrugged and smiled at the rest of them and followed Harv.

"Damn," Francis said, "he's even weirder in real life than he is on the boards. Tunnel Rat, I mean. Cutter seems to be okay."

"I wonder where Meat Grinder is," Fuchan asked. "This

was his idea. I hope he didn't get in a car wreck or something."

"Meat Grinder not come," Grandfather said flatly.

"What do you mean, Mr. Nomasaki?" Francis asked, feeling a shiver of fear at the tone in the old man's voice.

"He not come. He is sleeping, maybe dead."

"Grandfather! What do you mean?" Fuchan asked, her face stricken and frightened at the same time.

"Bad thing here," the old man said. "We go now."

"But, but we just got here," Francis said, "and I, we . . ." He looked at Fuchan, who was looking at her grandfather. "Fuchan, talk to him," Francis said. "I don't want to go home yet."

"Grandf . . ." Fuchan started to say. But he looked at her, and she knew it would be easier to change the course of the Mississippi than it would be to argue with him. "No, Francis, we should go now. If Grandfather says to go, we must go."

"Well, I'm not going anywhere," Francis said peevishly. "I don't get out very often and I'm sure in hell not going to leave because some old man tells me that bad things . . ." Then Francis looked at Hiro Nomasaki's incredibly wrinkled face and his coal-black eyes, which had a slight twinkle in them.

"Great Khan has temper like hot flame," Grandfather said gently, "and is spoiled like American child. Japanese children not talk about elders like disrespectful Khan, yes?"

Francis stared into the old man's eyes and saw nothing but kindness and love for him there.

"I'm sorry, Mr. Nomasaki," Francis said, "if you want us to go, let's go."

"Hai," Grandfather replied and put his hands on the back of the boy's wheelchair and wheeled him across the street, his granddaughter walking by his side.

Tom and Harv, standing in line at the snack bar on the river side of the butterfly, didn't see what was happening. And Tom was beginning to think that Dennis wasn't such a bad guy after all. A few minutes ago, when Dennis had enthusiastically started describing the computer equipment he had back in his apartment, Tom's opinion of the man had started to change.

Grandfather had Fuchan slide into the back seat first. He then lifted Francis in and pushed down the lock buttons on both doors on the passenger side. He broke down the wheelchair and put it in the trunk, then locked the other doors.

He handed Fuchan the keys. "No open door until I come back," he ordered. "No open door for anyone but me. Yes?"

"But Grandfather . . ."

"No argue, please. Do as I say, yes?"

She nodded, taking the keys in her hand.

He closed the door and made sure it was locked.

Then he started walking around the butterfly.

Wednesday, October 23rd, 6:17 P.M.

Mary Alice Sluice sat by her phone in her house, staring at it.

Dennis's number was imbedded in her memory, and three times now she had started to dial it. Each time, she had lowered the receiver before making a connection.

"This is absurd," she said aloud. "You're acting like a teenager who's calling for a first date."

She looked around her bedroom, surveying the furniture she had added over the last couple of years.

If I call him, she thought, I'm beginning something I'm not sure I want to begin. I can't call him and then back off like I did last night. If I call him, I'm going to get involved with him. Do I really want that?

She thought about the long, lonely nights over the past years, then picked up the phone and dialed a fourth time. When she finished punching in the seven numbers, she took a deep breath and waited. After a couple of seconds, a busy signal came through.

"Busy," she said disgustedly. "Wouldn't you know it?" She sighed, dropping the receiver back onto the plastic cradle.

Pacing the bedroom, she thought about von Neumann's final words, words that she had attributed to her emotional state at the time. Unfortunately, the videotape camera microphone had not picked up those soft words. And she hadn't mentioned them to anyone else on the project, afraid that they would have rejected them out of hand.

He couldn't have said it, she thought, it's impossible. But it was also impossible for a chain link to split the way she had seen in von Neumann's cage.

Wednesday, October 23rd, 6:19 P.M.

The small Japanese man walked up to Harv and tapped him on the elbow.

To Harv, it felt like someone had driven an ice pick through the bone, and he pulled back from the touch.

"We go now," Hiro Nomasaki said. He turned and looked at Tom. "You go too."

"I don't understand," Tom Barnslow said, "we just got here. What're you going for?"

"Great evil here," Grandfather said, staring fearlessly at Harv, who looked down at him disdainfully.

"I don't understand," Tom said.

"This man has become death," Hiro Nomasaki said, bowing at Harv.

"Screw it," Harv said, modifying his original plan on the spot. "If the crazy old Japper wants to split, let him split. Go on, Pops, take a walk. Real nice meeting you. See you soon, you hear?"

Hiro Nomasaki didn't blink but continued to meet Harv's eyes.

"I said I'd see you soon," Harv repeated, the challenge in his voice quite obvious now.

"Hai," Grandfather said softly but forcefully from his abdomen, bowing his head in acceptance of what was to come, knowing that the next time he met this huge man that he would have to take his stand.

Hiro kept his position until Harv acknowledged him by inclining his huge head.

"You go now," Hiro said to Tom. "Better you go. Death dances in this man."

Harv snorted.

Tom looked at Nomasaki, then at Harv.

"Up to you, Tom. Go with them or else stay with me and we'll shoot the bull about computers. Looks to me like the girl's got the hots for the cripple anyway."

Tom's forehead crinkled as he considered that idea. "I'm going to stay with Dennis," he said.

Hiro Nomasaki bowed sadly to Tom before he walked away on the balls of his feet, graceful as a young antelope.

"What was that all about?" Tom asked, his curiosity stirred.

"Beats the hell out of me . . . crazy old nip," Harv answered. "Well, since the picnic's such a bust, why don't we go over to my pad? We can grab a bite to eat there and I can show you my Macintosh and that voice-recognition program I was telling you about. Who needs those jerks?"

"Yeah," Tom said, angry with Fuchan for leaving so soon. "Why not? That sounds like fun. Computers are more interesting than people anyway."

"I think you'll get a real kick out of my equipment," Harv said, turning away, grinning fiercely.

Wednesday, October 23rd, 6:39 P.M.

Dennis sat by his computer, impatient for the file transfer to be completed. He looked at his watch. Even at 9600-baud, it would be after nine o'clock before all of the material would be safe in his hard drive. He thought about going out for a bite to eat but decided against it. If there was a protocol problem, he would need to be here to restart the transfer if necessary.

Wonder what the general's thinking, Dennis pondered, knowing that his old boss in army intelligence would find sitting still and watching a computer screen for almost four hours a major drag.

At the main lab, the director wasn't as bored as Dennis

thought. When Dennis had explained to him how long the transfer of two megs worth of information would take, the director had left the lab and had visited Al's Newsstand, where he'd purchased twenty dollars' worth of magazines. At the moment, his small feet propped up on the table next to the VAX, the director was thumbing through the latest issue of *Penthouse.* "God," he muttered, looking at one of the pictures, "what's happening to the moral fiber of America?"

Wednesday, October 23rd, 6:48 P.M.

"Does Great Khan want more food?" Hiro Nomasaki asked.

Francis spun on the revolving stool at the counter of the Camillia Grill on Carrollton Avenue, where Grandfather had taken him and Fuchan for supper.

"Gosh no, Mr. Nomasaki, I couldn't eat another bite," Francis said. "That was the best omelet I ever had."

"Wu?" Hiro asked, glancing at his granddaughter, who was on his other side.

"I'm stuffed too, Grandfather," she answered.

"I haven't spun on a stool in a long time," Francis said, using his good hand pressed against the side of the counter to turn himself in a semicircle, something he'd been doing ever since Hiro had lifted him up on the stool.

"Balance very good," Hiro complimented. "See, no legs no matter, yes?"

"Well, they matter, Mr. Nomasaki," Francis answered thoughtfully, "but I'm starting to accept the fact that I'm going to have to learn to live without them."

"*Hai,* very good!" Hiro stated loudly. "Great Khan fast learner like Wu." He stroked his granddaughter's hair fondly.

"May I ask a question, Grandfather?" Fuchan said, looking up shyly at the old man.

He frowned slightly, sensing what was coming. "Questions bad, no end to questions," he said, giving her his stock answer for when she was about to ask something he didn't want to answer or something he thought she should learn for herself.

"Why did we leave the picnic, Grandfather? Why did you say that stuff about Meat Grinder?"

The old man looked at her, his eyes sad and deep.

"We bring Khan home now," he said.

Wednesday, October 23rd, 6:53 P.M.

His voice full of excitement, Tom stared at Harv's computer lab, and gushed, "I can't believe this place. God, you've got equipment here that I've only dreamed about."

"Thanks," Harv said, pleased by the boy's enthusiasm. It wasn't often that he ran into anyone as totally computer-impassioned as himself, and Tom's reaction had tempered for the moment his plan for him.

"Sit down and take a load off," Harv said, motioning to the recliner. "I'll get us something to drink."

"Sounds great, Dennis."

Harv flinched slightly as he walked into the kitchen. For the first time in a long time, he was experiencing guilt about deceiving someone. The innocence of this kid was quite remarkable, and, for an instant, Harv thought about taking him under his wing

Returning with the bottles of cold sparkling water, Harv put them on the table by the recliner and then locked the lab. He pocketed the keys.

"Hope you're not upset about me posting that I lived in the Quarter," Harv said, dragging a computer chair into the center of the room so he could face the boy in the recliner.

"Of course not. You didn't lie nearly as much as I did."

"Well, actually, I did," Harv said, slowly putting his Perrier down on a cork coaster.

Tom's eyebrows raised a bit.

"Look, Tom, don't get upset because I like you, man, and I'm going to tell you the truth. Okay?"

Tom's face turned wary.

"Okay," he said slowly.

"I'm not Tunnel Rat. My real name's Harv Webster."

Tom thought rapidly, the list of the Surgeons rushing through his mind. Then he frowned. "I don't understand."

"I'm The Succubus."

Tom's eyes suddenly turned scared and he spilled a bit of Perrier water on his LaCoste shirt.

"Relax. I'm not going to hurt you. I like you, man. You're a cool guy. I'm comfortable with you. It was just a game."

"Yeah, but you threatened to destroy The Surgery. That's no game. You don't know how much that board means to me."

"I do. Now that I've gotten a chance to know you, I know just what that board means to you. It means to you what my lab means to me."

Tom nodded. "Yes, yes, that's true."

"I'm going to level with you. I'm a lonely guy. I've got a great mind for computers, but I've never been worth squat with people. I've always been, well, I've always looked like this. It's glandular. And kids made fun of me when I was in school and I developed this, shoot, I don't know, this shell or something that kind of protected me, you know what I mean?"

"Yeah," Tom answered, thinking about his own experiences with other people. Except for Fuchan and now Harv, he'd never really had a friend. And Fuchan had just dumped him at the picnic.

"Do you forgive me for all that Succubus stuff?" Harv asked.

"Sure, sure I do," Tom said, offering his hand.

Harv rolled the computer chair a little closer and shook hands with the young man.

"Friends?" Harv inquired.

"Friends," Tom answered.

Wednesday, October 23rd, 7:15 P.M.

Mary Alice finished her dinner, washed the dishes, bathed, and then tried Dennis Conlick's number again. It was still busy.

"Damn," she muttered.

She sat down at her computer and booted her spreadsheet program. Sticking a disk in the second drive, she quickly started to lose herself in all the data she had taken on von Neumann in the more than two years the lab had had the chimp.

Wednesday, October 23rd, 7:23 P.M.

"It's a remarkable piece of work," Tom told Harv. "The best voice-recognition program I've ever heard."

"Took me years to get it refined to this point," Harv said proudly. "I'm pretty happy with it."

"I'm glad you're happy, Harv," Teresa said through the speakers in the corners.

"Neat," Tom said. His eyes passed across one of the shelves above the counter across the room. "You sure have a lot of books. Which one's your favorite? Except for computer manuals, I don't read."

Harv removed a book from one of the shelves and tossed it to Tom, who fumbled the catch. After picking it up off the carpet, he looked at the expensive, leather-bound volume. "The Collected Works of St. John of the Cross," Tom read aloud. "Don't know it. Who is he?"

"The deepest Christian mystic," Harv answered. "Fascinating reading. He was hassled by the Spanish Inquisition, but he refused to play their game. He gives the most perfect directions ever given for finding God."

"Hmmm," Tom said. "Well, I'm not very religious. Religion's not logical."

"I'm not religious in the sense of church-going either," Harv said, suddenly very serious, his eyes fixed on the reproduction of Christ on the cross, "but I've always believed in a consciousness that exists outside the human ken. Christ was in touch with that consciousness, and so was St. John. I used to think that if you followed his directions, you could get in touch with God, too. That's why I read him. That's why I've tried to follow his directions. Before I became God."

"Before you . . ." Tom said hesitantly, put off by the zealotry in his new friend's remark. Tom tapped the cover of the book. "What does he tell you to do to get in touch with, to find this consciousness?"

"I'm glad you find this interesting," Harv said. "It's a subject . . ."

"It's very interesting, Harv," Teresa said, responding to the key word.

"Listening mode only, Teresa," Harv snapped. "See, there's still a few flaws in the program. Anyway, St. John is big on self-denial."

Tom laughed.

"What are you laughing at?" Harv asked, the smile gone from his face in an instant.

"Well," Tom answered, still chuckling, "this isn't the room of someone who's denying himself much." His hands spread out to include the thousands of dollars' worth of computer equipment. "Hey, no offense."

Harv's irritated look softened. "Yeah, I guess you're right. But he's not talking about that kind of denial. He's talking about physical denial and self-punishment."

Tom's face looked blank.

"You know. Stuff like sex and gluttony. Greed, the deadly sins."

"You don't look like you spare yourself any food," Tom said unthinkingly.

"I can't help this!" Harv shouted. "You think I like looking like this? You think I stuff my face to look like this? Hell, man, I probably eat less than you do."

"God, I'm sorry," Tom said, embarrassed. "I didn't mean to say that."

"Think before you open your mouth then," Harv snapped. In the back of his mind, a single word formed: betrayal. "You're not going to betray me too, are you? You're not going to be like the others I tried to make friends with who stabbed me in the back, are you?"

Tom shook his head rapidly, suddenly very much ill at ease. "God, no. I just spoke without thinking. I'm sorry. Really, I'm sorry. I like you. I think what you've done here is, well, it's magnificent. I want to be your friend. I want to learn from you."

Harv's florid face gradually returned to normal. "I'm glad to hear you say that. I'd hate to find out that you were like the others on the team."

"What's that equipment over there?" Tom asked, anxious now to change the subject.

"Over where?"

"Over there by the other IBM," Tom answered, pointing at the two prototypes of the Zeus connector.

"Those are the only two Zeus connectors on this planet," Harv said. "I designed and built them."

"Interesting name," Tom replied, lowering the recliner to its upright position and standing up. "Can I look?"

"Sure." As the young man walked across the room, Harv took off his stocking cap. His fingers scratched the small scabs on the top of his head.

Tom held one of the connectors in his hands. It was almost as light as stereo headphones. "What is it?" he asked. "A new kind of Walkman?"

Harv laughed and Tom turned to look at his new friend. He was shocked to see the glistening scalp.

"God, what happened to your hair?" he asked.

"I shaved it," Harv answered. "You can't hook up to the connector with hair. I haven't refined the sensors enough to do that yet. Working on it, but no luck so far."

"Not many teenagers are going to buy this if they have to shave their heads," Tom quipped. He held the device up to the light and looked at it more carefully. "I don't see any speakers."

"There aren't any. It's not a Walkman."

"What is it then?"

"It connects you to God," Harv whispered.

Wednesday, October 23rd, 8:15 P.M.

"I had a great time, Fuchan," Francis said on the phone, putting a period on the half-hour conversation they'd just completed. "But before I hang up, can I speak to your grandfather for a moment."

"Sure," Fuchan answered. "And I'm glad you came. We'll get together again soon. Maybe this weekend. You can come over and we'll play chess. I've written this great chess algorithm, and I'd like you to try it out."

"Sounds good," Francis said.

"Okay, good night. I'll get Grandfather now. Just a sec."

She placed the phone on her desk next to her IBM and went into the living room, where Grandfather was sitting in a straight-backed chair reading *The Sutra of Hui Neng*.

"I'm sorry to disturb you, Grandfather, but Francis wants to talk with you."

Hiro looked up and nodded.

"I'm going to take a bath," Fuchan said.

He smiled.

In Fuchan's room, he picked up the phone.

"Great Khan has words of wisdom for old man?" Hiro Nomasaki asked.

"Great Khan has words of apology for adopted Grandfather," Francis said softly.

"*Hai*, don't understand."

"Mr. Nomasaki, I'm sorry about those nasty things I said to you at the river. You're right. I am spoiled, and I was wrong to say what I said. I've been feeling bad about it. I just, well, I just wanted to tell you because I want you to like me."

Grandfather smiled. "Next to Wu, Khan is favorite child," the old man said. "Now forget quick words. They are gone, like smoke in wind, yes?"

"Yes, sir," Francis said, smiling broadly. "Thanks, Mr. Nomasaki. You make me feel a lot better."

"Sleep with clouds, Khan," Hiro said, adding, "good night."

"Good night, Grandfather," Francis said tentatively.

"Good night, Grandson," Hiro answered, smiling.

Wednesday, October 23rd, 9:02 P.M.

Tom looked up from the IBM monitor, where he was reading an introductory overview of a file entitled WEB-STER CONNECTION, Harv's compilation of every bit of information regarding the Zeus project, including his up-to-date schematics and the most recent version of the Zeus program and Cogglin's debugged Athena hypothesis.

"I don't understand much of this," Tom said, "but what I follow gives me chills."

Harv sat in the recliner and smiled. "Well, you've just read a précis of the entire project," he said. "I put it together for the book I'm going to write about the connection. It'll be more important than the Bible."

Tom lifted the smaller prototype again. "Does it work? Can it really interface a brain with a computer?"

"You want to try it?" Harv asked.

"Do you mean it?"

"Sure."

"You bet I do," Tom said, his grin wide.

"Okay, follow me."

Harv unlocked the lab and they walked into his living room. "The bathroom's that way," Harv said, pointing. "Go on in there. You'll find a pair of scissors in the bottom drawer."

"Scissors? What do I need scissors for."

"I can't shave your head until you cut most of your hair off, man."

Tom weighed for just a second the choice of being bald and trying the connector or of changing his mind.

"Bottom drawer," he said. "Got it."

Harv walked through the open door of the bathroom a few minutes later, two fresh bottles of Perrier in his right hand. He put one of the drinks down on the sink counter. "Good, I'm glad to see you're not a slob," he said, pleased that Tom was putting the clumps of hair he was removing in the plastic trash can and not dropping them on the floor.

"I hate slobs," Tom said. "I like things orderly."

"Me too," Harv said, happy to find yet another similarity with his new friend. He put down the cover on the toilet and sat down slowly, lowering his weight carefully. He brought the bottle of Perrier water to his thick lips and drank deeply.

"You know," Harv said a few minutes later, "I always wanted a brother."

"Yeah?" Tom answered, turning around and looking at Harv. "I always did too."

"What about your parents? What are they like?"

"My mom died when I was a kid. Dad's okay, I guess, but I don't see him much. He's always off making deals somewhere else. He thinks I'm weird."

"Rich, huh?"

"Filthy. He says he loves me, but . . ."

"I know what you mean."

"Are your folks still alive?"

"I killed them."

Tom's hand stopped in midair just as he was about to clip off another chunk of hair. "You're kidding me, I hope."

"What's the matter, Tom, couldn't you be friends with someone who killed his parents?" Harv asked, his eyes narrowing. Tom watched Harv's face as it was reflected in the mirror.

"I don't know," he answered honestly. "You're putting me on, aren't you?"

"Yeah," Harv replied, suddenly grinning broadly. "Do I look like the kind of guy who would kill off his parents?"

"Maybe," Tom said, smiling weakly.

"That's the right answer, man," Harv said.

Chapter
~~~~~~~
15

Wednesday, October 23rd, 9:07 P.M.

"Squirt a little more on there," Harv said, continuing to strop his stainless-steel straight-edge razor as Tom spread another blot of shaving cream on the top of his head. "Yeah, that's perfect," he said a moment later. "Okay, hold still now. Wouldn't want to slit your throat by accident."

Tom gulped and kept his head very, very still.

"You're going to look like one of those Hare Krishnas running around with a bald head," Harv said as he scraped the blade across the top of Tom's head, "but it's worth it. In a few minutes you'll have an experience like you've never had before."

"I can't wait," Tom mumbled between clenched teeth, intent on keeping immobile, watching in the mirror as Harv shaved his head.

Wednesday, October 23rd, 9:16 P.M.

Dennis broke the connection with the lab's VAX and looked at the hard drive on his worktable. It now contained two megs of encrypted information that could, if the Zeus project was what he thought it was, literally change the way things worked. If the team had indeed established a mind-computer link, as the director had hinted that morning, then almost every aspect of modern life would be touched in one way or another.

Just thinking about the possibilities sent a shiver through him.

He knew he needed to get to work on the problem immediately. Though encryption was fascinating, breaking an encryption scheme sometimes took months. It was the sort of challenge Dennis enjoyed because he could get so lost in it.

At the moment, however, he didn't want to get lost in a computer project.

After turning off his modem, he punched the buttons for Mary Alice's phone number. She answered on the third ring.

"It's Dennis," he said, "how are you?"

There was a pause from her end. "You sound different tonight," she said.

"I am different. Pulled myself out of a big hole today."

"You want to talk about it?"

"Yes. But not on a phone."

"I don't understand."

"I want to meet you."

"I'm on Fountainbleu Avenue," she said, "703 Fountainbleu. Small house. Third from the corner. Can you come now?"

"I'll be there as soon as I can get a cab," he said.

"Say chimpanzee when you come. See you soon, then," she said, lowering the phone.

Dennis hung up, puzzled by what she had just said, and then immediately redialed to have a cab sent to his apartment house.

Dennis went into his bathroom and ran a comb through his shaggy hair. "Months past time for a trim," he said.

As he grabbed his windbreaker and put his hand on the

door, he looked at the computer and hard drive and thought for just a second about the encryption problem.

"It'll keep," he said.

He opened the door and walked out.

Wednesday, October 23rd, 9:31 P.M.

"Look," Harv said, holding the prototype reverently in his huge hands. "I've beefed up the gain on this since the last time I tested it, and I want to make the connection first. After we try it on me, then you get your turn. Okay? If something goes wrong, I'd rather it happen to me than to you."

He sat down in the recliner.

"Sure, that's fine," Tom replied, an edge of disappointment in his voice.

"Okay," Harv said. "Now, here, help me get these needles in. It's kind of hard to do by yourself. Just slip them in under the epidermal layer. They don't have to go down to bone."

Tom inserted the microneedles, wincing as he pushed each one into Harv's skin.

"Don't be a baby," Harv said.

A few minutes later, all of the electrodes were in place.

"Now what?" Tom asked the huge man sitting in the recliner.

"Just like I showed you. Type the command and hit the return key. That'll run the Zeus program and initialize the connection."

Tom walked over to the IBM's keyboard. He entered the command Harv had told him to type.

"Wait," Tom said, "wait just a second. Tell me what I can expect."

"It's better that I don't," Harv answered. "That way we can compare notes when you break the connection. You're the first person in the world to observe the Webster connection, and when it's over I want an unbiased report of what you saw happen."

"Webster connection? I thought it was called the Zeus connection?"

"That's the director's name for it. This is the name it really deserves since I've done all the important work. Nobody's going to take the credit for my ideas ever again."

"I don't understand," Tom said.

"Look, do you want to shoot the bull all night or do you want to try this?" Harv asked, getting impatient.

"Try it," Tom said. "But I'm scared."

"Relax. It's wonderful, unlike anything you could possibly imagine. Go ahead, start the program."

Tom's index finger pressed the return key on the IBM and the Zeus program started to run.

As usual, Harv felt a tingling at the back of his head, the sort of feeling that comes when jerking out of sleep after having a dream about falling. It was decidedly unpleasant. Then lights of all the colors of the spectrum exploded inside his mind, which had become a huge cavern. It was like standing deep in a pitch-dark cave and looking out through the entrance, a long distance away, at a single star.

And then he was moving, all sense of balance obliterated, spinning, revolving, twisting, and the star was rushing at him with the intensity of a diesel locomotive.

He hit the light, was absorbed by it. His eyes, which had unconsciously closed, snapped open. He saw Tom sitting at the computer chair, watching him carefully.

"What're you seeing?" Tom asked, and the words reverberated in Harv's head as if coming from an echo chamber. The sound of Tom's voice was harsh and abnormally loud.

"Not so loud," he whispered, his own voice sounding like a shout to him.

Tom lowered his voice: "What do you see?"

Harv looked at the IBM, and he was the IBM. He became a single electron shooting through the various gates of the circuitry at the speed of light. He closed his eyes—the experience was too intense—but closing them did not stop the vision. He raced toward the central processing unit of the powerful computer.

Suddenly He was there.

Tom saw a look of wonder cross the man's face, which seemed to age years in a matter of seconds.

"What do you see?" Tom asked.

Harv's eyes slowly, fearfully, opened. A part of him was separating from the connection, screaming to him that what was happening couldn't be happening. He looked at the blank monitor.

Harv visualized the program that was running in the computer coming onto the screen.

And it was there, scrolling across the monitor too quickly to be followed by the human eye.

Harv felt like he could do anything now, that all barriers and limitations had been completely ripped away. He felt his mind growing, expanding exponentially outward.

Tom turned in the computer chair and looked at the cathode-ray tube.

The machine had dropped into the monitor, and now the Zeus program's code was scrolling past at an unbelievable speed.

And then the display cleared.

A single dot of light appeared in the very center of the screen. It grew in intensity, and then it exploded, flinging out from it thousands of other dots, like a heavy blanket suddenly being lifted to reveal a brilliant night sky.

A feeling of utter peace surged through Harv, and he felt weightless. His eyes rolled in his head.

"I am God," said the being that Harv had become, his eyes opening and staring into and through Tom, through the walls of the lab, through the apartment, through the very center of Mother Earth herself.

When he saw that horrible smile, Tom pressed the keys to disable the running of the Zeus program.

At that second, Harv felt as if a pickax had slammed into his chest.

His right hand flew up to his mouth, and he bit down on the fleshy part of his thumb to keep from screaming.

"Turn it back on," he gasped. "Turn it back on."

"No, that's enough," Tom said, his voice shaking.

"Turn it back on!" Harv shouted, his eyes rolling wildly in his head.

"No, it's too scary, something's not right!" Tom shouted back, rushing to the recliner. He put his hands on Harv's head to remove the electrodes.

"Turn it back on, damn it!" Harv ordered, his eyes filled with tears.

"Easy there, easy," Tom said, gently trying to reassure his new friend by patting him on the shoulders.

Harv's hands clutched at the front of Tom's shirt, ripping two buttons off. "You've got to turn it back on!" he shouted.

Tom slapped Harv's right cheek a hard, quick blow with his open palm.

The man's face jerked sideways.

Tears flowed from his tightly closed eyes. He sobbed uncontrollably, deep, rasping sobs coming from the depths of his being.

"Stop it!" Tom shouted.

Harv sobbed even harder, completely out of control. Then his huge body jerked in the chair as if hundreds of volts of electricity were passing through it. The recliner rocked, threatening to fall on its side.

Tom slapped Harv again. And again. And again.

Suddenly the man's obese body was still, paralyzed in a fetal rigor so complete his flesh felt like smooth, cold, water-aged stone.

"What's happening?" Tom shouted.

The air in the man's body escaped from his slightly parted lips in one long, slow, seemingly endless hiss.

Wednesday, October 23rd, 9:51 P.M.

Dennis paid the cab driver and walked quickly up the sidewalk to the front door of Mary Alice's house. He nervously put his hands in the pockets of his pants and just as quickly pulled them out again.

He rang the doorbell.

A few seconds later he heard footsteps.

"Dennis?"

"It's me," he replied.

"What did I tell you to say when I hung up a bit ago?" she asked through the locked door.

"Chimpanzee," he said, opening the screen door.

He heard her unlatch the chain and watched as the deadbolt withdrew from the space between the door and the frame.

She opened the door.

"What was that all about? By the way, I think I've fallen in love with you," Dennis said, smiling awkwardly, looking at Nelly Dean for the first time. She was everything he had imagined and more.

Her mouth opened but no words came out.

Their eyes locked together, and the same emotion swept through both of them.

She stepped back and gestured for him to enter.

He did so.

A second later, she was in his arms, holding him so tight he could barely catch his breath.

Wednesday, October 23rd, 9:57 P.M.

Tom removed the tips of his two fingers from Harv's fleshy throat. There was no pulse.

"Oh boy, now what do I do?" Tom mumbled, and for no reason a picture of Fuchan's grandfather suddenly came to mind.

He walked over to the IBM and turned it off.

He sat down in the computer chair, his body sagging with fear.

"He's dead," Tom said aloud, as if voicing the fact would finally make it real enough for him to do something. He knew he had to take some kind of action, but he couldn't think of what.

He turned the chair on its swivel and stared at the monitor, his eyes wide with shock.

Behind him, Harv's eyes suddenly popped open.

His huge body uncurled on the smooth leather of the recliner.

Silently, like a great python.

His arms spread wide and stretched.

He stood up and took several silent steps until he was standing just behind Tom.

Suddenly the young man felt cold fleshy thumbs on the back of his neck.

"I am God," Harv said, stroking Tom's jugular veins with his thick fingers.

Wednesday, October 23rd, 11:08 P.M.

Dennis sipped from the delicate porcelain cup, his finger barely able to fit into the thin ceramic of the curved handle.

"So, you see, Al Cogglin and I both served under the general in Intelligence in Vietnam for almost a year. Then I started getting kind of weird and asked for a transfer into the Tunnel Rat unit."

"Why on earth would you want that?" she asked.

"Good coffee," he said, holding the cup between his hands. "That's a long story, the story of my life, which I hope you'll now help me write. But, at its heart, was . . . and this'll sound crazy, I think, but at its heart was boredom."

"Joining one of the most dangerous units in the war because you were bored does sound a little crazy," she said.

"Well, I also had to prove some macho things to myself," Dennis responded, his eyes bright. "But the prime mover was boredom. Working for the general I got to do a lot of interesting things with computers and ciphers, but the war was happening outside, and there I was riding a chair in a concrete bunker with Al Cogglin and two other computer geeks breaking codes. I mean, it was fascinating working with those brainy guys, but, God, was it a drag."

Mary Alice nodded. Having worked with a team of similar men for the past three years, she knew just what he meant.

"So that's how my connection with the general got

started. He liked me because I got things done and because I knew how to keep my mouth shut." Dennis looked deep into Mary Alice's eyes. "You probably won't believe this, but I've never talked to anyone as long as I've talked to you tonight."

She covered his hand with both of hers.

A smile crossed his face.

"You knew Nelly but didn't know me."

"Well, I kind of knew you too, but I didn't know you were Nelly, if that makes any sense. You see, during the first month of the project, I ran extensive security checks on all of you for the general. Took a peek in some data banks that people aren't supposed to look into. Couple other things for him, like gathering some necessary material that wasn't publicly available. Stuff like that. Then I didn't hear from him again about anything to do with the project until the other night when he had me sweep the lab for bugs. Then, bam, he dumped this encryption problem on me this morning. Other than that, I've done a few minor things for some of his friends. He's got a lot of contacts with a lot of people, does a lot of favors and asks a lot of favors. That's the way men like him work—and it's why they get things done. He's what we called a *bottom-liner* in the service."

"And you're his electronic Sherlock Holmes," she observed.

"More like his beagle dog," Dennis corrected. "Don't get me wrong. I respect the general, but I don't particularly like him. He uses people."

"I've noticed that," Mary Alice replied.

She sipped her coffee thoughtfully. Then, looking at him over the top of her cup, she asked, "Dennis, just how much do you understand about what we're trying to do with the project and what we've accomplished?"

He thought for a moment before answering. "Between what I've read today of the original Zeus extract and from what the general told me this morning, it's obvious you're trying to establish a link, an interface, between the human brain and a computer. As for what you've accomplished, I don't know for sure since the general was evasive, but I assume something big has happened or else he wouldn't have me trying to crack the encryption problem." He raised an eyebrow at her. "Yes?"

She laughed. "Oh, you're a burrower all right," she said, lightly touching the hairs on the back of his hand. Then, seriously: "We have a working model of the Zeus connector which we've successfully used to interface a chimpanzee with a computerized robot."

"Good God," Dennis said, lowering his coffee cup and almost breaking the saucer.

"Careful with that cup," she warned, winking, "but that's not the best of it."

"No?"

"No. It's my theory that the connector not only interfaces brain tissue with computer circuitry but that it also enhances intelligence." And she then proceeded to tell him everything that had happened with von Neumann.

When she finished, Dennis was standing up, wandering around her kitchen. He stopped at the light switch, which he turned off and on a couple of times.

"Sorry about that," he said when he realized what he was doing and saw her puzzled look. "It's a bad habit I have when I'm thinking."

"Is it possible? Could the connector do something like that?" she asked. "I don't know enough about hardware to really say."

"I'd say it was impossible," Dennis answered, "knowing what I know about the current state of neural networking, but then I don't know what kinds of breakthroughs your hardware-and-software people have made. If Al Cogglin's been doing the programming, anything's possible. He's really bright."

"Yes, and Harv makes him look like a moron. Harv's the only legitimate genius I think I've ever met," she said, shuddering slightly. "He's a genius but a very disturbed human being."

"Tell me about him," Dennis said, pouring himself another cup of coffee and sitting back down at the small table.

"Okay. I need to go back three years ago when I first joined the project. The director threw a team party so we could get to know each other on a less formal basis, and . . ."

Wednesday, October 23rd, 11:30 P.M.

In his lab, Harv stood before Tom Barnslow, who sat, unmoving, on the recliner.

"You will be my first disciple, Tom," Harv said, his voice unnaturally deep and rich. "Together we will share the truth through the Webster connection with others. A select few at first, but we will grow, quietly, underground, spreading slowly but inexorably. And the boy in the bedroom will be second. Now I see why He told me to spare his life."

"I still don't understand," Tom protested, starting to get out of the recliner. "What boy in the bedroom?"

Harv gently pushed the young man back into the thick cushions.

"You can't understand, son. You can't know until you've received the connection. That's what we have to do now."

Tom's eyes grew as large as quarters as they moved from Harv's crazed face to the connector, which dangled in the huge man's right hand.

"I don't want that thing touching me," Tom protested.

Harv's face darkened. "Don't speak of the Webster connector that way. You must do it, Tom. Don't you understand? You can't join me without receiving the body. And you can only receive the body through the connector."

Harv's eyes stared at Tom, then at the connector, then at the IBM. His voice rose. "It's glorious. There are no words for the feeling, the experience of touching, of being God. It's beyond death, Tom." His eyes lowered and stared at the young man. "You *must* make the connection."

"Harv, I want to, I really want to, but I think I'd better wait until tomorrow. I'm just too upset right now."

The heavy flesh over Harv's eyes glowered at Tom. "It's now or never. Decide, for I grow impatient with you."

Tom stared at Harv, at his glaring eyes, his jerky movements. He stared at the connector, what was only a short while ago something he mistook for a Walkman headset and was now an embodiment of fear.

He shook his long head slowly. "I'm sorry. I really am. But I can't do it."

He started to rise from the recliner.

"Wait," Harv said, his eyes narrowing.

Tom sat back down.

"If you won't make the connection, at least let me lay my hands on you. You will feel the power that has come into me. And then you'll know. Then you'll see."

Tom shuddered, but he could see there was no use arguing. "Okay," he said, and closed his eyes.

Harv walked behind the recliner. He stopped when he was in place and lowered his huge hands to the hairless scalp of The Chief Cutter.

Tom felt as if slugs were crawling across the top of his head.

Then the thick fingers and fleshy palms lowered from the young man's head to his thin neck, and Harv strangled the life out of Thomas Barnslow.

"I'm sorry," Harv whispered a moment later into Tom's ear, "truly I am sorry, but I couldn't allow this betrayal."

Harv kissed Tom on the cheek before he picked up the long, thin body and carried it into the spare bedroom, over to the large horizontal freezer against one wall. He lifted the door of the freezer and pushed it back until it rested against the wall, then slipped Tom's body into the meat locker.

Condensation swirled around the room as the cold air from the freezer hit the warmer air, forming small fleeting white clouds.

Harv bent over and stared at Tom's face. The young man's eyes stared lifelessly back at him. Harv's thick fingers rested for a long moment on the delicate flesh of Tom's eyelids before he closed them.

On the bed, Jim Persall's scream was stifled by the band of electrical tape that covered his mouth. His muscular arms and legs strained to break the wire that held him.

Hearing the sounds from the bed, Harv turned slowly, his face flushed and his breath rapid.

"How nice to see you awake, Meat Grinder," he said.

He stepped toward the bed and Jim's widening, terrified eyes.

Wednesday, October 23th, 11:58 P.M.

Unable to sleep because of the pains in his back, Francis pulled himself out of bed and into his wheelchair. Adjusting his legs with his hand, he pushed the button to roll the chair over to the computer desk. He turned on his modem and booted his communications program to start autodialing The Surgery.

Once logged in with his account number and password, Francis hit the "C" button to get the Cutter into chat. Francis was quite surprised when Tom didn't respond. In fact, this was the first time that he could remember not getting an almost immediate response from the sysop.

Francis thought back about what Grandfather Nomasaki had said. I hope nothing happened to him, he said to himself.

A few minutes later, after reading a couple-dozen rather boring postings, Francis scanned ICU and found only one new message since he'd last posted, the message from Tom saying he'd changed his mind and would be at the picnic. Even though it was warm in his house, Francis shivered.

Bending over his computer keyboard, the boy typed:

```
[MESSAGE 24]: HOPE EVERYTHING'S ALL RIGHT
FROM: GENGHIS KHAN
DATE: OCTOBER 24
```

It's midnight as I write this, and, Cutter, I just tried to get you in chat but you didn't answer. Hope you were in the shower or something simple. Anyway, I hope you got home okay from the picnic. Fuchan and her grandfather and I went to the Camillia Grill for supper and had a good time. Hope you and Tunnel Rat also had a good time. Talk to y'all later, okay?

And as for The Succubus, where are you, chicken shit? Take a flying leap, dildo-head. You don't scare any of the Surgeons!

Genghis/Francis

Thursday, October 24th, 12:01 A.M.

After injecting Jim Persall with more sedative, Harv returned to the project lab, his body shaking with anticipation as he tried to keep his hands steady on the wheel of his car. He parked behind the lab, as close to the steel fire exit as he could get. Before entering the lab, he went to the dumpster at the back of the lot behind his car. He opened the double doors of the large trash container and was pleased to find it empty except for numerous cardboard boxes. Reaching into the bin, he removed most of the boxes and stacked them carefully to the side of the steel container. Then he entered the lab.

When he had unlocked the lab doors and was inside, he removed a three-and-a-half-inch disk from his shirt pocket. He put the disk in a drive and sat down at the main terminal of the VAX. He typed in a command, and the drive with the disk whirled for a second as the computer found the desired file. The modem clicked on and automatically dialed the phone number for Edward August.

"What is it?" came the director's sleepy, irritated voice.

"Don't interrupt me," the recording of Mary Alice's voice said. "I'm in serious trouble. He wants all of you here. Harv's holding me in the office. He's insane. He said he's going to test the prototype on me. Hurry, please, hurry! He's threatened to kill me and destroy the prototype if you call the police."

With a startled gasp of "What the hell?" from Edward August echoing over the telephone's speaker, the program disconnected the modem and hung up on the director.

Harv stifled a laugh, then adjusted the program so it would dial the phone numbers for Al Cogglin and Paul Brandais.

Three minutes later, the other two men had heard the same message.

Grinning insanely, Harv retrieved the disk with Mary Alice's digitalized voice on it and stalked into the animal lab. Using his key, he unlocked the medicine cabinet and removed a syringe and the vial of respiratory inhibitor that Mary Alice had used to put von Neumann to sleep. He filled the syringe with the poison and then pocketed the vial.

When he walked into the director's office, he took three of the general's lead crystal glasses from behind the bar and squirted a small amount of the deadly liquid into each glass. Then he put the glasses back behind the bar, whistled for a second, and sat down behind Edward August's desk to wait.

Thursday, October 24th, 12:32 A.M.

"What the hell is this all about, Harv?" Al Cogglin shouted at Harv as he entered the director's office.

"Wait until the others arrive, Herr Doktor," Harv answered, grinning wildly, his feet up on the director's desk and one of the director's manila folders open on his lap. He gestured for Cogglin to sit in one of the three chairs in front of the general's desk. Edward August and Paul Brandais entered the office a few minutes later.

"Get your feet off my desk!" the director shouted immediately upon closing the office door.

"Where's Mary Alice?" Paul Brandais asked, his eyes big and frightened.

"Relax, Herr Comrades," Harv said, slowly lowering his feet and standing up. "She's safe and will continue to be safe as long as you follow my directions."

"Ah shit, Harv, what's happened to you?" Dr. Cogglin asked, his face registering concern as he looked at the huge

THE HACKER

hardware expert's crazed eyes. "You've tried the connector on yourself, haven't you?"

Harv smiled then, the smile of a man who has just fallen in love. He nodded happily as he walked behind the bar.

"I have," he said simply as he removed the three glasses he had prepared, as well as a fourth. "And I'm going to tell you about it. But I think a drink is in order to celebrate."

"I don't want a goddamned drink," the director exploded. "Where the hell is Sluice?"

"Herr General," Harv said, his voice suddenly cold, "if you don't humor me, Fräulein Sluice is going to be deader than that monkey of hers."

"Do what he says, Ed," Dr. Brandais suggested, squirming nervously in his chair.

"Good advice," Harv said, as he sloshed a finger of scotch into each of the three glasses he had prepared and soda water into the fourth.

When he had distributed the drinks, Harv leaned his buttocks against the side of the desk. "To the Zeus project," he said, raising his glass, "bottoms up."

"The Zeus project," the other men said with little enthusiasm. They raised their glasses and drank.

Harv smiled beatifically. "You see, gentlemen," he said clearly as he watched the three of them carefully, "I don't need you anymore."

"What the hell are you talking about?" Ed August asked.

"And you told Cogglin I was expendable," Harv replied, giggling suddenly.

A groan came from deep within Paul Brandais's throat and the neurosurgeon slumped in his chair, his chin falling onto his chest. A wet sigh came out as his last breath.

"You son of a bitch," Al Cogglin shouted, realizing what was happening. He struggled to his feet, took two steps toward Harv, and then collapsed onto the carpet, dying with an ugly snarl on his face.

"What? What?" the general muttered as the poison started to shut down his respiratory system.

255

"Simple, Herr Director. You're dead," Harv said, and watched, fascinated by the speed and effectiveness of the respiratory inhibitor.

The director's compact body tensed. "Goddamn you, Harv," he said—his final words.

As Edward August's body tilted in the chair, Harv grinned. "No, Herr Director, God loves me."

Grinning to himself, Harv tossed the last of the bodies into the massive dumpster in the dark corner of the lab's parking lot. He looked at his watch and smiled in satisfaction. The garbage truck would arrive to empty the steel container in less than half an hour.

Using the keys he had removed from their pockets, Harv drove each of their cars to a self-service parking garage a block away.

Perfect timing, Harv thought as he got into his car and started the engine. Down the street, he could see the garbage truck heading toward the lab.

Fifteen minutes later, he was back in the computer lab of his apartment, taking off his clothes and slipping the monk's robe over his head.

Thursday, October 24th, 1:49 A.M.

"Fascinating," Dennis Conlick said, when Mary Alice completed her long summary of the project's three-year history. A great deal of the chronology had focused on Harv Webster. "Well, the guy certain sounds odd enough to be a genius." He frowned. "And I sure don't like that business that occurred at the lab the other night."

"I can take care of myself," Mary Alice responded.

Dennis nodded.

"And now they suspect him of stealing the schematics for the connector," she said, bringing him completely up to date.

He nodded slowly, thoughtfully. "I'll have to get down to business with the encryption, if that's the case. If the schematics aren't in the extract, the general's going to need to know as soon as possible. I still don't see what he'd have to gain by destroying them, though."

"I've been thinking about that," Mary Alice replied. "Of course, we can reconstruct it. As long as we have the prototype, we'll always be able to build another one. It'll take time, but— Oh God," she said, seeing the look in Dennis's clear eyes.

"The prototype is locked up, right?" Dennis asked.

Mary Alice shook her head slowly. "No. We've never secured it. The lab locks up tighter than Fort Knox and there never seemed to be any reason . . ."

Dennis stood up, pushing his chair out from the table's edge. "Where're your car keys?"

"In my purse in the bedroom. Why?"

"We're going for a ride."

Thursday, October 24th, 1:52 A.M.

Hiro Nomasaki turned restlessly in his bed.

In his dream, he stood before a robed and hooded outcast, a samurai who had betrayed his master. The hood of the robe was so deep that Hiro couldn't make out any features of his antagonist's face other than the eyes.

The eyes were of yellow fire.

Hiro unsheathed his sword and planted his feet firmly. He bowed. As he was straightening from the bow, his opponent drew his sword faster than a breath and swung it with all his might. Hiro Nomasaki watched his own head separate from his shoulders. He came out of sleep, his heart trip-hammering.

"A dream, foolish old man," Hiro muttered to himself, struggling to sit up, "it has no meaning."

He managed to swing his feet off the mattress and onto the carpeted floor. The solidity of the floor comforted him. A moment later, he opened the only drawer of his night stand. He took from the drawer a small Bayer aspirin tin, extracted one tiny pill, and placed it under his tongue.

A few minutes later, the pain in his chest returned to the

dark cave where it hid and waited, waited for the day it would triumph.

Thursday, October 24th, 2:03 A.M.

"What next?" Mary Alice asked. She and Dennis had been at the lab for only a few minutes before discovering that the prototype was missing.

"I don't know. I can't understand why none of the others answer their phones."

Dennis had tried the general's private home number, and Mary Alice had tried to contact Cogglin and Brandais.

"Dial Webster's number," Dennis said, nodding at the phone.

It rang twice and then was answered by a female voice: "Harv is unavailable at the moment. At the beep, please leave your name and number."

"Computer-generated, high-quality digital voice synthesis," Dennis mumbled to himself, nodding, impressed. "Sounds real, doesn't it?"

At the beep on Harv's line, Dennis said, "Hey, Succubus, this is the Tunnel Rat. The game's not over yet. I'm above ground, man, and I'm going to stave in your fat ass with a four-by-four. You've got something that doesn't belong to you, and if you don't return it, you're going to come up dead. Got it? I'm at the lab, hotshot. You've got fifteen minutes to call me."

Dennis lowered his thumb onto the plastic button and broke the connection. He smiled at Mary Alice.

"What was that all about?" she asked.

"BBS war style, eh?"

Mary Alice smiled her understanding.

"He won't call until after the time limit," Dennis said confidently.

In his lab, Harv said, "Teresa, replay the last phone message."

"Replaying last phone message," Teresa responded, and Dennis Conlick's voice came over the speaker, repeating the message.

Harv's head shook with laughter as the message ended.

He bent over the IBM and brought up his database on Dennis Conlick, a.k.a. the Tunnel Rat to the screen. A search through the veteran administration's computer a couple of days ago had revealed some very interesting things about the Rat.

"So you want to play, eh, Rat?" Harv asked aloud. "Oh, man, that'll make me very happy."

"I want you to be happy, Harv," Teresa said.

Harv walked over to the IBM and typed in a single command. "I don't need you anymore, Teresa," he said and hit the key that deleted the voice-recognition program he'd worked so hard on for so long from his hard drive. "You're history," he said happily as the hard drive whirred and destroyed the program.

Ten seconds past the fifteen-minute deadline, Harv called the lab number.

It rang twice. Dennis looked at Mary Alice.

"It's your play," she said.

Dennis winked at her and moved closer to the speaker. He nodded for her to start tracing and recording the conversation with the lab's complicated telephone and computer equipment, then pressed the answer button.

"That you, Succubus?" Dennis asked.

"Yep, it's me," Harv answered, chuckling deeply. "How long you been above ground this time, Conlick?"

"Been sneaking through my V.A. files, eh, Harv?" Dennis answered, unfazed by the question, adding, "I'm above ground to stay."

"You've said that before, according to the head peepers, Tunnel Rat."

"Yeah, man. At least five times to five different shrinks. But this time it's for real."

"Baloney. You nuts always slip off the edge."

"Here, Harv. I've got someone who'll tell you it's for real."

"Another shrink?" Harv said disdainfully.

"Better than that, Harv." Dennis nodded at Mary Alice and the speaker.

"It's true, Harv. Dennis is above ground to stay. But it looks like you've dug quite a hole for yourself."

"Oh my," Harv said, laughing again in that strangely deep voice, "so Nelly Dean's come to play too. How about the rest of your little group? Bet you don't have Meat Grinder or Chief Cutter with you. And how about Cogglin and Brandais? Are they around? Or the director?" Harv's laugh was almost hysterical.

"We're all here," Dennis lied, a frown crossing his face. "Bring the connector and the schematics back, Harv. There's a problem with the prototype."

"Yeah, I sure believe that. By the way, Nelly," Harv said, "if you're tracing this call, don't bother. I've got this phone wired through so many different switches you wouldn't believe it. You're going to be real surprised when the trace comes through." Harv laughed again. "Herr Rat, I'm out of this game. I'm leaving this one a winner, taking all the marbles with me, too."

"Not all the marbles, Harv," Dennis said, thinking furiously. "The Surgeons would whip your ass into foam if you had the guts to take them on. And you can bet your ass the director will prosecute for this."

Harv laughed for a long time.

"They're gone, pal. All gone. Sluice is the only Zeus player left. As for the Surgeons, have you seen Meat Grinder or Cutter lately? I have." And he laughed again, almost hysterically. "I offed the Cutter tonight, Rat. Got him in deep freeze. As for the other one . . . guess you could say he's just lying around." Another long laugh. Then he added, "The rest of you I was going to take out one at a time. Now there's no need. Besides, gods are compassionate."

"There's something wrong with the connector, Harv,"

Mary Alice said into the speaker, her voice very serious. "It killed von Neumann."

"Bullshit. I've had three more connections than the monkey had. My brain's better than ever." His voice quieted, became almost dreamy. "Clearer, sharper. I can carry thoughts further than I ever could before. I see things I've never dreamed of. You won't believe this, but I've become God. I have complete control."

Mary Alice shook her head sadly.

"You're no god, Harvey," Dennis said, "you're just a poor fat slob with an inferiority complex that's flipped you further off your rocker than even Freud would have thought possible. God? Ha! You, Elephant Ass Webster, a god?"

"Where'd you hear that, Conlick? Who told you about that?" Harv screamed into the phone, his voice shrill and excited.

"You think you're the only one capable of accessing government computers, Harv? Hell, man, I ran a check on you for the director right after you were hired for this job. I know everything about you, Elephant Ass. Everything from your compulsion for cleanliness to your religious mania. And you know what the shrinks say about you in your security-clearance files, Harv? Do you? They admit you're smart, but they also say you're nothing but a little frightened nobody hiding behind an ego and ass the size of an elephant!"

In his lab, the colors in Harv's mind expanded and soared outward. The anger in him boiled over, and his delusion that he was God grew into a conviction; he was invincible and could now control the minds of others.

"So you want to play another game, eh? Okay. The lab. Tomorrow night at midnight," Harv whispered. "Me against you and Nelly. For the connector." Harv chuckled. "And I'll even throw Meat Grinder in as a bonus."

"We'll be here, Harv," Dennis said, smiling and nodding, holding up a clenched fist in victory.

"I want the Surgeons there too. All of them. Khan and Wu

and the old Jap. Wu's grandfather. You see that camera above your head, Conlick?"

Dennis looked up at the videotape camera in the corner of the ceiling.

"Yeah, I see it."

"I'm tapped into it. You have the Surgeons in the lab by eleven tomorrow night. If you're not all there, the game's off, and I'm history."

"And if we're all here?"

"Then we play for the marbles, Rat. Winner take all."

"See you tomorrow night, Harvey," Dennis said, and hung up the phone.

He looked at Mary Alice.

She shook her head, watching the VAX spit out the location of the phone number of where Harv supposedly was. "According to the trace, we were talking to Harv all right. That was his voice pattern—deepened, but his— trouble is we were supposedly talking to him in Nome, Alaska."

"Bright boy, our Harv," Dennis said. "Is he too bright to walk in here tomorrow night with the prototype? Or will he leave the city tonight?"

"That's what I'd do if I were him, but I don't think he'll do it," Mary Alice said, her face flushed and suddenly beautiful.

"Why not?" Dennis asked.

"Because he's insane," she answered, "and because he can't stand to lose at a game."

They looked at each other, their eyes filled simultaneously with fear and love.

Chapter

~~~~~~

16

Thursday, October 24th, 2:36 A.M.

"They can't touch me," Harv said aloud in his lab, pushing the recliner back until it was almost flat like a bed. He had spent the last half-hour pondering the possibilities of finishing the game at midnight, and he saw no way he could lose.

His mind seemed to grow sharper with each passing second.

Suddenly he shifted his 295 pounds and straightened the recliner upright. Jangling his keys in his fat hands, he unlocked the lab and walked into the kitchen, where he got yet another bottle of Perrier water, his fifth in the past hour.

When he was again locked in the lab, Harv turned on his modem and dialed The Surgery. He picked up a carrier on the seventeenth attempt. Logging in as The Succubus, he went directly to the ICU, where he read Francis Schonrath's latest postings. He laughed. *Oh yes, the cripple and the old Jap and his granddaughter were going to get theirs. No doubt about it.*

"Goodbye, Surgery," Harv said aloud and pressed the proper sequence of keys to trigger the logic bomb he'd put in

Tom's BBS program so long ago. Then he broke the connection.

In Tom Barnslow's silent bedroom, the Apple IIgs received a machine language command that had been buried in one of the binary programs accessed by his BBS program during file transfers. This binary program loaded itself into main memory and immediately searched the system for all of its disk drives. It located three drives, a three-and-a-half-inch 800K drive, a five-and-a-quarter-inch floppy drive, and a twenty-meg hard drive. With the locations identified, the binary program jumped to a very simple subroutine which immediately destroyed the hard drive's directory, making all of the files inaccessible. A couple of minutes later, the logic bomb had formatted the other disks.

The series of programs that had once composed The Surgery, along with all its message bases and all its files, had ceased to exist.

Harv's logic bomb then erased itself from memory, leaving the computer alone, quiet, and silent in the shadows of the boy's room.

Thursday, October 24th, 2:42 A.M.

"You'd better get some sleep," Dennis told Mary Alice as they walked out of the lab together and into the early-morning air of New Orleans. "I'll get a cab home."

"You're coming home with me," Mary Alice said simply, taking him by the hand. "Now that I finally found you, I want to keep you."

"Sounds good," Dennis said, starting to hum as they walked toward her car. "Sounds real, real good."

Thursday, October 24th, 2:56 A.M.

Hiro Nomasaki silently eased himself out of his bed and opened the door just as silently. Walking down the hallway, he stopped in front of Fuchan's door. A light was visible through the crack at the bottom of the door.

Hiro turned the knob, opened the door silently, and entered her room.

Fuchan was hunched over her computer, her fingers flying across the keyboard like a concert pianist at work.

The old man padded up behind her and then moved to the side so he wouldn't startle her too much when she became aware of him.

"Hello, Grandfather," she whispered, and then turned and smiled broadly at him.

"Hai, very good. Your awareness grows. I moved silently as dust in air. Perhaps there is hope for you, after all."

"I saw your reflection in the monitor, Grandfather," she admitted. "I was not aware."

"Too bad," he said, shaking his head with mock sadness. "Wu must train harder. I not be here to teach forever."

"Are you feeling all right, Grandfather? Can I get you something?"

"Feel fine, but you must go to bed. Must get plenty sleep. We have long day and dark night coming."

"What do you mean, Grandfather? I have class tomorrow, same as usual, but nothing else is going on."

"Plenty else going on. Bad time coming. You must be rested. Sleep now, no argue. Sleep now. Turn off machine and go to bed. I sit with you."

She stared into her grandfather's deep black eyes, which were as serious as she had ever seen them. She nodded. She saved on disk the program she was working on and then shut off the computer. Gathering her cotton nightgown around herself, she crawled under the covers of her bed.

Hiro Nomasaki pulled her desk chair next to the bed. Straightening his back and planting both of his bare feet squarely on the floor, he started to clear his mind and concentrate on his breathing.

"Should I be frightened, Grandfather?" Fuchan asked. "Are you frightened?"

"Hai, Granddaughter," he replied enigmatically, and she

265

knew she was supposed to find the answer to the question on her own.

She folded her hands together on her small breasts and closed her eyes. She focused on her breathing as he had taught her to do, and in a few minutes she was sound asleep.

Hiro Nomasaki smiled and then slipped into *shikan-taza* to build his strength for what was to come.

Thursday, October 24th, 3:03 A.M.

"You're a beautiful woman," Dennis said, stepping out of Mary Alice's bathroom and finding her in bed, her hair down and flowing across the pillows.

"Hold me," she said, opening the covers.

"Are we going to come out of this all right?" she asked once she had snuggled into the crook of his right arm.

"The Tunnel Rat has never lost a fight," he answered, kissing her hair, which smelled of wildflowers.

Thursday, October 24th, 7:00 A.M.

The alarm started to beep.

It was turned off on the second beep, long before Mary Alice even heard it.

Ten minutes later, she awoke to the smell of fresh coffee brewing, and she slowly opened her eyes, rubbing them with the backs of her fingers.

"Good morning," Dennis said, walking in, dressed in his blue jeans and cotton work shirt. His hair was wet; his face, freshly shaved.

He placed the tray he was carrying, which held two cups of coffee and a plate of hot buttered toast, at the foot of the bed.

"How did I ever get along without you?" she asked, smiling brilliantly at him.

"You're even beautiful in the morning," he said, handing her a cup of coffee. He rubbed his face, which was slightly red. "Though you ought to change the blade in your razor more often. Hope you don't mind my using it."

"What's mine is yours," she said simply, sipping the hot coffee and reaching for a piece of toast.

He sat down on the side of the bed and looked at his coffee. She offered him the toast but he shook his head. "Not a breakfast person," he said.

"There's so much to learn about you," she said.

"We have plenty of time."

She lowered the cup and placed it on the saucer on the tray. "Do we?"

He smiled. "A lifetime."

"Even after tonight?"

"Especially after tonight." He leaned over and hugged her gently, stroking her long hair. "Don't worry, everything's going to work out fine."

"I hope you're right," she answered, but her eyes were uncertain.

Thursday, October 24th, 7:15 A.M.

"Wake up, Granddaughter," Hiro Nomasaki said softly, gently touching Fuchan's shoulder.

Her eyelids fluttered and she stretched under the heavy quilt. Opening her eyes, swimming up from sleep, she smiled at the tiny old man.

"Tea is ready and we must begin day."

She swung her feet out of bed and stood up. Looking at the clock, she realized how late it was. "Grandfather, I'll be late to class."

"You stay home today. We sit only."

Her eyes showed her puzzlement.

"But why?"

"Questions, questions," he answered enigmatically, gently pushing her toward the bathroom.

Thursday, October 24th, 8:00 A.M.

In the dream, Francis was once again with his sister, and the two of them were at the amusement arcade in the back of

Lakeside Shopping Center. Carol was playing Pac Man, and she had just beaten the high score on the machine. She shook her head, and her long hair twirled with the motion.

"Think you can beat that score, little brother?" she asked.

"You bet I can," Francis said confidently, and she moved out of the way to let him take a turn.

"Hey, Carol, where you going?" he asked, watching as she started to move away from him, walking backward down a corridor that was endless and black as a night without moon or stars.

"I have to leave you now, Francis," she said.

"Don't leave me," he begged, trying to move away from the Pac Man game.

He couldn't move, and he stopped watching his sister and looked down at his hands. His fingers were frozen to the control buttons, welded there as if glued to the colorful plastic.

He looked up again, and his sister was far down the corridor now, moving ever more rapidly away.

"Carol, come back," he pleaded. "I can't make it without you."

She smiled, her white teeth radiant in the darkness of the corridor.

"Goodbye, Francis," she said.

"Don't leave me alone," he pleaded.

Her voice, far away now and sounding as if she was in a cavern, could barely be heard.

"I love you, little brother," she said.

And then she was gone, swallowed by the night of the tunnel.

Crying, knowing his sister was never coming back, Francis turned to the Pac Man game. He would follow her, even if he had to rip the flesh off his fingers.

Looking once again at the game, he pulled on one of the buttons.

Suddenly a shrill sound started to come from the machine.

* * *

"Francis, Francis, wake up," his mother said, shaking him. "You were dreaming. Your alarm was ringing loud enough to wake the dead."

Coming slowly out of the terribly real dream, Francis looked at his mother's face. "Yeah, okay," he said. "I'm all right now."

"Good. Your tutor called. Her daughter's still sick, so you have another day to yourself."

He nodded. Another day to himself.

As his mother walked out of the room and got ready to go to work, he muttered, "I don't want another day to myself."

Thursday, October 24th, 10:00 A.M.

Mary Alice and Dennis sat at the conference table in the director's office. When they had first arrived, Mary Alice had gone into the animal lab and retrieved a videotape from one of the cabinets. The tape now rested on the table.

"Well, I can't contact any of them," she said, putting down the phone. "I'm starting to believe that Harv did what he said." She sighed deeply as Dennis nodded agreement. "And I don't think we should bring the teenagers into this. Harv's very dangerous. Particularly if what I suspect is true."

"I'm tougher than I look, Mary Alice." Dennis slapped his left shoulder with his right hand.

Mary Alice shrugged. "I wasn't thinking about physical harm."

"Enhanced intelligence? ESP stuff?" Dennis said disbelievingly.

"Maybe," she said. "Why don't we call the police?"

"I did that earlier. Reported that we couldn't contact the other team members. They said to give it twenty-four hours and then they'd check into it."

"They can do better than that. We can get some help here tonight." She reached for the phone.

He stopped her hand. "Not yet. I want to check with the other Surgeons first. I've got a feeling that I can't put my finger on. Something to do with the old Japanese man that Harv mentioned."

"Shall I call The Surgery and get their numbers?"

"I have their numbers up here," Dennis said, tapping his head.

Thursday, October 24th, 10:02 A.M.

The Zeus program was running, scheduled to stay on for twelve hours. The connector rested on Harv's head like a crown, its microneedles deeply embedded in the flesh of his scalp, flush with the hard bone of his skull. He sat and stared at the IBM across the room.

Colored lights danced on the monitor screen, producing the patterns he willed.

And then, suddenly, Harv was no longer bound by the computer's circuits.

"Let there be light," he intoned in his deep voice, a voice that sounded like it was coming from the bottom of a well.

A rainbow filled the lab, its colors flashing off and on like neon lights on the strip of Las Vegas.

The red spectrum separated itself from the others and circled the lab. Like a great dove, it hovered above Harv's head and then it lowered, surrounding his body.

"Yes," Harv whispered, warmed by the light as it filled him.

"Let there be sound," he said, looking at the speakers in the corners of the room under the counter. A high-pitched note formed and broke, formed and broke again.

Harv's forehead crinkled with concentration as he visualized the tweeters and woofers in the hardwood speakers. His mind saw and assimilated and became one with their circuitry.

The rich tones of Bach's "Ode to Joy" filled the room, the volume so intense that the speaker cabinets actually shifted on the carpets.

"Yes," Harv said, his breath coming rapidly, his heart pounding. "The power, I feel the power, I can control the power. I am the power."

Lights flashing everywhere in the lab now, and with Bach showering from the speakers, Harv partitioned his mind yet again and his vision settled on the bottle of Perrier that rested on the cork coaster on the table next to the recliner.

His huge hands, palms up, rose slowly from his lap where they had been resting.

Great beads of sweat formed on his forehead and dripped unnoticed onto the robe he wore.

The bottle moved almost imperceptibly from side to side.

Harv closed his eyes and visualized the green glass of the bottle.

He opened his eyes.

The bottle exploded.

"I am God," Harv intoned.

Thursday, October 24th, 10:06 A.M.

"Cross your fingers," Dennis said.

Dennis now sat behind the director's desk, poised to make the first phone call. The speaker was on so she could listen in on the conversation.

The phone rang once, twice, a third time.

"Nomasaki," a voice answered on the fourth ring.

"Err, hello, Mr. Nomasaki," Dennis said. "You don't know me in person, but I'm calling about something that's related to BBS, and I need to talk to your granddaughter. My name's Dennis Conlick. I'm also known as the Tunnel Rat."

"Glad Rat is man again. Granddaughter busy. Can't come to phone."

"It's very important, sir. It's about The Succubus."

"Hai," Hiro said, the syllable whiplike in intensity. "The great coward. Tell me."

Harv looked at Mary Alice, who shrugged.

"It's very complicated, sir . . ."

"Keep simple, please."

"He has Jim Persall."

"Yes."

"The Succubus wants all of the Surgeons to meet him tonight."

"This I know also. Karma. When and where, please?"

Dennis gave the address of the lab and how to get to it and then he said, "And we also need to have Francis Schonrath here. He wants all of us here at eleven P.M. Listen, Mr. Nomasaki, I want you to have this phone number in case you need to call."

Dennis slowly recited the seven numbers, enunciating carefully.

"Great Khan will come with me and Wu," Hiro said. "Please to have everyone together at ten-thirty. In private place. Goodbye."

"What on earth?" Mary Alice said curiously as Dennis lowered the phone. "It sounded like he knew what was going to happen before you even told him."

"I don't understand either," Dennis said, "but I intend to find out." He gestured to the general's computer terminal on the desk.

He turned on the machine and ran the terminal program, which automatically turned on the modem. He punched in a long string of numbers and then sat back.

A few seconds later, the connection into the host computer was made and the monitor filled with scrolling words.

Mary Alice leaned over Dennis's shoulder. "You're kidding me," she said, shaking her head. "Is this really Immigration's computer?"

"Yes. Their central data bank."

"You mean it's that easy to get into these things? Aren't any of these computers secure?"

"It's only easy if you know what you're doing. I've been doing this stuff for a long time, but most computer people would find it very hard to access a system like this at this point. A few years ago, well, it was easier then. Anyway, let's see what they've got on Nomasaki, shall we?"

Dennis typed rapidly, ordering the Washington, D.C., computer to search for all references to a last name of Nomasaki, living in New Orleans.

"Yeah, there we go," Dennis said a couple of minutes later when the name *Hiro Nomasaki* came up on the screen.

They both read rapidly.

"Fascinating," Dennis said, his eyes following the scrolling information.

"But hard to believe," Mary Alice said, feeling a sheen of sweat appear on her forehead.

"I'm going to print this out and then we'll take a careful look at it," Dennis said, pressing the proper keys to make a hardcopy on the printer to the side of the desk.

Several minutes later, he disconnected from the data bank and started to summarize the information for Mary Alice.

"Mr. Nomasaki brought his granddaughter here from Japan fourteen years ago," Dennis said. "Fuchan's parents were killed in a train crash, by the way, and he has raised her on his own since then. A pretty remarkable achievement in and of itself, which is significantly enhanced when you take into consideration her amazing school record. Seventeen years old, she's currently taking graduate courses in computer science at Tulane University. Her I.Q. is up in the stratosphere, and Mr. Nomasaki, before he left Japan, was, according to this information, one of the most highly respected Zen masters in Japan."

"This is an ignorant question, but what's a Zen master?" Mary Alice asked.

Dennis put the printout on the desk. Scratched his head. "I heard a lot about it when I was in 'Nam. Zen's a Japanese form of Buddhism, a fascinating derivation of the main branch which neither affirms nor denies the existence of God. It's a pragmatic faith which stresses a type of meditation called *zazen*. Through disciplined *zazen*, Zen Buddhists believe that individuals can realize their true nature."

"True nature?"

"Zen Buddhists believe that all things are one, and that all living things are interconnected."

"You mean like I'm God," Mary Alice said, smiling.

"A Zen master wouldn't talk in terms of God," he answered simply, "but I suspect he'd say that you could become aware of your cosmic connection to all living things if you weren't so wrapped up in your own ego to see it."

"Hmmmm," she said, nodding, serious now. "A Zeus connection without the connector and computer as middle men."

"You could think of it that way."

"What does Mr. Nomasaki do for a living?"

Dennis consulted the printout before answering: "He's retired. Eighty-two years old and failing health, asthma and a heart condition. Apparently he and his granddaughter live modestly in a small apartment in Gentilly. Immigration records show that he receives a small pension from the Japanese government."

Mary Alice nodded. The look on Dennis's face was one of puzzlement.

"Mr. Nomasaki was not surprised this morning when I called. In fact, it was as if he was already aware of what Harv had planned. Now, here's the point. When Immigration did a background check on Nomasaki-roshi, which is his correct Japanese name and title, they found out that he had a reputation in Kyoto, Japan, his home city, as a seer, an individual who could view the future. Several of his predictions, which he made public with the greatest reluctance and then only in an attempt to save lives, came true. Unfortunately, because they involved mass transportation, his warnings were not acted upon. Many people died who might have been saved if Nomasaki-roshi had been listened to. After his third correct prediction, a cult started to develop around him. Apparently he's a very modest and humble man. Soon after this idolizing began, he and his granddaughter immigrated to the West."

"A Japanese Cassandra." Mary Alice mused.

"We're just about finished," Dennis said. "This sounds crazy, but I think Nomasaki-roshi has had a premonition about Harv and that he's coming tonight to help us fight him. If that's the case, we may well be in for a lot more than we'd anticipated. Nomasaki is a great man in Japan. We must listen to him tonight."

Mary Alice's eyes widened. "It's possible, Dennis. It's possible. Especially in light of what I've suspected about the connector. Watch this tape." She turned on the VCR.

"See, see, right there," Mary Alice said, pointing at von Neumann. She put the machine into single-frame mode and ran it through again.

"Watch that link, there, right there," Mary Alice said, touching the TV screen with her finger.

She froze the frame.

"Just watch. Watch that one link."

Dennis watched where she pointed.

She clicked the button to move one frame ahead.

Dennis's eyes bulged as, on the next frame, the link split right down the center.

She advanced the tape.

In this frame the link separated, broke in half.

"That's quarter-inch chain link," Mary Alice said, quivering with excitement. "And von Neumann's hands and teeth weren't even close to it. Don't you see? He cracked it with his mind!"

"I don't know what to think," Dennis answered after seconds of silence, "but I do know it's coming after us at midnight. And if Webster's learned to control whatever the connector has let him tap in to, we could be neck-deep in big trouble."

"I know," Mary Alice answered in a whisper.

Thursday, October 24th, 10:36 A.M.

"Put Great Khan on phone, please," Hiro said into the phone on his granddaughter's desk.

"It's me, Mr. Nomasaki," Francis said.

"Thought it was man from depth of voice."

Francis laughed. "Guess my voice is changing, huh, Mr. Nomasaki?"

"Hai, man inside of boy soon break through shell."

"That'll suit me fine," Francis answered, wondering why Fuchan's grandfather had called him. Then he had a bad thought. "Fuchan's okay, isn't she? You're not calling because something's happened to her, are you?"

"You and Wu find problems in air, Great Khan," Hiro

answered, shaking his head wryly. "Wu is sitting. You come sit with us, yes?"

"I don't know what you mean, Mr. Nomasaki. Sitting? You mean you're meditating? Fuchan said you meditate a lot."

"Zazen, Khan. Not meditating. Very different."

"Whatever. Why isn't Fuchan at school? Sitting's pretty boring."

Hiro laughed, a long rich chuckle.

"Questions, questions. You and Wu have more questions than ocean has water. You come sit with us, yes?"

"Gosh, Mr. Nomasaki, I don't know. My mom might not go for that."

"I worry about Momma-san. You get ready. I pick you up in Dragonmobile in thirty minutes, yes?"

"Yes, sir, if you want, yes."

"Good. Let me talk Momma-san now."

"She's at work. You want her phone number?"

"Khan not so dumb after all."

Francis recited the phone number of his mother's office.

"Thirty minutes," the old man reminded the boy.

"I'll be ready, Grandfather," the boy answered.

Hiro lowered the phone and then dialed the number Francis had given him. As he had expected, Francis's mother freely gave her permission, ending the brief conversation by saying, "And thank you, Mr. Nomasaki, for all you've done for Francis. He's been a different boy since he met you and your granddaughter."

When he finished on the telephone, Hiro went back to the living room, where Fuchan was sitting on a plump *zazen* cushion, her posture erect, her *zazen* steady. "Five minutes *kinhin* now," he ordered, "and then resume sitting until I return."

She bowed from the waist but did not speak.

Thursday, October 24th, 11:30 A.M.

Nomasaki-roshi wheeled Francis into the living room of the small apartment where he and Fuchan lived.

Francis's eyes grew wide as he stared at Fuchan, who was sitting on a thick black cushion in an upright position that looked painful on the living-room floor.

"What's she doing?" the teenager asked.

"Zazen," Nomasaki-roshi replied.

"What's that?"

Instead of answering, the old man walked over to a bronze gong the size of a dinner plate, which he struck with the flat of his hand.

Fuchan swayed gently on the cushion in a circular motion, and then she stretched her head on her neck.

She turned around, her eyes intensely bright. She clapped her hands together sharply when she saw Francis with her grandfather.

"Good!" Hiro exclaimed, walking over to embrace her.

"What's going on?" Francis asked, and his voice cracked.

Fuchan walked over to his wheelchair and put her arms around the boy and hugged him.

He tentatively put his good arm around her neck.

He could feel her heart beating against his chest, slowly, amazingly slowly.

He returned her hug with all his might.

"Hai," Hiro said.

When Fuchan released him, she stepped back and bowed to her grandfather. "Do you wish food, Roshi?" she asked, her eyes lowered.

"No food. Tea only. Hot tea."

She bowed and walked toward the kitchen, her movements deliberate and light.

The Zen master knelt and sat back, his rump resting on the heels of his feet. His intense eyes searched Francis's face for several minutes. The boy, at first, felt uncomfortable with this unrelenting appraisal, like the old man was seeing everything about him, learning every secret, examining every thought he'd ever had. But then the feeling of discomfort passed, and Francis felt oddly at peace, almost as though he was losing himself in his adopted grandfather's unwavering examination.

Only when Fuchan came in with a wooden tray and three small Japanese teacups did the old man avert his eyes.

"Honorable Granddaughter perform tea ceremony," he said formally, and bowed to her deeply, his forehead striking the carpet.

Without consciously doing so, Francis too bowed, lowering his head as far as his injured back would let him.

"I am proud of both grandchildren," Nomasaki-roshi said, and clapped his hands sharply, once.

Fuchan bowed and began the ceremony.

Chapter

17

Thursday, October 24th, 11:35 A.M.

At one with the circuitry of the machine, Harv looked at the IBM and watched the Zeus program execute for a few seconds. Then he willed the monitor to go blank.

He stared intently at the hard drive that had held the voice-recognition program and brought the deleted file back into existence by rebuilding the directory track with his mind. Then he told the resurrected program to run itself.

"I love you, Harv," Teresa said, only this time her voice didn't come from the speakers in the corners of the lab. This time her voice came from Harv's mouth.

"Thank you, Teresa," Harv answered in his voice, looking at the monitor where Teresa's beautiful face stared back at him, her eyes full of love. "You've risen from the dead, you know."

"It's cold, something's different, Harv."

"Yes, everything is different. I've gone beyond St. John—far, far beyond him."

Harv looked at the Dali print of the crucifixion. He smiled sadly. "And beyond you, too," he said, nodding at the slick paper, which suddenly broke free from the thumb tacks that held it to the wall. It fluttered to the carpet, where it slowly crumbled up into a ball the size of a small fist.

"I am God now, Teresa," Harv said, his voice full of power.

"I am your Teresa," Mary Alice's voice answered, and the face on the screen dissolved for a microsecond and then reformed into a perfect reproduction of the psychiatrist's face.

"You will be mine, Teresa."

"Yes, God, I know."

Harvey Webster, satisfied that his control was complete, willed the Zeus program to stop.

It did.

Removing the connector from his skull, he pulled his bulk out of the recliner and left the lab. After locking the door, he went to the spare bedroom to sleep, resting for the midnight confrontation. Taking off his robe, he smiled gently at the terrified eyes of Jim Persall.

"I'm going to sleep now, son," Harv said, patting the boy's cheek, "and I need you to be still. If you don't stop squirming, you're not going to like what I'll do to you. I want you conscious tonight, so I'm not going to sedate you. If you want to see your friends again, you will be completely still until I wake up."

Jim's eyes closed slowly and he sighed through his nose. He nodded his head.

Harv set the alarm clock next to the bed for seven P.M.

Seconds later, he was sound asleep, immobile, dreamless.

Jim Persall, his mind frantic, thought about what he would do to the man next to him if only he could get his hands free.

Thursday, October 24th, 11:48 A.M.

Grandfather bowed to Fuchan, and she bowed back and then carried the teacups and tray toward the kitchen.

"Sit quietly," the old man said to Francis, leaving the living room and walking into Fuchan's bedroom, where he picked up the telephone and dialed the lab number that Dennis had given him.

"Yes?" Dennis said.

"Nomasaki. Speak Dennis Conlick, please."

"This is Conlick."

"He sleep until sunset," the old man said.

"I understand. Thank you, thank you very much."

"Hai."

"I look forward to meeting . . ."

But Hiro Nomasaki had already hung up.

"That was a beautiful ceremony, Fuchan," Francis whispered when she returned from the kitchen, "but what's going on?"

"I don't know. He's never done this before. I think he's trying to teach us something important," she answered, her voice also a whisper.

"Sit," the old man said, returning from the girl's bedroom and interrupting their brief exchange. Fuchan bowed and immediately returned to the cushion where she'd sat when Grandfather had wheeled Francis into their apartment.

"What am I supposed to do?" Francis asked. "I'm used to sitting because that's all I can do. Either sit or lie down. Are we going to do this long? What is Fuchan doing? Am I supposed to do something?"

The old man pushed the wheelchair between two cushions so that Francis would be between himself and Fuchan. Then he slowly resumed the full lotus posture.

Exhaling sharply because of the pain in his knees, he looked up at the boy. "Think of nothing," Hiro ordered, staring at the teenager intensely. "Follow breaths. On exhale, count 'one' in mind. On next exhale, count 'two' in mind. When reach 'ten,' start over. Simple. Yes?"

"Yes, sir, I can do that. But how long are we going to do it?" Francis asked.

The old man stared at him, his expression blank.

"I know, I know, too many questions," Francis answered.

Hiro grunted sharply and turned his face to the wall.

A second later, Francis took a deep breath. He looked at the wall. When he let his breath out, he thought, *One*.

"What was that all about?" Mary Alice asked.

"Nothing, he just wanted to make sure everyone would be here tonight."

"I'm going to the animal lab to review the data on von Neumann again," Mary Alice said.

Dennis nodded. "If I don't get some food, I'm not going to make it through the afternoon. I'll go grab something. Want anything?"

"No," Mary Alice said.

"I'll be back shortly," he said.

They parted at the door to the director's office.

Outside, using Mary Alice's car, Dennis drove to his apartment and illegally parked in a loading zone. He unlocked the door and, before sitting down even, turned on his modem and booted up his computer.

He cataloged his hard drive to make sure there was sufficient disk space.

Then he reached across the table and rummaged through a pile of printouts. He found the sheet he was looking for and memorized the number he had jotted down in a shaky hand at a time when he was just heading underground.

He typed the number into his computer, picking up a carrier on the first ring.

"Thank God," he said, entering the password he had hacked over three months ago, praying that it hadn't been changed.

It hadn't.

He had full access.

He typed a command to catalog the storage systems of the host computer.

A second later, his screen filled with the names of the files.

"Gotcha!" he said triumphantly, grinning from ear to ear and nearly shouting with glee.

He typed a couple of commands and then stood up to return to the lab.

Before he left, however, he opened a can of Vienna sausages and slapped the contents between two slices of bread.

Dennis took one lingering, hopeful look at his computer and saw the light on his hard drive signal that it was successfully receiving and saving the material he was downloading.

Munching happily on the dry sandwich, the Tunnel Rat closed and locked the door to his apartment and headed back to the lab.

Thursday, October 24th, 5:00 P.M.

"Well," Dennis said, sitting back after Mary Alice's in-depth review of all the data about von Neumann. "You've convinced me that the connector caused what appears to be paranormal phenomena."

"Any ideas on countering it?"

"Only one."

She looked at him quizzically.

"Look, if we can somehow get Harv to make the connection here in the lab tonight, I can hide a bomb, an endless loop, in the Zeus program that'll maybe disable him, maybe blast his goddamn brain to kingdom come. It's a dangerous alternative. Doing it could damage his mind. His great mind."

"But it's no longer the mind it was," Mary Alice said without hesitation. "I've listened to the tape of last night's conversation several times. There's no question that Harv's suffered a serious breakdown. Acute psychosis."

"Damn it, the man's a genius," Dennis replied, slapping the table with the flat of his hand. "I don't want to be responsible for destroying the mind that made the Zeus connector possible."

Mary Alice looked at him. "Put that bomb in the Zeus program, Dennis," she said. "It's him or us and the teenagers."

Dennis nodded. "I know."

He sat down at the terminal and worked for almost a

half-hour. When he'd finished, he wiped the perspiration from his forehead and turned toward Mary Alice, who had been silently watching him modify the program.

"Let's get something to eat," he suggested.

"Yes," she said.

Thursday, October 24th, 5:30 P.M.

Hiro Nomasaki clapped his hands together sharply.

"Dokusan," he said and walked gracefully, though his legs were hurting very badly, into his bedroom.

He closed the door.

"Now what?" Francis whispered.

For almost five hours, the three of them had been alternating between twenty-five-minute periods of sitting silently and five-minute rest periods when Fuchan and her grandfather had walked silently and slowly around the perimeter of the sparsely furnished living room, first one of them pushing the boy's wheelchair and then the other.

"In *dokusan,* students talk with their teacher," Fuchan explained quietly. "When you go to the door, knock. When he rings his bell, enter, close the door, and bow three times in front of him. When he rings the bell again, *dokusan* is over and you should leave."

"Don't you think this is kind of crazy, Fuchan?" Francis asked, grinning. "I mean, what's he supposed to be? Some kind of priest or something? Why have we been sitting here all afternoon? Aren't you hungry? I'm starved."

Fuchan's face was very serious. "He's roshi, master teacher," she said. "We are his students. It is a great honor."

Confronted by her seriousness Francis's grin disappeared. "I didn't understand," he said.

"It's all right. You go first. I will sit."

Francis pushed the button on the handle of his wheelchair and rolled to the bedroom door. He knocked softly and heard a pleasant tinkling of a bell in reply.

He opened the door and rolled in and closed the door.

Hiro Nomasaki had changed from the baggy pants and loose shirt that he normally wore into a soft black robe that was frayed at the tips of the long sleeves with a life's wear. The old man sat on a thick cushion next to his bed.

On the floor in front of him was a small bronze bell with a handle of polished cherry wood.

He looked at the boy but said nothing.

After several moments of silence, Francis cleared his throat and said, "I tried to count my breaths. It's very hard. I kept losing track, kept thinking of other things, about why you were having us do this."

"Mind is wild horse, very hard to tame," Nomasaki-roshi said. "You will continue with this practice."

"I'll try, sir," Francis said.

Hiro's hand lowered to pick up the small handbell.

"Wait," Francis said quickly. "Why're we doing this?"

"Old Japanese story. One day young man walked along mountain road. Suddenly great tiger leaps from behind rocks, ready to eat young man. Young man runs but comes to end of trail. Hungry tiger is behind him, steep cliff with long drop is before him. He sees root of old tree growing out of rock on cliff. He climbs down root so tiger can't get him, holds on tight. Patient tiger sits and waits. Young man looks below. Second tiger looks up at him, licking chops. Hungry mouse comes and begins to bite through root that holds young man. Young man looks around. There is nothing but single ripe strawberry growing. Young man picks strawberry and eats it. How sweet it tastes!"

The old man stared again at the teenager, who seemed puzzled by the story. "You ask more questions?"

"No, sir," the teenager answered. "No more questions."

Hiro reached down and rang the bell.

Francis bowed three times and rolled his wheelchair out of the room.

Fuchan, deep in concentration, didn't look at him. She knocked on the door, the handbell rang, and she entered, closing the door silently.

Francis rolled his wheelchair back to where Grandfather had originally put him. He took a deep breath, stared at the wall, and exhaled slowly, thinking, *One.*

In Hiro Nomasaki's room, Fuchan prostrated herself on

the floor three times. Then she sat up and looked at the opposite wall, her eyes unable to meet her grandfather's. "Roshi, my *koan* is *mu,*" she said.

"Show me *mu,*" he answered.

Her eyes downcast, she said, her voice full of shame, "I do not understand *mu,* Roshi. My concentration is good, but I haven't figured out what *mu* is."

Her grandfather pounded the floor of his room with his hands. Bang! Bang! Bang! Then he reached for his bell and rang it.

Fuchan bowed and returned to the living room. Without disturbing Francis, she sat back down, and resumed silently asking herself, "What is *mu?* What is *mu?*" A few minutes later, her concentration centering, she truncated the question to *"Mu, mu, mu,"* repeating the syllable that means "no" in Japanese with each exhalation of her breath.

In his room, Hiro Nomasaki fumbled at the night stand to get his small tin of tiny pills. Opening the tin with difficulty, he placed one of the pills under his tongue.

A few moments later, his heartbeat resumed the normal rhythm which had carried him through eighty-two years.

Accepting the pain, he slipped the small container of nitroglycerine tablets into a pocket inside his robe. Getting slowly to his feet, he left to rejoin the two teenagers in the living room.

Thursday, October 24th, 6:49 P.M.

"So this is the Tunnel Rat's burrow," Mary Alice said, walking around the small room, touching first his cot and then the cheap chest of drawers. They'd come to Dennis's apartment after stopping at her house, where they'd bathed and made love. She looked out the one window at the sky, which was clouding over.

"Yep, this is where I'd hang my hat, if I had a hat," Dennis replied, sitting down at his computer. The words "Transfer complete" were in the upper left-hand corner of the monitor's screen. "Would you see if there's anything worth eating in the refrigerator? I'd go with you, but I don't think it's big enough for both of us at the same time."

As soon as Mary Alice left the room, Dennis typed *Catalog* and pressed the return key. He checked the list of file names on his hard drive and found the one he was looking for.

Nodding to himself, he turned off the computer and monitor.

"Not much worth eating in here," Mary Alice said, wondering how this man she'd fallen in love with could live in such a cramped, unadorned space, "unless you like Vienna sausages and Spam."

Standing in the doorway to the kitchen, Dennis guessed at what she was thinking.

"Not exactly the Ritz, huh?"

Tears welled in her eyes, and then in his. She covered the six feet that separated them in an instant, and they held each other.

"To think I've known you all this time in BBS. If I'd only known you were living like this. And the things you posted—calling for help—I could tell, but I didn't do anything. And I was so lonely, too."

He stroked her hair. "Hey, it wasn't so bad. You should've seen the place before I cleaned it up." He pulled back and looked at her. "My lovely Mary Alice," he said softly, "the bad part's over now. You rescued me."

Using the tips of their fingers, they wiped the tears from below each other's eyes.

"Have any money?" Dennis asked a minute later, looking wistfully at his cot.

She followed his glance. Smiled.

"Later," he said. "We've got the rest of our lives."

"Yeah, I have money. In fact, I'm loaded. Been socking away my paychecks for years."

"Beautiful *and* rich. Well, spoil me. Let's go to Antoine's. I've heard a lot about that place."

She looked at his blue jeans and work shirt.

"You'll have to change. They won't let you in if you're wearing jeans. You'll have to put on a tie and sport coat too."

Dennis chuckled but there was an undertone of sadness in it.

"What?" she asked.

"Except for a duplicate of what I've got on, I don't have any other clothes," he admitted softly.

She raised her head and kissed him on the lips.

Thursday, October 24th, 7:00 P.M.

The alarm went off in the spare bedroom, and Harv was fully awake and on his feet immediately, his mind clear and precise, refreshed and sharp from his long sleep.

He smiled at Jim Persall. "Soon, son, soon."

Jim's eyes narrowed.

Harv turned off the alarm and walked to his bedroom, where he changed into a fresh robe and new pair of leather sandals. He removed his keys from the old robe and put them in the pocket of the new one.

He walked back to the spare bedroom, where he opened the large freezer and stared down at the body of Tom Barnslow. He was surprised to find the young man's open eyes staring back at him.

"Thought I'd closed them," Harv reflected, and put the thick tips of his fingers on Tom's eyelids.

Because the skin was frozen stiff, however, they wouldn't budge.

Wonder if I could raise him? he mused.

Harv removed his hands from the boy's face and lowered his head.

He stared into the cold, dead eyes of Tom Barnslow. "I blew up The Surgery, Cutter. Did you know that? It's not going to sit there in that room of yours and go on and on and on like you would have wanted. It's history, Cutter, just like you, just like all of them are going to be tonight when I finish with them."

Harv laughed softly to himself as he lowered the freezer door.

Then he turned to Jim Persall. "I lied to you, Jimmy," Harv said, lifting his robe above his knees as he crawled on top of the bed until he straddled the boy just above the waist. "You can't always believe God, you know."

His pudgy knees on either side of Jim's broad chest, Harv gently lowered his hands onto the boy's throat.

"I'm sorry, Jim," Harv said as his fingers tightened and squeezed. "You gave me a lot of pleasure."

Several minutes later, Harv got off the boy's body and went into the kitchen, where he removed from a drawer a large box of wooden matches, the type that light on anything. He opened the box and extracted a half-dozen, which he put in the pocket of his robe.

He left the kitchen and went into the bathroom, where he removed his robe and sandals and then relieved himself. He showered under cold water, then shaved his face and the top of his head with his straight-edge razor.

When he'd finished bathing, he stood in front of the large bathroom mirror and dry-shaved the cross in the hairs on his chest with a double-edged razor blade.

He opened the sliding medicine-cabinet door and took out a bottle of Aqua Velva. Flipping back the plastic cap, he splashed the aftershave liberally on the palm of his right hand and then rubbed the cool liquid across his scalp and chest, luxuriating in the burning pain that ensued.

He put his robe and sandals back on and left the bathroom.

Once he'd unlocked and returned to his lab, he opened a cabinet underneath the counter. He removed three single-gallon cans of wood stain, stain he'd had left over from when he built the counter. He put the cans on top of the counter.

He walked over to the IBM and picked up his enhanced Zeus connector and inserted the microneedles.

He did not run the Zeus program.

He opened his case of tools.

He picked up the original Zeus connector, the one he'd stolen from the lab.

"Teresa," he said.

"Yes, God?"

"Let's have a little music, shall we?"

"What would you like?"

"Your choice, my dear."

A second later, the room filled with the sound of a Mozart piano concerto.

"Very nice, Teresa," he complimented.

"I love you, God," she said.

"I know," he replied distractedly, taking a small screwdriver from the leather-bound case of tools. He began to disassemble the original prototype.

Thursday, October 24th, 8:00 P.M.

"Are you sure about what you did to the Zeus program?" Mary Alice asked when she and Dennis had reentered the project laboratory.

Dennis looked at her and walked to the terminal.

She nodded sadly. "We may not have to use it," she said hopefully.

"Yeah," Dennis replied.

"What will it do?"

"The program'll initialize and hopefully begin the process of whatever the hell it's doing, but then, after the first three minutes of the connection, it'll immediately jump to this subroutine, which is an endless loop that begins slowly and then picks up speed."

"Why have it pick up speed?"

"It'll unfocus him, and if we can get him to zero in on the loop, it should take more and more of his concentration as it increases speed. With the floating point processor in the VAX, this program will be zipping along at close to the speed of light by the time it optimizes."

"Yeah, yeah, I see," Mary Alice said excitedly. "Neat idea. That might do the trick."

"It's also liable to drive him completely nuts."

"Have you forgotten what he's claimed to have done? You keep forgetting that he's already around the bend."

"I know. I feel sorry for the guy."

Mary Alice walked over to the small table where they used to put the bowl that held von Neumann's bananas. The bowl was still there. She picked it up and turned it idly in her fingers.

Dennis joined her at the table. They looked at each other without speaking. Mary Alice put the bowl down, and Dennis pushed it with his fingertips.

She sighed.

Thursday, October 24th, 10:00 P.M.

Hiro Nomasaki clapped his hands sharply.

"We go now," he said, rising slowly to his feet. His heart missed a beat but then settled into its proper rhythm when he put his hands on the back of Francis's wheelchair.

Fuchan stood up.

Hiro turned Francis around. He looked at the two teenagers.

"Expect nothing," he said. "Keep eyes open, minds clear. Understand?"

Both of them nodded.

The old man walked to the small hardwood table by the apartment door and picked up the keys to the car. He opened the door and started walking down the hallway of the apartment building that led to the parking lot.

"He's barefoot," Francis whispered.

"He knows," Fuchan answered, putting her hands on the boy's wheelchair and wheeling him toward the door.

When they got to the car, Fuchan was surprised to watch Grandfather get in behind the steering wheel. He looked straight ahead, as if she and Francis weren't even there.

When he didn't move to help Francis out of his wheelchair, she looked at the teenage boy. He opened the rear door by himself, and, using his hand, pulled himself into the back seat. Then he put his hand in his lap and stared straight ahead.

Fuchan watched as his breathing slowed.

She rolled the wheelchair to the other side of the car, broke it down, and then lifted it into the back seat, placing it on the floor. It was a tight fit, but she managed to get both it and herself into the car. She put on her seatbelt as quietly as possible. When it latched, Hiro Nomasaki turned the ignition key and the car started. He pulled the car out of the parking lot and into the night.

A fine mist began to fall.

Thursday, October 24th, 10:15 P.M.

Hiro Nomasaki parked his car on the street in front of the project laboratory. Staring through the windshield, the wipers moving slowly back and forth, the old man took a deep breath and removed the tin of pills from his robe pocket. He opened the tin and placed one of the tiny pills under his tongue. A few seconds later, he felt himself stop sweating.

His heartbeat settled.

He turned off the engine.

"Hai," he said quietly but forcefully.

Fuchan asked softly, "Grandfather, are you all right?"

"Good!" he answered, proud of her awareness. He had been so deliberate in taking the pill that he knew she couldn't have observed the action only with her eyes.

He opened the door and stepped, barefooted, onto the wet asphalt of the parking lot across the street from the lab. Posture erect and strong, he waited, staring at the old brick building, which glistened from the night's steady rain.

Fuchan removed the wheelchair and reassembled it. Francis used his hand to push himself to her side of the car.

With her help, he got into the wheelchair.

Hiro Nomasaki, not looking at either them, started to walk across the street.

* * *

Dennis pushed the play button on the tape recorder they had used that morning to tape his phone conversation with Hiro Nomasaki:

"Nomasaki."

"Err, hello, Mr. Nomasaki . . . you don't know me in person, but I'm calling about something that's related to BBS, and I need to talk to your granddaughter. My name's Dennis Conlick. I'm also known as the Tunnel Rat."

"Glad Rat is man again. Granddaughter busy. Can't come to phone."

"It's very important, sir. It's about The Succubus."

"Hai, the great coward. Tell me."

"It's very complicated, sir."

"Keep simple, please."

"The Succubus wants all of the Surgeons to meet him tonight."

"This I know also. Karma. When and where, please?"

"And we also need to have Francis Schonrath here. He wants all of us here at eleven P.M. Listen, Mr. Nomasaki, I want you to have this phone number in case you need to call. 885-9273."

"Great Khan will come with me and Wu. Please to have everyone together at ten-thirty. In private place. Goodbye."

Dennis pushed the stop button. He looked at his watch. "They should be here very shortly," he said.

"He knows something," Mary Alice said.

"I think so, too," Dennis said. "Look, I've got a hunch about all this. When I was in 'Nam, I developed a deep respect for the Oriental mind. There's something about some of them that, well, transcends the ordinary, something about some of them that's hard to put a finger on. Just before I cracked up over there, I was down in a tunnel without any light for over nine hours, stalking, or so I thought, a North Vietnamese. Actually, he was stalking me.

293

The cat-and-mouse game was getting old, and we were both out of ammunition, and I decided to make a stand where the main tunnel bisected in two different directions. I was wedged against the back of the tunnel, a bayonet in my hands, when I saw a pure white light, soft but brilliant, coming from the main tunnel. Suddenly I didn't care about killing the guy who was coming after me any longer, and I did something that usually would have been very stupid. I stepped out of my hiding place. The light was coming from everywhere and nowhere at the same time. The North Vietnamese was maybe eight—ten feet away from me, and he had the biggest knife you've ever seen clutched in his right hand. But he too had stopped, and we crouched there in the light for I don't know how long. Then he smiled and bowed to me. I bowed back. He pointed to the branch of the tunnel that I hadn't taken, bowed again, turned, and went back down the main artery. I turned and the light started to fade. A few minutes later, I crawled out, safe, alive."

Mary Alice smiled through teary eyes at Dennis, who nodded at her.

"I'm not flipping out again, if that's what you're thinking," Dennis said easily, his voice confident and controlled, "and I'm not sure what the point is. Maybe there isn't a point. All I'm saying is that I had the same feeling when I talked to Mr. Nomasaki on the phone that I had in that tunnel, that some power, some power of good, intervened for just a moment to stave off death."

Nomasaki-roshi opened the door to the director's office and walked in.

His small hands hidden in the folds of his robe's sleeves, he moved aside as his granddaughter and Francis came in behind him. Fuchan closed the door. Nomasaki-roshi bowed from the waist and remained in that position.

Dennis returned the bow and, slowly, Mary Alice stood up and bowed.

When the old man straightened, he gestured for them to sit down on the floor around him. He radiated a power and serenity almost palpable in the room.

When they were seated, Nomasaki-roshi, in one smooth, effortless motion, sat down on the carpet with them. His small hands came out of the robe's sleeves and turned palms-up in his lap. His left hand went on top of his right hand and the tips of his thumbs touched.

He nodded sharply.

Fuchan mimicked him, and the others followed her lead.

The old man's eyes twinkled with humor as he looked at each of them individually. When he had finished introducing himself in that silent manner, he smiled.

"Good and evil do not exist," he said softly. "There is only this." His hands separated and moved out in a broad gesture and then returned to his lap. "Only this."

"Mr. Nomasaki," Mary Alice asked, "we know about what you predicted in Japan. Do you know what's going to happen tonight?"

"What will happen will happen," he answered, "and you must not become attached to it."

He paused for a second and then looked at Francis Schonrath before his eyes settled on his granddaughter. "You must not become attached," he repeated softly, staring deep into her wide dark eyes.

"Is there going to be danger?" Mary Alice asked.

"Hai, much danger."

"Is anybody going to be hurt?"

The old man nodded, his face calm.

"What can we do?"

"Do nothing. Sit quietly with concentration on nothing."

"It's almost eleven," Dennis broke in, looking at his watch. "He wanted us in the main lab at eleven."

"Hai, we go there now," Nomasaki-roshi said, gesturing for them to leave the room.

Mary Alice took the lead and opened the door. "It's this way," she said, putting her hands on Francis's wheelchair and smiling at Fuchan, who smiled back.

Dennis and Hiro Nomasaki were alone in the office.

Suddenly the old man faltered.

Dennis rushed to his side and held him up, helping him to the soft chair in front of the director's desk.

He reached into the robe pocket, opened the tin, and slipped another pill under his tongue.

"Heart?" Dennis asked.

Hiro smiled weakly.

"We'd better get you to a hospital," Dennis said, worried about the pain lines in the old man's face.

"No," Nomasaki-roshi commanded.

Dennis looked into the old man's calm eyes.

"Only this," Dennis repeated in a voice that wasn't even a whisper.

"Good!"

Dennis bowed.

"You take care of Granddaughter?"

"Yes," Dennis answered simply, adding, "but nothing's going to happen to you, sir. I won't allow it."

"I join you in minute," Hiro Nomasaki said from the armchair.

Dennis bowed and then left the director's office.

Hiro held his chest with both hands.

Thursday, October 24th, 11:35 P.M.

The one remaining Zeus connector on his head like a crown, Harv picked up his stocking cap off the table and said, "Teresa, access the camera at the lab."

"Working," she said, and he heard the modem dial the lab's number. A second later, he looked at the IBM's monitor. On the screen he could see the main lab through the camera in the corner of the ceiling.

What surprised him was the fact that Mary Alice, Dennis, and the two teenagers were sitting on the floor, their faces turned up and staring at the camera. The fear he had expected to see wasn't there.

In the center of the room, the old man stood defiantly, his hands on his hips. He too stared at the camera.

"Zoom," Harv said, and Teresa sent an electronic signal to the camera in the lab.

Hiro Nomasaki's face got larger and larger.

Harv memorized every detail of the old man's wrinkled

face and tight smile. His unblinking black eyes. His thin head of brittle gray hair. The large ears and strong chin.

Without realizing it, Harv shivered and sighed.

"Is anything the matter?" Teresa asked. "Can I do anything for you, God?"

Harv smiled then. "Yes, Teresa. Turn off the modem."

The picture from the lab faded on the monitor into nothingness.

In the project lab, Hiro Nomasaki looked at the others. "I go to office now," he said. "Will return when time is ripe."

"Grandfather, are you all right?" Fuchan asked, starting to rise to her feet.

"Sit!" he replied. "Build power. All sit. Concentrate!"

In the director's office, Hiro slumped into the soft chair in front of the director's desk. He opened the tin of pills and removed the last one, which he put under his tongue.

His heart slowed.

He waited.

Carefully putting the stocking cap on his head over the Zeus connector, Harv surveyed his lab. Chuckling, he opened the first can of wood stain and tossed the metal cap carelessly to the floor. Starting at the far end of the lab, he sloshed the stain onto the counter and floor. When the container was empty, he did the same thing with the second can, making sure the recliner in the middle of the room was saturated.

The only part of the room that he didn't splash with stain was that with the IBM. All the rest of the equipment, the other two computers, all the drives and modems, he covered thoroughly.

"And now the secrets are only in my mind," Harv said happily.

He unlocked the steel door to the lab. Standing in the doorway, he reached into one of the pockets of his brown monk's robe and removed a single wooden match. He drew it sharply down the laminated wood that covered the steel on the door.

The match ignited.

He tossed the match at the recliner, which burst into flames.

As the fire spread, he slowly closed the door and listened, a broad smile on his face.

"The temperature is now eighty-seven degrees and rising disproportionately," Teresa said. "We have a problem with the air control system, temperature, it hurts, God, it hurts . . ."

Harv slammed the door home and quickly threw the deadbolts.

He left his apartment without a backward glance, heading for his car in the parking lot, the enhanced version of the Zeus connector firmly wired into his scalp.

Chapter
18

When Harv entered the lab, sixteen-year-old Francis Schonrath gulped. Harvey Webster seemed even larger now than he did at the picnic. He was the biggest man the boy had ever seen. Francis stared at the man's huge head, which, he thought, was almost as big and round as a basketball. On his head, sticking out in weird places, was a yellow wool stocking cap. He wore one of those heavy brown robes like the monks in the movie *The Name of the Rose*, and his big pale hairy feet stood in sandals without socks.

Harv caught Francis staring at him, and he smiled crookedly, a grimace full of unevenly spaced yellow teeth.

The boy shivered and averted his glance.

Mary Alice looked down at her watch. It was almost midnight.

"Looks like a picnic," Harv said, smiling at the circle of people.

Rubbing his hands through the top of Francis's hair, Harv stepped into the middle of the circle and turned slowly, looking at each person for a second before moving on to the next.

"Where's the old Jap?" he asked.

"Where's Meat Grinder?" Mary Alice snapped.

"I sent him to a better life," Harv replied quietly.

Fuchan gasped loudly and Francis took her hand, squeezing it tight.

"I want this settled peacefully, Harv," Dennis said, shifting his weight as he sat crosslegged on the floor.

"But of course, Herr Rat," Harv answered. "I'm not one for violence. It's just a game, remember? For the connector, for all the marbles."

"What's the point, Harv?" Mary Alice asked angrily. "Why would you kill innocent people? I still can't believe you've done what you said."

"Believe it. They deserved it. Cogglin stole my idea for an enhanced design on that floating point microprocessor when I studied with him at M.I.T. You didn't really think I'd let him get away with that, did you?"

"That's part of the academic game, Harv," Mary Alice said.

"Well, this is my game. And I've won. I'm the only one with the secret of the Zeus connection," he said finally, removing the stocking cap carefully from his head and then tossing it on the floor.

They stared at the connector attached to Harv's bald head.

"I've improved it," Harv boasted, "doesn't even need a cable any longer, and you wouldn't believe what I can do with it." His voice lowered to a whisper and his eyes darted wildly from side to side. "I'm God now, you know."

"Look, Harv, let's make a deal, shall we?" Dennis suggested softly, his voice a study in composure. "There's no reason we can't settle this rationally."

"There's nothing to settle. I just dropped in to show you what my work has come to."

"You're sure full of yourself," Dennis said.

"Ahh, the Tunnel Rat speaks, eh?" Harv answered, turning to look at Dennis Conlick. "I'm surprised they let you out of the mental ward long enough to come to my little party."

"*His* mind's fine," Mary Alice snapped.

The obese hardware expert turned slightly and looked at the psychiatrist. His eyes widened as he looked from her to Dennis.

"I see," he said softly, almost to himself, taking a step toward her.

"Leave her alone," Francis said, waving his good arm.

Harv looked at him and then blinked. "So the cripple has some spine in real life too, eh?"

"Where's Meat Grinder? Where the Cutter? What did you do to our friends?" Francis yelled, his fingers locking into a fist. "You're nothing but a big, ugly scumbag!"

Harv's face reddened.

Losing his temper, Francis pressed the button on his wheelchair and drove right at Harv, swinging wildly with his hand, which grazed Harv's side.

Harv grabbed him by the shirt and lifted him bodily out of the wheelchair. He shook the boy in the air with both hands and then carelessly tossed him onto the hard tile floor.

Dennis started to get to his feet.

"No, no, you don't," Harv said, stepping toward Francis. "If you move, I'll stomp his skull in."

Dennis slowly sat back down.

"I think a demonstration's in order," Harv said, the redness in his face lessening, his eyes getting a distant look in them. "No, leave him alone," he ordered, and Fuchan stopped. She had started to get up, her eyes on Francis, who lay helplessly on the floor, his eyes squinting from the pain. "Miserable cripple," Harv muttered savagely.

Francis used his hand to wipe the tears from his eyes. Then he glared at Harv.

Watching them carefully, Harv walked to the VAX.

He typed rapidly.

Dennis shifted his weight.

"You want me to kill the cripple?" Harv asked, shifting in the chair in front of the VAX.

Dennis relaxed.

"That goes for all of you. No more warnings. Next time somebody moves, I ice little Genghis." He laughed at his own joke, thinking about The Chief Cutter in the freezer.

Harv's finger depressed the key to initialize the Zeus program.

It had never happened before, but this time, when the program started, the room lights dimmed for a brief second, as if the VAX had consumed a tremendous amount of additional electricity.

They watched as Harv's eyes rolled in his head.

Dennis jumped to his feet and charged at the robed figure.

He was within a foot of him when the huge man's eyes snapped open. Harv raised his right hand and pointed his index finger at Dennis. A ray of greenish light shot from the tip of the finger and hit Dennis square in the chest, knocking him backward. He stumbled and fell to the floor, the breath knocked out of him. The back of his head struck the tile and he lost consciousness.

Mary Alice's hands flew to her mouth.

"I am God!" Harv roared, his head flung back in ecstasy, "and you shall worship me!"

He pointed his finger at a shelf of lab beakers and test tubes. The glass shattered, sending slivers flying across the room. The others' hands jerked instinctively up to protect their eyes. He pointed at von Neumann's chair. The upholstery ripped loose in inch-wide shreds and the cotton matting burst into the air like ashes from an angry fire. He pointed at the video camera hanging from the corner of the ceiling. It rotated on its bearing and then repeatedly slammed itself into the wall until the lens cracked and split. A moment later, it hung there askew. He rubbed his hands together rapidly and then held them palms-forward at the portable electrocardiogram machine. The steel case of the heart monitor started to split. A second later, it ripped down the middle with a sound that the onlookers would never forget.

Harv planted his feet firmly and wide apart, placed his hands on his hips, and looked triumphantly at the remaining Surgeons. "You dare to challenge me?" he intoned, his voice a deep roar.

Mary Alice glanced at her wristwatch. Two minutes left before the bomb in the program went off.

The lights dimmed again, sharply, for a microsecond.

Mary Alice's mouth opened.

Harv's face turned, a beatific smile spread slowly. "You have something you want to say, Fräulein?"

"The connector, Harv, the Zeus connection, we built it to help mankind, not for this!" She swept her hands around the room to indicate the terror.

Harv's eyes widened and he pointed a finger at Mary Alice. "Now it's your turn, Nelly Dean. I can see what you've done with the Rat. You were going to be mine, but now you are stained. Tainted. Unworthy of me. So you shall join the others who betrayed me."

Fuchan screamed, and Mary Alice grabbed the young girl who was sitting next to her and pulled her body into a tight hug.

Francis, dragging himself across the floor with his hand, inched slowly toward the raving giant.

Harv threw back his head and laughed insanely.

Francis was now five feet away from Harv. His one fist was clenched tightly as his elbow pulled him across the tile. Anger and determination were etched into his young face.

"Look at the worm," Harv taunted, laughing.

Then Harv turned his attention to Mary Alice, who was holding Fuchan.

"Suffer the little children to come unto me," Harv said, holding his arms open wide, looking at Fuchan.

She slowly turned away from Mary Alice.

"No!" Mary Alice shouted, grasping at her, but Fuchan, as if her mind were no longer her own, started to rise.

Suddenly the lab door was thrown open, crashing into the wall, and Hiro Nomasaki, his hands buried in the sleeves of his robe, walked into the room.

Power seemed to flow from the old man, and the electrical energy in the lab intensified.

"Hai!" Nomasaki-roshi shouted from the depth of his being, and the single syllable seemed to turn Harv around as if he was on a swivel.

"So you were hiding?" Harv said, his deep voice full of disdain.

Hiro took confident steps into the lab. The old man's impenetrable black eyes seemed to radiate power as they bore into Harv.

For a second, a fearful look passed across Harv's face. Then he closed his eyes and concentrated on boring into the old man, to search out and find his weak spot.

Suddenly a smile rippled across Harv's thick lips and his jowls quivered.

"Your heart is speeding up, old man."

Hiro felt as if one of Harv's hamlike hands had reached into his chest and curled its fingers around his heart.

"Delusion!" Nomasaki shouted.

He felt the mental fingers inside his chest relax ever so slightly.

"Not real," the old man said, taking a step forward.

"I am God!" Harv yelled, also taking a step forward.

Mary Alice looked at her watch. Only a few more seconds. If only the old man could hold on for a few more seconds.

"I'm inside of you," Harv boasted, tentatively moving forward, not quite sure.

"I am you," Nomasaki-roshi said, his voice strong, "and you are me. We are one."

"No!" Harv screamed, his forehead wrinkling into knots of intense concentration.

The mental fingers seized the soft tissue of Hiro's heart, clamped down and started to squeeze.

"Now," Mary Alice whispered, the second hand on her watch indicating that the bomb in the Zeus program should begin.

"MU!" Nomasaki-roshi shouted with all his being, a single syllable that reverberated throughout the room, over and over and over again.

"What?" Harv said, turning for a second from the old man, relinquishing his mental hold on him.

Deep in Harv's mind, a small opening appeared, an opening that appeared to be the entrance to a narrow tunnel.

Harv's attention wavered when he saw the opening.

Hiro Nomasaki collapsed on the floor.

Francis crawled toward him.

An intense light seemed to be burning somewhere deep within that tunnel.

Harv's awareness of the lab dropped away, and he stared at the entrance to the tunnel.

On the floor, Mary Alice, Fuchan, Hiro Nomasaki, and Francis gaped in wonder at the huge man who seemed to freeze where he stood. His eyes moved upward and then rolled toward the back of his head.

"It's working," Mary Alice whispered. "The bomb's working. Thank God."

Francis reached Hiro Nomasaki and pulled himself on top of the old man to protect him.

Harv stepped into the tunnel, unable to ignore its pull.

Atop his head, the connector seemed to start to glow.

Suddenly the floor of the tunnel was moving, moving forward toward the light. He gathered speed, and part of Harv realized what was happening. His eyes snapped open and his hands rose upward, rose jerkily toward the Zeus connector. His eyes focused on Mary Alice and Fuchan, and a look of triumph came into them.

"No!" the psychiatrist and the teenager yelled simultaneously and, acting as if they were one, they came to their feet in an instant and charged the huge man.

Hiro Nomasaki, his heart released now by Harv's mind but unable to regain its natural rhythm, watched as the two women slammed into the obese man and knocked him off his feet. With Francis's help, the old man struggled to a sitting position. "Good!" he yelled, his voice powerful, hugging Francis tightly, even though his left arm felt like a hot iron rod had been impaled in it.

"Keep his hands away from his head!" Mary Alice shouted. "Don't let him remove the connector!"

The last vestige of conscious control slipped away from Harv even as he felt the women tearing at his hands and arms.

His body froze in time, becoming as solid as cast iron.

Wisps of steam came from the connector as chips overheated and started to burn as the mechanism seared into his skull.

In his mind, moving faster and faster, the tunnel now seemed to be going downward, down toward the center of the earth.

Out of control, Harv plummeted toward the light, which was flashing like a strobe.

On the floor, Dennis Conlick regained consciousness, his eyes fluttering open to see Mary Alice and Fuchan sitting on Harv's huge, flabby arms.

In his mind, Harv fell into the light, and, for a moment, a great peace embraced him as he thought, *Now I am truly God.*

Then he saw what he'd really become, and his mind screamed in horror. His body went limp under Mary Alice and Fuchan, and the breath went out of him in one slow, final exhalation.

"Grandfather," Fuchan gasped, releasing Harv's arm, her voice full of fear.

She raced to the old man, whose left arm moved from Francis to embrace her.

Mary Alice rushed to Dennis and took him in her arms. "I'm okay," Dennis muttered slowly, shaking his head, trying to clear it.

They turned and looked at Hiro Nomasaki. He smiled broadly at them. His body shuddered.

"His pills, give him a pill!" Dennis stammered, trying to get to his feet but unable to control his muscles.

Then Hiro's arms tightened once around Francis and Fuchan and he pulled them to his chest. He shook his head at Dennis and said, without regret, "Pills gone."

Their three heads touching, the old man whispered into Francis's and Fuchan's ears, "I am you. And you are me. All is one."

He pulled his head back and looked deeply into Francis's eyes.

"Hai, Khan is man now."

He pushed stray locks of hair back and kissed the boy's forehead.

He turned to Fuchan, and their eyes met and locked.

She laughed from deep within.

"I see, Grandfather, I see! I see *mu.*"

The old man smiled, the wrinkles on the sides of his eyes crinkling almost to his ears. A rich, full laugh came from deep within him. And then he was gone.

"No!" Francis shouted, feeling the old man go limp. "No, you can't die. I love you! You can't die." He pounded his hand on his crippled legs.

Fuchan gently lowered her grandfather's body to the floor. Then she pulled Francis into her arms and stroked the back of his head.

Mary Alice helped Dennis to his feet.

In a moment they were all gathered around the old man, who lay on the floor silently, an enigmatic smile on his lips, his face composed and peaceful in death.

Dennis reached down and picked up Francis, holding him tightly in his arms. "Get his wheelchair," he said, and Mary Alice went for it.

Fuchan bent over and kissed her grandfather on the lips.

Epilogue

Dennis, Mary Alice, Fuchan, and Francis were in Dennis's French Quarter apartment. It was four days since the night of Hiro Nomasaki's death, four days of meetings with police, meetings that had done next to nothing to explain Harv Webster's sudden spree of violence. The bodies of Jim Persall and Tom Barnslow had been found in the ashes of Harv's apartment, but so far the authorities had not been able to trace the whereabouts of the other Zeus project members. A government official, a dark-suited, anonymous friend of Ed August's, had shown up and listened silently to Dennis and Mary Alice's explanation of the loss of the project materials before going away again, but not after letting them know that he didn't believe their story.

Today they'd come to start moving Dennis's things to Mary Alice's house.

"This shouldn't take too long," Mary Alice said, shaking her head wryly.

"I guess Hiro would have called it living simply," Dennis replied, and she nodded.

"Yes," Fuchan said in agreement, evoking a smile from Francis.

Mary Alice sat down on the chair at the worktable. "I'm

glad it's over," she said, her fingers playing idly with the keys on the Apple IIe, "but I'm so sorry we had to lose . . . I really miss Paul Brandais."

"Why don't you two go have some beignets on me?" Dennis suggested, pulling a five-dollar bill from his pants pocket.

"I don't know," Francis said, his eyes traveling to the Tunnel Rat's computer setup. "I'd kinda like to check out your system."

"It's such a nice day," Fuchan said, smiling at Francis. "I'd rather go outside for a while. We can feed the pigeons in Jackson Square."

The boy's eyes left the computer equipment, and he pushed the proper button on his wheelchair to roll him to the door. "Let's do it," he said. "Pigeons here we come."

"Wonder if they'll like beignets?" Fuchan asked as she closed the apartment door behind them.

"Great kids, eh, babe?" Dennis observed. "No regrets?" He reached over her shoulder and behind the computer and booted its operating system.

"I sensed something wrong about the project from the first time we connected von Neumann," she said, "and I'm glad Harv took the secret with him. I'm just sorry so many people had to lose their lives."

"Well, at least Francis and Fuchan seem to be all right." Standing behind her, his hands rested lightly on her shoulders as she sat at the computer. His fingers played gently with her hair.

"She's a delight," Mary Alice said. "I never dreamed that I'd get a future husband and daughter in the same week."

"Instant family," Dennis said.

Mary Alice's eyes grew distant. "Dennis, could you duplicate the connector?" she asked.

"Probably. But I won't."

Then he bent over, kissed the top of her head, and typed the word CATALOG on the computer. "It's going to be Fuchan's graduation gift. I think she's got the sense to use it properly."

The hard drive whirled and listed its files on the monitor.

Mary Alice's eyes widened as she read the list on his drive.

"My God," she whispered, "is that what I think it is?"

Her finger moved slowly toward the screen and settled on one file name:

WEBSTER CONNECTION

"Yep, I lifted it right out of Harv's computer the day Hiro died. Remember when he called me at the lab? He wanted me to have it for some reason. I didn't understand then. Now that I'm getting to know Fuchan I know why he wanted me to have it."

Mary Alice's eyes grew wide. "You mean she'll be able to duplicate it?"

He nodded and lowered his head toward hers until their lips met.

In Jackson Square, Fuchan pushed Francis in his wheelchair.

"Look at that," Francis ordered, his hand pointing at a large white pigeon that had its body half-buried in a red-and-white cardboard popcorn box. The bird was trying to remove the last remaining kernels from the container.

As if hearing Francis, the pigeon pulled out of the box, cooed softly at them, its coal-black eyes darting nervously back and forth, then stretched its wings, and flew up, up, and up, toward the midday sun.

His hand protecting his eyes from the glare, Francis tried to follow the bird's flight. "That's beautiful," he said.

He felt Fuchan's cool hands rest lightly on the back of his neck.

"Hai," she replied.